TIME IS

GOLD

by Martin Knox

First Published – 2020
This edition published 2020 by Novel Ideas
Brisbane, Qld Australia
www.warmwittypublishing.com.au

 A catalogue record for this
work is available from the
NATIONAL
LIBRARY National Library of Australia
OF AUSTRALIA

The National Library of Australia Cataloguing-in-Publication

Creator: Knox, Martin, author.

Title: Time is Gold / Martin Knox.

ISBN: 978-0-6489930-0-1 (paperback)

Subjects: General fiction.
                    Contemporary fiction
                    Australian fiction.
                    Speculative fiction.
                    Sports fiction.

Editing by Denise Thomson
Typeset in Times New Roman 12pt by Donna Munro Graphic Design.
Cover artwork by Donna Munro Graphic Design. Dreamtime image author Vladimir Melnikov.
Printed and bound in Australia by Ingram Spark.
Copyright © Martin Knox 2020
htttps://www.martinknox.com
mpknox46@aapt.net.au

Reviews

TIME IS GOLD (2020)

Review by Brad Ahern, October 7th, 2020 - Science and Sports Educator.

Martin Knox is a chemical engineer turned science teacher who regards the entire universe as a laboratory for ethical experiments. He innovates novel solutions to deep problems. Across the past three decades, he has been one of the most gifted, creative and prolific writers of science works, beginning with resources for teachers and latterly writing speculative fiction about politics, industry and athletics.

REVIEWS OF MARTIN KNOX'S PREVIOUS BOOKS

SHORT OF LOVE (2019)

Readers Favourite, August 5th, 2019

Review by K.C. Finn Rating: 5 Stars

Short Of Love is a work of picaresque satirical fiction penned by author Martin Knox, which explores the notion of love and relationships, and how we treat other human beings when we view them as commodities for love rather than as individuals.

Author Martin Knox has created a fascinating parody of modern love and its effects on life, whilst also managing to stay true to the nature of many relationships where competition becomes a feature over compassion. Overall, Short Of Love will interest any reader who enjoys dissecting relationships and the notion of romance itself.

Online Bookclub Review, January 15th, 2020
Review by Stephanie Elizabeth

Short of Love by Martin Knox is a fascinating piece of satirical fiction. It explores love, relationships, and the moral impact of viewing people as commodities, rather than individuals. The story revolves around the exceedingly selfish Tom Archer, a student with his eyes fixated on a future as a successful engineer. But his focus wavers when he meets Vicki Hillstone. He becomes so wholly consumed by his desire for her, that he is driven to a whole new level of distraction.

Readers Favourite July 31st, 2019
Reviewed by Vincent Dublado

Martin Knox's Short of Love is an unconventional love story that spans decades dating back from the Jungian nightmare cycles of the 60s. First released under the title Love Straddle, this new and abridged version does not take away the essence and ambiance that make the story endearing. Every day we read a love story with a cookie-cutter leading man that sweeps readers (especially women) off their feet. But this novel offers something different with a misfit protagonist that we would find complicated except that his predicaments are downright understandable. Short of Love reads like a cross between a romantic story and an Idiot's Guide reference on relationships--an insightful delving into balancing love and a career.

Book launch address. September 15th, 2019
Editor Vesna McMaster

Short of Love is a complete re-working of an earlier work, Love Straddle. This predecessor was presented as a first-person narrative and was almost twice as long. One of the outcomes of this reduction in volume is that the pace of the novel is relentless. You won't be falling asleep over this one: it's been distilled to 100 proof.

Which takes me to the question of the novel's genre and place among literary works. I'm assuming most of you haven't read it yet. I'd describe it as a combination of Tom Jones, Catcher in the Rye, and St Augustine's Confessions, with a Beatles soundtrack. Tom

Jones for the rapscallion, picaresque aspect, and endless parade of jaw-dropping events. Catcher in the Rye for the unabashed use of raw unacceptability, dragging unsavoury things out of the shadows and into common view for scrutiny. And the Confessions for the overall aim (I think) of creating a malleability and a weakness in the reader, via the abasement and frankness of the creator, towards a consideration of acceptance and reconciliation.

I'd encourage you to take a punt on it, and be in on that first wave that gets to respond to a text before all the other critics with fat weight behind their names come in on the game. You get first pick. So if you haven't already done so, go and buy the book.

Thanks very much for listening.

PRESUMED DEAD (2018)
Readers' Favourite January 6, 2019
Reviewed by Grant Leishman; Review Rating: 4 Stars

Presumed Dead is a classic "whodunit" and author Martin Knox does a very credible job of describing in detail the investigative techniques of crime scene analysis that the character had developed in his years as a police forensic scientist. The story is well constructed, with possible "red herrings" thrown in at appropriate points.

The two principal characters of Jane and Phillip are well drawn and easy to relate to and empathize with. It is interesting that, as in real life, Knox has sought to bring two people with polar opposite personalities together in a romantic relationship. Jane, the firebrand extrovert with a passion for politics, and Phillip, the quiet, methodical, introvert who struggles to relate to people on a personal level.

I particularly enjoyed the political undertones of the story and the ideals of what truly constitutes democracy. The idea of scrapping political parties and independent politicians voting on their conscience every time has been floated often and I think even trialled occasionally. It brings a real modern-day relevance to the story – one only needs to look at the political turmoil in the US at present to see the dangers of partisanship and party politics. All in all, a very satisfying read and one I can recommend.

OnlineBookClub 21st May, 2020
Reviewed by Abacus; 4/4 Stars

The pace of the book is sedate, allowing for time to experience all the investigative techniques and the political power plays – so like politics today. Another intriguing aspect was Phillip's ability to understand Jane's mind by the movement and appearance of her left or right eye. The author was able to describe for us the conflicting emotions experienced by someone who suffers from post-traumatic distress syndrome (PTSD). The love story between Phillip and Jane also progresses during the chaos of fighting the council. We need a Jane and a Phillip now to solve the partisan American swamp politics.

I rate Presumed Dead **4 out of 4 stars**, for creativity, its focus on science, and the investigative techniques. It was a joy to read – educational and humorous. There are some detailed descriptions of an autopsy which may be too much for some readers.

I recommend this book to lovers of science, politics, crime investigation, love stories, authentic characters, and people who love a unique approach to a crime thriller.

Warm Witty Words, November 12th, 2018
Reviewed by Donna Munro

I've read all Martin Knox novels, and Presumed Dead is a standout. Though I'm not a political person, I felt what it was like to be amid councillors, throwing words in heated discussions on public concerns, bouncing them across the floor like ping pong balls.

It's impossible to tell which politicians are lying and who abducted Jane. The story twists and turns, particularly after part 4. The reader will be right alongside Phillip as he tries to solve the crimes and his faithful bunch of friends, give us some hope that honourable, devoted politicians actually care about their community and the greater good. Anyone who has an interest in politics will love this masterful story."

Pre-publication review September 8th, 2017
Reviewed by Phil Heywood, former Associate Professor and
Head of Urban and Regional Planning, Queensland University
of Technology.

'. . . a convincing and interesting story line on topics of currently seething public interest, including over-development of coastlines, political corruption and the roles of individuals and the media within contemporary society'

LOVE STRADDLE (2014)
Reviewed by Ian Lipke, October 4th, 2014.
Editor of Media-Culture Reviews at Queensland University of
Technology; author.

This novel by Martin P. Knox is vast in scope, scintillating in the brilliance of its conception and staggering in the creation of its hero. This is the work of a major talent

The concept is a straddle, a manipulation of the market in commodity futures:

'...*an investor in commodity futures wants to spread the risk between commodities that are substitutes for each other... when the price of one goes down, the other goes down as well.*'

Selwyn then applies such a concept to women and their affections to comical effect. It is in the teasing out of this idea into human behaviours that the originality of Knox's writing appears.

The last words in this review have to be delivered by the irrepressible Selwyn. Vicki has given him his marching orders and he has taken up with Helen.

'*Vicki knows what I'm like. Her place in my straddle allows her full freedom. If it becomes possible, I still want to close out my short on her and exchange my love for hers, at my best price.*

Until then, I also have a long position and am invulnerable.'

What a hoot! This book is recommended very highly. Get hold of a copy from Amazon. You'll enjoy it as much as I did.

THE GRASS IS ALWAYS BROWNER (2011)
Reviewed by Venero Armanno, December 10th, 2011.
Lecturer Creative Writing, University of Queensland; author of 9 best-selling novels.

'Martin Knox is the type of writer who knows how to tell a wonderful story and pose thought-provoking questions about life and the future. In his book The Grass Is Always Browner, Knox has managed to craft a political thriller, a romance and an allegorical tale of one man's prophetic journey towards enlightenment, all within the umbrella of a deeply satisfying work of speculative fiction. This is a novel to savour and Martin Knox is a writer to watch.'

QUOTES

If you can fill the unforgiving minute
With sixty seconds' worth of distance run,
Yours is the Earth and everything that's in it,
And—which is more—you'll be a Man, my son!

IF, Rudyard Kipling, 1895

The IAAF recognizes two world records for women, a time of
2:14:04 set by Brigid Kosgei on October 13, 2019 during the
Chicago Marathon which was contested by men
and women together, and a "Women Only" record of 2:17:01,
set by Mary Keitany, on April 23, 2017 at the
London Marathon for women only.

https://en.wikipedia.org/wiki/Marathon_world_record_progression

ACRONYMS

PB	Personal Best.
LAC	Little Athletics Club
IAAF	International Association of Athletics Federations

CHAPTER 1

'There's no limit to my running,' Maxi thought as she sped along a trail overhung by wild plants. *'My mind controls my body and my body is going to run faster than any female has ever run before. I am training to beat the World.'*

Leaves of castor oil plants swayed in the breeze from her passing. Her drone was ahead, 20 metres above, videoing and transmitting to the cloud. Her father pedalled his bicycle behind her, as he did for all her country runs.

A heart-rate monitor was strapped to her biceps.

'How is 155?' she called to him, wanting encouragement.

'Go up to 160. You're doing fine.'

He kept her below 80% of the maximum for 13-year-olds of 200 beats per minute. She didn't have to drive herself hard. She had been doing 10 kilometre runs at this pace for the past month. Earlier she had run faster and further, but she had stopped improving and he cut her back.

'You're stale,' he said. 'I am going to limit you to three 10-kilometre workouts a week. You'll run faster. Less is more.'

'Are you sure it will work for me?' she asked. It was a big change to her routine. 'The others are running further and faster.'

'It should work. Less training will prevent overtraining and burnout, cutting your injury-risk,' he said. She had melted down in a recent race. 'All you need do is maintain fitness. Your strength and speed are fine. Cutting back will take less of your time and you will be able to do your schoolwork.'

Maxi's programme included track interval running over various distances, short, mid and long tempos for different conditions of lactic acid disposal and fatigue. Today's trail run was on packed dirt

1

and sand. Tomorrow, her runs would be planned from analysis of today's performances and after adjustments to her pace and breathing.

When she competed in a 1500 metre race, she was alone, without Stan or the drone scaffolding her, a welcome relief from his over-supervision. She grappled with growing feelings of disloyalty to Stan. She had depended on him and trusted him, but lately, his control of her training and his old-fashioned methods annoyed her.

Maxi's mother had died when she was five years old. The cancer diagnosis had come out of the blue. Her exit had been a six-month hell of chemotherapies and hospitalisations. Maxi felt she hadn't done enough for her and might be responsible.

'It isn't your fault,' Stan had said. 'No-one knows what caused your mother to be ill.'

'Maybe he didn't do enough for her,' she thought. Her parents were not close and although he had nursed her at home, his care had been mostly physical. Maxi was their only interest in common. When her mother died, she and her father were bereft and they had clung together.

Her mother had wanted them to be together and close. Maxi grieved sometimes but Stan kept her feet firmly on the ground.

'Live one day at a time,' he advised her.

After 3 years, Stan had met Patti at a party. She was ten years younger, attractive at 40, with a pretty face, sultry looks, gamin figure, hair in a half-bob, short and brown on one side, the other platinum, swept over the top and falling over her left eye, giving an impression of shy concealment. Stan thought she was sultry and glamorous. Maxi thought she looked ridiculous.

'She's not like Mum,' Maxi said to Stan, 'not the way I remember.'

'I want to forget,' he said. 'We have to move on.'

Patti and her son Roly moved into their family home, with its large garden and space to keep pets and grow things. There was a tortoise, a guinea pig, a cat, a dog and her horse. Maxi loved to ride and explore along bush trails with her friends. They looked under

2

every rock and rotting log for small creatures, learning their names and their habits.

Patti had used to work doing make-up and costuming with singers and bands on the Australian leg of global tours, also ballets, musicals and operas. She prepared food for stage performers to their dietary specifications, including the fad foods they demanded. Her own diet was vegan and she soon converted Stan and Maxi. She had acquired a knowledge of nutrition, but her experience was in feeding performers vegan food, with more attention to their demands than to food chemistry theories.

She wanted to be a movie actress. When she was with celebrities, she was living her dream. She looked for opportunities to audition, but so far had won only small roles in advertisements. She posed and gossiped with friends at the local repertory company, where she sometimes had a walk-on part.

'She should do something worthwhile, like get a job,' Maxi said to her father.

'Patti has had a rough time,' Stan said. 'Please be kind to her.'

Patti's family life as a child had been traumatic. She didn't talk about it and was often moody. Years of going to rock concerts had affected her hearing. When people spoke to her, she sometimes misheard and took offence.

When it was Stan's birthday, she wanted to celebrate at home.

'I'll get a bottle of champagne,' said Patti going to the fridge. 'Where did you put it?'

'I didn't buy any this week,' Stan said.

'Why not?'

'I'm a bit short,' he said. 'I needed the money for food.'

'I don't eat food,' said Patti.

'Maxi and I do.'

'I drink. What did you get?'

'Cigarettes for you,' said Stan. 'Vegetables, salad, fruit, pizza, pasta, veggie burgers, baked beans, nuts, yoghurt, soy curd, soy milk and Gatorade.'

'Is that all?'

'I said I would get foods for Maxi's running. I did and that's why I didn't get any Bollinger.'

'I must have some.'

'Have a glass of plonk.'

'I need champagne.'

'Who is going to pay for it?'

'I have connections,' said Patti. 'There is usually someone with money.'

'Not this time.'

'Could Maxi get a job?'

'No way. She is studying and training.'

'She should contribute to her upkeep.'

Patti was jealous that Stan favoured Maxi.

Maxi was going upstairs when she met Patti coming down.

'Where's Dad?'

'Why?'

'I'm going on a run.'

'Okay. Go.'

'He always comes.'

'Not today. You can run by yourself.'

'I want him to come with me.'

'Tell him about it when you get back.'

'I'll ask him.'

'No. He's resting.'

'He won't mind. Get out of my way.'

Maxi tried to push past her stepmother and she pushed back.

'Get your hands off me, bitch,' Maxi said. 'You can't force me to do what you want.'

'I'm your stepmother. I have legal rights to control you.'

'Not to stop me speaking with my father.'

Maxi did speak to him. He got up and accompanied her run.

She had found her niche in distance running naturally. By the time she was six, her family friends and classmates knew that her destiny was to run. She ran, skipped, hopped, jumped and leapt with

4

deliberation and persistence, as if her aim was to hang in the air. She had the body of an ectomorph, tall and light, with the narrow frame ideal for long-distance running. She could run like the wind, her head still, her lithe body leaning forward, her straight legs angular, taking impossibly long strides, her arms pumping forwards and back like perfectly coordinated pistons. Her paces were strong and precisely balanced, a human machine designed for speed and endurance, straining to excel, as if from the exultation of possessing such an able body.

When she saw a YouTube of an Olympic marathon race, she was hooked. The winning woman's courage was the bravest thing she had ever seen and she wanted that adulation for herself.

'An Olympic marathon is the worst possible ordeal for mind and body,' her father said, warning her. 'It can be life-threatening and you must be careful.'

Stan had been a marathon runner but had retired from it. His advice, tersely and bluntly delivered from under his broad-brimmed sun hat, was wise with experience. He had learned to run marathons at a private boys' school known for military-like discipline. He had turned out to train at dawn, followed by shouted commands, peer pressure, cold showers, with beatings for slacking and cutting corners. His involvement in distance running followed from disliking team games in which his slender build made him last to be picked for rugby and rowing teams. In the summer, he came last in the cricket batting order and he spent Wednesday afternoons sitting in the pavilion. He wanted to be active. Running was his way to independence. The running track went around the cricket pitch and fielders called to him as he ran past.

'Fleet, you're a wanker.'

'Sissies play cricket,' he said.

It was mutual acknowledgement and they left it at that.

Now he saw himself as protecting Maxi. His harsh commands provoked her to want to rebel, but she respected him too much.

'What are you now?' Stan asked from behind her.

'157.'

5

'Try and stay at 160. Keep a steady pace; the others will let you lead.'

'Does my every minute need the same exertion?' she thought. *'It doesn't seem like it: time drags sometimes and flies at others. I have to be vigilant to keep a steady pace.'*

She was comfortable, with her mind detached and floating nearby, enjoying the surroundings. The trail was eroded in places and had an occasional rock to step over. Luxuriant greenery grew right up to the path and she smelled the pungent odour of leaves crushed by others, smelling like the basil Patti put in vegetarian Bolognese sauce for pasta. She wound up a hillside and over a ridge, going from one side of rain shadow with dry woody scrub and charred stumps, to rainforest, lush and green, on the other.

She padded quietly through a tunnel of trees, cool and dark. A whip bird's call split the silence. A scrub turkey scooted across, its guilty head low, peering for a path to get away.

They emerged into sunlight along a road between paddocks. Cattle grazed, attended by white egrets, one riding on a cow's back. Adorning the roadside were colourful patches of paper daisies and foxtails.

Leggy bees crawled across flower heads and their hum droned in the quiet, between her breaths. A small grey bird, a spotted pardalote, hopped between the magenta flowers of a eucalypt tree.

Coming the other way was a runner, a few years older. Maxi didn't remember her. She might be new in the area.

'Hi,' Maxi said as they passed.

'Hi.'

It was standoffish, but there wasn't time to be friendly. When she had seen her a couple more times, they could stop for a chat. Maybe they could train together.

'Could she be a faster runner than me?' she thought. *'Maybe her body could endure better, or she could be more determined? I'm pretty good at those. Running is what I do best. I could be wasting my time, but I don't want to do anything else. I want to improve.'*

She wanted to be the best and knew that she was doing the right thing by training hard. She was fortunate she could train in pleasant surroundings.

Their house was on the outskirts of Caloundra, a town of 50,000 on Queensland's Sunshine Coast, with surfing beaches and near the Glasshouse Mountains. She rambled with her friends and ran for hours along trails through scrub and gorse. The hilltop was often in cloud, the vegetation damp with the odour of rotting leaves. They would run to exhaustion, collapse onto a mat of moss, joining clover blossoms into chains to go around their heads and wrists.

Most days Maxi played after school with the neighbouring children, snacking on the move. They played tag and climbed trees. They rode their bikes, scooters and skates and made kites and cubby houses using cardboard boxes, tarpaulins and ropes.

They had music from a speaker and danced energetically. Maxi practiced cartwheels, her straight arms and legs like the spokes of a wheel. She could do handsprings and walk on her hands. They held athletics contests, with high jump and long jump, hurdles, javelin, bow and arrow and shot put. Maxi ran against them: she skipped, loped, pranced, cantered, trotted and sprinted, but it was running distances fast that fascinated her.

She would run with the wind behind, pushing her along, bounding with her feet barely touching the ground. Sometimes it blew so strongly that Maxi felt herself being lifted off. It would buffet her face, her skin would redden and she would imagine she was a wild animal fleeing from pursuers.

She went to the beach with her father, stepmother and stepbrother. They sat next to each other on the picnic blanket. She smelled the sweet scents of bodies and sunscreen against the fishy salt smell, as she dug her toes into the damp sand, squinting in the sun, feeling its warmth on her skin.

When boys went past, Maxi pulled the blanket over her body.

'You don't have to cover up,' said Patti. 'You're too skinny for them.'

'How would you know?' Maxi said. 'You're too old.'

7

Patti had been a groupie following a heavy metal band, then worked as a model for advertisers. She was a poser, attention-seeking and vain. She liked to dress up and flirted with men, covertly when Stan was there.

CHAPTER 2

Maxi and Roly went to the local State secondary college. He was a low-achieving student and waiting to leave school when he would be 18 in two years.

'Woodwork is your favourite subject, isn't it?' Maxi said, trying to help him engage with school work. 'Why do you skip class?'

'They want me to make stupid stuff.'

'What?'

'Book ends.'

'What do you want to make?'

'I dunno.'

'Could you work with another student?'

'They don't want to.'

'You don't try. You need to show you can do something.'

'I can do what I want. I don't need no school results.'

'What do you want to do?'

'Hang out at the beach.'

'What will you do?'

'Surf.'

Roly seldom surfed.

'Yeah, right. What will you do for money?'

'I'll get it from Mum. If I go to job interviews, Centrelink will pay out.'

'Don't expect to get anything from me.'

Maxi had tried to help Roly. He had no ambition. Maxi thought it had something to do with being unhappy. He had no self-control and simply took advantage of her.

'A sister should help her brother in need.'

She had tried to cheer him up, but without success and was impatient with him.

'Get off your fat arse, you lazy shit.'

Roly could not settle into schoolwork. He had tantrums in class. The tentative diagnosis was ADHD. He was on medication and had a remedial teacher. When he became too much of a distraction to the others, he was withdrawn from class and supervised in a group with troublemakers. When he conformed, he was allowed back. Then the cycle repeated.

Roly ate too much and refused to exercise. He stole food and money from shops and from other students. His misbehaviour was infamous at the school and embarrassed Maxi.

Stan was a biology teacher at the school. After his wife's death, he had focused on marathon running and won the national open. He had taken up with Patti that year. She expected he would stay famous, but it only lasted one season. When there were no more invitations to hold inspirational talks and conduct workshops for runners, he returned to science teaching. Patti regretted marrying Stan. He had little interest in her and was critical of her dissipated lifestyle, lazy friends and bizarre fashion choices.

Now he was retired from running and coached the school's running squad, including Maxi. He was a commanding figure, ramrod straight, lean, muscular and well-proportioned. He was an experienced instructor, knowledgeable about biomechanics and physiology, sporting a moustache. He supervised her daily training, setting tasks and giving tips from his experience.

He devoted himself to science teaching. He was an independent thinker who embraced science with fervour and rejected other influences: aesthetic, religious and psychological. His beliefs were sometimes eccentric or controversial.

He was frequently at odds with his teaching colleagues and with parents of students and was regarded as old-school and extreme. Maxi suffered from his strange ideas about running, training and coaching.

Yet Maxi was close to her father. Their personalities meshed: he was enthusiastic about discipline and planning. Maxi was a performer. She longed to show what she could do and loved being in the spotlight.

'Your body should be straight and leaning slightly forward, with your head upright and balanced comfortably,' he said.

'That's what I do,' she said.

'Usually, you are good; when you're tired, you hunch up, put your head down and slow up.

On the hockey field, Maxi had serious competition from Angela, who was shorter, stocky and nimble, with experience from club fixtures. When the two were on opposite sides and Angela bested Maxi, at first, there were tears but Maxi learned to dig in and fight back.

She sometimes went to school friends' houses for birthday parties. She took the lead in organising games. Maxi liked to get her own way and sometimes the sparks flew.

She was at a party at Angela's place and organised the crew of a space ship to colonise Mars, assigning Angela to the engine room as mechanic. Matters came to a head when Angela refused to go below.

'I'm not going to be shut away, by myself,' she said.

'You have to do what you're told, or you can't come,' Maxi said.

'Who said you can decide who goes?' Angela asked.

'Don't come then, stupid.'

Angela complained to her mother.

'Maxi is bullying us.'

She ended the game.

When Patti came to collect her, Angela's mother told her: 'Maxi is too big for her boots. You're going to have your work cut out with that one.'

Patti spoke to Maxi. 'You should have considered how Angela would feel,' she said. 'Would you like it if you were shut away?'

'No, but I'm different.'

'In what way are you different, Maxi?'

'I don't know. But I am.'

'Try to fit in and understand how others feel.' Patti paused. 'It's not easy fitting in. It is what I should have done at your age, instead of getting into trouble.'

11

Maxi was naturally a ringleader and tried to get her own way, but she accepted Patti's advice and stayed out of trouble.

In the playground, the boys chased the girls and kissed them. Depending on which boy it was, a girl would run, scream and fight him off. Fast and elusive, Maxi had her favourites who she allowed to catch her.

She was always hungry, watched her weight and snacked carefully. Maxi's favourite food was prawns. She regularly dreamed of binge eating, imagining shovelling in hamburgers, chips, cheesecake, chocolate and coke. She knew these foods would slow her down and she never gave into her food yearnings, sticking to the foods her stepmother prepared for her. Patti was strict with Maxi's food but condoned Roly's overeating. He was two years older and unfriendly. Maxi put up with him for her father's sake.

Roly's paternity was uncertain and Patti felt guilty. Her first marriage had soon failed, followed by brief affairs. An unexpected pregnancy had produced her only child. Unlike Maxi who dieted to run, Roly ate himself to a standstill, with legs like tree trunks and a massive behind. Maxi knew that Roly's problem was his mother. With Roly, Patti's interest in nutrition was overridden by her inability to say no to him. She overfed him, excusing his slack and disruptive behaviour, giving him money, turning a blind eye to his stealing and waiting on him hand and foot.

'Patti has made Roly into a foodaholic,' Maxi told Stan.

'She depends on his approval,' her father said. 'She thinks she's being kind. He is such a mess.'

Patti thought Roly was depressed. He had good reason to be. He had wrecked his body with excessive eating and smoking weed, hanging with a bad crowd and usually in trouble with the police. He spent his days on the beach at the surf lifesaving club with his loser friends. He was too overweight and uncoordinated to ride a board.

'Here's some chocolate,' he said to Maxi, knowing she never ate any. 'You need energy to win.'

It was tempting.

'No, thank you. Get off my back, Roly.'

Another of his ploys was to hide her shoes or take out her laces.

12

'He's jealous of my running success,' Maxi thought grimly.

Patti would not allow Stan to be firm with his stepson. He had no time for Roly and showed him dislike. Roly didn't do anything at home or try anything worthwhile at school. He sat on the side-line, complaining of injuries or pains to excuse not joining in. His tantrums in class caused him to lag behind, despite extra attention. At age 18, when his enrolment at school expired, he lacked achievement. To get unemployment benefit, he had to attend interviews for jobs. He was offered an apprenticeship making surfboards, but he was lazy, took offence when corrected, walked off the job and went to the beach. He was popular with the group at the surf lifesaving club because he bought weed with money stolen from his family and shared it with them.

His stepmother had not given up hope. 'Roly is finding himself,' she said.

Maxi showed him the need to work by her example, but he was too far gone to change his behaviour.

Patti and Roly were close, as were Stan and Maxi. Stan withheld his attention from Roly and showered Maxi with praise.

'How was your lunch today?' Patti asked Maxi.

'I only ate the fruit. I don't like soy.'

'I'm a nutritionist. I know what you need for running. Runners eat soy. You eat it.'

'No.'

'While you live in this house, you will do what I want. Is that understood?'

'I don't have to,' Maxi said. 'Ask my father.'

Maxi liked to have Stan choose between her and Patti because she usually won.

'Please try and get along with Patti,' Stan said to Maxi. 'She means well.'

'I doubt it.'

Patti avoided exertion except for the camera. Her career in nutrition had been spasmodic, feeding actors. After she had watched a movie (25), she had become vegan. Feeding Stan and the children gave her a new interest. At first, there were hiccups.

13

'Why do I have to eat vegan all the time?' asked Stan.

'Because a plant-based diet is better for your health, strength and athletic performance.'

He got used to it. Maxi was resistant too.

'My stepmother wants to help,' she said to her friend Jocelyn, 'but she tries to control me all the time. Her vegan food is bland and boring. It is annoying.'

'Is it healthy food? Does it affect your running?'

'Hmm. I suppose I do feel lighter. I have noticed I have more energy and strength.'

'You shouldn't complain, then.'

'It's her lack of choice that gets to me.'

'What else does she do?'

'She nags me to change my running routes because she imagines attackers. She even tells me how to dress.'

'What do you do?'

'Sometimes I go along, but I flared up the other day. Her negativity is driving me crazy.'

'Does she like it when you win?'

'Not much. I think she'd prefer me to stop running altogether.'

'Does it make you want to run more?'

'Running puts a distance between us and I simmer down.'

'You run to get away from her?'

'Her only interest in my running is to brag to her friends about my winning.'

Maxi made a few good friends at school, mostly girls. Maxi always competed strongly in class, but running was her greatest talent. Her friends were in awe of her running success.

'If I put more time into my homework, I would top the class,' she said. 'But I prefer to spend my time running.'

She was satisfied to be in the top academic group. Almost every Monday at school assembly, she would go up to the stage to receive a running award and the applause of staff and students. On Awards Night, she came away with many of the prizes for athletics. She learned to accept acclaim with modesty and her growing fame did not 'go to her head'.

14

'They say I am great,' she thought. *'But how would they know? How can anyone know when I have only run in local races?'*

'Am I special?' she asked her face in the mirror. 'No, but I will be special. I'll find ways to improve until I am the best.'

She was offered a place at a private boarding school with a prestigious athletics record, reputable coaches and alumni who were champion athletes. Her parents declined the offer.

'We want you to live at home,' Stan said. 'They produce losers as well as winners. You'll be safer here with us.'

'Okay. I heard it's pretty grim there.'

'I would miss you,' said Patti, 'a bit.'

Maxi was pleased her relationship with Patti had improved.

Her father took her to the Little Athletics Club on Wednesday afternoons and Saturdays, for club competitions and gala events. Maxi's exceptional running ability attracted interest from Henry, the club coach. He decided which events Maxi should run in and planned her training programme with Stan.

Maxi's disaffection was known to her father and he encouraged her to take responsibility for improving her performance. Making training choices empowered her.

'You need to run 40 kilometres a week. I'll go with you as much as I can. The drone can be your pace-setter and report on your safety, vitals, and results.'

When training made demands on her resolve, her self-confidence sometimes faltered.

'I may not have the equipment to be the fastest female on the planet,' she told her father. 'I don't have a freakish body.'

'Your body is good enough,' he said. 'It's your mind that has to be unique.'

'My mind isn't unique,' she said. 'I have doubts and fears the same as other runners.'

'You're spending too much time dreaming,' he said. 'You'd be better off thinking how to run faster. If you have your head in the clouds, you won't know what your body is doing.'

'I'm finding it difficult to concentrate.'

'It will get easier. With practice, you'll reach your goal.'

15

She knew he wouldn't lie to her; he never had.

'I am getting better. Thank you for all your help. Do you really think you can lift me up that high?'

'I can try or find someone who can.'

'Thanks, Dad.'

He persuaded her of the need for regular and intense training. She didn't know any famous athletes or sports stars, apart from her father. When Cathy Freeman came to her school, Maxi escorted her on a tour and chatted with her.

'They told me you can be a champion,' Cathy said. 'You are special. Most people never get the chance and would give everything to be in your shoes. Don't waste your chance! Do you have a goal?'

Maxi told her she wanted to win the marathon at the Olympics.

'That is an excellent goal,' said Cathy. 'Don't waste your time dreaming about it. You have to put everything you have into your training.'

Maxi trained hard, but when doing routine exercises, she sometimes lost interest.

'Are you sure my training is extending me enough?' she asked Stan during a break in her training at the school track. Her father's ideas about coaching were from a bygone era. 'Shouldn't I be doing other things?'

'Stop stressing,' Stan said. 'To build running ability, you have to do it over and over again.'

'What's the value in repeating it?'

'It stays the same, but you change. You do it better.'

'I'm not speeding up much. Shouldn't I be trying new things?'

'We can add some exercises, but you already have great skills. You need fine-tuning, not making over.'

'It seems to be taking forever. How long will it take?'

'Until your next race. After that, you begin again, pushing harder and ratcheting up your effort. It will get tougher and tougher. It can take years, but you have time.'

'How can you be sure this is the way? Is it scientific?'

'I believe in you.'

'Thank you. I believe in you too.'

'I may not be good enough to help you all the way. You'll need someone else.'

'Don't worry, Dude. You're good enough for me now. That's what matters.'

CHAPTER 3

Jack Cram and his non-identical twin brother, Sebastian, lived with their hippy parents near Kings Beach Caloundra. Their mother, Sarah, designed lift systems for new buildings, working three days per week. Their father, Brian, worked three days as an air traffic controller at nearby Brisbane Airport. There was always a parent at home if either of the twins chose to stay home from school, as they did sometimes. The Cram's lifestyle was Bohemian. The boys were required to choose free-spirited activities that valued science, art and self-expression over status and excessive belongings, respecting others, consuming little and conserving the environment.

Both boys helped their parents grow food and take care of livestock on their acreage. Jack investigated how things worked, using microscopes, cameras and telescopes. He took things apart and put them back together again, sometimes with repairs or improvements. He realised his own character happily and gained self-respect.

Sebastian grew vegetables in the house garden. He helped Jack with his experiments and kept things organised.

Jack was about 180cm, moderate build, his torso narrowing to slim hips, his posture upright. It was the body of a sports player, moving fluidly and briskly in a straight line, pushing other pedestrians to use their half of pathways. His face was pale and oval, surmounted by locks of brown hair swept back from a square hairline, a high forehead, large penetrating eyes, stubbled cheeks and smallish ears, narrowing down to a pointed chin.

At school, he and Sebastian sat together and worked independently of the class.

'Hippies,' jeered their classmates.

The boys' projects were ahead of the others' and more creative. When the class learned computer coding, Jack showed outstanding high ability. He astonished his teacher and parents when he designed a digital model of the Universe, including the constellations and a mathematical model of the solar system.

'I'm getting to know where I live,' Jack said.

'Astronomy nerd,' his classmates scoffed. 'Get a life.'

However, within a few years, they had changed to admiration.

'Jack's inventions are cool.'

Sebastian helped him but was content with a back seat.

The brothers sat an entrance exam for an elite secondary college that prepared students for university entrance. Jack won a scholarship, but Sebastian was assigned to a vocational school to learn a trade. He was labelled 'the dumb one'. Although they were together at home and on the bus, their separation was unfortunate, affecting both boys badly.

'They are grieving, like from loss of a limb,' a psychologist told their parents. 'Singletons who have never experienced separation anxiety cannot imagine the painfulness.'

Neither of them made friends at their new schools and they kept to themselves. Their parents appealed to Jack's school to take Sebastian too, but they refused.

It jolted Jack out of his childish complacency. He had entered an adolescent world without ready-made rules where he was alone. The joy of his liberation was diminished by discovering that his social freedom could be encroached on by arbitrary and unfair actions of adults who could attack him, like a savage dog that breaks its chain. His freedom was restricted arbitrarily and unpleasantly by a ceiling of adult authority requiring him to comply with an arbitrary moral code.

He was angry that Sebastian's schooling was inferior and blamed his mother for the separation because the entrance exam had been her idea.

'I wanted you both to have the best opportunities possible,' she said.

19

Their mother comforted Sebastian but Jack switched his affection to his father.

He became a troubled adolescent out of step with his classmates. He did not work with others, preferring solo achievement.

'Jack, you must work in with the other students,' his teachers said.

'I don't want to be with them,' he said bluntly. 'They would hold me back.'

The others tried to bully him, but he won fights and they left him alone.

At age thirteen he opted to learn only maths, physics and chemistry. Discoveries in science interested him but so did the arts and humanities. He regretted having to make this choice. He chose science, but when the arts students discussed the motives of Shakespeare's characters, Rembrandt's use of light and the significance of the Magna Carta, he was envious. His schooling seemed unfairly narrow.

He asked his year coordinator if he could transfer from Chemistry to English Literature.

'Only if you are top in Chemistry.'

'Why?'

'You have to refute the hypothesis that you want to change because you are lazy.'

He topped Chemistry, but the coordinator would not let him change class.

'You would have to repeat a year,' he said. 'Is that what you want?'

He didn't want to repeat. He was resentful they had moved the goalposts with a new condition.

'All they care about is themselves,' Jack said.

He brooded that administration at the school was arbitrary and separation from his brother was unfair. His interest in school work declined, he refused to kowtow to the school's uniform dress rules and he defied punishments.

He quit doing the work, performed badly in assessment and was put into a slow class.

20

His father let him hunt using a .22 rifle. When he grew bored blowing apart hares and kangaroos, he set his sights on jet airliners thundering past overhead, going to and from Brisbane Airport. He hated the world and, even more, he hated himself. He put the muzzle in his mouth and imagined ending his life.

'I want to shoot myself,' he told his father.

'If you did that, I would blame myself.'

He couldn't do it to his father, who was kind to him.

Brian quietly observed his surly son and suggested he read author Albert Camus, who rejected suicide as an illogical response to an absurd world. Jack realised he should make the most of his life.

The media had prophesies of gloom and doom that worried Jack. The superpowers were in a new nuclear conflict, causing instability around the world.

'The world is run by inexperienced, narrow-minded, bigoted adults,' he thought. *'When will youth get a fair say?'*

Time dragged interminably at school. His teachers were old and slow. Their modelling of critical thinking skills and logical rigour was woeful. His thirst for insights was like trekking across a desert.

'Young people would be better at negotiating an end to conflict,' he thought. *'They would solve the problems by innovating, instead of reiterating past failure.'*

His accomplishments at school were limited to science, maths and sport. The drudgery of study and revision was punctuated by exams, from which his class position was calculated and announced as if his value was decided by his exam marks. His formative experiences were at home, where his father encouraged the boys' physical development and coached sports skills. Jack received a javelin for his sixteenth birthday and was in his school's athletics squad.

He gave up trying and started hanging out with the bad-ass kids. Teachers found his laconic commentaries during their classes offensive and disruptive. He would break school property and once pierced his hand with drawing compasses.

'Everything sucks,' he said.

21

Large, strong, irresponsible, wild and dangerous, he was sent to the office for fighting. At the School Athletics Carnival, his javelin almost speared a judge.

'Jack has a chip on his shoulder,' they said.

It seemed deliberate and they sent him away to a juvenile residential detention centre. Teachers had all the authority and resources. He had to conform, never acting positively from choice, only by flight.

At first, he felt defeated and contemptible. He could not will himself to do what he wanted and felt defeated. He wanted to be ignorant of himself and lose self-consciousness. He was fearful of engaging in any project. He tried to forget himself, to be ignorant of himself, but the nothingness inside him was also his awareness of himself. His negativity was revealed positively as anguish, desire, appeal and laceration.

He realized he was in the world as a blind uncontrolled force which anybody could control, even him. Either he turned back toward the world of his parents and teachers or he adopted the boys' perspective of what the world was about, what was wrong with it and how to negotiate with it. He identified with the boys' values, adopting their opinions, sheltering behind a label, adopting the prison language, emotions and sentiments. There were ready-made anti-group roles that enabled him to risk engaging and take refuge in group activity.

As his individual freedom was shredded, his solace was that his conformance was contrived and a means to an end. He had put aside his quest for uncompromised freedom and would stalk it patiently using his conformance to negotiate as best he could. He despised himself for slaving away at meaningless tasks, indistinguishable from his peers, but he had no choice. His satisfaction was from knowing that his obedience was merely a means to an end. His intent was to serve his time and regain his freedom.

He worked with his group of troubled adolescents at practical outdoor tasks. Gradually his anger was replaced by self-respect. He discovered he could choose to be who he wanted, that it took steady effort, but was worth it. He yearned to one day have a good job, a fast car, overseas travel and a beautiful girlfriend. It was up to him.

When he returned to the school from the detention centre, he was a changed boy. He became a conscientious, hard-working student. Aiming for a technological career, he resumed the science subjects he had spurned and applied himself diligently, astonishing his teachers.

He was chosen for the first XV rugby team and was able to vent his frustration in legitimate violence. He hung out with the guys, relinquishing his inclination to be nerdy, detached and alone. After a game, he would come from the showers into a maths class, fall into a seat nursing injuries and quietly solve the problems set. But he preferred javelin and pole vault, solo activities that investigated biomechanics, body dynamics and trajectories.

Jack competed at athletics meets as a member of his school's squad. He admired the focus of the distance runners and framed his Year 12 studies as an endurance event, with a series of obstacles to overcome. His teachers cajoled and threatened him to jump through the hoops of calculus like a circus pony, deducing oxidation reactions and predicting simple harmonic motion. The light-bulb moments were few. Time dragged endlessly between school bells but he maintained a steady effort.

His studies at school seemed interminable. Incarcerated in the classroom at a desk, day after day, he asked himself: 'Who cares about chemical equilibrium reactions? Does anyone use Newton's Second Law to calculate the angle to fire an artillery gun? Why would anyone ever need to know the area beneath a quadratic curve? His subjects seemed a procession of lifeless dogma. He wondered if a full-time job would be any better.

Because he was captive, he consented to live under these restrictions. He was not oblivious to freedom but hunkered down declining opportunities that came his way, even those that attracted him. He felt dishonest, excusing himself by renewing his dedication to his studies. They were a means to his end.

He travelled to school with Sebastian and together after school they cared for the animals. Hours of homework followed. He ploughed through his textbooks, checking his responses with the model answers, enjoying accomplishment. He imagined each problem that he solved would bring him closer to finishing school and getting off this merciless treadmill.

His mother Sarah was a staunch advocate for delayed gratification.

'Work hard now and you will be able to enjoy yourself later.'

His parents distrusted impulsivity and dictates of the ego. He worked hard without enjoyment or material reward. He focused on the moment, solving problems one after another, hour after hour.

Jack visited a university, attended a lecture and watched the students at study and play. *'I wouldn't mind being an academic. All I have to do is put up with this school shit until the end of the year.'*

His ranking at exit gained him entry to study physics at the University of Queensland.

His school studies had been arduous, but he had learned to enjoy self-directed learning. He left school with a restive mind and a strong analytical ability. He could multitask several threads simultaneously. He developed a passion for theoretical physics. His ambition was to become a researcher in physics. He had a passionate but vague interest in uniting mankind and was trying to find a role in which he could contribute. The world was in a mess and that bothered him.

CHAPTER 4

Maxi was in Year 8 at the secondary college, a lively teenager with a blonde ponytail and long legs, a distinguished distance runner who posed and strutted, turning heads wherever she went. She exulted in her superlative physique. She was the centre of attention at running meets, leading the others in staging pranks. Her boisterous frolicking sometimes pushed against adults' boundaries. When a parent complained her behaviour was riotous at a pool party, her coach at Little Athletics Club (LAC) gave her a personal warning.

'You're becoming a brinkster,' Henry said. 'Do you know that word?'

'No.'

'If you were younger, I would have said precocious. You are behaving in ways not expected until you are older. You are testing limits. You can test your limits on the track by running fast and breaking records, not by playing up and getting into trouble. Watch your step, young lady!'

She went with her parents to the athletics championships for the area. There were runners from a handful of clubs of various ages. Maxi had run against them earlier in the year and had been first or second to finish. Her personal best in the 1500 metres had steadily improved to 5 minutes 15 seconds.

Boys and girls ran together at each age. In previous club competitions, Maxi had often outrun the boys, but this year they were bigger, faster and she might not win. The winning girl and winning boy would go forward to separate races in the State Championships the following month.

Stan had no son. During his lifetime, females' capabilities had been realised. Women had started distance running only recently and had been allowed to compete in the Boston Marathon for the first time as late as 1972. The gender gap was closing. He tried to have gender-neutral expectations of students, in both science and athletics. He accepted that Maxi's running ability was equal to or superior to his own.

Behind the starting line, there were twelve girls and seven boys spread across the track.

'Move over,' a voice said rudely, jostling Maxi.

A girl elbowed in beside her. It was a foul to interfere with another runner. Surprised, Maxi let her in. She wasn't sure if it was Amy, a girl who had pushed in in an earlier race.

'Get set.'

They all stepped forwards and toed the line.

'Bang!'

Maxi lunged forward with the pack and ran as hard as she could. Amy elbowed her hard in the ribs and when Maxi hesitated, pushed past her. It was a foul. Maxi stayed behind her until they had opened a lead with only a couple of boys in front of them. The sprint slackened a little and time dragged. They were in single file now and Maxi was tucked in at fourth in the inside lane, her long smooth strides and arms working in perfect synchrony.

It was a race of three 400 metre laps, plus three-quarters of a lap, to make 1500m. Maxi felt strong and decided to burn off Amy. She kicked out to go around her and shot forward, but as she came back into the inside lane in front of Amy, her foot caught hers and sent her sprawling. The track was grass and there was little damage to her knees and hands. She jumped up with her eyes focussed on Amy's receding back. Pushing her anger aside, she gritted her teeth and homed in, catching up and drawing alongside Amy, who tried to stay in front. Maxi was stretched out and flying with more power than Amy could match. Maxi passed her, panting oxygen to ease the pain in her starved muscles.

Maxi was no stranger to pain, for Stan detested 'softness.' He had made her do long hard runs, steep hills, bad weather, cold showers and late lunches. He ignored her when she complained of pain and treated minor injuries as malingering. His coaching had toughened Maxi. It was his way of showing love.

The boys in the front positions made a weak attempt to hold their lead, but Maxi ignored the worst hurt she had ever experienced and shot past them. She crossed the finish line fifteen metres ahead, her legs rubbery. Her time of 4m40 was a new under 16 club record by a large margin, below the boys' record too.

The boys stared at her in awe and a small audience of parents whooped and yelled.

'Way to go, Maxi!'

Her big toe was sore, but there was no sign of bleeding or bruising. There was a trickle of blood from one knee and from scratches on the heels of her hands. Maxi glared at Amy but she turned away. Maxi was sure she had tripped her deliberately. It was the trailing runner's responsibility not to contact a runner in front and Amy had been at fault. She thought of speaking to her but thought it would do no good.

She limped across to the race officials' tent.

'Excuse me,' she gasped. 'Amy Stark fouled me three times. She elbowed me when we lined up at the start, she cut me up as we got away and in the third lap brought me down with a deliberate trip.'

Coach Henry had known Maxi for years from their weekly training sessions.

'I didn't see a trip,' he said, 'but I believe you. Someone else has complained about Amy. I'll have a word with her.'

Maxi saw him talking to Amy.

When he came back he said: 'Amy denies tripping you. Are you sure it was her?'

Maxi felt her face flushing.

'She's lying,' she thought.

'She did trip me.'

'Could you have imagined it was her?'

'No.'

'Could it have been someone else?'

'I crossed over in front of her just before my foot was tripped.'

27

'Did you see her face?'

Maxi hesitated. She wasn't good at faces. Sometimes she mixed people up. There had been other runners near them and they were all wearing club colours, so it was difficult to tell who was who.

'It looked like her.'

'Could it have been one of the others?'

Maxi paused. Amy's face was like the others.

'I don't know.'

'Unless you are certain it was her, I can't do anything, sorry. Anyway, you are through to the State. In future, before you call a foul, be sure you know who did it.'

Henry turned away. Maxi felt cheated, but at least she was through to the State. There would be stiff competition. Winning today had taken everything she had. She would train hard. She would show everyone her ability and they would respect her too much to try anything on. Her success felt good and she wanted more.

CHAPTER 5

Henry introduced Stan, Patti and Maxi to Margot, the state junior distance coach. She discussed Maxi's outstanding performances and her running future.

'Maxi has rare talent and she should have the opportunity to get as far as she can,' said Margot.

'How much training should she do?' asked Stan.

'Five or six hours daily.'

'It's too much to fit between her subjects.'

'Can she go to school part-time?'

'No, the School won't allow it,' he said.

'Is there a school for athletes?' asked Patti.

'Only for older students,' said Margot. 'Could she do home education next year?'

'What study would she do?'

'There's a distance education school with online lessons.'

'Going to a school is social conditioning,' said Patti. 'Don't kids need that?'

'She'll have enough social contact through running,' said Stan. 'She can be with friends at the club and at weekends. In year 9, she won't be missing much of importance at school. Girls tend to mark time, gossip about boys, discover pop culture, suffer teenage angst and get into trouble. She'll be better off with homeschooling.'

'Dad's right,' Maxi said. 'Going to school is a waste of time. There's so much distraction with kids playing up; it's difficult to get any work done in class.'

'That's not the point, Maxi. If you continue at school, you won't be able to do the training necessary to get to the top. Do you want to get to the top?'

'Yes.'

'You can run mornings and do schoolwork in the afternoons,' Stan said with enthusiasm.

'Who will keep an eye on her when she's out running in the middle of nowhere?' asked Patti.

She remembered her own wild adolescence and was less interested in protecting Maxi than controlling her.

'She can't go out on her own,' said her father. 'She must be supervised at all times. It was okay when I was keeping an eye on her track work, but she has started doing twenty-kilometre runs. Riding with her on my bike takes a lot of time, when I should be preparing lessons. It could be too much on top of teaching.'

'She'll need more and more training,' Margot said.

'She's self-motivated and coaching her is a joy,' said Stan. 'She has the opportunity of a lifetime. I want to support her running as much as she needs and oversee her studies. My drone can go with her on some training runs. I can set exercises, demonstrate techniques, monitor her performance and help her to improve.'

'How are you going to cope, Stan?' said Patti. 'What about your job?'

'I'll take leave. Maxi's grandmother left some money for Maxi to have opportunities she wouldn't get otherwise. I know she would have wanted Maxi to have this opportunity. Ten years from now, Maxi will have retired from running and I'll go back to teaching.'

'Will we have enough money?' said Patti.

'It will be tight.'

'I can get a job,' Patti said, 'in nutrition.'

Stan and Maxi looked at her in amazement. So far her interest in employment had been limited to auditioning.

'I wonder what her agenda is?' thought Stan. *'I haven't seen her weighing in to help Maxi before — although she has been good with preparing vegan meals for us.'*

Maxi put her arm around her stepmother.

'Thanks, Patti. Could you continue looking after my food, please?'

'Yes, I'd like that,' said Patti. She turned to Stan. 'Will she be able to keep up with her school work?'

'She'll have to send work in regularly,' said Stan.

'It's a long shot,' said Patti. 'but will it be worth it? Distance running has few rewards. What if she loses interest, gets injured or simply doesn't run fast enough? When she has to get up at 6 am in the winter, she could lose interest. We can support her, but the motivation has to come from her. What do you say, Maxi?'

Stan realised that Patti expected Maxi to quit running and she would help her to fail. His preoccupation with Maxi's running would end and he would switch his attention to Patti.

'I want to do it,' Maxi said.

'Can she try it and see how she gets on?' asked Stan.

'She is going to be very busy,' said Margot, 'and so are you, Stan.'

Margot looked at Maxi, Patti and Stan. 'So it's decided?'

'Maxi, it's home schooling for you next year!' said Stan.

'Wow! Great,' she said.

'You'll be training six days.'

'Bring it on.'

In the new year, Maxi started Year 9 distance education at home and Stan took leave to supervise her. She was always first up in the morning and eager to run, whatever the weather.

Each day had different activities. On Mondays she did cross-training in the gym and pool, for 1 to 2 hours; on Tuesdays she varied from easy running, to tempo, Fartlek and hill running, again 1-2 hours, on a monthly cycle; Wednesday was a rest day, with schoolwork all day; Thursdays she had runs of 1 or 2 hours, with up to 8 repeats of high effort brief intervals; Friday was rest; Saturdays had a run of an hour at race pace including intervals; Sunday was a longer run, at least 1 hour at easy pace, increasing as an event neared, to 3 hours at race pace.

Stan spent mornings with her at the school's running track or accompanied her in the Glasshouse Mountains, or along coastal trails at Kings Beach. He coached her to develop her style with exercises on the school's track.

'To improve your coordination, I want you to sprint, pace, lope, stutter, prance, canter, trot, step, skip and run backwards,' he said. 'Follow me. The purpose is to stretch your body, achieving flexibility and strength. Li Cunxin, the ballet dancer, spent hours forcing his body into new positions at the barre before learning new movements. The pain was enormous but screaming would have brought severe punishment. Hurting is not the purpose, but it is necessary.'

Other exercises developed her stride length, foot strike, posture, gait, cadence, breathing, cell respiration and circulation. She did circuit work in the gym and swam in the pool to strengthen her body and muscle responses.

She ran all morning and in the afternoon did her school subjects. The arrangement worked well. Both her running and her schoolwork were improving.

CHAPTER 6

Jack won a scholarship to study physics at the University of Queensland. He rented a room near the university with his earnings from ride-share driving and started a new life. He had been root-bound at high school, without space to grow into who he wanted to be. At university, he was free to develop independently of parents, adults and peers. He could have a girlfriend if he wanted and he did, going on dates that relieved the tedium of study.

Sebastian left school at the same time. When Jack went off to university, he stayed at home and worked as a warehouseman in a logistics depot beside the motorway.

Their lives seldom coincided. The earlier rejection of his brother by his secondary school impelled Jack to make the most of his own elite education. He wanted his learning to bring wealth and influence that could alleviate Sebastian's toil, to make up to him the opportunities that had been denied.

Physics was what Jack liked doing best and it felt like his intellect had found a home. He had spent his school holidays building racing carts, tree houses and flying foxes. He had dammed the local creek, constructed rafts, punts and canoes, installed a waterwheel with an electrical generator to charge batteries, made a solar still and modified farm machinery. He had a thirst for technology and used every opportunity to learn as much as he could.

He hoped studying physics, maths and computer coding at university would lead to a job in IT. Concepts like relativity and string theory fascinated him. He delighted in drawing diagrams and using mathematics to tease out metaphysical concepts of space and time.

At the commencement of the first year, students in his class received a warning.

'This year's intake is too large for all of you to go on to second year. Students who do not achieve will be dis-enrolled at the end of this year.'

There were sixty-three students in Jack's cohort. Peer pressure and competition didn't bother him. He could shut out the world and give his full attention to one thing at a time, not letting feelings and emotions get in his way.

Half of his time was taken by lectures, laboratory work and tutorials, with the other half available for study. Time had dragged at school, but it flew past now he was able to follow his interests and satisfy his curiosity. For the first time, he enjoyed studying.

He was grazing on the savannah of learning, moving with the undergraduate herd. Tutors and postgraduates seized his ideas like predators. He was flattered and happily showed them his work, developing his proficiency.

In second year, he moved into a hall of residence. He made several friends. Alice Lamont was a psychology major; Blake Holocene was an engineer; Corvid Feir was a neuroscientist.

Alice was leaving the hall with a backpack one Sunday morning and he walked beside her.

'What are you doing today?' he asked, expecting her to say: 'Bushwalking'.

'A base jump.'

'Wow! Where?'

'In the mountains. There's a cliff.'

'How will you get there?'

'We'll drive in and then go up in a helicopter.'

'How many jumps have you done?'

'Heaps. I have to go now.'

'Can we talk later? I want to find out about it.'

'Okay.'

He was having his evening meal with Corvid when Alice joined them.

'How was your jump, Alice,' he asked.

'Great, thanks.'

'Tell us about it.'

'It was about 1000 metres vertically. I wore a lycra bodysuit with a hood and a parachute pack. The arms have webs, like stubby wings. I ran and dived out from the top of the cliff and steered with my wings to pass down through a chasm. I was falling almost vertically. I came out over the landing ground, pulled the ripcord and dropped on to my feet.'

'Did it hurt?'

'Not at all. I have been dragged before, but today it was gentle.'

'How long did it take?'

'About 20 seconds.'

'What did it feel like?'

'Out of this world. There's nothing like it. It's tremendously exciting. At first, your mind races with thoughts. But then time crawls as you look around at the awesome spectacle of mountains rushing towards you as your time crawls to an end. It drives everything else out of your head.'

'Is that why you do it?'

'I get a rush, a huge buzz, beyond anything else. It's like being reborn with new awareness of the world.'

'Was it like a near-death experience?'

'Maybe it was: I could have died.'

'So is it the danger that attracts you?'

'No. It's fun and about as dangerous as crossing the road.'

'Were you frightened?'

'The first time I was petrified, but now I'm used to it.'

'A kilometre in 20 seconds is 180 kilometres an hour,' Jack said.

'I was at terminal velocity, as fast as air resistance would let me go,' said Alice.

'How quick did it seem?'

'Not quick at all: it was serene. Those 20 seconds went on and on, for longer than every other 20-second interval I have ever lived. Can neuroscience explain that?' she asked Corvid. She was a Goth, in long black clothes, with earring and lank black hair. She was reputed to possess spiritual and even mystical occult skills.

'Did it seem as long as a 200-metre dash, about 20 seconds?' Corvid asked.

'Longer.'

'It's the Kappa effect,' Corvid said. 'People overestimate elapsed time when stimuli are repeated at equal intervals with the distance traversed increasing.'

'Do you mean I was beguiled to believe I was operating constantly, an illusion?' Alice said.

'You assumed you had taken more time than you really did, because you were going further,' said Jack. 'You were going faster than you expected, so it seemed to take longer.'

'So that's how it works,' said Alice. 'Jack, you are one cool piece of work. Every cell in your body is doing physics all the time.'

'Yeah,' said Corvid. 'We have met-a-physical.'

'How do our brains keep time?' Jack asked Corvid, because she was a neuroscientist.

'Who says they do?' she said. 'Maybe thoughts take as long as necessary.'

'When we do a lot of thinking,' said Jack, 'our brains have to speed up.'

'What if brain time could stretch to fit it all in?' Corvid asked.

'Could it?'

'No-one knows. Brain time can't be measured.'

'If brain time could stretch, we could get more done in the same time,' said Jack. 'Maybe there's a way to stretch it.'

'For a computer's central processing unit to do more in the same time, it has to be reprogrammed. Alternatively, the completion time has to be delayed. What if the computer has its own time and can stretch to get done without delay?'

'Computers have clocks. They can't stretch their time.'

'Brain time can stretch when it has to.'

36

'It may have to adjust perception to match certitude.'

'Then it can seem to bend,' said Alice, standing up. 'Perhaps sky-divers and glider pilots are time travellers too. I have to go. See you later.'

'What are you going to do now?' Corvid asked Jack when she had gone.

'I've been researching some ideas.'

'What about?'

'Time.'

'Why are you obsessed with time?' Corvid said. 'Are you on a schedule or something?'

'I suppose I am,' he said. 'I'm trying to find out how to use my time best.'

'Like what things to do?'

'Time can be determined by definite activities,' said Jack. 'For me, time is an intangible, malleable and personal element in my work, most valuable when my work is independent.'

'How are you aware when you are independent?'

'When I can do what I like, free of attachments.'

'Don't you like attachments?' she asked.

'Not usually.'

'Me neither,' said Corvid. 'It's why I'm going to do a PhD.'

'To be independent? Are you breaking out from something, or away from someone?'

'I like to be contemplative, detached, free.'

'Me too,' Jack said. 'What do you contemplate?'

'How brains work.'

'Me to. I want to learn how they regulate our sense of time, how people can control time.'

'Wow! That's ambitious.'

'Many people have to perform feats quickly without looking at a timepiece. They may get their idea of speed as an impression. I want to find out about runner control over performance time in distance running.'

'That seems like something worth knowing about. I thought runners monitor performance with wrist devices.'

'They do, but the bigger problem is how they can best use that information. Do you think about how brains control our time?'

'Never! I don't think about it; I connect with the world spiritually, by meditation.'

'Mindfully?'

'Mindlessly.'

'You're kidding!'

'Yes. I stick to lower order thinking: TV, food, sex, drugs, whatever.'

'You're taking the piss.'

'Get a life, Jack.'

He smiled. Corvid was attractive. If he could get to know her better, perhaps they could get together.

'I have to go,' she said. 'I'm on a schedule, a lower order one. Bye.'

CHAPTER 7

A few days after her success in the 1500 metres at the Area Championships, she drove with Stan to a local park to prepare for the State competition.

'Today is Saturday, when we practice race-pace running,' he said. 'I want you to follow this trail for half a marathon, that's 7 of your 1500s, as fast you can.'

'Why so far and so fast?'

'You're up against some good runners. When you've run hard for 10 kilometres, hard running 1500 metres will seem like a doddle.'

Maxi trained with earbuds, her mobile and a mike at her waist. She could press a button and speak to Stan, where he waited at the start. Her drone watched over her. A phone app, Strava 7, relayed with the drone and calculated her GPS position, keeping stats like distance, time, calories and active minutes, uploading them to her Fitbit.

As usual, Maxi's self-talk was reflection, a conversation in her head.

'It's 5 kilometres each way,' she thought as she ran, 'but already I am giving it a big effort. I have set my level high, like the last lap of a 1500 metre race. I have to do two more 1500 metres and a bit more to halfway. Doing it again coming back will not be too far at all.

' I've been going for only 10 minutes, but time is dragging. It is taking forever. I can't even remember what I was doing earlier today. Oh, no! Another runner. Should I wave? Why not? Oh, they didn't wave back. Maybe she'll think I'm a dill. Maybe I am a dill. Fuck them. I'm not going to wave at anybody now.

'Telling myself helps my concentration, keeps me focussed.

'It's getting easier. Maybe my dad is right, you do get a second wind. Oh, it's downhill. If I had a heart attack here, no-one would come for ages. Then they might run right past me. What if there was a body on the ground around this next corner? This isn't such a great place to run. It may be better to run in the street. Then I could look at myself in shop windows. Is my posture okay? My legs are too long and my ass is too small. I'm built for going down hills, not up.

'That last section went quickly. I've turned around and I have three more 1500 metres to do. It should be easy after that. Oh no! Here's a hill. Where did that come from? It wasn't so steep going down. I'll pretend it isn't here. Christ, this is hard going. My legs don't want to bend. I've had enough. Why did I ever start running? There's no point to it. You just go around in circles without getting anywhere. I might as well be dead. This is getting too negative.

'I have to finish at race pace. God, it is taking everything to keep this pace up. Hard running is a like a bottomless pit I can't get out of. Next time I'll have a time goal I can aim for. This open-ended running is the pits. Not much further.

'There's only another 1500 metres to go. I've been running for half an hour. If I did a half-marathon, it would take about 70 minutes. Maybe I'll do that one day. Oh, this is good. I'm overtaking someone. I'm not even going to look at him. Oh, he said hello. How nice is that? We both stopped. His name is Ken, he lives near the garage and he's new in the area and has just started running. He's friendly and maybe hot. Running is pretty good. We're both runners. Look at us running. Not much further now.

'Stan saw me stop and talk to him. He won't be pleased. Too bad. There has to be some fun for me to stay interested. Phew. I've finished.'

'Good work,' said Stan, waiting by the car, 'Only a little time wasted stopping there.'

'I think of it as a reward for running hard.'

'It was good practice. Lack of fuel didn't slow you down, so you could have run harder. We'll do it again next week.'

'I can't wait.'

'Atta girl.'

Maxi thought of herself as a runner. Running absorbed her. It was the centre of her life. She felt privileged when she was enjoying it and when she wasn't, accepted it was necessary. To get to her goal, she expected hardship. She ran, studied, ate, slept and suffered.

Patti was less occupied. She sometimes sat stunned or stoned staring into space. She would shake out a cigarette, light it, hold it with long fingers and blow the smoke up to the ceiling. She smoked and drank profusely.

Maxi wondered what went on in her head.

'Are you doing mindlessness?' she asked her.

'You wouldn't understand,' said Patti.

They traded insults regularly. Maxi knew she should be sympathetic but Patti seemed like a poser.

'Would you not smoke in the house?' said Maxi. 'That goes for your joss sticks too. Dad doesn't like them.'

'Stan doesn't mind, do you Stan?' Patti said. 'He accepts that people can have differences.'

Stan was reading and was silent.

'You shouldn't impose harm on innocent people,' said Maxi.

'Everyone does,' Patti said. 'Can you hear that noise? It's traffic and planes. Its obnoxious but it happens anyway. Get used to it. When you're older, you'll be more tolerant and a nicer person.'

'You're not nice. You don't tolerate my need for fresh air.'

'You blame others, Maxi,' said Patti, 'because you only care about yourself.'

'Lung cancer kills many people,' Maxi said. 'Don't you think it's inconsiderate to suicide when your family want you to stay alive?'

'Dramatizing it doesn't make it harmful. Smoke is part of the natural environment. Modern humans have evolved around smoky fires. Genetic types unable to cope with smoke died out long ago.'

'Smoke can cause anyone to have lung cancer.'

'Sensitivity to smoke has been selected out,' said Patti. 'In moderation, smoke is not a problem.'

'Would you please choose a less anti-social way of indulging yourself?' asked Maxi.

'Vitriolic bitch,' was Patti's reply.

'We all have cancer in us and cancer cells are activated by smoke particles when there is anger, anxiety, depression or pessimism,' Maxi said. 'If you want to live you should reduce these emotions, particularly your anger. Cutting out smoking is the first step.'

'Would you please reduce your anger about my smoking,' Patti said.

'Maxi,' said Stan interrupting. 'I want you to stop hassling Patti about her smoking. She has the right to kill herself if she wants.'

'Thank you very much for your concern Stan,' said Patti.

A few days later, Patti changed to vaping.

'E-cigarettes allow me to absorb more nicotine,' she said. 'The effect is wearing off and I'm looking for something to replace nicotine.'

'Why don't you try strychnine?' Maxi said.

'If I had some, I would put it in your food.'

'Living here with you, I would eat it.'

They looked at each other and burst out laughing.

CHAPTER 8

As the State competition approached, Stan stepped up her training. He was dour and demanding, increasing her running volume, requiring her to train every day at the Club and solo one day at the weekend.

Stan's coaching assumed she would be encouraged by his esteem and warm fuzzies, her main reward being public acclaim when she raced. Punishments were doled out as harsh words, silences and extra laps. He believed that training had to be hard enough to hurt a lot. He thought a coach's task was to motivate the athlete to endure suffering or to shame them when they quit. It was behavioural conditioning which assumed Maxi lacked self-control and as a coach he had total control. It was authoritarian and Maxi resented it.

'Don't save yourself,' Stan said. 'Give it everything you've got.'

Maxi was doing more practice running for the State Championship than for any previous race. Stan expected her to adhere closely to the training programme they had agreed, with no authority to make changes. She logged her times for each run, next to her target times, to discuss her achievement with Stan.

Every day of her 14-day cycle began with a run of 8 kilometres in their neighbourhood, followed by fartlek runs and interval running on the school track, with pace increasing and rests decreasing. Two weeks before her race, she tapered off.

On the day, Stan drove with her to the QE2 stadium, taking in his car several other competitors from the Club. She spent the morning in the stand, yelling for her friends. The 1500 metres was after lunch. There were fifteen girls in her race. She knew a couple of them and chatted as they waited to be called to the start.

'These girls are quicker than any you have run against this year,' Stan said, leaning over the fence. 'Stay with the frontrunners if you can. Remember your training and don't try to run flat out all the way. Keep some petrol in your tank to get in front at the end. Your last lap should be faster than your first.'

In the dressing room, she chatted with Artula Crawford. Maxi had beaten her, narrowly, in the State final the previous season.

'I've broken all the rules of training this year,' Maxi said to her. 'I may fall into a hole and never get out again.'

'Have you trained to run hard all the way?' asked Artula.

'No,' said Maxi, lying.

'That's good,' she said. 'I'll be taking it easy too.'

It seemed like Artula wanted to lure her into a pact that Artula expected to win.

'My contest is with myself, not against Artula,' Maxi thought. *'I want to improve on my time of 4m40 at the Area.'*

She walked out on to the track wearing an oversize man's shirt and a baseball cap back-to-front. Her smile showed no trace of nervousness. She went through her last-minute preparations and took a mouthful of water. She removed her street clothes revealing white top with a strappy back and bikini bottom underneath. She did stretches and shoulder flexes with the other girls as they lined up.

'Set.'

The gun fired.

Artula was in front from the start, setting a scorching pace. Maxi's plan was to shadow the leader in the first lap, staying glued to her hip through the second, then moving into the lead for the finish. For the first lap, her time was 65.3s. She felt strong and took the lead, departing from her plan. It was hot in the bright sun and perspiration ran from the girls' faces. Artula was close behind.

In the second lap, Artula challenged her lead twice, but Maxi hung on, with the next lap at 65.1s. The race was a little faster than she had prepared for, but she was able to sustain the pace. She put everything into it and the two of them were 50 metres ahead when Artula dropped back. The third lap was 64.4s and then at the start of the fourth, with three-quarters of a lap to go, everything hit Maxi all at once. A pain stabbed in her chest, her quads seared and convulsed, her calves cramped, her ankles felt sprained and she seemed to have marbles in her shoes. Overheating, she gasped, her body begging to quit and she slowed to a walk. She had encountered these hurts separately in training, but they were all together now and she was stunned. Never in all her races had she felt so spent, so far from the finish line. She staggered to a halt and squatted, her senses reeling.

'Pain is in your head, not your body,' Stan had told her. 'The initial causes of pain are unknown to science. Experience of pain is less frequent as living standards and medical technology improve and people have become soft. A runner is allowed to be squeamish, sensitive or even cowardly.

'Treatments vary widely and for the same symptoms, authorities may recommend either complete rest or continuing as usual. Toughness and machismo are less admired these days and distance runners and sports players learn to deal with pain. They disrespect it: because its source is uncertain; or because its warning has too large a safety margin; or because response needed would be involuntary. Your body will prevent itself from being injured. A champion distance runner succeeds because she has dealt with pain better than her rivals. You don't have to kowtow to pain.'

His words were small comfort to her now. She was familiar with his mind-over-matter obsession. Pain was an evergreen topic amongst runners. No-one seemed to understand it. It was her pain and it was her choice what she did about it. Her realisation of having choices was never so real and she agonised whether to quit or finish.

Artula and the others went past her as she bent over, her hands on her thighs. Her desire to finish overcame her misery, she stood up and resumed running. She was too far behind to catch up, although she gained twenty metres and was fourth across the line, with 4m55 in fourth place. She collapsed on to the track near Artula, Vandergris and Stewart. Medics took care of her and she quickly recovered.

'I blew that,' she said to Stan as they drove home. 'Did I hit the wall or what?'

'Maybe not: you didn't collapse.'

45

'What then? Was it because I didn't follow my plan? I must have used up all my energy.'

Stan hesitated.

'I'm not sure,' he said. 'There are several possible causes and it's impossible to know definitely.'

'Does it matter?'

'Yes. You need to know what to do next time, but you can't be sure.'

'That's not much help.'

'You have to guess and take your chances,' he said.

'What do you think was the problem?'

'You go first.'

'Perhaps I should have eaten more carbs?' she said.

'No, it wasn't that. I think you went under for psychological reasons. You were chronically fatigued from overtraining and you melted down. But I could be wrong.'

'How much training is overtraining?'

'You could have tried too hard. Training is to learn something new, not try hard. You could have feared relaxing and went at it too hard. The advice I gave you was wrong, causing you to overtrain. I can see it now. The way we copied competitors' schedules and fad training methods was wrong.'

'How much training should I have done?'

'The programme I set was too demanding,' Stan said. 'I should have left it more to you. Paula Radcliffe learned to self-trust, observing herself and how she was feeling. She reverted to minimal training and broke the world record. Would you be more comfortable with less training?'

It was a first for Maxi to have Stan admit he had been at fault. Previously he had blamed her when things went wrong. He was overly critical and this said more about his negativity than about her shortcomings.

'I would prefer to do less,' she said. 'Training alone all day every day is lonely and stressful. I seem to have all my eggs in the running basket. At school, I was with other students, talking about everything, realising the importance to me of running and

46

strengthening my resolve to train. Instead, I have to look for reasons to strive and sometimes I don't find them. I am tired of driving myself.'

'You should do as much as you feel like. It's not how much you do; you have to do it well.'

'I wasn't hungry enough in training.'

'It was my mistake, I pushed you too hard,' Stan said. 'We'll know in future. It was a good experience today. What are you going to do this weekend?'

'Hang out with the girls from the Club.'

'Enjoy yourself. You did okay today - you could have won.'

But the idea that she had failed lingered.

'You need to withdraw from your training habits and make a new start with a different orientation,' said Stan.

'Am I hiding away after my meltdown?'

'Not at all,' said Stan. 'You didn't stuff up. Overtraining happens often. You used hard work as a security blanket. It's my fault. We had been using best-is-less to excuse doing as little as possible. We went too far the other way. I thought working hard would be enough but your unrelenting hard work detracted from confident mental preparation. It didn't work out as I expected and I have learned from it. From now on, your training will learn from performance, not from ideas about how much work to do.'

They had talked several times about the possibility of Stan exchanging jobs with a science teacher overseas, who would live in their home while they lived in theirs, with Stan teaching their classes.

'How would it be if we went to London for a couple of years?' Stan asked the family at breakfast a few weeks later. After the disappointment of her performance at the State Championship, Maxi leapt at changing to a different scene. They discussed it, made inquiries and accepted.

In the months winding down before they went, Maxi wanted to socialise. She was 'that distance runner', a girl with a ponytail and long legs, shy and awkward. But her nature was to push against boundaries. Maxi sneaked out from home and let go of her social inhibitions as she never had before.

Maxi told her stepmother she had gone to the gym, but she joined some school friends in a séance. They went skinny-dipping with the male students, taking a boat and dancing naked around a fire. At a sleepover party, the girls lit Roly's bong, toked and choked on the smoke. Then they watched a porn movie. Her stepmother smelled the weed and went ballistic. Her friend Angela, another leader, was banned from their house.

Another time, she went out secretly on a date. Stan was furious. He cancelled her going to the State athletics training camp she had enjoyed in previous years.

'You have other things you should be doing, like riding. If this happens again, I'll sell your horse.'

After that, she was not allowed out except with her group at a movie. She went with a boy to Angela's place where they kissed and touched. Her father found out from her brother.

'Maxi, you are 15. You aren't old enough yet for sexual experimentation,' said Stan. 'It will be several years before you will be able to be in a situation like that.'

'I like boys,' said Maxi. 'I want a boyfriend.'

'You're not old enough.'

'How will I ever learn to talk with a boy?'

'You can talk with boys at the athletics club.'

'All they know about is running.'

'What do you want to talk about?'

'Everything.'

'Your school subjects?'

'That too. I need help with physics.'

'How would it be if I could find a student to tutor you in science?' Stan asked.

'That would be good. A male.'

'Don't get any ideas. He would be a science tutor. But it's not worth starting here — we're leaving for the UK in three months. I'll find someone for you over there.'

She resented that Stan had sanctioned her as if the rights she would gain when she turned 16 next year meant nothing. A child she was not. He sold her horse anyway, because she had stopped riding it. She didn't mind the horse going to someone with time to ride it. Her priority was running.

CHAPTER 9

Jack was not at university to pass. He wanted First Class honours. A top degree in physics would get a good job, a high salary and classy females. He wanted to be an oil tycoon, to pilot his own plane, ski, sail, dive and drive a fast car. To do these things he needed a high paying job obtained with a first-class degree.

Jack imagined a three-year marathon of study. To qualify, he would have to finish in the front group that accomplished assignments with highest competence, reported practical work above the required standard and solved problems in examinations displaying the skills taught.

He asked a friend who was a long-distance runner: 'What should be my strategy to succeed?'

'Your perceived effort must endure the unremitting pain of high effort while sustaining enough resources to get to the finish,' he told Jack. 'You need to establish superiority early, conserve energy, stay with the leading bunch and win the final sprint of exams.'

'I can equal anyone on this course,' he thought, *'because I am able to tolerate more study and keep on going when they quit.'*

They began the course work at a blistering pace, tightly bunched. It was difficult to pick the frontrunners because some hung back to conserve their strength. He kept notes on opponents' traits that might indicate high ability: assiduous note-taking; high quantity library borrowing; and interaction with lecturers outside class. He offered to trade answers to assignments with them, but the high flyers were reticent and those who reciprocated were mediocre. He persevered and people started coming to him for help. After a while, he was regarded as a pace-setter.

Jack's individuality had more individual attention at UQ than at school. He had more freedom, but the tasks required more concentration, resilience and stamina. The ordeal was a long negation of himself, with agonizing self-denial at times. His future held dark and terrifying spectres, but he had nothing to lose and he persevered with growing awareness of himself.

His antidote was to study obsessively. He had rolled over his study habits from school and thrived in a self-imposed routine. He was in heaven doing physics. His goal was to complete as many as possible of the physics units, going for A's in assignments, putting in long hours of study and sacrificing his recreation time. He worked fourteen hours a day for six-day weeks and observed peers losing motivation and dropping out. They disapproved of his working so hard and tried to entice him away from study. When they went in a group to the Students' Union bar, he studied. When they went to parties, he studied some more.

Girls were plentiful and attracted his attention. He eased off his studies a little, to everyone's relief. He allowed himself one night off per week. He dated a series of girls. He liked Corvid but she wanted him to go to rallies and cultural events that didn't interest him, demanding too much of his time.

'You need to get involved in some uni communities and the counter-culture,' she said.

'All they do is talk and complain,' he said. 'I want to make a difference.'

He changed to going with Ophelia, a second year at the hall, sleeping with her on one night at weekends. He had metamorphosed from the nerdy schoolboy he had been, dragging himself from hated task, to hated task. Now he thrived on learning, intoxicated by it.

He met Blake at the hall, an engineering student.

'I feel privileged to be learning physics,' Jack told him. 'It's sublime.'

'This is what Coleridge wrote,' said Blake.

'For he on honey-dew hath fed
And sipped the milk of paradise.'

51

'I envy you your rapture,' Blake said. 'Your diet of physics could have as many delights for you as Xanadu, with its stately pleasure dome.'

'Physics is wonderful,' Jack said. 'When most people try to play a piano, the sounds are separate notes. Legend has it that when Mozart was a boy, he could play whole pieces immediately. Physics ideas come to me naturally and I realize both the richness and the poverty of their origins.'

'Hmm. You do seem quite composed. Perhaps you're a genius.'

'Do you think I have exceptional intellectual ability?'

'No. I think you're a swottie nerd. Isembard Brunel was a genius. He was well-rounded. He studied art at uni, as well as engineering. All you do is physics.'

'Physics is aesthetic.'

'Oh?'

'The proofs and maths are beautiful.'

'Not for me they aren't: they take the fun out of life.'

'That's because you are an engineer who believes in the senses and reason, whereas most humans live by intuition.'

Jack and chatted with Blake often. He wanted to invite Blake to go home with him in the vacations. But he knew the disparity between his twin brother Sebastian's life and his own would resurface, spoiling the visit. He didn't invite Blake but went home and spent time with his parents and twin brother.

Seb lived at home and worked in a warehouse, distributing groceries, from a glass-sided building 4 kilometres long and a kilometre wide, constructed recently by GroCom on a greenfield site where arterial motorways intersected with a ring road around the city of Brisbane. 70% of Queensland's population lived within a 4 hour drive. The warehouse was surrounded by spacious grass lawns, gardens and trees.

He gave Seb a lift to work.

'Drop me over there,' Seb said, directing him.

He stopped at an inconspicuous door in a vast glass wall.

'What do you do in there?' Jack asked him.

'We pack groceries for customers.'

52

'What customers?

'They order online and their groceries are delivered to their homes from one of our 85 distribution depots.'

'From the closest one?'

'It could be from farther away, if they are out of stock.'

'Where do GroCom get the stuff?'

'The trucks arrive in the dead of night from wholesalers and manufacturers nationwide and overseas. They reverse into receival bays, where fork-lifts unload the pallets. I'll tell you about it later. I had better get inside, or I'll be late. Thanks for the ride. See you this evening. Someone'll give me a lift home.'

When Seb arrived home, Jack was writing an assignment on his laptop.

'How did you go?' Jack asked.

'Okay.'

'What did you do today?'

'Packing mostly.'

'Did you fill boxes with groceries?'

'No,' said Seb. 'A robotic cart goes to the storage area to fetch an item. It stops on the track above a storage bin, reaches down and brings up a crate. It takes it to have the item picked out, boxed and despatched, all automatically. You should see it. There are hundreds of carts scooting every which way, on a grid the size of 4 football fields. They navigate along tracks in straight lines, turning at right-angled intersections. They go to and fro between 1500 storage bins. They use GPS navigation to cross paths without colliding.'

'Is there anything for you to do?'

'I check that the items ordered are being brought together okay. Things can go wrong, like a package spilling its contents.'

'Then what do you do.'

'I remove it and order another one.'

'Don't you get bored?'

'Sometimes. Today was about as bad as it gets. I asked for a roster change. Tomorrow I'll be at the receival station, which is more interesting.'

'What happens there?'

'The goods arrive on pallets, in packages with barcodes. We use hand scanners to track them. Each item has an exact storage location and a cart takes it there and puts it in a crate. The crates can be stacked vertically to save space. High demand items are placed at the top to reduce the amount of digging.'

'It sounds like hell,' Jack thought.

'Do you like working with robots?' he asked Sebastian.

'The pay's okay and I only work 3.5 days.'

'You job share?'

'Yes.'

'Is there much theft?' Jack asked.

'No. We would be found out.'

'Do the customers get what they ordered?'

'Always. That's our top priority. GroCom call it a Fulfilment Centre.'

'Because the boxes are filled full?'

'Haha.'

'What is there for you to do?'

'Things can go wrong. The other day a customer accidentally ordered 100 packages each with 20 toilet rolls. There was a massive traffic jam of carts.'

'Why wasn't the order rejected? No-one does that much shitting.'

'People put in some strange orders. They hoard obsessive quantities of milk, or olives, or baked beans.'

'Do you supply retailers?'

'Not at our prices.'

'Wouldn't you rather be coding the instructions for the robots?'

'I would have to do a programming course. I don't like computers and I'm not much good at study. Not like you. Don't you get bored studying?'

'Sometimes.'

It was painful for Jack to admit it. Going to university was supposed to lead to more interesting work, but there was frequent tedium. He loved physics, but it was hard to see it leading to the adventurous life he had wanted when he enrolled.

'I don't know how you can sit in front of a screen all day,' said Sebastian. 'I'd rather be in the garden.'

'I like coding. I never do the same thing twice.'

It was true. Jack hated routine and revelled in self-directed learning. Perhaps any day now his physics would reveal an exciting new world of possibilities. He doubted Sebastian enjoyed his work as much. He wanted to ask him how he felt about not having a fair chance to get to university.

'I won't ask him,' he thought. *'It would be a loaded question as if he might have less right to be happy. He seems to be happy enough, though. Am I an educational snob? Perhaps Sebastian will rise in GroCom and his career could be more prestigious than mine.'*

'Do you think the way you deliver groceries is more efficient than the old way when a grocer assembled customers' orders by hand?'

'Oh, yes. It would take hundreds of people. There are only about 20 of us.'

'Can you get promoted?'

'Yes, but no one's pushy.'

'Are they friendly?'

'Very. I get asked to parties. Some of the girls are hot. Instead of being bored, I imagine what I am going to do on Saturday night and time flies.'

'It sounds like you're having fun,' he said. He thought: *'He's having more fun than me.'*

He realised reluctantly that Sebastian was not necessarily worse off.

University studies had disappointed him lately. The lecturers' pedagogies were deficient and off-putting, lacking insights. They pitched the ideas to the least common denominator, students of low intelligence, with simple situations and over-reinforcement. Assignment instructions were provided piecemeal, rather than as a coherent whole, wasting his time. Jack had begun to dislike his university. Fortunately, this was his last year. Next year he hoped to get an interesting job.

CHAPTER 10

The Fleets flew to London in October.

'When you resume training here you will be able to make a fresh start,' Stan said to Maxi.

'How will it be different?'

'You will learn to run faster, not just try harder. We will ratchet up your speed and endurance.'

'Are you saying I have to push myself more?'

'Exactly. Imagine you are wearing a headset repeating 'faster, quicker'.'

Stan was an exchange teacher at a secondary school and coached their running squad part-time, at the Linford Christie Stadium in West London. Maxi joined in with them afternoons. She also ran in local parks and along trails, tracks and road verges. Her father usually rode with her. When she could, she ran in a group with other athletes, but it was difficult to find others able to keep up with her because she ran faster and further.

'The girls who go to school every day think I'm crazy training all day,' she said. 'They think they are cool hanging out at the shopping mall, fooling around, making smartass comments to passing hot guys and daring each other to chat-up boys. That is such shit. They can't imagine the pleasure I get from achieving something I want.'

In the afternoons, her father oversaw her distance education work in the five subjects required of senior students.

'The work she does is excellent,' her online maths teacher emailed her father, 'but she misses out whole exercises. Why is that?'

'I stop her doing them,' Stan said.

'Why?'

'Her ego must not feed on anything other than running,' her father said. 'If she won an award for maths, she wouldn't get out of bed at 5.00 am and run 10 kilometres in the cold and rain. She has to train hard every single day. I allow her to be successful, but only at running. Running has to get all her attention and any other approval would undermine it. When she loses, she realises that being ordinary is not sustaining and she redoubles her efforts at running. She will be able to take up maths later when she retires from running.'

'Is it ethical to make her so vulnerable?'

'Greatness is nurtured by austerity, not by pampering.'

'It is a high price to pay.'

'Greatness is priceless,' he said. 'By missing out on academic success, she won't lose anything nearly as valuable as becoming a running champion. If she wasn't exceptional, you would have a point, but she's a winner. With our help, she can achieve greatness. It's worth it.'

'I don't agree with what you're doing to her, but I respect your right to do it.'

'Don't worry,' he said. 'She's having a ball. Your instinct is to make her into an ordinary child. You mean well, but your premise that she can be ordinary is flawed. A mundane adolescence would break her spirit. She is not ordinary and she's doing well. It's what she wants.'

Maxi found home schooling uncomfortable at first. She missed the school routine with its sociality and regular feedback from all her subjects. School friends tried to catch her up on their ideas and attitudes, but she began to be left out. She felt vulnerable as if she was out on a limb and could fall off.

When she won a race, she realized that her experiences were as good, if not better. A runner trains and competes for various reasons. She did not have an obsession, nor an addiction, nor was she doing it to please someone else. She ran partly for self-aggrandisement, showing off, attention and kudos. But Maxi also enjoyed how her body and mind felt, alive and healthy. She was fulfilling a dream, self-actualising with opportunities opening for fame, travel and a lifelong career. This was a true self-expression of who she was. Her lack of sociality was amply compensated for by the growing independence of her lifestyle.

She progressed up the 1500m hierarchy, against competitors who put her out of her comfort zone. This was not trial and error. She adapted and her improvement was by carefully trained development of her skills to race faster.

Each coach had a different ethos. Stan was an authoritarian, closely controlling Maxi's training regime and Patti was jealous.

'Hey Stan, when are you going to pay me some attention?' Patti asked.

'Why?' he asked. 'You know I love you.'

It wasn't enough but she had no choice and had to make do with it.

Her son Roly was now 18 and had enrolled with the London County employment agency. When they found him a job, he would be able to obtain a work permit.

Maxi was still 15 and continued her Queensland Year 10 subjects by internet. She did her track work with Stan at the Stadium and at the Hammersmith school occasionally, using the pool, weights room, laboratories and science equipment. Her studies were almost always at home alone. Previously, when she needed help with a subject, she had asked her classmates, but in the UK she only had her father to turn to.

'I'm a biologist and I can't help you much with physics and chemistry,' Stan said. 'I'll try and find a tutor who can help you with the Australian syllabus. I know it's tough for you, but keep soldiering on, like you would in an endurance race.'

It took her a couple of months to get used to the new conditions in the UK.

'I have realised I'm not depressed,' she said. 'It's the low light that's gloomy.'

She missed the Queensland sun. The sun in the UK appeared only briefly and palely between clouds and rain, unlike the dominating Australian sun blasting down from a blue sky.

'I can't get used to the sun being in the south, nor west being on my right when I face the sun,' she said. 'I need a map to find my way home.'

But she liked the running conditions, typically wet and cold.

'Rain in my face is better than Australia's glare and heat,' she said. 'They sapped my energy.'

'The constancy here will help you to improve steadily,' said Stan. 'We are progressively building you up with longer and faster runs.'

She trained every day except Sunday. On the track, she sprinted 100, 200, 400, 800 and 1500 metres, with repeats after recovery times that reduced with practice. She varied from 70% effort allowing her body to adapt, to 80% effort when she developed her style and cadence at race pace, to 90% effort for sustaining effort at above race pace (24).

'Short, fast repeats improve your oxygen economy at a given pace,' said Stan. 'Think of it as getting better gas mileage – you can go longer before running out of gas.'

'Fartlek' was Swedish for 'speed play'. It was visceral training demanding faster running. On alternate days, she did fartlek runs, with short bursts of speed varying between 70 and 90% effort, for about an hour.

It was a gruelling regimen. When her performance was sub-standard, Stan invoked remedial punishments, such as extra laps. After several months, she became tired and began to lose interest in running.

Stan didn't have enough to do. His substitute teacher work was infrequent and he had become negative. His constant criticism of Maxi's style and pace wore her down. He was a perfectionist and too demanding. She compensated by slipping back into the overtraining that had been her downfall when she melted down the previous season.

The other runners in Stan's squad sometimes gave her a cold shoulder, because she was so much better. Their rejection leveraged her dedication to training. But because she had little contact with others of her age, her self-confidence diminished and her enjoyment faded.

She couldn't talk to Stan about it. Disillusioned, she sneaked away several times, going into the town with the others to a coffee bar.

'What runs did you do this afternoon?' Stan asked her abruptly.

'A couple of 1500s and a 3000.'

'Liar!' he barked, slapping her hard across the side of the head. 'You were at a coffee bar in town!'

He had struck her before in rages, but never as hard as this. She was shocked.

'I needed a change,' she said, weeping. 'It's not compulsory to train every day!'

'It is when I am coaching you. If you want a break, you ask me.'

'When I asked you before you said no.'

'When I told you no break, it wasn't up to you. My coaching requires you to do what I say, always. The main learning from training is to keep doing it, even when you don't feel like it.'

Maxi felt confused and ashamed and said nothing more to him. If she protested his rigid discipline, it would merely press Stan's buttons. He didn't understand when she asked him to relax his unnecessarily strict training. Perhaps he imagined that because she was a girl, she was soft without self-control.

'It is consuming my spirit, forcing myself around the track at top speed, again and again,' she told Patti later. 'I'm becoming an empty husk. My true self has gone. I'd rather be taking it easy and doing other things.'

Patti must have spoken to Stan because that evening he knocked on the door of her bedroom where she was studying and came in. He sat on the bed.

'I'm sorry, Maxi,' he said. 'I have been a bit down lately and I didn't notice you were unhappy.'

He told her of difficulties with his position as an exchange teacher. She was sympathetic, but he seemed to be putting pressure on her, rather than dealing with the inflexibility of his training schedule.

'Do you like training with the Stadium and Hammersmith school group?'

It was once a week.

'Yes,' she said.

'I'll see if you can do more with them.'

A week later, he came out on to the track where she was training.

'I've arranged for you to train with the school squad every day,' he said. 'That will be more fun for you.'

'Thanks, Dad. I love you.'

'Love you too, Maxi.'

In the days that followed, he obtained a part-time teaching job and was happy. Nothing was said about his slap and Maxi put it out of her mind. Her training returned to normal. Stan nominated her for the County U16 1500 metres championship. She had not raced since her meltdown in Australia.

'I'm dreading this run,' she said. 'What if I meltdown again?'

'Don't let it worry you,' Stan said. 'You'll be fine. Every runner melts sometime.'

His coaching became positive and supportive, reassuring her that she would not injure herself by ignoring pain and warning her of perils that could cause injury.

Once or twice a week she would jog over Kew bridge into the Gardens, with wonderful buildings, large Victorian glasshouses and beautiful landscapes. She ran along wide smooth paths through woodlands. There were 14,000 trees from all over the World. As she ran, she admired the unique foliage, colours and flowers. She pondered why leaves and stems had different shapes and sizes. Why did some plants seem more friendly than others? Which plants were foreign or alien? A gingko tree, her favourite, had been planted in 1762.

She passed runners who smiled or nodded, as if sharing in something. The Gardens were extravagantly elite, a minority interest funded from the public purse and she felt privileged. She strutted and preened as she ran, in a ballet with the garden's peacocks.

She jogged over Hammersmith Bridge to Richmond Park, west of Wimbledon Common, along the 11.6 kilometres Tamsin Trail and around the 1000 hectare park, or alternatively, along a 5 kilometres loop starting close to Bishop's Gate, where she sipped lemonade at a friendly pub.

'I'm averaging 60 kilometres per week at racing pace and it doesn't seem too hard,' she said to Stan. 'I'm enjoying myself.'

'Nice going,' he said. 'We'll time your next run to check you are improving.'

Maxi ran into first place at the West London Schools Championship in 4m35. A month later at the Southern Counties Championships, she was second with 4m30. At the Nationals, she was first in 4m26.

'You're unbeaten by any other Under 16 1500m runner in the UK,' Stan said. 'Your future in distance running looks bright.'

Because Maxi was improving, there was not much incentive to change her training programme. The effects of change could not be predicted with confidence and it was a case of 'leaving well alone.' They kept her training routines as constant as they could. Even so, she ran into a problem that tested her capacity to endure pain.

CHAPTER 11

She was on a 20 kilometres run along a winding trail, below the steep north-facing scarp slope of the South Downs weald in East Sussex. Stan had driven her down for an outing into the countryside, to a track favoured by half-marathoners. It was Winter, cold and muddy, as she bounded down the trail between wet chalk rocks. Then her left foot slipped and all her weight went on to her right leg. Her right foot tried to stop her falling, but it twisted under her and she felt something give in her knee as she went down. She was able to limp slowly to where Stan brought the car.

She used ice, elevation and rest immediately and stopped training for a week.

Stan's tough love rejected medical treatment by a GP or hospital, preferring to treat her himself. He wanted her injuries to heal naturally, without pharmaceuticals or surgery, to make her more tolerant of pain and disability, able to complete races independently under adversity. His treatment for her pain was that she ignore it. When it hurt too much, she could slow down.

She was able to walk and seemed to be recovering. Traversing their local high street, she had a sudden spike of pain, her knee seemed to pop out and she fell on to her hands and knees in the road. It happened again a couple of times before she went to a specialist. An X-ray showed a possible torn meniscus in her right knee.

'It is in a stabilising structure and difficult to see,' said the surgeon. 'We want you to do provocative therapy here in the hospital.'

'What is provocative therapy?'

'It provokes an injury to reveal intermittent symptoms. I will examine you when it happens to be sure your knee is popping out.'

It was the cruellest test imaginable. She lifted progressively heavier weights, strapped to her right leg until her knee gave way with excruciating pain.

'The Xray shows a right medial cartilage tear. We'll have to remove it.'

'How?'

'It's a simple operation. You'll be in hospital for a week.'

'When?'

'That's a problem. Maybe in about three months from now.'

'3 months? I can't be out of action all that time. I'm in training for a race.'

'Sorry. There's a shortage of beds.'

'What if someone cancels? I can come in immediately.'

'I'll note that down for the admissions staff. Good morning.'

Next morning her luck was in. The hospital phoned for her to come in for the operation immediately. When she woke up from the anaesthetic, she was in a ward with a physio talking to her.

'How are you?'

'Okay.'

'How does your knee feel?'

'It aches a bit. Is the cartilage gone?'

'Yes.'

'How will I manage without it?'

'It absorbed shocks and lubricated between the femur and tibia bones. They say it quickly grows back as good as new.'

'Great.'

'We need to get you up and about. You won't get better lying around. There's a shortage of beds. I want you to sit up, swing your legs over and stand up.'

'But I only just had the surgery. Doesn't it have to recover for a bit?'

'No. The sooner you start moving it the better.'

'Isn't pain a signal to take care of a hurt?' she said.

'No. Pain is an unreliable guide to injury. It is subjective.'

The physio explained that she would get used to pain by confronting it. He told her an anecdote about his scientist friend who worked in a burns research laboratory for the Ministry of Defence. He and another researcher shaved the bellies of guinea pigs and held them under boiling water in a tank. The skin would blister and they tested salves to find the best one to treat battlefield burns. After a week, the two researchers were so sickened by the creatures' screams they transferred the test to their own forearms, which they held under boiling water. It was very painful at first, but they got used to it. Their arms healed in a few days. Over the next two years, they repeated the test many times.

'So you see Maxi,' the physio said, 'pain is subjective. Your knee will be painful, but we want you to start walking and go home tomorrow. We need your bed.'

Maxi tried but couldn't stand up.

'It's in your head,' she told herself. *'The pain signals are to stop you leaping down another rocky trail. They are not to stop you walking out of here. You will get up and walk.'*

She walked out gingerly the next day and Stan took her home. For the rest of the week she got used to walking around the house, gardens and up the stairs. Her knee ached, but with pethidine, she could concentrate on her lessons.

She went to a physiotherapist who cleared her to start slow jogging and after a couple of weeks, she got back into her training runs and gradually sped up to full speed. She didn't compete at all that year.

In the afternoons, Maxi rested her body at home, studying five Queensland Year 11 subjects.

'How are you getting on with your subjects?' Stan asked.

'Year 11 is harder,' she said. 'I'm doing okay, except for physics.'

'What's happening there?'

'I don't get some of the theories. I need to have someone to talk with.'

'Perhaps I could help you?'

'Thank you, but no Dad.'

'It isn't cool being helped by your father, is it?' he said. 'You have done well to get this far by yourself. I haven't come across anyone who could tutor you yet. Are you sure you need someone?'

'I need help with the questions,' she said. 'Next year they'll be even harder.'

'Year 12 is full on and having a tutor could help a lot. I'll post an ad on the school website.'

CHAPTER 12

It was convenient for Jack to continue in the residential college in third year. Blake, Alice and Corvid and his girlfriend Ophelia were there too. He studied prodigiously. Those in his year who had failed earlier in the course had disappeared quietly. There were 52 survivors doing physics in competition. He was in the straight to final exams, revising three years' work and investigating additional topics rumoured to be examinable. His friends had exams too and didn't have time for socialising, except in the dining room and with Ophelia for one night each weekend.

The others in his class took time off for evenings out. When they asked him if he wanted to go with them, he thought they were being friendly until he realised they wanted to stop him getting ahead. He worked steadily. The more revision he did, the more he felt compelled to do. By searching for patterns in previous exam papers, he identified likely exam questions and prepared answers.

Jack had been hitting the books all night when he met Blake in the kitchen, making himself a hot drink. He was a night owl too.

'Are you having a good time?' Jack asked him.

Blake raised his eyebrows sardonically. "Why, yes, I'm having great fun.'

'Me too.'

Jack wasn't lying. It seemed like a paradox to him that his lonesome vigil, mustering obscure theories, could be so pleasurable.

He had retained energy to take final exams on the burst. He sat exams every day for a week. As soon as one exam ended, he began swotting for the next. Afterwards, he got drunk with the others and waited for results to be announced.

'Jack Cram, First Class Honours.'

It was a relief, vindicating his hard work.

He was pleased that his parents and Sebastian came to his graduation ceremony. Their support meant a lot to him. Afterwards, he went home to be with them as he started looking for a job. He wanted work where he could apply his exceptional physics skills. He filled out application forms to work for IT companies and waited, hoping to be called for an interview.

With the hot-house of intense study ended, as they were finishing at university, Ophelia became demanding. His coming-of-age was when he lost his virginity and became socially and politically active. She was impossible to please and it was a relief when she proposed they separate. He went on a graduate work experience programme to Central America for several months. There he encountered poverty, becoming aware that his life had been privileged. He confronted questions such as who was being exploited and whether he was an exploiter. He became interested in socialism.

He resolved to avoid keeping bad faith with himself by acting out his beliefs. He had only ever been an 'underman', contrasting with Nietzshe's overman who had been his idol. He would pick up the gauntlet of freedom. Back in Australia, looking for a job, he joined his friends in protesting racism and drove an ambulance for a war in Israel. He had a taste of freedom and it was good.

Jack returned to his school for its 50th anniversary reunion and ran into Stan, back in Australia from teacher exchange in the UK. He was Jack's favourite teacher, although slightly eccentric, but agreeable and able to think 'outside the box'.

'Hello, Mr Fleet.'

'Congratulations on your First, Jack!' Stan said.

'Thank you, Mr Fleet. How much longer will you be in the UK?'

'A couple of years, probably. My family are busy doing various things or they would have come with me. Maxi, my daughter, runs in the mornings and studies at home by distance education. If she can get a good exit ranking, she wants to do a degree in sports science. She is finding physics a bit difficult and I'm looking for a tutor.'

'If I get to London, perhaps I could help.'

'What are your plans?' Stan asked.

'I'm looking for work doing math modelling. I am thinking of trying in the UK, but I would need a work visa.'

'There's heaps of IT work in London. It's where the private sector does its research. Top physics skills like yours are wanted. You would get a visa.'

'Thanks for your encouragement,' Jack said. 'I'll start looking.'

'If you do come, get in touch. Here's my number.'

Two months later, Jack was in London. He called Stan.

'You said to let you know if I came over, Mr Fleet.'

'I remember. Have you found work?'

'I have landed a job with Oilco and started last week,' he said. 'Do you still need a physics tutor?'

'Yes. Maxi is struggling.'

'What physics is she doing?'

'Queensland, year 12.'

'I did it 4 years ago. Too easy.'

'Good. Where are you staying?'

'At Hammersmith. I'm sharing a flat with some Oilco people.'

'We're at Shepherds Bush. It's not far. Could you come over here?'

'Okay. When would suit you?'

'How about Wednesday,' Stan said. 'You could make a start on some physics and then stay for dinner.'

'I would like that.'

'See you next week.'

CHAPTER 13

It was 6.30 pm, the time arranged with Stan when Jack rang the doorbell at the London house the Fleets had exchanged for theirs in Caloundra. It was modern and detached, with a well-kept garden.

The door was opened by a teenage girl, probably a sixth-former. She was in a pink T-shirt, brief shorts, long shapely legs and Birkenstocks. She was polite, pretty and engaging.

'Hi,' he said. 'I'm Jack Cram, about physics.'

'Where have I met her before?' he thought.

'I'm Maxi Fleet.' She offered her hand, which he clasped briefly. It was soft and warm.

'Pleased to meet you,' he said.

Her gaze was polite and respectful. 'Come in.'

He followed her in, through a hallway, adorned with outdoor clothing hanging from hooks and shelves crowded with trophies, ornaments and photos. He took off his jacket and she showed him where to hang it.

She was about 175 cms and lithe. He followed her into the dining room. She seemed to float along effortlessly. She called through the door: 'Dad, the tutor's here.'

Stan bustled in and pumped his arm vigorously. Patti followed, proffering a hand and mild interest.

Jack's face had discrete features, seeming arranged by Identikit. In profile, the slope of his forehead descended to a longish nose, an inverted blade like an axehead. Under it, a thin, humourless mouth bordered a cliff-like chin that dropped vertically below. He smiled perfunctorily and although his demeanour was courteous, it was inscrutable.

He remembered he had met her the previous week, when they had danced passionately in the gloom of a pulsating night club. She put a surreptitious finger to her lips and he knew not to mention their meeting.

He assumed she didn't acknowledge him because her parents hadn't known she had been there. He was delighted to renew contact with her. She was even more entrancing in this setting than he remembered.

Finding her was like finding the princess who had fled the party at midnight. He recalled how closely they had danced, her small but firm breasts against his chest and the sensuousness of her slender body. Patti sidled forward.

'ow are you finding London, Jack?'

Her attempt at Cockney talk and her forward manner grated on him.

'Cold but otherwise pleasant, thank you, Mrs Fleet.'

'Call me, Patti.'

'Thank you for coming, Jack,' said Stan. 'On time too.'

'Physicists know about time,' said Patti, smoking a cigarette, appraising him.

'Time is relative,' Jack said. 'If you're moving at the speed of light, your time would stop and you couldn't be late.'

'Maxi would like time to stop, wouldn't you love?' said Stan.

'Too right,' said Maxi. 'I don't have enough time for anything except running and schoolwork.'

'You're doing okay,' said Stan.

Jack remembered from school that Stan was a reinforcer, not out of kindness but as a shaper of others' behaviour.

'Maxi trains for running in the mornings and does her subjects in the afternoon,' he said. 'She wants to do sports science at uni, don't you Maxi?'

She gave a small nod.

'Could physics help her run faster?' Jack asked.

'Possibly,' said Stan. 'But I don't want her to get into physics theory, just practical problems.'

71

'He doesn't want her to become a physics nerd like me,' Jack thought.

'Okay,' he said. 'But she will need a working knowledge of the theories.'

Stan was a science teacher. He nodded, acknowledging he knew what Jack meant.

'Okay. Do what you must. She needs to pass.'

Jack was puzzled by Stan's reticence with theory. He didn't want Stan supervising his tutoring.

'Could you make a start on some physics now?' Stan asked him. 'You can have dinner with us afterwards. Oh, how much should I pay you?'

'I've no idea. I'm doing it for fun. Oilco are paying me scads.'

'Hmm. Is 30 pounds for an hour enough?'

'It's heaps.'

Jack pocketed the 30 pounds.

'We'll start with that and see how it works out,' said Stan.

'Great. Thank you.'

Stan left them together.

Maxi and Jack sat side by side at the dining table.

He wanted to be a good tutor. His favourite teachers had used a wide range of techniques. He looked forward to the challenge of tutoring Maxi. He would start by establishing a rapport.

'It's so good to see you a . . . ' Jack began.

'Shh . . . My parents didn't know I was at that club,' she whispered. 'I had told them I was at a girlfriend's home for a birthday party.'

'I see.'

'It is good that our relationship is already sharing a confidence,' he thought.

'You're a runner?' he asked.

'Yes.'

'What distance?'

'I ran 10 kilometres this morning. I've been running 1500 metres races but I'm changing to 3000 metres. I have the Counties next month.'

'Could you win?'

She hesitated.

'I have been injured and haven't run for a year.'

'What has that been like?'

'Deadly dull. Training isn't enough without racing. I need a challenge.'

'Will you be able to get back to it?'

'I am hoping to. In my last race, I won the National 1500 metres.'

'Terrific. What are you aiming for eventually?'

'The marathon record at the Olympics.'

She said it quietly, looking coolly into his eyes. He wondered if she was having him on.

'Wow. A huge ambition.'

'Yeah,' she said. 'Running is my life. I train every day. My PB is 1500 metres in 4 minutes and 26 seconds.'

'That's 20 kms per hour: marathon record speed,' he said.

He liked to show off his ability with numbers.

'Yes, but I have to keep it up for 28 times further,' she said. 'It will take years to get there, but I like training.'

'She is genuinely going for the world record,' he thought. *'How extraordinary!'*

'Do you do schoolwork every day?'

'Yes. On 5 days I do schoolwork from 2 to 5 pm, then I eat and study again from 6 to 8 pm.'

'You must be about 18?'

'Yes, in November.'

'Stan told me you're doing Year 12 at the Brisbane Distance Education school?'

'Yes.'

'Could you have been in Year 8 at Caloundra Secondary College when I was there in Year 12?'

'I don't remember you,' she said.

'In year 7, you wouldn't have come across me. I was always in trouble in year 11,' he said. 'In Year 12, I quietened down. I played rugby, drove a car. Did you go to school discos?'

'No. Year 11s and 12s were like gods. I didn't get to know any.'

They told each other their home addresses.

'It's strange that you lived only one kilometre away and then we meet over here.'

She doodled on her pad in heavy black biro. It was a drawing of a mountain with a stick figure climbing it.

'What subjects do you do?'

'Physics, biology, applied maths, physical education and English.'

'What will you do when you finish?'

'I want to get into the Queensland Institute of Sport. Their coaching is the best and I could get a UQ degree. If I can win at the Australian nationals, I could get a scholarship. I'll have to go home to run at the end of the year.'

'Passing your subjects would help too, wouldn't it?'

'Yes, they want that. But QIS would have me training every day and all day. It would be a lot of hard work. I'm not absolutely sure I'm up to it.'

'Like climbing that mountain?' Jack asked, pointing to her sketch.

She shifted in her chair, self-consciously.

'I've never climbed a mountain,' she said.

'If you did, how would you do it?'

'The same way I run, by putting one foot in front of the next.'

'Would you look up at where you have to get to?'

'Never. It would seem too far, too hard, impossible.'

'Will getting the Olympic record be hard?'

'It would be if I thought about it, but I'm not going to. I just train and study.'

'What are you doing just now?'

'The laws of motion.'

'They could be important for a runner to know. Have you done gravity yet?'

'We touched on it.'

74

'What can I help you with?'

'The assignments,' she said. 'I am stuck with the questions.'

'Okay. Let's start on them.'

He set his smartphone alarm for an hour.

She showed him her lesson materials online.

'Would you read, please?' he asked.

She read several screens and he asked questions to check her understanding.

'You learn well,' he said. 'Now let's see how you go with the exercises.'

She answered multiple-choice questions on her laptop while he used her logins to get into the school's website and scanned her lesson material.

'Finished,' she said after 20 minutes.

Most of her answers were correct.

She was bright and interested, vibrating with energy. He found her adorable and it was hard to concentrate on physics.

'That's awesome,' he said.

He explained where she had gone wrong with a couple of the problems.

'Now tell me: How do we describe an object's motion?'

'By its velocity and direction?' she said.

'Correct. So how do we know when a runner is moving?'

'When their velocity is not zero.'

'Correct,' he said. 'How could a runner's motion be changed?'

'By a force.'

'If there is no force acting on her, what would she do?'

'Stay at rest, or in motion at constant speed.'

'Good. What property causes that?'

'Her mass.'

'That's right. What do we call the tendency of a mass to move at constant speed in a straight line?' he asked.

'Inertia.'

'Excellent. Is there anything else we need to know about a runner's motion besides velocity, direction and inertia?'

'Would it make any difference what substance her mass is: like lead or feathers?' she asked.

'What do you think?'

'Maybe mass is all the same and what her body is made of wouldn't change her movement.'

'True. But what about shape? Could a person's body shape matter?'

'I don't know. Could it?'

'Yes. Different shapes have different inertias. Would a long rod and a round ball, each of one kilogram, roll the same on a sloping surface?'

'No. A long rod can't roll in all directions the way a round ball can.'

'Correct. Anything else?'

'Would a ball continue rolling further?'

'Yes, it would.'

'Correct. It can store more rotational inertia.'

'I see,' she said. 'So if they increased the diameter of the Earth somehow, say with tall buildings like on the battle planet in Star Wars, Earth's rotation would slow down.'

'It would,' Jack said. 'The same as a spinning ice skater holding out her arms would slow her down to a stop more quickly.'

'Or pulling her arms in she would speed up?'

'Yes.'

Maxi's understanding of physics impressed him. He remembered Stan's caution to discourage her from taking a theoretical interest. It was unfortunate because she had an inquiring mind.

'Why are distance runners usually ectomorphs, like you?' he asked.

'Lower mass is easier to speed up, to keep going, to climb hills and has lower wind and ground friction.'

'Correct.'

'Perhaps you can swerve and go around corners better too?'

'I think so.'

'Tell me, Maxi, what is your body mass?'

'50 kilograms.'

'50 kilograms of what?'

'Water, muscle, fat, bone . . .'

'In physics, mass is just matter. Now, what is your weight?'

'Where?'

'Here.'

'Gravity is about 10kgs per second squared, making my weight 10 times 50, which is 500 Newtons.'

'If a force acts on your body mass, what could happen?'

'I could speed up, slow down, stop or change direction.'

'What else happens?'

'An equal reaction force acts in the opposite direction to the action.'

'When Earth's gravity pulls on you with 500 Newtons, what reaction is there?'

She puzzled.

'I don't know.'

'When you push on the ground, what else happens?'

'The ground pushes back.'

'It does unless you slip because there is insufficient friction between the soles of your shoes and the ground.'

His alarm sounded.

'That's an hour. We'll stop there for today. I have enjoyed our tutorial, Maxi.'

'So have I. Thank you, Jack. Would you please tell me what I can leave out? I have so much training to do. I only need to get a pass.'

He recoiled from that idea, but went through her lessons, telling her the most important topics and exercises.

'Would you like to have dinner now?' Maxi said.

They joined Stan, Patti and Roly in the dining room.

The conversation at the table was a little strained, with Patti rather over-familiar and Roly unfriendly, but the food was good and plenty of it. Stan did most of the talking.

As he left the Fleets' house, Jack's mind was filled with the loveliness of Maxi. She seemed enveloped in an indistinct aura, as if her presence was unreal. As he went out the front door, down the path, through the garden gate, past houses in her street, everything had a surreal quality as if he was dreaming.

CHAPTER 14

When Jack next visited, Patti told them about the app she had been developing in her work with a London Borough Council.

'We are using social media to persuade people to run, jog or walk to work,' she told them.

'For their health?'

'To reduce congestion on roads and public transport.'

'Why do they need a nutritionist like you?' asked Stan.

'People need an inducement to change to active transport. We will credit their apps with free food. My role is to select the food rewards they can win and design app advertisements that will nudge them to try it and take it up.'

'Fast food?' said Jack sardonically.

'Haha. Healthy food. Vegan.'

'Why would commuters trust you?'

'We are the government.'

'It might work.'

'People are interested. This could take off. It's great to be in on the ground floor of something that could be great.'

Patti worked long hours. She was well paid and enjoyed the family's dependence on her.

'I work my fingers to the bone for you,' she said to Maxi.

'Thanks, Patti. I like what you're doing.'

She said it without rancour and their antipathy was over.

Maxi made Jack a cup of coffee after the tutorial. They sat quietly in the lounge. He was feeling used and abused after a long day at Oilco. Her magical aura continued and he relaxed.

'How's your job going?' she asked.

'There are 20 systems graduates and we have been on an orientation programme for a month. I've been assigned to one of the departments. The hours are fixed. No-one starts work before 8am or later than 9am. Everyone stops for tea at mid-morning, then we stop for lunch at 1.00pm and everyone goes home at 6pm.'

'Have you tried arriving late or staying behind?' she asked.

'I stayed late once but they practically forced me to leave.'

'It seems very controlled.'

'Yes, it is,' he said. 'There's a right way to do everything. I know where I must be and what I must do. Most activities are routines. Variations are discouraged. If I put the right spin on my work, my supervisor is pleased with me.'

'That's okay, isn't it?'

'No. It's brainless and stultifying. It's so Post-Truth.'

'What happens?'

'We all stand around in a circle with our coffees and the supervisor will talk about an item in the news. Then the race is on for the rest of us to suggest ways Oilco can make money from it.'

'What's wrong with that?' she asked.

'Someone puts up an idea and makes an emotional appeal. It gets approved without proper consideration or reasoned debate.'

'It's not critical but if that's their culture, maybe it works,' said Maxi. 'Not everyone is as clinical as you.'.

'I used to think that the worst thing in life would be to end up alone. It isn't. The worst is to end up with people who pretend to be your friends. I need intelligent discussion. I feel alone. I am like a fish out of water. I don't think I'm going to succeed at Oilco. The focus is on money and everything else is ignored.

'The solutions they prefer are the easiest to do. Problems are solved recklessly. When I take work home, my efforts are deprecated by the others. My brain is slowly atrophying.'

'You're paid well, I expect?'

'It's different from being a student' said Jack. 'Every second Friday they put a large sum of money into my bank account. At uni I did more work but got no reward and even had to pay fees.'

'You shouldn't complain then.'

'My work lacks authenticity,' he said. 'I don't enjoy my pay because I haven't earned it. I want to be creative, but there's no opportunity to do anything except trivia that no-one cares about.'

'You sound a bit precious, a snowflake, trying to be unique and special, when you're simply decaying organic matter like everyone else.'

'I'm not precious but I am an individual,' said Jack. 'I long for a project of my own. To get into creative work I must claw my way up the hierarchy and become a project manager. There's competition for promotion, but eligibility and rules of play are not advertised and no-one talks about them.'

'Perhaps promotion is by invitation.'

'It is. The work that interests me is given to people with doctoral degrees.'

'Maybe you should do a PhD.'

'Maybe you're right.'

'You don't seem to like your job.'

'I like it less each day. The Oilco people are mainly interested in themselves and getting ahead. The culture doesn't allow me any dignity or worth.'

He collected his things to leave. He felt better for sharing his concerns with her and hoped his candour would not reduce her respect for him. Her success was important to him. He was enjoying being in the UK. Although he was unhappy at Oilco, it was experience and he would continue with them until he had a better career plan. He would try to fit in.

He was gaining proficiency but there were others with more highly rated skills. They got the plum jobs and he was overlooked. He couldn't pursue his ideals at Oilco. It was a wrench that freedoms he had enjoyed as a politically active volunteer were taken away.

'Anything goes,' he thought. *'I will be indifferent.'*

But he found he couldn't do it. It was like being back in the correction centre. He simmered with ambivalence, rejecting the values of his co-workers. Pretending to conform was agonising. He wanted the cake of freedom without having to enslave himself to eat it.

He was dangerous, wanting to become a tyrant, dishonestly ignoring the subjectivity of his choices and the freedoms of others, becoming a fanatic who would oppose Oilco, on behalf of others like him, taking refuge in disputing the serious, but not the ambiguity of his own position. Oilco would not allow him sensitivity, intelligence and humanity. He was forced to abdicate his freedom and accept slavery. Quitting Oilco and going to a different corporation with equal slavery was not attractive. He was stuck.

'Why should I quit? I have been ready to do what I am told but they have been wasting my time.'

'Maybe you have expected too much too soon,' said Maxi.

'I expected to have some freedom, but I have none.'

'Be patient. Can I do anything?' asked Maxi.

'Keep up your physics! Thank you for listening to my complaints.'

He liked talking with Maxi about his job. He didn't have anyone else he could tell. She understood his challenges, was non-judgemental and made sensible suggestions. Articulating his difficulties always helped him to resolve them. He was grateful to Maxi and he wanted to reciprocate, but she kept her feelings about her running to herself. He felt slighted, as if in her mind he was a physics nerd, without human understanding or common sense she could trust. Although she flirted with him, he wondered if she cared for him.

CHAPTER 15

I discovered the miracle that was Maxi in our weekly tutorials. She was an adorable, sensitive and humorous interlocutor, with an inquiring mind. It was delightful that she joined me in indulging in my passion for physics. But her main interest was in running and her mind was seldom away from it. I accepted that and we connected well.

We knew the two of us had something between us beyond physics, some sort of chemistry. We quickly had a rapport and seemed to enjoy each other's company. I often reacted to her with delight. Her parents didn't leave us alone together for long and discouraged liaison between us outside tutorials. Fate seemed to have brought us together and I couldn't stop thinking about her. It was unprofessional for a tutor to be interested in a student outside the curriculum and although I tried to keep her at arm's length, I was not oblivious to her femininity. She would be 18 in November, four years younger than me, but old enough.

We had met on a dance floor but I didn't hold her or kiss her again in public. Now that I was her tutor, a relationship with her was illicit. I desperately wanted to hold her again and kiss her, but I would have to wait. It wasn't easy to keep my hands off her. I would watch her entranced, my manhood stirring. I don't know why Maxi triggered in me a sexual itch I couldn't scratch. It happened when I was with her and not with others, as if I had subconscious connection with her.

After tutorials, I usually had dinner with her family. 'Jack, are you with us?' Patti prompted as I continued to watch her after she had stopped speaking. 'Maxi certainly has your attention.'

It wasn't just her talk that attracted me. I liked the way she sat, stood and moved, sometimes languorously, at times excitedly and at others with poise. A simple action, such as trying to scratch the middle of her back entranced me. I was spellbound by the coincidence that had brought us together in this exact place at this precise time. Could it have been ordained? Physics had no answer. Our meeting was so unlikely and so perfect, the possibility of intervention by a higher power was a bond we acknowledged without mentioning it.

I was jerked back to reality when Stan interrupted my thoughts.

'She's not allowed to have a boyfriend, Jack,' he said. 'Your tutorials are for her to learn physics.'

I respected her father's wishes. Although physics was our preoccupation, I lived in hope that we would eventually become partners.

She was not allowed to be out, except to go to a movie in a group. I went with her and her friends to the Tate Modern and we walked through the galleries together, liking some paintings and disliking others.

'This one is amazing,' she said, showing me. 'The expression on that woman's face tells us her thoughts about him are not at all kind.'

'The artist is in love with her. She doesn't care for him.'

I was projecting my feelings for Maxi onto the painting. I wanted to tell Maxi I loved her, but daren't.

'An artist is usually in love with himself, isn't he?' she said. 'He might be jealous.'

'Probably. To impress his own perspective on reality, an artist must have a narcissistic inclination, projecting his emotions into subjects for others to admire and buy his work.'

Maxi poured herself into viewing each exhibit, halting for up to 10 minutes at each. She would stand facing a painting, with her hands on her hips and her legs astride as if she was a work of art too. Her poses were self-conscious as if she knew I was watching her. Her hair was in bangs today, a different frame for her pretty head. I marvelled at her clean lines, smooth skin and pert nose. She would peer closely, then step back, as if the different viewpoints could add to her understanding of the work and the artist's intent.

I would read about the piece on the wall plaque. As we stood side by side, our shoulders touched and sometimes our arms and hands brushed against each other and I tingled with excitement. I adored her indolence and was irresistibly drawn to her, although I was conflicted about taking advantage of her age, limited by my role as her tutor.

It had to be done in secret. In an empty gallery, I held her roughly by the shoulders, then tenderly by the temples, inclining my head over her lovely upturned face, pressing my lips to her mouth and tasted her. It was a long kiss and we stopped when people came in. She wouldn't go public. We kissed furtively, rapt in each other.

CHAPTER 16

He rang the doorbell.

Maxi opened the door. 'Yes?'

'It's me, Jack.'

'Oh,' she said, embarrassed. 'Hi. I didn't see it was you. Sorry.'

'Maybe I've changed,' he said, trying to explain her gaffe.

'No, it's me,' she said. 'I'm not good at faces. Come in.'

She was in skimpy tight shorts and a halter top, revealing a taut midriff.

'How did you get on at the County?'

'I was first, in 8m55.'

'Congratulations!'

'Thank you. I was pleased. It was my first 3000 metres.'

'After a year off with your knee, that's excellent. Maybe the rest did you good?'

'It wasn't all rest. I trained hard.'

'Well, it's a feather in your cap. How did you go with the physics we did last time?'

'I got an A+,' she said.

'Well done. What's the topic this week?'

'Gravity. I've done some of the questions. The work we did on mass has helped me a lot.'

'Have you memorised the universal law of gravitation?'

'Yes.'

She recited it to him.

'Excellent. What do you know about the force on a person standing on the surface of the Earth?'

'Where?'

'At the equator.'

'It would be about 9.6 kilograms per second per second.'

'And at the north pole?'

'More?'

'Correct,' he said. 'Earth is an ellipsoid, flattened at the poles and the gravitational pull is greater there.'

They talked about the gravitation theory, as some people do about a favourite cake recipe. She spoke clearly, with a slight tongue clutter. Her curiosity charmed him, showing enthusiasm for a theory he loved. Best of all, she was playful and kicked concepts around with him, for the fun of it.

'Will the Olympics ever be held at La Paz, Bolivia?'

She thought for a moment. 'No. It's too high.'

'How would that affect an athlete's performance?' he asked.

'Running could possibly be speeded up by moonwalking and bounding,' she said.

'But more breaths could be needed to pull in the thin oxygen required,' he said.

'Yes, but thinner air would have less wind resistance.'

'Correct, there could be several factors affecting speed, some making it faster and some slower,' he said. 'It might be more difficult to speed up and go around corners, because lower weight reduces friction between your shoes and the ground.'

'An Incan might win,' she said.

He smiled. 'It's quite likely. Incans have evolved to escape by running from conquistadors on horseback. Now here's a question: Are speed and velocity the same thing?'

Jack had borrowed the question from her text.

'No,' she said, scanning and finding her answer. 'Velocity is the rate of change of position in a straight line from A to B. Speed is the distance travelled along the path from A to B, per time unit, as an average.'

'Does the difference matter?'

'Yes,' she said. 'If I run a lap of 400 metres on an oval track, my velocity is zero because there is no overall change of position. On the other hand, if I used an app on my wrist that calculated at 10-

metre intervals, my speed for a 60-second lap would average . . .' she used her calculator '. . 6.7 metres per second.'

'Great. If you wanted to speed up, what force would you use?' Jack asked.

'I would push harder with my legs to take longer and faster strides,'

'Can you speed up as quickly as you want?'

She looked at him, puzzled.

'Sometimes.'

'When you give it everything you have?' he asked.

'Then I would accelerate as fast as I can.'

'Yes. Would a person having twice your mass have to push harder with their legs?'

'Twice as much push.'

'Correct,' he said. 'If your mass was half, would you have an advantage?'

'It would take half as long to get up to speed.'

'How would running up a hill make a difference?' he asked.

'It would take less effort than a vertical climb, but I would have to go further.'

'Is gravity the only force the runner has to overcome?'

'There's air and ground friction too.'

'Yes. Is it better to zig-zag up a hill, the way cattle do?'

'If it is steep,' she said.

He was watching her mouth, how she used it to convey her feelings, pulling it this way or that with doubt and compressing it to show she was considering. He wanted to kiss it.

'Why do cyclists change to a lower gear to climb a steep hill?' he asked.

'For a better cadence.'

'Yes,' he said. 'They select a rate of working that is comfortable.'

'Bicycle seats are always uncomfortable,' she said, smirking.

'When you have a bony bottom.'

'Haha,' she said uncertainly as if it might be a criticism.

'Would you select a gear for maximum power,' he said.

'What is power?'

'It is the rate your muscles can work at when supplied with energy.'

'What if your energy runs out. Would you hit the wall?'

'Yes,' Jack said. 'In boxing, they say you are gassed, like running out of petrol. Then your body clunks to a halt and shuts down.'

'Runners usually call it a 'bonk',' she said matter-of-factly, looking for his reaction.

'Really?'

'No-one gets confused.'

'How can a runner avoid 'bonking'?' he asked, trying the new word out.

'I'm not sure,' she said. 'Tell me.'

'I imagine by greater efficiency, conserving energy and reducing power.'

'How would I do that?'

'Run smoothly and make the most of your kinetic energy, avoiding jerks.'

'I do avoid jerks,' she said, grinning.

He grimaced, showing patience. 'For example, if your legs and feet are springy, you can bound along using stored elastic energy.'

'Would a kangaroo use less energy hopping than a horse would galloping?' Maxi asked.

'I'm not sure,' Jack said. 'A kangaroo might be able to outrun a horse over a short distance. It is a good question. They have evolved divergently. Hopping could be faster in scrubland and galloping in grassland.'

'Did dinosaurs hop?'

'Probably some did,' he said. 'Birds are descendants and they do. Not emus. Only a few quadrupeds are bipedal and hop, like kangaroo rats and spring hares.'

'Not elephants,' she said. 'They lollop along.'

He laughed.

'What are some other ways I can save energy when I run?' she asked.

'Wear the right clothes for comfort, for heat loss and for reducing wind friction,' he said.

'How can I save energy going down hills.'

'You can glide down, overcoming ground friction by floating above it.'

'What about slip-streaming another runner?'

'You can lower the effort you need to overcome air resistance by running in someone's wake, maybe down to 80% on a still day and by more when there is wind.'

'Does being slipstreamed slow down the front runner?'

'Probably not. It could even speed her up, by breaking the vacuum in her wake and improving her fuel economy.'

'I wouldn't like to be behind someone who is breaking wind,' she said.

They laughed together.

'What can I do to reduce ground friction?'

'Choose shoes with a suitable tread for the surface and place your feet on a smooth path over and around obstacles.'

'There's a lot to get right.'

'Learned helplessness is lack of control, letting bad things happen to you,' he said. 'When you are running, you have many controls, such as your pace and stride length. By actively choosing the right settings, your running will be faster and more enjoyable.'

They stopped then and went through for dinner with her family. Their time had gone quickly. Once again, she her ability had astonished him.

'How's your job going, Jack?' Patti asked. 'Are you still finding it inauthentic?'

'I am living with three young male dudes from Oilco in the penthouse of an apartment building. Sean is an Irishman, a systems analyst. Guy is an economic forecaster. Ross is a marketer and plays rugby with me at Chiswick RFC. We hang out together and swap notes on how we think Oilco works, or rather, doesn't work.'

'Good,' said Stan. 'Playing rugby will relieve your stress from work.'

'I hope so. Oilco is a jungle teeming with brutal relationships and I doubt I have the in-fighting skills needed to survive in their dog-eat-dog world. The change from university has made me anxious. I prefer a detached role as an observer or investigator, but to get respect, you have to network and self-promote.'

'Maybe in time you'll get used to it,' Maxi said.

'I don't want to fit into their world,' Jack said. 'They're encouraging me to consume and spend what I earn. They would like me to have a house and a mortgage with the company's bank, to dedicate my life to the job, to socialize with company people and enculturate from the managers. Good results could bring promotion, privileges and respect by the hierarchy and by colleagues. By striving, I would climb status ladders. My life would be dominated by Oilco. It would be difficult to leave because the lifestyle requires so much money to maintain.'

'Hmm. Many people seek a lifestyle like that,' Maxi said. 'I don't think I would want it though.'

'Give it more time,' said Patti.

'That's the problem,' Jack said. 'I don't have time to waste.'

Starting his first job at Oilco had brought economic and material freedom when what he wanted was to use his skills to make a difference in a troubled world. He had stepped onto a low rung of a tall hierarchy. He wanted to be someone that counted in the world, by his own standards. His lack of agency at Oilco gnawed at his self-esteem. He knew he wasn't being true to himself and his health suffered, developing a stomach ulcer. He was stuck as an underman, without any freedom and he couldn't see his way free.

Frustrated, he would have resigned, but he hung on, hoping it would get better.

He phoned his parents every second week and spoke with Sebastian too. His conversations with them were stilted and he was losing touch with his families. He would return to Australia as soon as he could.

CHAPTER 17

'How's your running going?' Jack asked Maxi at their next tutorial.

'I'm through to the National,' she said.

'Wow! When did that happen?' he said. 'Congratulations!'

'The Regional was on Wednesday, at Crystal Palace.'

'What happened?'

'I led all the way. My time was 8m50.'

'Fantastic!'

'Why didn't she tell me she was running?' he thought. *'I would have liked to watch her. Perhaps she didn't want me there because it was only her second 3000 metres and she might not have been confident.'*

'Will you be able to do it again in the National?'

'It will be tougher,' she said. 'I melted down in Brisbane 3 years ago.'

'It will be cooler here,' said Jack.

'It will be twice as far.'

'Who else is in it?'

'Artula Crawford. She was 2nd in the U17 1500 National last year.'

'How far ahead of her were you?'

'20 metres.'

'That's quite a bit.'

'Only 3 seconds. It could be close. She beat me in the Southern Counties the year before.'

'What training are you doing?'

'A variety of distances, speeds and terrains, with reps and pace changes.'

'Where do you train?'

'At the club track, Kew Gardens and Richmond Park.'

'When do you run?'

'I start about 5 am, at first light. I have a break at 9 am and then continue until 1pm.'

'That's 7 hours. Wow. How do you do it?'

'I love it.'

'Could I watch your race?'

'It's at Leicester.'

'When?'

'Hang on.'

She consulted her mobile.

'Saturday June 12th at 7.30 am.'

'I'd like to be there.'

'I'll ask Dad if you can come in the car with us.'

She had never before invited him to watch her run. It would have been intrusive to turn up uninvited as if he might be stalking her. He had waited to be asked.

'That would be terrific.'

'It's just a footrace. What's your interest?'

'You. I want to know all about you and your running. I also have some ideas about the metaphysics of time. I want to investigate how an endurance runner responds to time.'

'Am I a science experiment or something?'

'Not likely,' he said. 'You're too uncontrolled for that. It could be that I fancy you, a bit.'

'Haha. You don't seem very sure. Tell me, how old you are?'

'I turned 22 in August.'

It was four years older.

'He's not too old,' she thought.

She had never had a boyfriend, not counting some furtive kissing and groping with a classmate from school at Angela's party. Jack's longing for her was evident and with a thrill of excitement she remembered their kiss in the gallery. Maxi wanted more of his attention, if they could conceal it from her parents.

Her U16 meltdown three years earlier haunted her, but when she watched a video of the American runner Steve Prefontaine, she knew she wanted to race with his total commitment. His trademark was to lead for the whole race. He bragged like boxer Muhammed Ali, who had declared 'I am the greatest'. Pre was not popular, but his toughness was legendary, training hard for long distances every day. In the 1972 Olympic Games, although he came 4th in the 5000 metres, he had made two gutsy comebacks in a performance famous among distance runners. His exploration of himself to the extreme limit inspired Maxi.

'I'll give it everything I have, from beginning to end,' she thought.

Jack went to Maxi's club to watch her train. It was in the grey light of dawn that he arrived at 6.30 am. She was the only runner lapping the track.

'70 seconds,' Stan called from beside the track. 'Your pace is good.'

He stood with Stan and they talked as they watched her. Her pace for the lap was only a little slower than the record. Her programme was the one she had followed the year before, modified for the longer distance.

She had run this programme with Stan for the past two years. When she changed from 1500 metres to 3000 metres, she maintained the same training with distances doubled. It was a gruelling schedule. She was running 4 x 800 metre repeats at 3000 metre pace, then 4 x 400 metre repeats at 1500 metre pace, then 4 x 200 metres at sprint pace. In between each repeat, there were 3 minutes of passive recovery, reducing to 2 minutes and 1 minute for the shorter distances.

Today she was tapering off to be fresh for competition.

'You have seen today what she does,' said Stan after a while. 'She has to concentrate and you are distracting her. That's all there is to see here. You'll see what it's all about at the National.'

Jack left then, feeling somewhat rejected but pleased that he could affect her.

In preparation for watching her at the National, he read everything he could find on distance running: media interviews with winners, biographies, memoirs, coaches' analyses, race reports, scientific investigations and research studies. He wanted to find out methods runners like Maxi could use to endure and win.

CHAPTER 18

Maxi was midway through her final year of schooling and although we were close friends, we had been hands-off all year.

Our interest in each other had not gone unnoticed.

'We can see what is going on. You two won't be getting involved sexually,' said Patti archly, 'or tutorials will be cancelled.'

Despite the distraction, our tutorials were a great success. We had a great rapport. Our time together was devoted to physics. I fought to suppress my lustful interest in her body. I would lie in bed at home imagining our bodies intertwined. Maxi's schooling would soon be over and I could wait for her.

'Let's go to the school's disco,' Maxi said.

'Will your parents let us go?'

'They have said no but we can sneak out. They'll know me from training and let us in at the door.

'Your parents will find out.'

'It's a fancy-dress disco. We can wear masks.'

'It's dangerous.'

'We won't be there long. I have to run the next day.'

They let us in and we danced together in near darkness. It took self-control to keep from holding her. I wondered how long I would be able to restrain myself.

At tutorials, I noticed her watching me sometimes, smiling. It was a good sign. My experience with Ophelia in Australia had been a one-night-per-week relationship for sex. With Maxi, it was different. We met only once each week with her parents there. I liked her a lot and she was important to me.

Maxi was adorable. Her appearance, her behaviour, her talk and her ideas all fascinated me. I wasn't trying to fall in love with Maxi, but it happened anyway. An emotional involvement with her would not be illegal and although she was my student, the tutorship was a private arrangement and not subject to any institutional or guardianship strictures. Our interest in each other deepened and widened and she began to let me into her life.

'I have a physics problem you might be able to help me with,' she said. 'Is it better to run barefoot or in joggers? I have tried both. I prefer bare feet on smooth surfaces. My father favours joggers. What do you think, from a physics point of view?'

'When do you need to know by?'

'Next week?'

'Okay. I'll do some research.'

Helping her was a pleasure. I hardly knew her, but she seemed pure and good all the way through.

I obtained information about barefoot running from the Runner's World Magazine online. The topic was a hot potato.

'You don't want to injure yourself,' I told her. 'Barefoot running seems to be a rallying cry for masochists.'

'That's unkind. Natural running is a beautiful concept.'

'Marathon running is hardly natural. Maybe its appeal is partly masochism.'

'No more than other endurance sports, like mountaineering.'

'I agree. A little masochism may be good for us.'

'How would you know?'

'Quantum physics has flagellation built-in.'

'How could it be good for you?'

'It humbles me to realise it could be a figment of my imagination.'

'You mean you don't understand it!'

'I understand running shoes,' I told her. 'Barefoot has less weight to transport and takes advantage of the natural elasticity of your feet. The elasticity of joggers transfers energy from heel-strike to toe-off less efficiently but gives a better transition of weight on to your foot. Running shoes provide foot protection, support and abrasion reduction. If your feet roll onto the inside, cushioning can prevent pronation that overloads the big toes. In a medium distance race on a kind surface, you might be better off barefoot. For a road marathon, well-designed joggers are probably better.'

'That agrees with Stan's advice,' said Maxi. 'Thank you, Jack. I'll do it.'

I was pleased that my indulgence in helping her had been appreciated. My help had been an amae, a Japanese device of bonding, that Ross had explained.

'An amae is a gesture of selflessness,' he said. 'She will feel you are caring for her.'

It was my first practical advice to her and Maxi began to rely on me. I enjoyed helping her win races. I wondered if she desired me enough yet. I was wrapped around her little finger. Her presence kept me on cloud nine. I had to stop myself ogling her pert breasts, shapely bottom, sleek femurs and slim legs. It was frustrating to have to stay physically uninvolved.

Whether she smiled, pursed her lips, pouted or grimaced, my eyes were glued to her looking for signs of approval. I wanted to tell her I loved her, but playing hard to get was probably a better strategy. My attempts at feigned indifference failed miserably. She found me out. It seemed that the sweetest apple grew on the highest branch and I knew getting her was precarious.

'Fortune favours the bold,' I thought.

The memory of our first furtive kiss at the gallery seemed like a dream and I looked for opportunities to kiss her again, but she was evasive.

'No, Jack, not here.'

Our involvement had to be concealed, kept apart by something like the 'keepers' used to separate two magnets that would cling strongly together.

We tried studying together in silence, but usually we talked.

'Do you watch Netflix?' I asked.

'No. I have important things to do.'

'Like Facebook?'

'I talk on the phone.'

'Do you ever go out with friends?'

'Every week, we do something together. Would you like to come dancing with us?'

I went with Maxi and her friends back to the night club where we had first met. The music was loud, the dancing energetic. Several of them were runners and well-coordinated. After one dance, she wouldn't dance with me again.

'Thank you for the dance, but any more and my parents could find out.'

I wasn't interested in dancing with anyone else.

'You could dance with someone else,' I said, hoping she wouldn't.

'I think we need to talk.'

I sensed there was something different and more demanding about Maxi, as if she had decided something important and was locked on to getting it. We found a quiet corner. There was a lot I wanted to know. Did she like rap music? Was there a psychic dimension between us? When could I kiss her again?

She had questions for me too. Did I prefer introverts or extroverts? Did I prefer to be with males or females?

'I prefer to be with females,' I said. 'Can I get you a drink?'

'Yes. Water. That's all I drink.'

'I'll join you,' I said. 'You can get the next round.'

'The waiter doesn't approve.'

'He'll get used to it.'

I brought a water bottle and glasses.

'Why are you on water?' she asked.

'Wine gives me a pain in the guts.'

'Is that why you look pained?'

'Do I?'

'Yes. Have you seen a doctor?'

'Yes. He said it could be an ulcer.'

'Why would you have an ulcer?'

'Anxiety.'

'Do I make you anxious?' she asked.

'No. My job does.'

'What have you got to be anxious about?'

'I told you. Oilco is driving me nuts.'

'Maybe you should change your job.'

'I agree. My project isn't going anywhere. Oilco are going to miss the boat.'

'Does that matter?'

'I need validation. I feel useless like the driver of an empty bus. My CV is suffering from lack of action.'

In a band break Maxi pressed up against me.

'This music is great,' she said. 'If we start dancing, I won't be able to stop.'

'Let's call it a night.'

I walked Maxi home from the station to the end of her street.

'Goodnight,' I said.

'Goodnight. I had a lovely time, thank you.'

I wanted her to be my girl forever.

I had a feeling Maxi's parents would uncover our involvement and try to stop it.

A few days later, I went to an athletics club party where Maxi threw herself into dancing in a group. Afterwards, we waited at a bus stop in the rain and I kissed her. She hesitated, then kissed me back. After a while we were gasping and grinning at each other, holding each other in the drizzle. For the moment, it was enough.

CHAPTER 19

Stan's car had L plates. Maxi was at the wheel, driving Stan and Jack.

Trees writhed in blustery winds.

'This wind is shit,' Maxi said. 'I haven't trained for wind. It takes a lot of energy.'

'Don't go too fast,' her father said. 'Keep an eye on the clock.'

'I want to lap at 70 seconds.'

It was the first time Jack would be there to see her run and he listened as she and Stan discussed her strategy. Since coming to the UK, she had replaced her feeling of being an underdog with 'all or nothing' bravado, coming first in her County and Region. Like her hero Steve Prefontaine, Maxi planned to control the race from beginning to end.

Now it was the National championship for U18 over 3000m. There would be two runners from each of the eight regions. Maxi was early, jogging and doing stretches in the assembly area. The announcer gave time checks at: 30 minutes before the gun; 15 minutes; and 10 minutes. As they waited to be called to the line, a runner waved and Maxi walked over to her, embarrassed.

'I know you, but I can't remember where from?'

'The 1500 National last year. You beat me by 20 metres.'

'Of course! You're Artula Crawford! Sorry, I'm bad at faces.'

'You were great, Maxi. Are you going for the record today?'

'There's too much wind.'

She told Jack at the barrier she had spoken to Artula.

'Could she set the pace?' he asked.

101

'Maybe. I beat her last year, but she beat me earlier when I melted down in a 1500.'

'That was ages ago' Jack said. 'You've prepared thoroughly and you won't have any problems today. Don't let her hurry you.'

While they were talking, the announcer called: 5 minutes; then 4 minutes; 3 minutes; 2 minutes; 1 minute; and 30 seconds. Maxi jogged over and took a position near the front inside. The last warning was at 15 seconds before the gun and Maxi half-crouched.

Jack was with Stan overlooking the start, halfway back in the stand. He had been in the UK six months, but it was his first time watching Maxi compete. She was in a white singlet and black briefs, with Artula next to her in the inside lane.

At the air horn, they got away in a bunch and Maxi stayed with the group until the second lap, when she moved forward. She passed below them, 20 metres ahead of the field. He was amazed and thrilled. She reminded him of a film he had seen with a war party of African Masai, who ran fast and focussed across the harsh Kenyan savannah. Maxi was such a warrior, the acknowledged leader of the pack. He felt his hair prickling erect, excited by her singleness of purpose, her fixed gaze, her self-control and her atavistic intent. Her movements were precise as if every muscle in her body was finely tuned to deliver optimum, effortless performance. Her bare arms, legs and midriff revealed her musculature, tendons and arteries. She had told him she had a predominance of striated muscle that contracted smoothly and continuously at relatively slow rates. He could see etched in detail those muscles working, actuating the biomechanical machinery of her body.

Jack shivered, chilled momentarily by the thrill of her athleticism. Etched on her body were glimpses of her interior with its 600 muscle bundles, 4000 tendons, 900 ligaments, 360 joints and 206 bones. Her heart was pumping blood and oxygen to them all. Every component had its own role and had been trained to be strong, fast and coordinated with the rest of her body. Her head was poised serenely on her straight vertebral column, her brain anticipating events and controlling her performance.

102

Her body reminded him of a cathedral pipe organ, a system of many parts, operated by the mind of the organist. Her running was like a cantata by Bach in full flight, soaring resonantly and repetitively through 100 pipes, varying from large rumbling basses to small reedy trills, querulous at one moment, next rhythmical and harmonious, with crashing and thundering notes pondering below. He imagined her mind mirroring the organist's exuberant joy, as her anatomy revelled in the delights of performance.

Maxi was a performer through and through. She had rehearsed diligently for this race and now basked in the worship of the stacked faces.

Her running was optimised for efficiency and speed. Every pace was identical to the one before, her legs striding powerfully, her arms swinging with perfect balance, her heels striking precisely, her weight rolling forward onto the plantars of her soles, launching her toes smoothly. There was no hint of limitation by endurance or of an imperative to conserve energy. She looked as though she could run like this forever.

'She's going too fast,' said Stan.

As if she had heard him, Maxi eased off and for the next 6 laps she merged into a group of four, 50m ahead of the field, with the remainder spread back along the circuit, their friends cheering them on. At the bell for the final lap, Maxi was in 2nd place behind Artula, with everyone screaming Go! or Yay! or Woohoo!

200m from the line, Maxi shot forward and drew abreast, but Artula increased her lead and drew away to cross in 8m35. Maxi's time was 8m40.

'For fuck's sake,' Stan said to Jack. 'She let her have it.'

Jack thought Stan was unkind and felt angry. He had not seen any evidence that Maxi's effort was less than her utmost. He had felt Maxi's pain as she strove to pass Artula.

'She went well,' he said to Stan and turned to Maxi. 'You were brilliant. It was a close thing and a big improvement on your PB.'

Stan slunk away and Jack waited with her for her award.

She recovered her breath.

'Thanks, Jack. Dad is not happy.'

103

Stan came back. 'You could have won!'

'I tried but I'd left it too late.'

'That was a choke if ever I saw one. You should have been up with her earlier.'

'You ran well,' said Jack. 'Second in the UK is terrific.'

Stan glared at him. Maxi walked among the other runners, having a word here and there, in her chosen environment. He was reminded of a cheetah he had seen at a zoo. The sleek animal exuded a wild strength of purpose as it sauntered restlessly around its enclosure. Maxi seemed caged too, able to unleash herself fast at any time. She was fabulous and a mystery. He observed her with awe.

When she came back, Jack said: 'Until the last lap, you seemed to be biding your time. I expected you to pounce.'

'It seemed like that to me too,' she said. 'I left it a bit too late at the end. I'm not a sprinter. I won't let that happen again.'

'You should be pleased with your personal best.'

'Stan doesn't think so,' she said. 'He thinks I had more running in me.'

'You did what your body would let you. He thinks he knows better.'

'Who is right?'

'No-one is right. It's a difference we have to deal with.'

It had taken Jack many hours of study and much reading to begin to understand her. Today he'd learned more. When she unleashed herself, she ran well naturally.

He turned away, not wanting to get into a quarrel with Stan.

On their way home in the car, Stan was grumpy.

'To get into QIS next year, you have to be a winner, not a choker,' he said.

'Maybe I'm not good enough,' she said.

'You need to train hard,' he said. 'Winning will be worth it. The distance running programme at QIS is the best anywhere. You can enrol for a degree course at UQ. To get a QIS scholarship, you'll have to run in Australia. We will have to go home and enter you in the Open 3000 at Area level.'

'I want to stay over here,' Maxi said, eyeing Jack. 'Do I really have to go back?'

'To get into QIS, you must run in Australia,' Stan said. 'Anyway, my exchange here will finish soon.'

'Do you have to stay?' she asked Jack.

'My job is crap, but I don't want to quit yet: I've only done six months and I'm still on a steep learning curve. It would look bad on my CV. I'll go home soon.'

'We'll see,' she said and turned away.

CHAPTER 20

When he joined Oilco, he had expected personal freedom and adventure. Although he was proficient, the best project opportunities were given to obsequious peers. Nor did he obtain any encouragement to pursue his passion for truth. His critical questioning of managers was resented. Without answers, he stopped believing in what Oilco was doing.

In the Oilco office, everyone was working on delegated or self-generated projects. Managers were hungry for money-making ideas to take to their superiors, who would submit them for approval by the Board. Jack contributed to his team's proposals for their monthly meeting. New ideas were dressed up in misinformation and hyperbole to attract board members' interest.

'No decision, guys,' said Wayan his team leader, wearing shirt sleeves, coming from the Board meeting to address them at their desks. They swung around to face him. 'They didn't look at it.'

There were sighs. The team's carefully prepared proposal for development of a new mine had been by-passed yet again. This had happened repeatedly over recent months. Jack felt exasperated that his time and effort were being wasted. There would be no reward until their project was taken up.

'Is there a problem?' he asked Wayan.

'The usual. They thought other matters were more urgent.'

'Didn't our return on investment of 20% per annum get their attention?' asked Jack.

'They had other fish to fry, such as what to do about the workers' union. Maybe Jubilee Mine will get up after the election.'

'What do you want us to do?' Jack said, gesturing to the other five engineers.

'Fine-tune Jubilee so we can fast track it when we get the go-ahead.'

He had been working on the Jubilee Mine plan for months. At the start, every day had been a joy, creating designs. Time whizzed past and he stayed behind at work, putting in many extra hours. Detailed plans for the mine had accumulated steadily, but the Board overlooked them. It seemed that Oilco lacked courage for this large project and preferred to spread their risks. Jack was pessimistic: the project might never go. There was no Plan B. He would have to hide this episode in his CV.

He resented preparing plans for projects no one was interested in. He was being treated like a circus animal, doing tricks that demeaned his ability. It was a dysfunctional workplace, where fear and favour ruled. He was aware that his supervisor bypassed head office directives, allocated resources his own way and claimed other supervisors' successes as his own. When Jack copied him and ignored central policy, the hypocrite reported him and he was reprimanded.

'I'm not getting much satisfaction from working for Oilco,' he told Ross. 'Are you?'

'None at all, but I don't expect to. I make enough money for my ego to get pumped up by my social activities.'

Jack wasn't motivated by money: he needed the validation of practical outcomes. He asked for more innovative work and they assigned him to building a numerical model of coal to oil conversion and sent him on a World tour of plants in Germany, Holland, UK, South Africa, USA and Japan. His task was to identify the best investment opportunity for a project in Australia. His cynical conclusion was that technology companies were in a fake competition for government handouts.

'No-one believes the technology will ever be profitable,' Tom said when he returned and reported to his supervisor.

Instead of moving him to another project, his boss left him stranded with technology that was hopeless. He became frustrated and angry.

He had willed himself to be a mover and a shaker, but Oilco was restrictive and he lost confidence that management was moving forward.

'When I delivered my negative evaluation, they should have taken me off the project,' he said to Ross. 'It doesn't make sense that I have to waste time and effort on a non-starter.'

'You're their fall guy. No-one wants to cop the blame for backing a loser. They're making like ostriches until the sand storm of commercial disinterest blows over and they can pull the pin without getting their asses kicked.'

His physics tutorial with Maxi was the best part of his week.
He showed Ross a picture of her. 'This is Maxi.'
'Hey, cute. Why is she frowning?'
'She's concentrating. She's taking a drink during a hard run.'
'She's a runner? Who coaches her?'
'Her father. I'm her physics tutor.'
'What's she like?'
'Smart. Fun. I think I'm falling for her.'
'She's too young for you.'
'She's 17.'
'Do her parents know you want her?'
'Not really. I tutor her.'
'What are you going to do?'
'Nothing. I will wait for her.'
'Carpe diem, my friend. Waiting is a mug's game.'

On the phone to Australia, he told his parents about her. She was the first girlfriend he'd mentioned to them. They tried to seem not over-eager to know about her. It was a milestone to have a son disclosing his affections for a girl, no less than it was strange for him to be telling them about her.

108

Sebastian was more open about it. 'Is she a goer, is she? Nudge, nudge, wink, wink?'

Seb's presumption to intrude with these words taken from a Montepython skit annoyed Tom. Jack knew that Sebastian was not short of girlfriends, but he doubted his experience was as advanced as he pretended. His relationship with Maxi was private and he ignored Sebastian's intrusive questioning. He had held back while Maxi was still at school, but in a few months time she would be leaving.

CHAPTER 21

The end of Maxi's final year in distance education neared and online exam papers arrived at her local library for her to sit. At our tutorial, I asked revision questions to check her understanding of electrical circuits, but she was in a playful mood.

'How can you find resistance?' I asked her.

'I would look underground,' she said, 'in France.'

'Haha. You divide the voltage by the current. Would a conductor have few or many ohms?'

'None. Conductors are ohm-less. They sleep rough on the back seat.'

'Haha. Shall we finish there today?'

'Are you an ammeter? Can you eat a ham sandwich?'

Her parents were away for the weekend. She was laughing and teasing me, flirting. She came around the table, took me by the hand. Usually, I took the lead, but I didn't mind. I had been hanging back because she was younger and I was her tutor. It had been excruciating waiting for her but she had been adamant that she had to be sure. I wanted her badly and was overjoyed she was taking the lead.

She led me up to her bedroom.

Patti had suspected something was going on and wanted to end our tutorials.

'I don't think Jack is helping you, Maxi,' she had said, when we were both there.

'I've been getting top grades for my physics assignments.'

'That's not what I mean,' Patti said. 'Maxi, you're too young to have romance in your life yet. You're only a teenager. A boyfriend is a distraction.'

'We aren't involved,' Maxi protested.

She could have reminded Patti that she was 17 and old enough to decide her sexual activity, but that would have made it worse. Patti wanted to prevent Maxi being trapped by pregnancy the way she had been with Roly. She wanted to prevent Maxi becoming pregnant and me absconding, but my view wasn't asked.

We hadn't had sex. I had never been to her bedroom before. It was tidy and carefully organised, with posters of athletes on the walls, shelves of trophies and her clothes in racks. It was late afternoon and I closed the curtains to the street.

We helped each other undress. I tortuously unbuttoned her blouse wanting to rip it off. She wasn't wearing a bra. It seemed wrong that such beauty was covered. Her nipples were pink and hardened to my touch. We stood naked facing each other, looking curiously. She was awkward and embarrassed, with her legs crossed and an arm concealing herself.

'I've never done this before,' she said.

I believed her.

'I hope you will like it.'

I gazed at her taut young body and thin limbs, my arousal embarrassingly obvious.

My arms felt her silky skin as she nestled up to me, firm and slender, our thighs intertwined like vines. I surrendered to the world of touch, exploring the shape of her mouth with my tongue and lips. It was a long and searching kiss, like savouring the sweetness of a fruit. Her tongue teased mine, playing catch me if you can, as I tried to corner it. My hands marvelled at the curvature of her back and the firmness of her perfect buttocks. Her boldness seducing me was a very pleasant surprise.

She was slender and young and my conscience troubled me.

'What right do I have to take her virginity in her parents' house?' I thought. *'Am I certain my intentions are honourable?'*

111

'Yes. I'm certain I'll behave honourably,' I thought, *'whatever happens.'*

I drew her down onto the bed and we pressed together. My every contact point sizzled with excitement as I felt her body, smooth, lean and firm, pressing against me. Shyly and reverently, we touched each other. Her hand was soft and kind. Her fuzzy mound disclosed secret pleasures and I could wait no longer.

'We need a condom,' I said.

'I'm on the pill.'

'When did you start?'

'When I turned 16. It was a birthday present from Patti, just in case.'

'I wish you'd told me,' I said. 'We've wasted almost a year.'

It was a joke, but she didn't laugh.

'I'm sorry your time was wasted,' she said stiffly.

'I mean we could have been having fun — more fun.'

'It wasn't right until now,' she said.

'I'm getting a mixed message from Patti,' I said. 'Is she expecting us to have sex?'

'No. But she is realistic. Dad is the fanatic. If he catches us, there will be hell to pay. No more tutorials.'

'There's no time to lose,' I said.

'Where did you learn the art of seduction — from James Bond?'

'From Lady Chatterley's Lover.'

'Well, don't be coarse,' Maxi said. 'I want to be on a pedestal.'

'Very good, my Lady.'

We were hesitant and a little awkward, even clumsy. I didn't feel like a learner who should proceed with caution. Nor was I a veteran who knew exactly what was wanted and where. We were experimenters. She offered herself to me and I took her gift gratefully.

'Ladies and gentlemen of the jury, it was consensual. I did not force myself on her. She seemed to enjoy it. How do I know that? She held my thighs with her legs, pulling me into her and matched my every thrust with hers. This continued until she cried out and then when I was spent we stopped.'

We rolled apart.

'Have I taken advantage of her?' I thought.

I knew if it came down to her word against mine, her version would be believed. She was innocent and vulnerable.

'I never thought it would be like this,' she said.

'How do you mean?'

'I liked it. I didn't think I would. It was pretty special.'

'It was for me too.'

'It is so shared,' she said.

'Like a conversation.'

'It's called intercourse.'

'A reciprocated interaction,' I said.

'Like knocking up at tennis.'

Where did she get her ideas?

'Like in a long rally? Getting on top?'

Maxi was thoughtful.

'No, not a contest,' she said. 'Wanting to keep it going, evenly matched. There has never been anything like this for me before.'

'Nor for me. Perhaps we both won,' I said.

'Were we good together?'

She wasn't sure whether what we had done was good.

'Okay for beginners,' I said, playing along.

'Practice makes perfect,' she said.

'No. It was perfect,' I said, kissing her gently.

She was young and irresponsible and perhaps saw this as sexual experimentation. For me, though, our sex meant more, like something we'd created together and shared. It was unique, seeming like ascendance in my dream since I met her.

I wondered what came next. I wanted more. I felt committed to her, with admiration, longing and respect for her presence and humour. Could our physics tutorials continue? We would have to conceal our deeper involvement. She was going back to Australia and we only had a short time. Looming separation threatened. I seemed powerless to change my plans to prevent it as if it would be a just retribution for my ecstasy.

113

Maxi had been running as an Under 18 in the UK but she heard from the AAA that when she returned to Australia she would be in the Open category.

'Whoopee-doo,' she said. 'The QIS selectors could be easier to impress with a good performance in the Open,' she said. 'Are you coming with me?'

'I would like to go back to be with you,' I said, 'but I want to stay at my job here for a while.'

'You said you hated it.'

'It has been frustrating, but it might improve. How would it be if I stay here for a while, then come over?'

'I don't want to lose her,' I thought. *'We've known each other for seven months as student and tutor. Being apart will test whether this is really love.'*

'How long do you think?'

'Under a year.'

'That's a long time to miss you.'

'We can talk every day on Facetime or Skype,' I said.

'It's not the same. We've been doing a lot together.'

'Including sex.'

'For me it wasn't just sex,' she said. 'It was sharing our lives and being happy together.'

My heart leapt. 'It was for me too,' I said. 'If what we have doesn't last for a year apart, then what we have isn't special.'

'You make it sound like you want to stress-test our relationship to see it's strong enough. Do we need to do that?'

'If we last, it would be by choice, not convenience,' I said.

'Could you have chosen me for my physics?' she said.

'Your physique?'

'Well, for that too.'

'For all of you, Maxi. Let's make the most of the time we have left.'

We spent a lot of time in bed, sometimes getting up to go out for meals, then coming back to continue where we left off.

On the second day, it came to an end.

'I think I'm getting a cold,' she said nasally. 'I'd better rest.'

I went home. The next day when we talked on Facetime, she was croaky.

'It's getting worse,' she said.

I felt sorry for her, but there was nothing I could do but wait until she got better. It seemed to take forever.

'Perhaps we could go out for a drink,' I said the following weekend.

'Okay, but it will have to be with my friends.'

'I want to be intimate,' I said. 'When are your parents going away again?'

'I don't know.'

There were few opportunities to be together in our last two weeks together. It was bittersweet, as though our emotions could forestall a parting that could be forever. I surrendered my mind to sensing her, appreciating she was exquisite. What Maxi and I shared was authentic, between the two of us and no-one else. It was beautiful.

The Fleets marked her 18th birthday with a house party. Her running friends' and family's levity seemed to me forced, as if it was a farewell party and I might never see her again.

I was in a love relationship, for better or for worse and we would soon be parted. Our time wound down unpleasantly, even though it was short with time dragging like waiting in a departure lounge before boarding a plane. When she was gone, I'd have nothing to look forward to.

CHAPTER 22

Roly was reluctant to quit his gardening job in a London borough park.

'Why do I have to go to Australia?' he said. 'I want to stay here.'

'You haven't lived alone yet,' Patti said. 'You can move out from home when you have a job.'

'What if I can't get a job in Australia?'

'It might take a while, but you will. You've done so well here.'

Roly's interest in gardening had opened new vistas for him. The three years away had been good for all the Fleet family.

Patti's job with the run-to-work campaign in London had ended. She didn't know what she would do back in Australia.

'Something will turn up,' Stan said.

Jack was sad at the airport as he farewelled the Fleet family. When he reached the departure gate with Maxi, it seemed like an ending and he was emotional. He hugged her and kissed her.

'It seems wrong to separate now,' he said. 'It feels like a mistake.'

'Like we should stay together,' she said. 'I want that.'

'I'll see you in Australia, just as soon as I can sort out employment.'

'Keep in touch,' she said, pulling away, their fingertips lingering.

'Everyday,' he said.'

Maxi's parents thanked him for his tutoring. They didn't know their daughter had been having sex with Jack, unless they had guessed and said nothing. They were happy the two had separated before there were unwanted complications.

The Fleets' had been in the UK for 3 years. Back in Australia, Stan would coach Maxi and if she was accepted at QIS, he would be free to resume his teaching job.

Running in the open category, she would be up against older runners having more strength and greater will to win than in the UK schools' competition. On arrival, she began training immediately for the Area 3000 race in October.

'It's good to be back,' Maxi said to Stan as she took off her tracksuit after a first lap of Stan's school oval. 'Being able to count on fine weather is such a boost.'

It was a typical September morning in Queensland, with a cloudless sky, cool in the shade and warm in the sun. It was like discovering an exuberant new country. The light was bright everywhere, the sun following her like a hot inspection lamp. Seagulls clock-worked in a flock on the grass. A training run meant going into the oven outside for a space walk unprotected from solar radiation, without wind or shade.

She trained three days with the University of the Sunshine Coast Athletics Club at Sippy Downs. It was 20 minutes' drive from home. Stan sat with her as she practised her driving and she soon obtained a licence.

Stan coached Maxi on the track every morning. The training rehearsed and gradually improved her skills such as longer striding, more efficient cadences and faster pacing. Weeks of practice increased her endurance and reduced her perceived effort.

She followed Stan as he modelled goose-stepping, jumping, skipping with and without a rope, striding long and stepping fast. He wanted her to always be aware of what she was doing with her body and controlling it, finding the fastest ways to run by fine-tuning her running action during a race. His participation was to demonstrate to her the various skills. His were declining with age while Maxi's improved, surpassing his proficiency.

'Excellent,' he said. 'You've nailed that!'

On other days she ran near home, or on trails in the Glasshouse Mountains. She enjoyed the variety of terrain, surfaces, vegetation and fauna along the different routes.

She talked with Jack on FaceTime most days. Since watching her at Leicester, Jack wanted to know all about her runs. He asked her about her strategy for her coming race.

'Will you take the lead early and then drop back, like you did in Leicester?'

'I'd planned to lead all the way, but I dropped back when I thought I was going to bonk.'

'What was there to fear? You'd been there before. You told me you melted down years ago.'

'Not really. At QE2 I kept going and came in 4th. At Leicester I almost stopped but fell over the line at 2nd.'

'Stan says you choked.'

'It was close to the finish and the line between choking and quitting is fine.'

'You did keep going, though, so it was a choke.'

'Okay. Choking sounds better. Anyway, I need to be first across the line to get a QIS scholarship.'

She told him on the phone results of her races. In the Area Championship, she had led for most of the way, but in the last few metres, she faded and was overtaken, coming second with 8m20.

'Close again! Maybe if I had been there watching and cheering, you would have won?'

'The change from the UK threw me,' she said. 'My training was hurried and I found I didn't have the strength I needed at the end. Maybe I was still jet-lagged. It was a repeat of Leicester.'

'What did Stan say?'

'No much. He probably thought I choked again.'

'That is unfair. You did very well after arriving back so recently.'

Maxi trained hard and at the State Championships in Toowoomba in November, won in an improved time of 8m17.

'Way to go!' said Jack on the phone. 'Nothing can stop you now.'

In December Maxi, Stan and Patti flew to Melbourne for the National Championships. She won in 8m10, a record time. After the race, an official from QIS told her he would nominate her for a scholarship. Maxi was thrilled.

She told Jack on FaceTime.

'Congratulations,' he said. 'It's been your dream to go to QIS, hasn't it?'

'I've wanted it for years. They prepare you to be a champion.'

'How far have you been running?'

'I tapered down from about 30 kilometres to 10 kilometres per day in the week before the final.'

'How did it go?'

'When I lined up, I was feeling stronger and more confident than before my meltdown at QE2.'

'That was three years ago. You told me you melted down because Stan had over-trained you. How was it different this time?'

'I was less anxious and less tired from training. I was more in control.'

'What did you do that was better?'

'At Leicester, I had tried to do a Prefontaine and hold the lead all the way. I melted down because I began too fast and faded at the end.'

'Stan said you choked.'

'The label doesn't matter. This time, I held back and had enough left to sprint at the end.'

'You were more confident today?'

'I understood what I had to do better. You've helped me with that. I wish you were here.'

'I wish I was there too, to celebrate with you.'

'Here's a kiss,' she said.

'Is it a tongue kiss?'

'Yes.'

'Do I suck?'

'Definitely. Even though you suck, I like you.'

'I'll call tomorrow.'

CHAPTER 23

We took turns to phone, talking every day online at 8 pm Australian time. Our conversations were jokes, laughter, swapping of anecdotes and trivia. We told each other the events of the day and our plans for tomorrow. I would recount my trials and tribulations at Oilco and she would tell me about the delights and pains of her training runs and about the athletes she had talked with. Our chat was often about how we were feeling and especially how we missed each other. I was lonely without her and our conversations could become querulous as I complained about my lonely life in the UK without her.

'It's no good feeling sorry for yourself,' she said. 'You need to meet people.'

'The Roman philosopher Cicero said he was never less lonely than when he was alone.'

'He must have been self-sufficient. He wasn't the type to have a goddess girlfriend like me. He probably had slaves looking after him.'

'He spent most of his time in the senate debating.'

'Those senators were a shifty bunch,' she said. 'No wonder he preferred being alone.'

'Possibly. But it is more likely that he trained himself not to feel lonely. Psychologists say loneliness is like a person who has a dog phobia. With gradual exposure to dogs and loneliness, they get over it.'

'Are you getting used to being without me?' Maxi asked.

'Yes.'

'Well, don't take it too far!'

We laughed together.

'I was late for my lecture this morning,' she said. 'It was difficult to find a car park.'

'Get a bicycle,' I said. 'It's convenient, uses less energy and frees up parking for others.'

'It isn't safe,' she said.

'I use a bike and it's safe enough.'

'Cycling is safer in London than in Brisbane.'

'Bike lanes in London are separated from cars by barriers,' I said. 'If Brisbane had barriers for bike lanes, would that be safe enough for you?'

'It would be safer and faster,' she said. 'Brisbane traffic is at a standstill.'

'It would be public-spirited of you to ride.'

'If people were more like me, there would be more room on the roads,' she said.

'How come?'

'My driving gets to places more quickly. Some people faff around, blocking streets.'

'They have less purpose than you,' I said, humouring her. 'People travel unnecessarily.'

'People need goals,' she said.

'Not everyone is going for Olympic gold.'

'No,' said Maxi, 'but they should have a goal, if only to get a pass in a subject they are studying, or a promotion.'

'They won't have a goal if they could fail. They risk less by getting stuck in the traffic. Your best bet is to ride a bike.'

'I'll try it.'

Maxi made choices, living her life full-on and joyfully.

Sometimes Maxi and I would play with ideas, taking variables to ridiculous extremes.

'I bought fast food for lunch today,' Maxi said, 'from the Institute café.'

'Was it fast enough to improve your running?' I asked.

"Haha. Their food is getting faster. Soon all food will be precooked.'

'It's cooked in a factory now.'

121

'Like airline food.'

'Totally packaged.'

''Eaten in front of a screen, not at a table,' she said.

'No conversation.'

'Good. I don't like dialogue.'

'Why not?'

'Conversations go on and on,' she said. I waited. Eventually, she said: 'Don't you find that ironic? Oh, I want to remind you about the jacarandas being in flower here. I wish you could see how beautiful they are.'

'I do remember.'

'It's not the same. I do remember you, but I still want to see you and talk again soon.'

'I'm working on it,' I said. 'I'd better be doing. I love you. Bye.'

She put her lips to the phone screen and so did I. I felt valued. We were still connected.

Maxi's life was her running. When I would be with her again, I wanted to be more involved in her running. I envied Stan his coaching her.

CHAPTER 24

Jack stayed on at his job at Oilco in London. He followed the leaders and their rules. It was like swimming in a school of fish, swerving in unison to go in a new direction, then another. He had few choices and found it anxious, claustrophobic and oppressive.

He had been trained to engineer first designs, but at Oilco everyone tried to be second, or later. Oilco wouldn't risk adopting an innovative design and preferred off-the-shelf technologies that had been demonstrated elsewhere. The ethos at Oilco was to maximise corporate profits, ignoring possible effects on the environment, without regard for effects on communities and individuals. Creativity was mostly in seeking government handouts and tax exemptions.

He lacked experience in mining and his teammates played a practical joke on him. He received a faked request from the government to supply 'clean' coal. His colleagues sniggered when he requested details of the order and discovered that 'clean coal' was a politically correct euphemism invented to disparage ordinary 'dirty' coal. 'Clean coal' didn't exist. Jack was annoyed how his time had been wasted.

Jack wanted his team's mine design to make efficient use of the mineral resource but none of the others cared about that.

'Our greatest resource is government relations,' a manager said. Oilco was superficially deferent to the government, but the interaction was sycophantic and secretly contemptuous.

Jack's work would mainly advantage shareholders. He wanted to make a difference, but he was aware citizens who trusted Oilco would benefit little or lose. He was reluctant to exploit people the way Oilco expected.

They transferred him to a team developing a coal seam gasification project, sending him on a world tour of technically advanced operations. His work was to code a numerical model of process dynamics. He quizzed their boffins. There was insufficient data and models had so many variables that the predictions were no better than guesses. He returned disillusioned.

'Garbage in, garbage out,' Jack said at a company conference. 'Modelling coal seam gas gasification is too hard: it's like trying to model the weather.'

His flatmate Ross was there.

'You have put your foot in it,' he said to Jack afterwards. 'If the project folded, people would lose their jobs. You can think it, but you can't say it.'

His disaffection had rocked the boat and he was ostracized and withdrawn from the project.

'How's the engineering going?' Maxi asked Jack on the phone.

'Okay.'

'Did you think you would be doing this when you chose to do physics at uni?'

'Not exactly.'

'Are you making a difference?'

'Our project would meet customers' demands, build useful infrastructure, create jobs, provide incomes, support a community.'

'What about the bad stuff,' she said, 'like harming the environment, taking land and water, polluting air, threatening wild life, displacing indigenous people and disrupting country life?'

'People who are disadvantaged would get compensation.'

'Can a farming family be compensated for losing their home, their land and livelihood?'

'We would move them to an equivalent farm, or better.'

Maxi changed tack.

'How long does a mine keep going for?'

'20 years.'

'What will happen when you run out of coal?'

'We can mine deeper, or find new deposits nearby.'

'After that would you close down and walk away?'

'Yes.'

'What about the mess you leave behind? Who would restore it?'

'The government collect money from us to landscape it, with lake sanctuaries for water birds and a water skiing park.'

'Would anyone still go there?'

'A few people would stay. The workforce would be fly in and fly out, so the town would be small. The existing houses would continue to be lived in.'

'Will the locals let you do it? Don't people want their patch left alone?'

'It could be a fight. There could be stories about effluents, emissions, endangered species and burial grounds. They regard Oilco as fair game and would take as much from us as they can get. It is not about rights and compensation; it is a zero sum game between the interests for and against the project.'

A few weeks later Maxi asked him again about his job.

'How are you getting on at Oilco now?'

'My time is wasted.

'Is there any enjoyment?'

'Yes. Sometimes, when something I have worked on is developed.'

'Why does that matter?'

'It vindicates my hard work. I want to make a difference.'

'Maybe your people don't care that much,' Maxi said. 'Isn't your large salary enough for you?'

'No. I want recognition from people who will benefit.'

'A trophy for your ego?'

'The same as when you run in a race. I want a place on a podium too.'

'It isn't the same really,' he thought. *'I'm not achieving anything that matters, not for myself nor for anyone else. Maxi's achievement is real. She's a role model for others and she's getting more pleasure from her exertions than I am from mine.'*

Jack's frustration grew. He denounced Oilco's neglect of public interest and he criticised company policies. He ignored his boss' instructions and openly challenged management at a department meeting.

'It's wrong to neglect the public interest,' he said. 'This project is futile and unethical.'

His whistle-blowing was branded disloyal. At a meeting convened to consider his future, it was decided to transfer him to the USA, as a tame boffin and of little consequence. He refused to go. He delayed completing tasks assigned to him and worked on problems that interested him. Soon afterwards, his in-tray emptied and he had nothing to do. His boss ignored him and he was sidelined. He had been careful not to contravene the terms of his employment or they would have fired him.

He would have preferred to be contributing, but he was too independent-minded. He was internally motivated, not needing affirmation or reward. His principles guided him and he wanted to engineer something that would benefit people. While the company was deciding what to do with him, he was content to follow his dreams, completing his design for converting coal to oil, for when the company came to its senses.

Jack expected events would vindicate his criticisms. But it soon became apparent that his days at Oilco were coming to an end. He took legal advice from a law firm that defended whistle-blowers. They advised him to stay put and record evidence of discrimination. The damages he could win would be sufficient for him to pursue further university studies.

Earlier, when his ideas had met with approval, they had expanded the size of his desk, with chairs and a small table for meetings with visitors in his office. He had been awarded a patterned carpet, a potted shrub and paintings on the walls.

Now they tried to drive him out by removing his privileges. They took away his car parking spot in the basement carpark and he had to buy expensive parking outside. His cubicle was medium size, with head-high movable walls. They moved the walls in, until he was barely able to squeeze in behind his desk. They removed his chairs, table, pot plant and paintings. It was a fate others feared and they stayed away from him. His ignominy deterred others from rocking the boat. Ironically, he had more free time than he wanted.

It was a difficult time for him and Maxi's support by telephone kept him going. He didn't mention it to his parents. He felt they wouldn't understand the machinations of the corporate world and would worry about him.

CHAPTER 25

Derek Tracker was head coach of athletics at the Queensland Institute of Sport. He was a former national sprint champion, a household name and an activist for rights of Indigenous people. He had joined the QIS faculty only recently.

He was an experienced coach with a quiet and humble manner. Maxi walked with him from the administration building across the arena to where a woman of oriental appearance, wearing a white tracksuit, stood in the runway holding a javelin and talking to a group of javelin throwers. She stopped as they came up.

'Good morning, Doctor Tracker,' she said.

'Good morning,' he said. 'Sensei, this if Maxi Fleet. She is a distance runner. Maxi this is Sensei Riko Minami.'

'Pleased to meet you,' said Maxi, giving a small bow.

The teacher turned back to her class.

'It must be purposeless and egoless,' she instructed in accented English. 'Allow the javelin to fly. It doesn't matter how far it goes.'

She took a javelin, walked back a few paces and held it by her side. Standing straight, with her eyes closed, she meditated for a few moments. Raising the spear above her shoulder, she pulled it back as far behind her as she could. Running forward with long smooth strides, at the line she planted a foot and levered her torso forward, launching the javelin with a long propulsive force, until it left her hand at the last possible moment. Minami hopped to a stop short of the line and stepped off the runway, turning her back. The spear's trajectory was a high arc, seeming to float as it flew, descending gradually to land with the point slightly down, marking the ground.

It was a longer throw than most of them had ever seen.

'The way you throw it is important; how far it goes is not,' she said.

They took in turns to throw. As each stepped out of the runway after throwing, she said a few words.

'That was right.'

'Aim infinitely far ahead; don't release it; don't open your hand on purpose; release the javelin when the fruit is ripe and it drops.'

When they had all thrown, they faced her again.

'Do not grieve when you do a bad throw,' she said. 'Forget it. Clear your mind. I want you to practice, with repetition of practice, followed by repetition of the repeated. A spiritual state of throwing will take time to master. Good morning to you.'

She made a small bow to the group and turned away to where Coach Derek and Maxi waited.

'Dr Riko Minami is our spiritual coach,' Derek said to Maxi. 'She's a Japanese Zen master. As you'll have heard, she won the Boston Marathon two years ago. QIS is very lucky to have her. Zen and science go together. She may accept to coach you. I'll leave you two to discuss it. Maxi, will you let me know when you start with her?'

Derek left.

'Now Maxi, would you please tell me about yourself,' Minami asked. 'What running have you done?'

Maxi summed up her career highlights and recent placings in competition.

'You have done well,' Minami said. 'Congratulations. It took me 10 years with my Sensei to master Zen running. I specialised in 10,000 metres and later changed to marathons. The Zen technique can be applied to throwing, to archery, to swordsmanship, to martial arts and even to ink brush painting. How do you think I might be able to help you?'

'I want better mental control,' said Maxi. Riko's serenity had captivated her.

'It would take several years for you to become a Zen master,' she said. 'I would be your Sensei and try to transfer my mental skills to you. The word Zen means concentration. You will learn to see into

129

your mind as into the depths of a crystal-clear pool of stilled water, with attentiveness. Do you want to do that?'

'Yes, very much.'

'You can fine-tune your body the way a Zen bikie tunes his motor-cycle, with reverence. Did you read that book?'

'I've made a start.'

The book Zen and the Art of Motorcycle Maintenance (10) was on her reading list.

'I request you read it right through. By focussing on your body, you will reach new heights of performance. I will set you tasks to do and exercises, that develop your running skills and mental control. I will expect you to follow my advice. Do you have any questions?'

'No, thank you.'

'I will be here for you at 8.00 am tomorrow. Do you agree?'

'Yes, thank you, Sensei.'

The next morning, Sensei Minami watched her do several short runs. She made several constructive comments on her style.

'The pieces are good but they don't fit together right. Run as if all of you is in one piece, make yourself comfortable. That's better.'

'I can learn from her,' Maxi thought.

Afterwards, she left a note at the office.

Coach Derek,
I've started with Dr Minami.
Thank you.
Regards,
Maxi.

For her next lesson, Dr Minami took Maxi to the Institute's Shinto garden and Buddhist temple, donated by a Japanese corporation. It was about a hectare, with a traditional lake fed by a burbling stream crossed by ornate bridges. It was bordered by large rounded boulders, with trimmed camellia and azalea bushes in bloom, with delicate russet branches from a Japanese pine reaching overhead. Maxi loved the peacefulness of this sacred place.

Riko had brought two bows, quivers and a target. She set the target up 30 metres away on an island in the lake reached by a bridge. They knelt on mats in front of a gazebo, gazing across the water at the target.

'I want you to learn the correct forms of Zen archery (25), with me watching you closely so that you will be able to follow the same process when you are running and I cannot see you.'

Maxi copied her movements as she performed a ritual of consecration and purification, then prayer and obeisance. Following Sensei Minami, she 'nocked' an arrow and held the bow with arms outstretched in front and above her, with the arrow aimed at the target. She drew it back so far it seemed the bow must break.

'Do not release the arrow. It must release itself.'

Maxi's arms shook until the arrow unleashed itself.

'It is of no consequence where the arrow went,' said Riko. 'Do not look. Your mind controls your body. Remember that archery is not meant to strengthen your muscles. Your arm and shoulder muscles must remain relaxed, as though they look on impassively and let your hands do the work. Only when you can do this will your drawing and shooting be spiritual.'

Sensei Minami showed her the hand positions and guided her through the phases of movement. It took concentrated strength and Maxi's arms were trembling, her breathing laboured. Her drawing and shooting did not become spiritual, no matter how hard she tried.

'Relax! Relax!' said the Sensei. 'Concentrate entirely on your breathing.'

In the following weeks, Maxi learned to control her breathing.

Sensei Minami introduced exercises to develop her balance.

'For the arrow to hit the target, the base must not move. Your stance must be in full control of your body position.'

One day Riko applauded her shot.

'You did 'It'!' said the Sensei.

The arrow had missed the target, but Maxi knew she had experienced the sublime self-control Riko had told her about.

'Your action was correct; later you will hit the target. It is not important at this stage of your training that it hits the bull. Your collapse at the Gold Coast does not matter: you ran well.'

All that summer her training continued. She could unleash an arrow effortlessly. On the track, Sensei Minami honed her running as precise action with tolerable effort under conditions that simulated racing.

It was mental training that Riko explained to Maxi.

'Learning to play a guitar is as demanding as learning to perform well in an endurance run. Both have demands that are physical and mental.

'When you learn to play a guitar, you encounter pain in your fingers from pressing on strings that are thin and taut. You grow protective calluses and become habituated to the pain. Eventually, in a virtuoso performance, you may not notice any pain.

'While learning and developing skills, neither a guitarist nor a distance runner have their attention primarily on performance. Their focus is on achieving the correct forms. Like a novice guitarist who puts body, arms and fingers in the correct positions at the right time, without worrying about the sound, a novice archer and a novice runner both strive for technique.

'Your performance may improve, but not as a reward for effort. Striving alone won't help. A runner's speed results from achievement of the forms. You are learning to control your body, your breathing, your running and your mind.

'For many years, competitiveness is of low interest and a Zen archer does not check if he or she has hit the target. Sounds made by a guitarist are not important until the correct positions have been achieved. It may be several years until a runner finds herself at the front of the field. Just as the arrow finds its own way to the bull, so virtuosity and best performances will inevitably result. The art of Zen is artless, by total mental control.'

Maxi's Zen archery practise laid the foundation for her mental control in endurance running, with Riko correcting her form and watching for her to achieve 'It'.

'Zen training takes a long time,' Maxi said to Jack. 'I am learning to be patient. I used to dream of winning gold at the Olympics. Now I seek mental control and sleep soundly.'

CHAPTER 26

The front page of the Queensland Institute of Sport's newsletter announced Maxi's arrival, with her photograph and this story.

GOING THE DISTANCE

Many top runners do more training than studying but for Maxi Fleet, 19, beginning at Queensland Institute of Sport on a three-year scholarship, her training will be balanced by lectures. She has lived in the UK for the past 3 years. In the UK in June, she placed 2nd in the U18 3000 with a time of 8m40. Back in Australia at Melbourne in December, she won through to take out the 3000m Open Championship, with a PB of 8m10, a new Australian record.

'This year I plan to run half-marathons,' she told me. 'I enjoy the challenge of endurance and I'm looking forward to running longer distances.'

The QIS programme supports around 150 athletes every year, across a range of sports, competing nationally and internationally. The program is designed with a holistic approach and individualised programmes.

A sports scholarship at QIS includes competition and training expenses, lectures, tuition, one-to-one coaching, group workouts, elite athletic skills workshops and training of strength, speed and flexibility. Athletes also have access to physiological support; sport psychology; nutrition consultation; sports massage; physiotherapy and sports medicine.

'A half-marathon is more than 7 times further than the 3000 m,' Maxi said. 'I'm in the Open category, with athletes who are more mature and stronger than the school students I've been running

against. I'm finding the training more challenging and requiring careful mental preparation.'

Our best wishes are with Maxi in the Brisbane half-marathon championships at QE2 stadium on March 23rd, starting at 7.20 am.

'It will be my first ever half-marathon in competition,' Maxi said. 'My goal is 1h 30.'

Members of the public are welcome to attend. I hope you can come and encourage Maxi in this significant next step in her running career. See you there.

Victoria Langthorne,
QIS Athletics Writer.

Coach Derek Tracker coordinated Stan and Riko with preparing a training programme for Maxi.

Maxi had heard from other QIS runners that Derek was infatuated with Riko Minami. At QIS socials, he sought out Riko and stayed with her, oblivious to the stares and cold shoulders of other staff who were friends of his wife and had met their children. Maxi tried not to let Derek and Riko's relationship affect her response to their coaching.

'They're sleeping together for sure,' she said to Jack. 'Too bad he has a wife and kids.'

'I'm not going to take sides,' said Jack. 'We don't have the right to make a moral judgement, unless it affects their coaching.'

Stan supervised her when she was at home on weekends. He was sceptical about Riko's coaching.

'The Zen method is fanciful,' he said. 'A runner discovers style by experience. When your PB improves, that's when your style improves.'

She ran the Brisbane Area half-marathon in 1h25, well within her goal, coming in 3rd. It was her first half-marathon and she was happy with her performance.

'Other runners set my pace,' she said. 'Sometimes I wanted to speed up and at others I wanted to slow down, but I stayed with the front group. Next time I will run more of it at my own pace.'

Maxi's programme was gruelling, with several half-marathons each week.

'You need to increase your tolerance for pain,' Stan said. 'When you're habituated to suffering, your perceived effort will reduce and you'll speed up.'

'There are stories of runners who have wrecked their bodies,' Maxi said. 'Are you sure I can ignore pain signals without risking harming myself?'

'You won't ignore pain until you have investigated it,' Stan said. 'You can discover your limits carefully in training by science, without any possibility of injury.'

Maxi threw herself into training. It limited her recreation and she missed out on social activities.

'The girls at QIS understand when I can't go out,' she told Jack. 'Some of them go to parties, drink, sleep with guys and wreck themselves. I have to stay in top condition for what I do.'

'Yeah, you should hold off on sleeping with guys until I get back.,' he said sardonically. 'Don't even think about wasting yourself.'

She was second in 1h15 at the State Championships in Cairns, but in the National in Wollongong, after leading for most of the race, her big toe ached and she became dizzy. She came in 6th but still managed an improved time of 1h12.

'Did your toe slow you down?' Jack asked on FaceTime from the UK. She hadn't seen him all year. She tried to keep him informed about her progression from Area to Region to the National in the half-marathon, but his questioning could barely keep up with what had happened.

'I faded. I couldn't keep going.'

'Was it a choke?' Jack asked.

'No,' she said. 'I was feeling a bit off and had to slow down. My big toe was the last straw.'

'You were physically able to keep going, so it seems like it was a choke,' he said. 'How come you let a toe get to you like that?'

'I didn't,' she said hotly. 'It sort of took over. You think I could have kept going, don't you?'

136

'No. I'm sure you did the best you could. What was the worst your toe could do to you?'

'Get gangrene and be amputated,' she said, indignant.

'That isn't likely,' said Jack gently. 'It must have been very painful. That type of pain comes and goes. How is it now?'

'Swollen, red, hurts,' she said.

'Could you have ignored it?'

'In the race reports I've read, winning distance runners generally disregarded pain,' he thought.

'Yes,' she said, humouring him. 'I suppose I could have ignored it, if I had wanted to keep going badly enough and had overcome my fear of injury and surgery, which were irrational.'

'Is she putting me on?' he thought. *'Or is this the self-talk of learning to suffer?'*

'Overcoming fear is what it takes to deal with pain, Maxi! You kept going and ran well.'

'Do you think so?' she said, liking his stroking.

'I do. It was the National half-marathon, a big step up from 3000 metres. Coming sixth was well done. I wish I had been there.

'I was pleased to finish.'

'Next time you'll do better.'

'Yes.'

We talked everyday on Facetime. She would tell me what she had been doing and I would try and make her laugh.

'My back is sore,' she complained.

'Could you have annoyed it?' he asked sarcastically.

'You are supposed to be supportive.'

'Would you like a back support?'

'My injury is no joke!'

He could tell she was holding in a laugh.

'Sorry.'

'Saying sorry won't do. Put some real sorry into it.'

'I am very, very sorry.'

'That's not enough.'

'What do you want me to do, cry?'

'Okay.'

He thought for a moment, missing her.
'Perhaps I'll come home soon.'
'Great! What about your job?'
'It's cactus. I am going to quit.'
'That would be excellent.'
'I will be back supporting you.'
'Haha.'
'Here's a kiss.'
'Here's one back.'

CHAPTER 27

Maxi had just leapt out of bed in her room at the university, propelled by her goals, when I called her from the UK on FaceTime. For me, it was evening, before bed.

'What are your plans for today?' I asked.

'Track intervals with Derek, then Zen with Riko. This afternoon I'll work out in the weights room and at the pool.'

'What exercises have you been doing with Riko?'

'I've been sprinting flat out with her watching.'

'How is that different from Derek's intervals?'

'Riko's a perfectionist and demands my utmost flat out, whereas Coach Derek keeps me at one effort level. I am increasing how much work cardiac muscles can do more before lactic acid accumulates. QIS are religious about monitoring my physiology. He's training me to take advantage of my oxygen reserves.'

'You poor thing, having to fight your natural instincts to eke out your oxygen. Are you ever frightened?'

'No. I trust Derek and Riko. We are doing it in stages too gradual for any harm.'

'Which do you find hardest, accepting the hurt or finding the will to go on?'

'That's like asking me what I am developing most, my mind or my body?' she said. 'I don't know.'

'What do you think makes a car go, the engine or the wheels or the fuel?'

'All of those.'

'Coaches have you train one part more than others,' Jack said. 'Stan would say: train your body.'

'Coach Derek would say: train your mind's willpower,' Maxi said.

'Riko would say: train your spirit.'

'Then I should train all three,' Maxi said. 'Anything else?'

'It sounds like you're having fun. What other training are you doing?'

'I do half-marathons with Stan at the weekend,' said Maxi. 'I love running in the country here. The runs bring all the training together: body, mind and spirit.'

'You are in good hands. I wish I was there with you.'

'I wish you were here too. When are you coming home?'

'Hmm. I want to. I'm missing you a lot. Maybe I will.'

For half marathons, she had shortened her pace length, from the loping strides she had used for 3000 metres, to a shuffle. Shorter, quicker strides were more efficient and easier on her legs. But her times were slower than she wanted. She trained harder and ran further. In the months following, Maxi averaged 100 kilometres per week, much of it at race speed.

CHAPTER 28

Jack's job was precarious. When he made rebellious waves, management pointedly ignored him. He imagined they lacked the courage to fire him because he could whistle-blow. He was not cut out for the type of work Oilco wanted and it would be only a matter of time until his position on the employment-consumption treadmill would end. He had an idea to go back to university. He resigned his job, bought an air ticket to Australia and said goodbye to his friends.

When he arrived in Brisbane, Maxi and his parents were at the airport. Jack wanted to be with Maxi, but he was tired and went home for a couple of days. His conflict with Oilco had been stressful. It was great to be home with his parents and Sebastian. When he explained his difficulties with Oilco they were sympathetic.

'They treated you badly,' his father said. 'You were right to challenge them and leave when they tried to bully you. Working for corporations isn't for everyone.'

'I like your idea to go to university,' his mother said. 'Research could suit you very well. I did a major in philosophy and I would love to hear your ideas.'

'I'm not very far along with them yet,' said Jack. 'But I would be happy to tell you what I have done so far. My interest is in personal time control.'

'Time is metaphysics, isn't it?' she asked. 'Is it calculated by dividing a distance moved by the speed?'

That was Newton's idea. Einstein widened it out, for space curved by gravity.'

'How do you explain it?'

'I think it is an amount sensed, measured or calculated relative to observations in different time frameworks. It's Einstein's relativity.'

'How do you imagine personal time control?'

'Maybe if a person was in a fast framework, perhaps by speeding up, another person who is an observer would see them moving slower and they would be able to do more work in the time.'

'That's a good idea. I think you are on to a good thing. Many people would like to have increase their performances.'

His mother had a critical mind and he welcomed her interest. Their discussion had clarified his ideas and given him new threads to follow.

Jack wanted to be with Maxi, but boyfriends were not allowed to be in her room at the university overnight.

'Would you like to come to my parents' place for a few days,' she offered. 'We can be together.'

'Won't they mind?'

'No. Dad and Patti have come around. You've passed their authenticity test.'

Jack spent the weekend with the Fleets. He was hungry for Maxi but had to wait until her parents were out.

'It's great to be with you again,' he said, as he lay in bed gasping. 'I had forgotten how switched on you are.'

'I'm not a sex robot.'

'I mean passivity is not in your repertoire.'

'I don't sit around.'

'Have you put on weight – just a little?'

'You haven't lost your eye for detail,' she said. 'As a matter of fact, I am a bit over. I stopped training because of my toe, but now I am preparing for another half marathon and my weight is coming down.'

They lay in bed and talked then about her running. He had tried to keep up with what she was doing by phone, but now she filled him in with the details of her training and performances. She talked about her family, friends and feelings. He listened entranced, his adoration interrupted by their love making. Then he went to his room to sleep.

142

In the city, he was staying at Blake's place, his friend from undergraduate physics days, who had rented an apartment in a deconsecrated church. Jack slept on his couch.

'Thanks Blake,' he said.

'There isn't much room to spread out, but you can stay here until you get somewhere.'

Jack spent the week inquiring about jobs and university courses. At the weekend, he went to Maxi's again.

'I'm looking for a place where you can stay with me,' he told her. 'Until I know what I'm going to be doing, we aren't going to see as much of each other as I would like. I want to be with you as much as possible.'

'What are you going to do for work?'

'I'm not sure yet.'

'What decided you to quit Oilco?'

'We had a falling out.'

'You said you didn't like the work.'

'My job was pointless except to get money. I broke their rules and had to quit.'

'What rules?'

'Management policy.'

'Did you behave badly?'

'No. I exposed that they were unethical.'

'That wasn't smart. Will you get a job here?'

'Not a full-time corporate job. I want to work for causes I value with a life outside the office. I couldn't be myself at Oilco. I want personal freedom.'

'Perhaps a different type of job would suit you better?'

'I don't think I'd be happy with a change of job or a change of company. I want to reduce stress, spend less time worrying about possessions, commit to self-education without possibility of disruption by my employer. I want to be off the treadmill. I want freedom, creativity and culture.'

'Will you have money for that?'

'I have applied for a research grant to study physics.'

'Not a bad life,' she said. 'What research are you going to do?'

'A PhD.'

'What topic?'

'Relativity.'

'Connecting with relatives is relatively important, isn't it?' she said mischievously.

'That's not it.'

'Oh,' she said disappointed. 'What is relativity then?'

'If an object is moving a lot faster, an observer would see it arrive earlier.'

He had enjoyed studying relativity as an undergraduate and had explored it online. He wanted Maxi to glimpse its splendour.

She was silent, thinking.

'If astronauts were paid by the hour,' she said, 'they wouldn't want any relativity or their pay could be docked. They would want a contract for the voyage there and back, taking as much or as little time as they want! The old wind jammers that sailed the Atlantic in competition with steamships won cargoes by speedy delivery. I doubt their crews were on a daily rate. Early delivery needed payment in full.'

'Einstein's relativity idea was that at high speeds, time would stretch.'

'You said stars moving away from us have their light stretched to lower frequency, causing a red shift. Do we get red light at sunset because the light waves are stretching?'

'Nice try, but the red shift is a frequency change of light waves. Einstein predicted a slowing of any object near the speed of light. The speed of light has been measured precisely and it is always the same. Our fastest spaceships can only get up to 2% of light speed.'

'Constancy of light speed isn't obvious,' Maxi said. 'It can't be tested, because it takes light and time to measure its speed, which would be circular and invalid.'

Jack smiled delightedly. 'Brilliant. You are correct. This is not a physics theory. It is metaphysics and a matter of belief.'

'Do you believe it?'

144

'Yes. There is evidence from space that is unable to be explained except by relativity. I hope to find more evidence of relativity affecting everyday life.'

'How long will that take you?'

'A PhD normally takes 4 years.'

'How will you earn enough for food, rent and university fees?' Maxi said.

'Because my degree is first class, the State will give me a scholarship to do a PhD. Also, I can do tutoring.'

'You could tutor me!'

'You would have to pay me. Would it be okay if I was your gigolo?'

'No, not when I can get you free.'

They laughed and kissed.

'But about your research, will you have the freedom you want?'

'I think so. A PhD student can explore physics topics freely, under a supervisor.'

'It sounds like you would enjoy it,' Maxi said. 'If it was me, I would have to have a definite goal.'

'Because you want to be the best?'

'Don't you want to be famous?'

'No. I want to discover something that people can use.'

Jack enrolled at UQ to do honours followed by a PhD in physics.

For two years he had been at Oilco's beck and call. Free of Oilco at last, and with a definite goal, Jack threw himself into the academic life. Now he could do what he liked. He would be the hero of his own life, an adventurer whose mind was open to exploring not only physics, but other subjects that touched on his interest in personal time.

'Maxi tells me you want to do research in physics. Isn't that for dreamers?' Sarah asked him.

'The frontiers for exploring in physics are space and particles,' he said. 'I want to explore time, where metaphysics overlaps with psychology and neuroscience.'

'Is it science?'

145

'Partly,' he said.

'You will need a supervisor whose bow has several strings.'

'More than one supervisor is possible, but one would be enough to get started.'

The cohort of new research students met with the Physics research staff to allocate supervisors. Dr Baxter, a charismatic and good-humoured lecturer with an interest in relativity of time agreed to take Jack as his student.

To help him deal with the subjectivity that physics abhorred, Jack scoured the campus to find philosophy researchers interested in time phenomena. Blake, Alice and Corvid, who he had kept in touch with since they were in hall together as undergraduates, were now doing PhDs that related to his interest and they suggested ideas that he could follow up.

He felt he was on the cusp of something new. He made a list of everyday situations when time was of the essence, like when a person had little control, for example, waiting for a bus to arrive. There were other situations when a person controlled occurrence of an event, for example, going for a walk. He put 100 different time situations into a ranking, from those with most personal control down to least. The list was headed by activities with much personal control, such as individual voluntary work, down to involuntary imprisonment and capital punishment, without personal control. At the top of his list was a person volunteering her time, with beginning and ending the activity under her total control. Examples were solitude, meditation, enjoying entertainment and engagement with nature.

'I want to find out how a person can best use their time,' he said to Maxi.

'Don't we all,' she said.

'Some good uses seem timeless and therefore must be best.'

He looked for other self-controlled situations when the passing of time was most enjoyable. At the top of his list were time-friendly situations. Transcendence could be achieved through practice of religion, by Hindu mantra chanting, or by Sufi whirling dervishes. His research also led him to states induced by ingesting hallucinogenic substances. He developed a rich palette of subjective experiences of time and composed a landscape of personal time control.

Eventually, he became interested in endurance in extreme sports, as adventuring at new frontiers of human accomplishment, by going long distances, moving fast, or for long durations. He questioned: *'What perspective of time did endurance performers adopt during their feats? How did personal control relate to endurance? Was it cause or effect?'* He would investigate an endurance runner's time perspective to discover whether people in other walks of life could adopt an endurer's perspective and benefit. He would investigate Maxi's endurance running.

CHAPTER 29

Maxi was starting her second year at QIS when Riko Minami came out on to the track where she was training.

Riko's exercises always began with slow and deep breathing.

'When's your next race?' the Sensei asked after the breathing was done.

'The National at the Gold Coast in two months' time.'

'What's your goal?'

'I want to reduce my PB to 1h10.'

'Good. Forget about that for now. You need to develop purposeless running.'

'How can I? My purpose is to improve my PB.'

'Put your PB out of your mind. Your Zen running action must be purposeless and effortless, expressed as an artless art. Your goal can be in mind but must not control your strides. Be alert, concentrated and serene. Now I want you to run 4 laps with 30 second breaks.'

'How fast?'

'As fast as you can.'

'I can't do 'fast'. You have to ask for a time.'

'Just run as fast you can. You don't have to have a time. '

Maxi was doubtful. 'I'll try it.'

She sprinted the laps. In the breaks, she rested with her hands on her knees.

'What were my times?' she asked, panting.

'I don't know, I didn't measure them. They don't matter. How did it feel?'

'It was strange without knowing times,' she said.

'Were you fast?'

'Like the wind . . .'

'Did you feel uncomfortable?'

'I was at my pain limit.'

'Did you forget you were hurting?'

'Only once, on the last lap. . .'

'. . . when you knew you were going to make it?'

'Yes.'

'Your confidence overrode the pain. Could you have had less pain earlier when you had more confidence?'

'I don't know.'

'I would like you to try it. Your running action was efficient but your posture was straining a little. Your breathing seemed a little forced. You have to be comfortable to get into 'It'.'

'What do you mean, 'It'?'

''It' is a special spiritual state in which you perform better.'

'Should I relax or slow down?'

'No, you have to run fast, but without straining,' said Sensei Minami. 'Like when you knew you were going to make it. You forgot about hurting.'

'She is messing with my thinking,' thought Maxi. *'Where is this going?'*

'I want you to run 3 sets, each with 4 laps, as fast as you can, with 3-minute breaks. I will meet you afterwards, at midday tomorrow.'

'Coach Derek has scheduled me for a series of short runs, tomorrow morning.'

'How fast does he want?'

'100%. Should I do them before yours?'

'No. You could be worn out. Do mine first.'

Maxi wondered if Riko was upstaging Derek, her lover, in a power play. It was an awkward situation and if it obstructed her training she would complain.

She wondered if Zen was benefitting her, as she had not yet experienced what her Sensei called 'It'. She had asked Sensei Minami several times how she could achieve 'It'. Her answer was always the same: 'Don't ask, practice!' She lacked courage to

149

continue asking. She trained day after day, doing more training than her programme required. She enjoyed running as fast as she could, without the silent criticism of a timepiece. She embraced the uncertainty as freedom to perform her art.

CHAPTER 30

Jack was in the rear seat, with Maxi at the wheel and Stan beside her in the front, driving to the Gold Coast for the State half-marathon championship.

'Don't take the lead,' Stan said. 'You might not have the stamina. You've been over-training.'

'Gloria Zeto will probably lead. She broke the national record earlier this year.'

'Don't let her force your pace. Run comfortably.'

At the start, Jack and Stan watched as Maxi crossed the mat with the herd and ran along the road next to Southport waterway in a bunch. Her hair was a tawny mane, with orange highlights restored by Australian sunlight from brown acquired in the UK. He thought she looked splendid.

'It's up to her now,' he thought. *'She can do anything, provided she follows the set route and has no assistance. Competitors can use any training method, or eat any food, except prohibited performance-enhancing substances.'*

He ran with Stan to his car to drive the 5 kilometres to the first drinking station. They were waiting when she arrived in the leading group. He was beside the road with a paper cup of Gatorade.

'Maxi! Well done. You're on target.'

She ran over and had a mouthful. He offered her a Mars Bar.

She shook her head. 'Not now.'

He could see distress in her face.

'What's wrong?'

She wanted to cry and tell him it had been harder than she expected and how she doubted she could finish. But she kept her anguish to herself because she wanted him to think she was strong. Girls from her school were watching and she had to keep going for them.

She gave him a smile, grabbed a paper cup of water, sloshed it over herself and set off to run 16 kilometres more.

'Go Maxi,' yelled Jack and Stan.

'Something's bothering her,' Stan said as she ran off.

'What do you think it is?' asked Jack.

'I don't know,' Stan said with a shrug. 'She could be under-confident.'

At the halfway turnaround, they had waited 15 minutes when she hove into view.

'Maxi, over here!'

She slowed to a jog, limped up and halted in front of Jack. She rested with her hands on her knees and burst into tears.

'What is it?'

'I can't do it.'

'But you're halfway and coming 2nd. You've done this before in training. Why can't you do it again now?'

'It's killing me.'

'The others are hurting too. It won't get any worse. Put the hurt out of your mind. You'll be over the moon when you finish!'

Maxi stopped sobbing and sniffed. The white noise of crickets rang in her ears. Perhaps it wouldn't get any worse. She could put up with it for another half hour.

'What's my time,' she asked Jack, taking deep breaths.

'35m17,' he said. 'You're on schedule.'

Maxi breathed normally.

'Who's in front?'

'Gloria Zeto and 5 others are about 250 metres ahead,' he said.

'I'll try to catch them,' she said, drinking from a water bottle. 'See you at the finish.'

She was gone.

Jack was at the finish when the front group climbed over the horizon. He was amazed to see Maxi 10 metres ahead of the bunch. She had caught up and passed the leaders.

As he watched, Maxi staggered on jelly legs, labouring to remain standing. The others ran past her as she melted down. Jack sprinted to her along the road parallel. When he reached her, she was flat on her back in the road, her arms spreadeagled like a Da Vinci science drawing, her eyes open but sightless.

'Call an ambulance,' Jack ordered paramedics who were standing back, in case she would continue in the race. 'Who's got a phone?'

Several keyed their devices.

He hadn't seen her like this before and he fought panic, with tears leaking out.

He didn't touch her.

'Maxi, can you hear me? It's Jack.'

She sat up at the second attempt and looked around.

'I'm going to finish,' she said gruffly.

Her head bent over as she took off her shoes. The crowd watched and waited.

After several minutes, she stood up and with bare feet hobbled along, putting down each foot carefully.

'Come on Maxi,' a spectator shouted. 'You can do it!'

Without warning, she collapsed on the grass verge. She waved Jack away and the stretcher bearers stayed back waiting to see if she would continue. After a minute, she got to her feet uncertainly. She jogged towards the finish amid loud cheers.

A few metres further on, she staggered as though she'd taken a stiff jab to the chin. She raised her arms skyward as though beseeching the wondering throng lining the course to tell her what the hell was happening to her. She bent over with her hands on her knees.

A runner coming through stopped and spoke to her. Maxi set off jogging beside her. When she heard the roar of the crowd ahead, she sprinted to the finish and lay flat on the track. Zeto had won in 1h14. She came and knelt beside Maxi and threw her arms around her. Maxi was 23rd in a time of 1h25.

153

When she had recovered, she sat by the road with Jack and Stan, her head hanging.

'Is this how you felt at Wollongong?' Stan asked. In her previous race, a foot injury and dizziness had slowed her down.

'Today is much worse,' she said. 'Maybe half-marathons are too far for me. I'm sorry.'

'It isn't your fault,' said Stan. 'It's not irreversible and it only affected the last part of the race. Overall, you ran well. It's only your fourth half.'

'I don't understand it. I put in the training,' she said.

'How far have you been running?' Jack asked her.

'100 kilometres per week.'

'It's more than we planned,' said Stan.

'I enjoyed it, so I kept on going,' she said.

'You could be addicted to running, wanting to do more and more,' Stan said. 'Maybe you've lost the big picture.'

'Like I was obsessing instead of training? Jesus! That's a mean call when I have been enjoying Zen training.'

'Zen is shit,' Stan said. He had expressed this point of view to her before and to Riko. But Maxi's Zen training had continued.

No-one said anything for a couple of minutes.

'How are you feeling now,' said Jack.

'Getting there. Hungry.'

He peeled a banana and gave it to her.

'It is so good,' she said, eating.

He gave her an energy bar and she munched on it, drinking Gatorade.

'The pain in my legs was too much,' she said.

'You knew what to expect.'

'It was worse than when I trained.'

'Perhaps you were thinking too much about yourself and not enough about finishing the race,' Stan said.

'No, it wasn't that.'

'Self-absorption is an aspect of addiction,' Stan said, persisting. 'I blame myself - I should have noticed your training coming off the hinges.'

'Can we talk about this with Riko and Derek when we get back,' Jack asked, trying to stem the negativity. Post-run analysis was supposed to be positive.

Jack was disturbed by these events. It was the first time he had seen her run a half marathon. He hadn't realised the brutality of it. Up to today, his interest in Maxi's running had been at arm's length, investigating how her personal control affected her performance. But her meltdown refocussed his interest on helping her to win. Achieving her Olympic goal would take all his help.

CHAPTER 31

Maxi was sitting with Jack, Stan, Derek and Riko in the QIS coffee shop.

'Maxi, what happened at the Gold Coast?' asked Coach Derek. 'Jack's message was that you melted down.'

'It's pretty embarrassing,' she said. 'When I lined up, I felt good. The competition was tough. There was Zeto, the New South Wales record holder and Singuna, who won the Area 3000m two years ago. My friend Marigold was there too. I'd trained hard and I thought I was in with a chance.

'After the gun, it turned into a sprint. We were like a shoal of fish, pouring around obstacles, staying together. I kept my eyes on the people around me, getting bumped and nearly tripping. I was soon breathing hard, but I kept up as we galloped through the tunnel of spectators.

'I felt good and took the lead. The pace was quick and no-one challenged me. After about a kilometre the pace slowed. I was running at 68 minutes, a little quicker than my training target of 70 minutes and behind the national record of 65 minutes.

'As I approached the 5 kilometres water station, my legs and back began to feel like they were being struck with blunt weapons, causing sharp pains. I hadn't had this before. I felt desperate and was doubtful I could continue.

'Jack gave me a drink. He offered me a sugar hit too, but my carbs were finely balanced and it would have upset them.

'I wanted to walk up the hill but kept up my pace and coasted down the other side. I got into a steady rhythm with the pace good for a new PB and let a group go past me. I reached the turnaround

156

and began the second half. Below my waist, everything was throbbing. My legs were painful and heavy like lumps of wood. A second group passed me. It was turning out to be faster than I'd expected. I hadn't prepared for either the intensity or the duration of hurt.

'I looked for Jack in vain. I was going to quit. When I didn't see him, I was about to sit down and take off my trainers to ease my swollen feet.

'When I found Jack I blubbed. He cheered me up and set me back on the road. I wanted to do my best for him and my father. They'd given countless hours to my training. I had to finish this race, for them.

'The day had warmed up and the sweat coursed down my neck. I was feeling better and better. I sped up and began to overtake runners, working my way forward through the field into second place. I concentrated on running efficiently, allowing my mind to roam and take in the roadside, spectators and competitors.

'The heat was unbearable. Sweat was running into my eyes and blinding me. I said to myself, 'This won't stop me.'

'I heard crows cawing as if they were jeering. With half a kilometre left to run, I'd just taken back the lead when I hit the wall. My whole body became heavy and out of control. I staggered along the track. I was trying desperately to keep going, to hold on, but my thoughts were blurring and the sweat in my eyes stopped me seeing. I felt stupid stuck there. I wondered if I was ill. My legs were like blocks of concrete, thudding down jarringly. Stomping as though on a trampoline, I was gasping as I lay in the road. I sat up and took off my shoes to ease the pain in my feet. Zeto blasted past, followed by several others. After a few minutes, I walked on in bare feet.

'I became dizzy, tripped on the kerb and fell down on the grass. Jack and some race officials surrounded me. Medics brought a stretcher, but I sent them away. More of the field zoomed past. Fans leaned over the barrier and urged me on. Then I got up onto all fours, into a crouch and levered myself vertical. I set off in a sort of stumbling jog.

'I ran into a wall of pain again and pulled up. My skills had quit on me, like they say happens at the anaerobic threshold. The heat was terrible. I took a few wobbly steps, then bent over with my hands on my knees.

'My friend Marigold stopped to help me.'

''Run with me,' she said.

'I thought I was dreaming. I trotted beside her, shuffling along. I wanted to hold on to her but knew I'd be disqualified. Within a short distance, I started to pick up. Soon I was running smoothly and feeling okay again. The crowd struck up a thundering chant of 'Maxi! Maxi! Maxi!' I overtook some at the back of the field and scooted over the line like a spring lamb. I came 23rd in 1h25. I lay down on the road.

'After a while, I sat up and talked with Jack and Stan. Then I changed, went out and watched them photograph the winners and present cups.

'I had trained hard, but I hadn't prepared for the heat. I'd expected it to be easier. I ignored my body's limitations. They brought me down. In my opinion, the training was the problem. I should have prepared for the worst, not the best.'

'Your Zen training was the problem,' said Stan.

'Zen doesn't ignore body limitations, Maxi,' said Riko. ' It trains you to overcome them.'

''It was me,' Maxi said. 'I got the big picture wrong. I didn't do what Riko told me.'

She looked down, embarrassed by her confession.

'You ran okay, Maxi,' said Sensei Minami. 'Your style was good. It doesn't matter if the arrow didn't hit the bull this time. Next time, you will win.''

Jack felt annoyed that not one of Maxi's coaches had picked up that Maxi's performance would crater in this race. Each coach had ideas from their own discipline and they lacked a framework in common to articulate their views and combine the training exercises. Maxi had been left to coordinate her own training.

'Your coaches only took responsibility for their own advice,' Jack said, his voice steady although he felt aggrieved. 'No-one saw this coming.'

'I was supposed to bring it all together, but I didn't,' Maxi said.

'It was too difficult for you alone. Don't blame yourself.'

Stan, Derek and Minami were silent, guilty.

Jack continued. 'If you agree, I will get the others to train you sharing your time and efforts between them. I will coordinate a unified coaching programme and help you prepare a plan for your next race. My lack of coaching experience gives me an advantage: I don't have an agenda and can coordinate the others.'

'Are you going to bully me?' she said in a small voice.

'No. You'll have full control. I propose that we all meet regularly and agree a joint programme. So far, your coaches have worked independently but I want to bring you all together. You need a holistic approach. It will prevent you over-training and collapsing again.'

She looked at him quizzically and he nodded, encouraging.

'Okay, let's do it,' she said.

'I would like to meet with each of you separately to get your ideas,' Jack said. 'Then I'll combine the strands into a united programme for Maxi and the group to consider, to amend and approve at a meeting. It's too much to attempt in one go.'

Jack set a date for the first meeting in several weeks' time. Maxi's coaches were experienced and now their training would be concerted by Jack.

CHAPTER 32

We had the house to ourselves and Maxi had an idea.

'Let's do it in my parents' bed,' she said grinning, leading me upstairs.

I was surprised and reluctant: it seemed disrespectful. The bed was unmade, with a musty odour of recent occupation.

'I like your bed better,' I said.

Maxi would not be diverted.

'This is where I was conceived,' she said as if it was natural to bring a lover to the fecund nest of her parents. 'Doing it here is such a turn-on!'

Usually, we liked each other's ideas and responded to each other's proposals positively, but I balked at this fantasy.

'I have too much respect for Stan, Patti and your mother,' I said. Patti had told me that she still thought about her mother, who had died long ago. 'Your father would be angry.'

'You have been okay with sharing their food and sitting in their chairs,' she said. 'What line would we cross by making love in their bed?'

'Using someone's bed without their permission would be presumptuous, like using their toothbrushes.'

'They wouldn't know.'

'It's underhand.'

'You're not much fun.'

We went instead to her bedroom. She allowed my more mature integrity to overrule her capriciousness. We had fun anyway.

I wanted to understand everything about Maxi, especially her use of personal time. Alice suggested I investigate Maxi's personality to find out her goals. I asked Maxi to complete a survey of Enneagram Personality Type. Alice sat next to us as Maxi keyed in responses to 126 multi-choice personal questions. At the end, her rating was Type 3.

'Your psychological type is Achiever and Performer,' said Alice, reading the information on the screen. 'That's no surprise. You always push to be best, fear worthlessness and are vain.'

'Am I narcissistic?' asked Maxi.

'No,' said Alice. I was glad she was helping us interpret Maxi's character. I could easily offend her. 'You like being out front when people are watching, but offstage you're fragile.'

'Fragile?' Maxi said, disbelieving.

Alice changed the topic. 'You like to have your own way. Your type values honesty in others, but can be deceitful.'

Making love in her parents' bed seemed in character.

'I haven't noticed her being deceitful,' I said, defending automatically. 'She can be mischievous though.'

'She's always honest with me,' said Alice. 'She's a runner who achieves by reducing her performance time.'

'It's straightforward.' I said. 'She is very honest. I want to help her reduce her time.'

'Through training?' asked Alice.

'Some training methods have been tested scientifically,' I said. 'Most suck.'

'You need to explore what her coaches do with her and how it affects her performance.'

They surveyed me and found I was Type 5, an investigator.

'No surprises there,' Maxi said.

She was beginning to trust me as her coaching coordinator. We often discussed ideas about running. She asked me questions that went beyond physics, sometimes with hilarity.

'When I run, perhaps I could bound along,' she said. 'I want to conserve energy like a spring.'

161

'Good idea,' I said, 'but wouldn't you get wound up?'

'True,' said Maxi. 'I'd alternate between compression and deflation.'

'They might ban you from bounding, like they did with swimmers when they took up the Australian Crawl.'

'That was to protect breast-stroking,' Maxi said.

'A noble cause,' I said, with a straight face.

Maxi hooted.

'Have new running techniques ever been stopped?'

'They haven't banned anything yet. They've controlled footwear, clothing and slip-streaming. They haven't controlled different striding, foot placement, arm swings, posture or cadences. Paula Radcliffe set world marathon records with what looked like a hiccup in her stride. But nothing as radical as bounding has come in yet. Go for it!'

'I might try it,' she said with a smile, 'sometime.'

'You should strengthen your Achilles',' I said. 'Kangaroos have long ones for bounding.'

'Perhaps my strides could be one-legged bounds.'

Maxi had ideas that were more innovative than accurate, about where energy came from and where it went to. We discussed how to conserve energy and lose heat, using physics of motion and heat transfer.

'I'm wearing tight briefs and a singlet to stay cool,' she said, 'and a sports bra.'

'You could be cooler in loose clothing that flaps and lets air convect.'

'Wouldn't it slow me down?'

'Maybe a little.'

'A little is too much,' she said.

'Does your bra stop your breasts jiggling?'

'Yes, it controls bounce on foot strike and wobble when I swing my arms.'

'I thought arm swing was bad technique.'

'It is, when it's sideways. Arm swing forward and back causes wobble too.'

162

'They could bounce from inertia, causing friction and even pain.'

'You're a well-informed young man.'

'I keep abreast.'

She continued to run in tight clothes. She had other ideas that I couldn't reason away.

'I'm getting an ear-stud,' she said.

It was an announcement, not a question. I wasn't being asked for my opinion. I knew I had to be circumspect. She had anticipated my opposition and overridden it. She seemed to be testing the limits of my control over her.

An ear-stud had personal meaning for her. She revered it, whereas to me it was an affectation, a distraction as if there wasn't anything better to do. Such irrationality was beyond my comprehension and it felt as though we came from different worlds. It was a deal breaker and discussion ended.

Installed on her ear, the stud was prominent and I looked at it askance. It was like looking in a mirror with a crack in it. I couldn't ignore it. The stud symbolised her personal freedom to perform for herself regardless of others. It announced that she was the one who decided what went with her body. It was an ethos shift and I was gradually habituated to it as an accessory to her lofty independent ambition. It signalled Maxi's assuming control of her training and racing.

Maxi's races were her performances. Although she didn't always win, she ran in large international fields and was always in contention. Over the past year, her successes had attracted the interest of the half-marathon social set.

She was recognised as one of a small group of runners with prospects. At venues before her race started, she struck poses and adopted facial expressions that embellished the charisma she exuded. Such prominence in a novice caused excitement.

She wanted to be valued as the best and was gloriously vain. Running fans were drawn to watch her train and follow her progress. Contrasting with athletes who behaved wildly, she was scrupulously honest, law-abiding, civil and decent. Sports journalists competed to interview her. She received invitations to celebrity sports events.

Maxi and I sought happiness in different and unusual ways. Neither of us wanted to satisfy hedonistic appetites on an employment-consumption treadmill, nor material gain, nor stoical achievement. We were too preoccupied with our activities to have time for spiritual connection. My happiness derived from making a difference to the public good. Maxi's happiness was from running optimally in the moment of performance. Our outlook was existential, not reworking the past or speculating unduly about the future.

She was a vigorous lover. My experience was of girls who reciprocated slowly and warmly in a subdued way. Maxi participated vibrantly, with an intensity equal to mine. She climaxed as abruptly and noisily as me, usually simultaneously. Although we now had a professional working relationship, the bottom line for us was our love-making, in Maxi's cosy room at the university. There, our affections had full play, until we fell back sated.

CHAPTER 33

Before the first meeting of the coaching team, Jack moved into a room near Blake's in the old church. Alice and Corvid had lived with Jack and Blake in residence hall as undergraduates. They too were doing PhDs.

Jack's room had been the sacraments room, where altar cloths, candles, robes, chalices, offertory wine and sacred wafers had been kept. It had a gothic stained-glass window of St Augustine, who was reputed to have been an avid party-goer before contrition. The following prayer had been attributed to him: *'Lord make me chaste but not yet.'*

Jack introduced Maxi to his neighbours.

'Maxi plans to stay with me on weekdays,' he said. 'She's a distance runner at QIS.'

They were interested in her running. Corvid ran too and Alice was investigating willpower in runners. Blake was investigating limits on repetitive task performance by industrial workers.

Realising that there were many different perspectives on endurance, Jack thought it would help Maxi to consider alternative training methods.

'Let's meet in the community room here one evening' he said. 'Maxi's coaches can propose their training ideas. Everyone can have a say. I hope you can come.'

They gathered on a weekday evening in the former transept, sitting in pews that had been dragged into a square. Maxi and Stan arrived together from a training session. Patti parked her red Mustang on the front lawn, big noting herself as usual. Coaches

Derek Tracker and Riko Minami sat together, holding hands. On the other side, Blake, Alice and Corvid were having a neighbourly chat.

'Welcome everyone,' he said 'Maxi, this is your show. Don't make me chair — I'd rather be pitching ideas.'

'It will have to be you,' said Maxi. 'This meeting is your idea. You're my coaching coordinator.'

'Thank you for your trust, Maxi,' he said. 'I will do my best. Coordinating Team Maxi is a big responsibility. I want all of you putting your weight behind this adventure.

'Now I want to introduce everyone briefly.

'As most of you know, Maxi is on a 3-year scholarship at the Queensland Institute of Sport. During the week, she does track work, distance running at QIS, training with the squad, weights, swimming and classroom studies at UQ. At weekends she's at home with her parents. Stan has coached her since primary school. He used to be a champion marathoner but now only coaches. Patti is a nutritionist and feeds Maxi vegan, for health, strength and performance.

'Maxi trains at QIS under the coaching of Doctor Derek Tracker here, a national sprint champion and with Dr Riko Minami, our Zen master, who won the Boston Marathon two years ago.'

'Blake here,' Jack said, 'lived next door to me in hall when we were undergraduates doing physics, but he's now doing a PhD in management engineering.'

'I'm here because managers have to perform and endure too,' Blake said. 'Perhaps I can help set Maxi's goals.'

'Alice Lamont was in hall with us too,' said Jack.

An attractive brunette, Blake's girlfriend, smiled at them.

'Alice is doing a doctorate in psychology about willpower and is a base jumper. We expected her to jump out the hall window. She had enough willpower but not enough height.'

They laughed.

'Finally, Corvid Feir is doing a PhD in neuroscience about human responses to pain and stress. She was in hall with us too.'

She was tall and rangy, in her later 20s, with frizzy black hair.

'This is my cat, Satan,' she said proudly, proffering a shiny black floppy object. 'I hope you don't mind me bringing her. She's a sprinter like the big cats, with fast-twitch fibres that enable her to surprise prey. Animals that pursue, like hyenas, hunting dogs, wolves and humans, are different. They exhaust their quarries, with slow-twitch smooth muscle fibres for endurance. A fit human has smooth muscle and can outlast nearly all mammals in a pursuit. The pursuits of early hunters lasted up to 6 hours, covered 15 to 25 kilometres in temperatures over 38°C, too hot for conductive cooling, with furless bodies and increased sweat glands for evaporation. Other adaptations include a narrow pelvis, short toes, expanded attachment for the gluteus maximus. It's a physique like Maxi's, ideal for endurance running.'

'Her butt looks pretty good too,' said Blake.

People laughed.

The cat's cold double-barrelled stare pierced each person in turn.

'It is interesting that Maxi is supposed to be dogged, not explosive,' Jack said. 'I'll remind her next time she gets toey.'

'Buster, so far you've had it easy,' Maxi said irritably.

'She's a sweetie,' said Jack. 'Let's get down to business.

'Maxi's goals are my goals and we want you to make them yours. Maxi needs your different inputs. My goal is to bring your ideas together into one training programme.'

Jack wanted his coordination to be unambiguously respectful of their goals and he would have to subordinate his own. He wanted to dispel any possible suspicion that his goal was to make his fortune, to obtain glory, or to get the girl. Obtaining their trust was paramount.

'Would you please consider this question. How will we know if we have been successful?'

'When Maxi achieves her goals.'

'Does anything else matter?'

'Our involvement in this group should be harmonious.'

'What should I do if someone is out of line?' asked Jack.

'There are ways of persuading people,' said Blake with a sinister laugh. 'You have to hold the group together.'

'I see my role as group facilitator,' said Jack. 'My idea of how to proceed is by a group conversation, with one person at a time contributing, with talk directed to me as chair, to prevent interaction becoming interpersonal. Is that okay?'

'Okay, let's begin. Whenever you have any concerns, be sure to voice them. I would like us to 'Put up or shut up'. No carping. I might have to remind people that we are all going to be winners if we can pull this off.

'Maxi, would you remind us what happened in your half-marathon two weeks ago?'

Maxi spoke humbly. 'I disgraced myself at the Gold Coast: When I was in the lead half a kilometre from the finish, I collapsed. I staggered in at 23rd.'

'You ran well up until then,' Stan said, 'maybe too well.'

'My time was 1h25. I needed 1h20 to qualify for the National.'

'You may still be accepted,' said Stan. 'Your previous time at Wollongong was 1h12. I'll apply to the Regional committee for special consideration.'

'What caused you to collapse?' asked Alice.

'We think she overtrained,' said Stan. 'She was running 100 kilometres per week and the running took over. She couldn't 'let go''.

'I don't get the 'letting go' idea,' said Maxi. 'What is it?'

'Letting go is like when a monkey puts its hand into a jar of lollies and grabs so many its fist gets stuck,' said Alice. 'The monkey is trapped by its own greed. To succeed in a race, you have to settle for realistic achievement and let go of the rest. A runner has to avoid grabbing too much.'

'How much should I grab?' said Maxi.

'No more than you can get away with,' said Alice. 'You have to be absolutely sure you can achieve it.'

'Is such confidence possible?' said Maxi.

'Your training should rehearse you until you are confident,' Jack said. 'Could your races repeat training experiences?'

'Didn't you do it before?' said Stan. 'What happened?'

'I had to stop,' said Maxi. 'I didn't have a choice. I bonked.'

'Bonking is when you run out of energy and you hit the wall,' Stan said. 'That didn't happen, did it?'

She shook her head.

'She had energy to go on,' said Patti. 'She'd eaten enough,'

'Choking is fear of success, losing self-confidence,' said Coach Derek. 'Maxi, you may have misunderstood what was happening to your body. Could you have over-reacted?'

'I'm not sure if I ran out of energy. I became dizzy and slowed down. Perhaps I did over-react and choke. Maybe I did it last time out too, at Wollongong.'

'Can we consider Maxi's goals are, first, to prevent her choking next time?' said Jack. 'Maxi should have an internal goal. Isn't that right Riko?'

'That's correct,' said Riko Minami, speaking carefully. 'Thank you for asking me this evening. The Zen way is to internalise a goal. What that means is that in Maxi's mind her running enacts achievement of her goal during every moment of the race. Maxi has to have a goal.'

'Maxi, do you have a goal for Sydney?'

'63 minutes,' said Maxi. 'It's 9 minutes below my PB.'

'Her instruction in Zen with Riko can aim to achieve this goal,' said Coach Derek. 'Riko is helping her reach a new level, without worrying, focussing on how her body feels right now and controlling it to operate correctly in the race.'

'Maxi is learning to concentrate in the Zen way,' said Riko.

'I am trying to reach a new level Riko calls 'It',' said Maxi, with a nervous laugh.

'This Zen stuff needs to be balanced by a focus on self-sustaining,' said Stan.

'I agree. Maxi can sustain goal achievement in the Zen way,' said Riko. 'She can improve her endurance. 9 minutes is a big improvement, but she can do it.'

'Maxi, there's plenty to be going on with,' said Jack. 'Derek, Riko and Stan, can we get together now with Maxi and come up with training activities that will develop engaging with her goal and enduring? I think we can stop there, for today. Let's all meet here again in two weeks' time to review progress. It's a month until her race in Sydney.'

'Excuse me.' said Maxi. 'I have to go. I have a big day of training tomorrow.'

'Can you stay for a short while?' said Jack. 'We need your ideas and agreement for the training.'

'Okay,' said Maxi. 'It will have to be quick because I am tired and need to rest.'

'This first meeting has gone well,' Jack thought. *'Although everyone's perceptions were different, by sharing them we will analyse Maxi's running results and get ideas for her training.'*

CHAPTER 34

Maxi, Stan, Patti, Derek, and Riko stayed with Jack at the table as the others got up and left.

'Maxi, you have been running brilliantly, but Stan and I are concerned that you might be choking,' Jack said. 'Because choking is underachieving, it is a difficult topic even without intending any criticism. It is a common experience of runners and we need to address it openly. It would be disloyal to talk about it behind your back. You'd prefer we talk about it here openly, wouldn't you?'

Maxi was surprised and puzzled. She nodded automatically. 'I don't know what there is to talk about.'

Jack continued. 'I'll get Stan to start the conversation because he has spoken to you about it before.'

'Bluntly, but not unkindly,' Stan said. 'Maxi has been coming first, then lost several times. She's come in 2nd or 3rd or 6th or 23rd.'

No-one said anything.

'I've come in first a couple of times too,' said Maxi, defensively. 'I admit to choking in a couple of races, but in others it is arguable it was choking, rather than hitting the wall. When I stopped, it was not under my control.'

Jack broke the silence. 'You have run some great races, Maxi and we think maybe you sometimes lack self-confidence.'

'In my experience, choking is a phobia, a fear of trying something new,' said Coach Derek. 'It could be fear of bonking. You may fear going past the point of exhaustion, right up to falling over the finish line.'

'Bonking is dangerous, isn't it?' said Jack.

171

'Not for runners who build up to it gradually,' said Coach Derek. 'All my athletes have bonked without adverse consequences. Athletes sometimes see their opponents collapsing with heart attacks and disabling injuries and misinterpret those as bonks. Bonking has little risk for a fit athlete who has built up to it gradually.

'Her body will try to get her to stop by increasing the feeling of pain. When that doesn't work, it will reduce muscle fibre recruitment to force her to slow down. When that doesn't stop her, there could be a complete shutdown, a fail-safe mechanism that will lie her down horizontally, where blood can flow more easily to her brain, instead of pumping against gravity when she's upright.'

'I hate this idea of deliberately bonking and lying on the track,' said Maxi.

'When these steps of the bonking sequence become familiar to you by experience, there is no risk,' said Coach Derek.

'Must she bonk?' asked Jack. 'Making her collapse seems drastic and unkind.'

'It is not for us to make her do anything. We can inform her of the consequences and leave it up to her.' Coach Derek was a democratic coach who wanted runners to decide activities.

'Otherwise, she'll continue to choke from fear,' said Riko.

'Cognitive behaviour therapy can raise her awareness and reduce the choking,' said Alice.

'I propose that we set her demanding challenges, so she will anticipate and experience bonking,' said Coach Derek.

'Like exposing someone to spiders to overcome arachnophobia,' said Alice.

'Is that like making a fearful person hold a spider?' said Jack. 'Will familiarisation with the stimulus extinguish the unwanted response?'

'It's worth a try,' said Stan. 'I can simulate bonking in a race by getting her to run on soft sand at the beach.'

'That would be perfect,' Coach Derek said. 'If you will get her to bonk on sand, I will get her to do the same on the track. Maxi may have choked through lack of half-marathon experience. She has to deal with tough running situations by unhooking from dreaming,

172

fixating on performance and regulating the hormone cortisol to manage her stress response.'

'We don't want to overkill with mental deconstruction,' Stan said. 'Siri Lindley started winning when she was physically able to risk bonking, not because of a psychological rebuild.'

'It's arguable,' said Coach Derek. 'Frank Sutton treated Siri Lindley's phobia of bonking by setting her a series of challenges that provoked her to perform at her best. She became accustomed to operating her body close to bonking without choking.'

'Maxi has to give everything she has to the point of bonking,' said Riko. 'If it is enough to win, so much the better.'

'It takes a trained mind as well as a trained body,' said Coach Derek. 'We have to provide her with the experience she needs.'

'We seem to have agreed,' said Jack. 'Derek and Alice will help her overcome choking cognitively, while Stan can habituate her to bonking by running on the beach.'

'I'll teach her the Zen way of concentration,' said Riko. 'She will learn to sustain against bonking.'

'I can make sure she is carrying enough energy to push her boundaries,' said Patti.

'We have a plan. Jack, can you put it all together for us?' said Maxi. ''I have to go.'

'Yes, I'll be pleased to,' he said. 'We've made good progress in our first meeting. I'll coordinate with each of you on her training programme. We'll meet again after her next half-marathon, in the new year. Shall we call ourselves Team Maxi?'

They agreed.

'Thank you, everyone,' said Maxi and left.

They stayed chatting for a while. Maxi's running was forging friendships.

CHAPTER 35

Stan set Maxi water-running challenges at the QIS pool. Held upright by a flotation belt, her legs churned and propelled her along the lane. Stan walked at the side, staying abreast.

'Give it 80 percent effort for a minute,' he said.

When the pool clock reached 60 seconds, she had gone almost a length.

'No break,' said Stan. 'Now turnaround and do 30 seconds at 90 percent.'

She went for half a length and was panting.

'Take a break for 10 seconds, then let's have 100% for 15 seconds.'

Treading water slowly, her brief respite prepared her to run again. When she unleashed her energy, her body rose vertically until her shoulders were well above the surface, her legs threshing below and pushing her up.

'I could fake it and take it easy,' she thought, *'but I must aim for exhaustion after 15 seconds.'*

When she finished, she was blowing, but Stan didn't give her a rest.

'Good work. Now do it again.'

This time she misjudged and used her energy too fast, becoming exhausted and fading after 12 seconds.

'That's not 100 percent,' Stan said. 'Don't choke! Give it everything you've got. Do it again, properly.'

He walked away to the pool shop for an ice cream.

Maxi repeated, giving it 100 percent effort and hurting badly but ignoring it. Without warning, pain overwhelmed her, shutting down her body. She reached for the side of the pool a metre away and clung to it gasping, her body leaden.

'Is this a heart attack?' she thought. *'What have I done to myself?'*

When Stan came back, her yell was a croak.

'WTF was that for? You could have killed me.'

'No. You bonked,' he said, laughing. 'It won't kill you. You ran out of petrol. You're refilling your energy now and you'll be back to normal soon. Your glycogen stores got so low, your body shut down. You must learn to recognise when a bonk is coming on and eke out your energy, using your reserves up gradually, bonking just as you cross the finish line. How did it feel?'

'Weak, tired, nausea, sweating, blurred vision, anxious, awkward, shaky.'

'Were your muscles shutting down?'

'My arms and legs felt heavy.'

'Pain?'

'In my head.'

'Did you get confused, light-headed, irritable, emotional, hallucinating?'

'Yes, some of those.'

'Everyone experiences it differently. Remember what it felt like and next time, when it starts, ease off a little to avoid it.'

'Maybe by then it will be too late. It came on fast.'

'You'll have time to slow up.'

'It will be hard to keep going, risking another bonk. It was bad.'

'To be a winner, you have to dice with bonking. We'll do some running exercises on sand.'

'I can't wait.'

The next day, Stan called her. She had been on a 10-kilometre run with him that morning and she wondered what this was about.

'Let's go. We'll push your running limits on sand, the way we did water running yesterday.'

'No bonking, I hope,' Patti called from the kitchen.

Maxi had told her about the bonk at the pool and Patti was concerned. She was out of work, spending her days with her sister at high-end department stores and boutiques, going to lunch at trendy restaurants, forgetting to look for work, unable to shop with her cards, out of credit and with nothing to do except social media. She had two mobile phones, which she checked constantly, one for family the other for friends.

'You bonk when your carbs don't produce enough blood glucose for the intensity and duration of your run,' said Stan. 'Without enough glucose, when a high level of effort is required such as climbing a hill, you'll feel tired, lose motivation, become lethargic. You might want to stop and lie down. It's not dangerous, although you could fall and hurt yourself.'

'Prevention is by correct nutrition,' said Patti.

'Also by habituation,' said Stan. 'When she has bonked running, she'll know what is happening, slow down and gain energy to continue.'

'Many athletes have never bonked. She doesn't need to experience it. Why are you doing this to her?' asked Patti. 'Is it worth it?'

'Most marathon runners have bonked,' said Stan. 'If they haven't, maybe they have been choking. My role is to challenge Maxi to push her boundaries.'

'What boundaries?'

'Physical.'

'What about mental? She should be developing her goals and willpower.'

'Bah. Psychology might develop her thinking but thinking won't win races. Her body needs to overcome physical challenges.'

'Is winning worth all the suffering?'

'Yes. She's a performer. As a champion she could have a good lifestyle now — worth getting out of her comfort zone.'

'She won't get there by training alone,' said Patti. 'She has to eat. I'm giving her pasta for energy. That's the best way to deal with bonking.'

'Good. She doesn't need protein. Muscles would weigh her down.'

When they got to the beach, there was a cool wind and Stan hunkered down in his parka, his craggy face partly concealed under a peaked cap. Maxi wore a track suit.

She steeled herself to deal with his negativity.

He leaned against a rescue boat as he spoke to her.

'I want you to run from this flag, along the beach to those rocks and back in under 15 seconds, 50 times.'

It was about 100 metres there and back. The sand was dry and soft. It would be heavy going.

'Holy shit,' she said. 'Are you serious? Why so many times?'

'This is how you can improve your running.'

Maxi shrugged, took off her tracksuit and stood ready to start.

'Ready. Go.'

She ran as hard as she could and Stan logged each lap.

'39,' he said. 'Don't slow down.'

"That's all I can do,' she gasped.

She threw herself down on the sand and lay on her back panting. This was a new extreme in her experience of Stan's tough coaching.

'That's all the running I'm good for,' she said.

'Are you quitting?' he said, with disdain. 'Perhaps you don't have the patience to be a runner?'

'What's patience got to do with it?'

'You don't win by quitting. Why have you quit now?'

'I bonked.'

'No you didn't. You choked.'

'I couldn't go on.'

'You could have gone on, but you gave up,' he shouted. 'You're a loser.'

'Why are you so mean to me?'

'You think you know what you're doing, but you don't,' he screamed. 'You can run a lot further than that. Tell me, what do you think would have happened if you had continued just now?'

'I'm not sure. Bad stuff.'

'The worst that can happen is you'll pass out like you did in the pool on Monday. You would recover with no damage done. You have to face your fear. If you do, it will change your life forever. Fear is holding you back. You are quitting too early in the piece.'

'I did my best. It was cruel.'

'I want to find out what you can do when you really try.'

'What's it to you?'

'I'm not going to spend my time coaching someone who gives up when it gets tough. Unless you give it everything you've got, we're both wasting our time.'

'You can fuck off whenever you want to!' she said, weeping.

He slapped her face and shoved her as if she was beyond reason. Maxi was humiliated.

'When I race, I do give it everything,' she sobbed.

'It's too late by the time you're in a race,' he said quietly. 'You have to face your fear now, on this beach. You must find your fear every time you train and laugh at it. It will change you and be the beginning of a new and good life.'

Maxi said nothing. Her father was a bully who used violence to get his own way when reason was absent. Part of his treatment was to brainwash her with his strange ideas about endurance. She hated having to walk on eggshells in case she might set him off.

"You can try again on Thursday,' he said, glowering. He got into the car to drive back and she got in.

Two days later, Maxi stood with Stan on the beach at the foot of a soft white sand dune that rose away from them to 20 metres high.

'Why can't I run along the beach like I did on Tuesday?'

'This is not about what you want to do, it's about discovering what you can do.'

'I can't run up this fucking dune man, no way.'

'I want you to run to the top and back here again as fast as you can, 50 times. If you take more than 30 seconds, it doesn't count and you have to do it again.'

'You're joking. It's a huge task.'

'I'm dead serious,' said Stan. 'You want to win? You have to endure. You won't win by choking. You have a choice: do it my way or you're on your own.'

She hesitated.

'Why does it always have to be your way?'

'A coach's job is to get the best from an athlete. You won't get far by yourself.'

'I could get Derek, Riko or even Jack to coach me.'

'They'd give you an exercise to do just like this one. You heard them agree to me habituating you to bonking. That means getting used to it. I have more coaching experience than they do. This will improve your running. Now show me what you can do.'

She shrugged and stood ready to start.

'Go.'

Maxi had completed 38 climbs when she fell down on the sand beside him and sobbed.

'I can't do it.'

'Why did you stop?'

'I'm not strong enough to go on.'

'You quit again,' he said. 'You must never quit while you can stay upright.'

'It was too difficult.'

'Did you try harder than yesterday?'

'Yes. Today it hurt way more. My feet are slipping in the sand. My legs are like concrete.'

'When you start something, you have to finish it. Never quit.'

'Why are you making me do this?' Maxi asked.

'You haven't faced your fear yet.' said Stan. 'It'll take everything you have. To win, you must be tough. You're learning the moves you need to defend yourself against bonking.'

Sometimes Maxi thought he was insane, but she had thought that earlier too and had been proven wrong. She trusted him.

'What do you mean, moves?'

'In your head. You'll win by superior thinking.'

'How can I get that?' asked Maxi.

'You have to give everything in training. When a bonk is looming, recognise it, get smart and put your remaining energy into getting to the line.'

'It seems risky to run along the knife-edge of a bonk.'

'In what way?'

'It risks hitting the wall.'

'Bonking scares you, doesn't it?' said Stan. 'Fear of the unknown is a natural protective reaction, but you are learning to manage it. The unknown will become familiar and you'll cease to fear it. There isn't any risk. You'll enjoy giving everything.'

'Is it safe to run so hard?'

'Running won't kill you, you'll pass out first.'

'That's a theory. It could be different for me.'

'You're right to be cautious,' Stan said. 'You haven't experienced bonking while racing yet. We're trying it with a medical safety net. When you've worked up to it and been stopped by it, your fear will go. It's like a Formula 1 driver who corners on the edge of spinning out, with skills to stay safe, sliding out a little but staying on the track, going fast enough to win. A downhill skier uses all his strength, going as fast as possible, on the edge of crashing. His skill is to control his speed up to the limit of his own strength. Your skill will be to run on the edge of bonking. You need to have bonked to know when you're at the edge. When you are no longer scared by it, you won't fear it.'

'Courting bonking seems dangerous.'

'It won't be,' said Stan. 'Pain is subjective and coaches differ on how a marathon runner should deal with muscle stress. You have to recognise it, observe it, respond to it and endure it. My way is to familiarise you with it, so you can go to the edge and keep running.'

'How can I run at the edge?'

'Have you noticed how the hurt increases as you get closer to bonking?' asked Stan.

'Maybe. I'm not sure.'

'Look for signs that a bonk is coming,' Stan said. 'You can't let go. To stay in control, you need to be familiar with it. We'll work on that. You will run at the edge subconsciously.'

180

'I'm worried about bonking.'
'You need more experience of it.'
'That's what worries me,' she said.

CHAPTER 36

Maxi would turn 20 in November. Her run time at Wollongong the previous year had qualified her for the National Half Marathon Championships in Sydney. She was diligently following her training programme prepared by Jack and Team Maxi.

On the plane to Sydney with Stan, Jack said: 'You've prepared thoroughly, haven't you? You can unleash yourself today.'

'It's going to be fun,' she said.

It was strange for Jack to be on a flight as a private individual. Oilco had moved him about like a pawn on a chessboard. On this flight, he was his own man. He had paid the economy class fare from the last of his savings and felt good about what he was doing. His coordination of Team Maxi and this trip to watch his girlfriend compete were enjoyable diversions from his work as a doctoral research student.

He mused and wrote in his notebook: *'How should I live? What should I do with my time? Is it better to be madly active or succumb to sloth? How can I get more of what I want? What is it about personal time I value most? What lifestyle is best for me?*

'I'm investigating the best ways Maxi and I can use our times. I've stopped using calendars, clocks and timepieces. I've noticed when I am highly mentally engaged, I don't notice time passing. I'm not sure why, but I aim to find out.'

They arrived in Sydney and stayed in a hotel near Olympic Park. The next day they took a short taxi ride to Cathy Freeman Park where the half-marathon would start and finish.

'Whatever happens today,' Stan said to Maxi, 'you must not choke.'

He had not let Maxi forget her meltdown at the Gold Coast earlier in the year. 'You must give this race everything you have. Unleash your mind, like Siri Lindley did, focussing on your goal of 63 minutes, making sure you achieve it. We know you can do it because you've practised sustaining a fast pace.'

Maxi went to the athletes' changing area and came out on to the track, waving to them where they sat overlooking the start. She jogged with the other runners, loosening up. It was a fine Autumn day, cool and pleasant.

Summonsed to get set, her thoughts took off following a thousand threads. *Today my mind is calm and I'm poised to go. I'm visualizing the course. We're off. I'm through the melee. Now the road is clear and I can faintly hear my footsteps, observe my breathing.*

My body parts are in harmony and I'm focussing on my cadence, feeling each heel-strike and my weight rolling forward until lift-off from the plantar, then a brief interlude until the next heel strike. I step around the lumps, cracks and dents in the road. My monitor is recording 180 steps per minute with 30 breaths per minute. I count 6 steps while I inhale and exhale, then count the next 6. The rhythm is calming and I relax.

That large crowd at the start is thinning out now. We're in the country and my monitor shows 20 kilometres per hour, which is my goal. Can I keep this up all the way? I was in front for 5 kilometres but three runners passed me just now. The first looked like Hoogly but I'm not sure — I didn't see her bib. Another is a Kenyan, maybe Theodore Kirwan. Her PB is 1h10 and mine is 2 laps behind at 1h12. She isn't that far ahead now, about 40 metres. I'll speed up a little to stay with her.

I'm passing a vineyard with ripening green grapes. Mmm, the delicious smell of Chardonnay. I'll celebrate with a few glasses if all goes well.

We've settled down to a brisk pace. One of the leaders, the one I think is Hoogly, has dropped back. I'm 3rd and on target. I must concentrate and not let my thoughts rove around. I need to stay alert. I won't meltdown like I did at Southport. I had a big lead and should *have slackened off. Stan reckons I choked, but it was a bonk. My willpower had driven my body harder than it could sustain. Today I will run as hard as I can without bonking.*

Two of the best half-marathon runners in Australia are in front of me but I'm not out to beat them. It's not about ego and winning, but effectiveness and efficiency.

Riko watched me last week and was positive about my style.

She told me my running is good and said if I concentrate, I'll get to my goal.

My knee seems good. It has been three years since they cut out the meniscus. I had some pain a few weeks ago but I went easy for a few days and it got better.

Uh-oh someone is trying to get past me. It could be the Canadian. That's okay, I can take the lead again later. I can stay at my target pace - I don't need to be in front. My monitor's showing 21 kilometres per hour. The numbers work out just right for this 21km race. I'll be done in an hour. I'm not sure if it's accurate, because the split is one kilometre long and I could have sped up and be going faster than it shows. If I keep up this pace, my time will be just over 1 hour. The World record is 61m36. My goal is 63 minutes, one minute below the national record of 64m27. My will is keeping me at this pace but I'm nearing my physical limit. When I've caught up with the leaders, I'll ease off to conserve energy.

I'm on automatic and letting my feet, stride, arms, breathing and posture look after themselves. My body knows what to do. Must keep up this pace. Here's a gentle rise. When I catch up with the leaders, I'll slow down a bit and enjoy it more.

There, I'm back to 20 and more comfortable. My effort level is how I remember Wollongong when I slowed down and came 6th. My goal today is a huge 9 minutes faster. I don't have to think about moving up yet. We've done 10 kilometres, coming to halfway. When will the leaders ease off? The sun is in my face and sweat is rolling down my sunscreen.

Still at 20 and on target. I am focusing on running skilfully, not on breaking the record. If it's meant to happen, it will.

I want to keep some energy in reserve but I am pushed now. I won't forget to drink water at the next station as I did at the last. If I tuck in behind third, she can part the air for me.

This pace is still too fast. Kirwan and another are 20 metres in front of me, with the Canadian behind. Kirwan is strong and I could have to fight her for the lead. When I choked at the Gold Coast she had a leg injury and didn't start. Her legs seem fine today and she's led for most of the race. It's been fast and she may want to slow down and comeback at the finish.

My thoughts keep returning to the hurt in my legs like my tongue to a toothache. My muscles are screaming for mercy, from femurs to metatarsals. I'm trying not to listen, but I'm starting to stumble along rather than springing like the gazelle I was earlier. Shit. Must remain calm.

I want so badly to listen to my body's pleas for mercy, but for Siri Lindley that was the road to hell. I'm watching out for a bonk. Provided I keep to my race plan, I'll succeed.

I'm in the hardest part of the race now but feel better than at the Gold Coast. I've been steady while the others have burned up their carbs contesting the lead. I've been here before. Jack and Stan's training has increased my perceived effort threshold by giving me the freedom to let loose and do what I feel like.

I hope I'm choke-proof. We've done 15 kilometres. My pace is a comfortable 19 kilometres per hour and I'm enjoying myself, time slipping by. We're getting to the business end of the race, up a hill to the 15 kilometres water station. Here's Jack smiling, whooping and clapping me.

"You made it!' he says. 'You're ahead of your target time and nearly there. Kirwan is 50 metres ahead.'

I pause only briefly and set off again. The cruise down the hill is unpleasant, my legs heavy and stiff. This pace takes too much effort. I can't get enough air, my knee is hurting. I could be bonking. This is horrible. Maybe I can't run this distance. I was better at 3000 m. I've slowed down. This is the dreaded bonk. I'll have to pull out. I should have taken up tennis.

No, I won't let myself think why I let myself in for this. My goal is 63 minutes. The time on the media truck is 54 minutes. Ten more minutes to go. If I can keep up this pace I'll finish in 63.20. Awesome. I've got it in me to improve my position. I just left a spent runner in my dust. I'm pretty sure it was Bettana Namabo of Ethiopia. The rest are too far back to see. I could try to pass both the Canadian and Kirwan — if it is her — with a sprint. If I contest the lead, I might tire more than they do. But if I take the Canadian first, she might not fight back. I'm digging as deep as I can to fend off her comeback. She has dropped back. I can stay 2nd and replenish my energy for the last lap when I'll try to take Kirwan in a long sprint to the line. She may be a better sprinter than me over 100m, but I could be faster over 400m. I've caught up to Kirwan. Here goes!

I can see the finish. Kirwan is trying to fight me off. I'm almost out of energy as we run shoulder to shoulder towards the line. The motion seems slowed. I can see Jack jumping up and down in a wall of spectators at the finish.

"Go Maxi, Go!' he yells.

I've got nothing left to overtake with. She gets ahead of me and crosses the line a few metres in front in a time of 62.28. I'm second with 62.31.

There's applause and calls of 'well done, Maxi' from my friends who start towards me. I go over and congratulate Theodore.

In the distance, I see my father hunched over as if in pain, angrily kicking a post, throwing his cap on the ground and stamping on it. His outburst embarrasses me. I hadn't seen him attach so much importance to winning before. He knows I'm watching and it hurts me that I've disappointed him. I feel my mood sink.'

Maxi sat with Jack as she recovered.
'I'm so proud of you, Maxi.'
'I'm worried about Dad. He could snap.'
'It's an act to make you feel bad about how you ran.'
'He doesn't need to carry on like that. I feel bad enough.'
Maxi rested with her hands on her knees, breathing steadily, perspiring.

186

Later in the car on the way home, Stan was horrible.

'You could have won,' he said. 'Coming second won't get you into the Olympics.'

'I was 23rd last time. This time I was 2nd. I didn't choke.'

'You did choke,' he said, his voice raised. 'You could have taken the lead, but you quit trying.'

'I didn't have it in me. I couldn't do it.'

'You were keeping to your target rate on your monitor, instead of unleashing yourself. You could have run faster.'

'No, I couldn't. I was at my target rate.'

'Your monitor is for training, to learn what goal achievement feels like. In a race, you have to vary your pace.'

'I tried to get in front of Kirwan, but she sped up.'

'If you had challenged her sooner, you would have succeeded.'

'I tried. She was faster.'

'How do you know that?' he said angrily. 'I asked you to give it everything but you didn't. You feared bonking and gave up. You'll never be a winner.'

'If Stan wasn't my father, I wouldn't bother with him at all,' she thought. *'He is opinionated and harsh. His coaching is old fashioned. I know he is trying to do what is best for me and I respect him for it, but his criticism is unfair.'*

'I don't want you coaching me anymore,' she said, yelling the words.

He said nothing. There was a long silence in the car.

'Jack can take over,' Stan said quietly at last. 'I'll tell him what I would have done with you.'

Maxi was forlorn but knew she had done nothing wrong. She had lived with Stan all her life on reasonable terms until the last few months, but this harshness was new. He was not a person who talked: he stated opinions. She was not able to discuss anything, or give her view, without provoking a dispute. She wanted her performance to be respected, but he was uncompromising.

187

CHAPTER 37

'I am not the right person to take Maxi on further,' Stan said to me after she had finished with him. 'It's difficult for her to respect my experience when it seems to her out of date. Why don't you take over coaching her?'

'But I'm not a runner!' I said.

'Her running technique is good and she needs self-control to fine-tune it. Because she loves you, trusts you and wants to please you, she will learn self-control from you.'

I was flattered and wanted to do the best I could for Maxi.

'Not being a runner limits me from relating to some difficulties you have,' I said to her, 'but I can think outside the box. We can try some new ways.'

I could hardly believe my good fortune in having beautiful Maxi as my girlfriend. Other men noticed her and I had to stifle my jealousy. She could have any man she wanted and I feared she might tire of me. I couldn't imagine being without her. Her running preoccupied her and I was a secondary interest. I had to make the most of her while I could, because my involvement with her might not last.

It dismayed me when Maxi was distant, but there seemed nothing I could do except finish with her, if that was what she wanted. Feeling neglected, I wondered idly if Alice would be a more reliable partner, if I could get her away from Blake. It would be the end of Team Maxi. Without Maxi, I would have to rebuild my life.

The four of us went out for a meal and Maxi sat next to Blake. They were talking and laughing and I was jealous. Blake had charm and could take Maxi away. It was bad form to steal a mate's girl. If that was what he was trying to do, it was disrespectful. Perhaps there was already something between them? His view would be that who Maxi wanted to be with was up to her. I realised that I had to reorient our relationship into a warmer, more caring and supportive relationship.

With her living at the university through the week and going home at weekends, our relationship was bumping along. I decided to make a move.

'I want you to live with me and spend more time with me,' I said.

'Would it be an experiment?' she asked.

'No, I am really hopeful that it will be the start of a very long relationship.'

'What if I want to leave?'

'It would be up to you, of course. I would be sad.'

'Can we start in a small way and see how we get on?'

Maxi stayed in my apartment on weekdays, going to her family home with me at weekends. We were together as a trial and she kept her room at the university in case she wanted to move back. She moved some things into my place. I possessed little, mainly books, because taking care of things was a burden and things would eventually be abandoned. My family used to tease me for having a stingy streak. But I liked having her things at my place. It was commitment of a sort.

It was different between us now because we had chosen to live together, rather than associating as a by-product of our coaching relationship. She stopped flirting with other men, as if our relationship had changed to real. We were together most of every day and our lives were intertwined. I awoke when she crawled out of bed into the shower and shared many parts of the day with her, until we tumbled into bed again.

When we were at her home on the weekend, where she had grown up, I noticed the jumble of her things. She had clothes, shoes, posters, photos, make-up and keepsakes in profusion. At some time past, she had arranged them tidily and now they had begun to stray. Perhaps my influence was to disorder her tidy world.

One morning at her home, we had the kitchen to ourselves and Maxi was trying to cook eggs and bacon. I like my bacon crisp and eggs sunny side, but Maxi had created a rubbery omelette.

'Is that okay?' Maxi asked as she deposited the melange onto my plate.

'It is interesting,' I said. 'Is it your own recipe?'

'Next time, you cook,' she said, in a strangled voice and threw down the spatula. She sat at the other end of the breakfast bar, drinking coffee, not eating, oceans apart.

'I'm sorry,' I said. 'I wanted to make you laugh. It wasn't a criticism.'

'Well, it sounded pretty negative to me.'

'I'm totally positive about you,' I said. 'You're amazing.'

'No. I'm quite ordinary. Your expectations are too high.'

She wasn't often moody like this. I wondered how to change the topic.

'When you've finished putting yourself down, could we talk about your snoring?' I asked.

'Do I snore?'

'If you do, I don't hear it. That's pretty positive, isn't it?'

'It's another put down,' Maxi said. 'What's wrong with you? You're totally insincere with me. Just because I am your science experiment doesn't mean you can heap shit on me whenever you like. Not anymore. You can fuck off.'

'Trying to speed up your running isn't using you!'

'If you loved me,' she said, 'you wouldn't find fault with my cooking, snoring and running. All you care about is pumping up your ego with physics.'

'All you care about is winning races. I only mentioned those things for fun. They were to make you laugh, but you have taken them the wrong way. I am not a humourless schmuck.'

'Stop it,' she said. 'I'm not using you. I love you.'

'Do you really?'

'Yes,' said Maxi. 'You're the best thing that has ever happened to me. You give me a scary feeling that I am going to wake up and find you gone.'

'Perhaps you really want me gone?'

'No. I sense that we can't get as close as I would like. Will we live together and have kids one day?'

'Maybe,' I said, pondering.

'If you don't love me, you should leave now.'

'I do love you, but I'm not quite ready to settle down yet.'

'Do you realize how hurtful that is?'

'Maybe we can't talk honestly without some hurt,' I said.

'I think we should take a break from each other and you can think about what you want,' she said.

'Don't snap at me.'

'Don't scold me as if you have the right.'

'Okay,' I said. 'Have you thought that maybe you're too demanding?'

'Demanding? Would you leave please!'

I had heard that coaches were often in conflict with performers but it was no consolation. I wondered if she would come back, or whether I should go and get her, or accept we were over?

When I was home, I felt very alone. An important part of my life had ended. I'd been honest but Maxi had taken me by surprise. I'd refused to make a commitment and missed an opportunity by reflex rather than lack of interest. I wanted Maxi, but perhaps it was too late now.

We went to the Team Maxi meetings separately and didn't speak to each other. The others noticed the ice.

'I'm sorry you and Maxi aren't hitting it off,' said Blake. 'What's the problem? You've been good for each other.'

'Lack of trust and commitment.'

'Yours or hers?'

'Both. We're having a timeout.'

'Total commitment should happen naturally. It can't be forced.'

'Thank you, Blake.'

Maxi was doing all her training at QIS and the progress of my work was slow without her to discuss my ideas with.

After three weeks I called her.

'I'm missing you,' I said. 'It isn't getting easier.'

'Nor for me either.'

'Can we talk over dinner?'

'Okay.'

We met at a restaurant.

'How's your training going?'

'Stan has me on a schedule,' she said.

'Are you happy? Because I'm not. I really want you in my life.'

'For casual sex?' she asked.

'No. For love. I want to be with you,' I said.

'Remember when we protested against war with Iran?'

'You were the fervent one.'

'My parents didn't approve of us protesting. Patti said: 'Just because you feel passionately about something doesn't make it right.''

'You were such a hothead, a pretty hothead,' I said.

'Aren't I now? Pretty?'

'Yes, very pretty Maxi and still hot-headed.'

'Who are you to criticise my emotions?' she said.

'Perhaps I'm not emotional enough,' I said. 'Is that what it's all about?'

'No. I love you.'

'Couples do lose interest in each other.'

'We love each other, don't we?' she asked.

'Perhaps it's the sex that keeps us together.'

She swung a fist at me.

'Just kidding,' I said. 'The sex is pretty ordinary.'

She tried to hit me again and I held her in a bear hug.

'The sex is good for me,' she said. 'I've longed for you.'

'I've wanted to forget you, but I can't,' I said. 'I'm tied to you. What I mean is that I do love you. I think about you continually. Could we live together?'

'Hmm. Where?'

'You could move into my place properly.'

'What about the sex?'

192

'You said it isn't important.'

'Hmm. Could we try it for a few days?'

'Definitely. Could you come over this evening to make a start?'

'I'll come for a short while, say at 7. Is that okay? I'm going now.'

She kissed me hard on the lips.

'I like being kissed by you.'

'There's plenty more where that came from. See you later.'

'Bye.'

Her interest in my research inspired me to create concepts and build theories. In Team Maxi, she showed pride in my expertise that helped gain the respect of the others. My attention to her winning and my pride in our association validated her. The different textures and hues of our passion were like ornamental gardens, where we strolled at leisure.

Although she was at odds with Stan, he helped me with coaching her and coordinating her training programme with the others.

'How can I help her best?' I asked him.

'You can become her best friend, whom she trusts, confides in and who helps her realise the best way forward.'

CHAPTER 38

Maxi was hurt that Stan had been critical of her narrow defeat in the National half-marathon. Since yelling at each other, they hadn't talked.

'Blaming me is unnecessary, unfair and cruel,' Maxi said to Jack. 'I was well inside my goal, yet he is treating it as a personal betrayal.'

Jack was sad to see Maxi and Stan giving each other the silent treatment, after coming so far together. Maxi could not overlook Stan's abuse. Jack tried to cheer her up.

'Don't worry about what Stan said,' he told Maxi. 'He didn't mean it. I'll help you mend your bridges with him. I believe in you and I know that you gave the National everything you had. He had no right to talk to you like that: coaches are often critical, but he has gone too far.'

'He has hurt me badly.'

'He was trying to sting you, to stop you choking. Frank Sutton did it with Siri Lindley, making her angry with him. You're a different type of runner, less needy, wanting more respect and Stan blew it. Don't let it bother you.'

'I don't need his shit. What can I do to improve my running?'

'You could do better in full marathons.'

'Why?'

'They're less tactical. You'd be running against yourself, rather than trying to outsmart rivals.'

'Are you saying I'm not a tactician?'

'I'm not saying that, but you do run races your own way, don't you?' said Jack. 'In a full marathon, you would set your own pace and be less likely to get into a sprinting duel at the finish. Compared with a half marathon, you'd use your energy more slowly for twice as long, sustaining rather than jostling for position. You're a controlled runner and a full marathon could be your optimum race.'

For the second Team meeting, Jack and Maxi were first to arrive. They waited for the others to come in and take their seats.

'Maxi has stopped training with Stan,' Jack said, beginning the meeting. 'I've taken over what she was doing with him. Today we're going to plan Maxi's run in the Brisbane Marathon.'

His pale blue-grey eyes roved around the group, searching for contributors. He would listen with concentration, interposing questions, then holding forth with his ideas. He knew to keep their participation and support he had to avoid slipping into rhetoric, dogma and contradiction. He would have to sacrifice some of his own ideas.

'A full marathon puts Maxi into a new world. She's been very successful in half marathons. In the national championship, she was only a whisker away from winning. How do think you went, Maxi?'

'My time was 62:31, well under my goal and near the national record of 62.10.'

They applauded enthusiastically.

'Congratulations Maxi,' said Jack. 'What do you think about running twice as far in Brisbane in August?'

'It will take more willpower than I usually have,' said Maxi. 'My goal will be to finish.'

Jack said: 'There has been a brain revolution in endurance sports and the most important finding is that a runner cannot improve except by changing her relationship with perception of effort. 'The brain has to increase physical capacity by increasing tolerance for pain, by increased motivation and by will. Did anyone see the movie 4 Minute Mile?'

'I saw it,' said Stan. 'It's fanciful to believe that a runner can run on mind alone. Fitness is essential.'

'I agree,' Jack said. 'The movie shows it from the other side, that prior experience can condition a runner mentally to cope with discomfort that would otherwise be too much. No matter how fit Maxi is, she'll run better if she has encountered and overcome the race conditions beforehand.'

'It's a theory, ' Stan said, 'and it can't be tested.'

'Psychology is always difficult to test,' said Jack, careful not to be drawn into an argument. 'Dr Minami, how can Maxi increase her tolerance for pain?'

Riko Minami stood up and went to a window with views of the distant city.
'Would everyone come over here by the window, please.'
She showed them an apple.
'Imagine I am a runner and my goal is to grab this apple.'
Riko went outside and placed the apple on the sill of the window, outside the glass. She returned inside, pulled on a heavy glove and stood in front of the group, beside the glass looking out at the apple.
'Maxi, suppose there is an invisible barrier stopping me getting to my goal, represented by this glass. To achieve it I must break through the glass and seize it.'
'Why must you break the glass? Why not go out through the door and get it?'
'I have to make an effort to break through. By acting it out here in training, my attitude can change. I can find out I am capable of smashing through a barrier.'
Riko Minami fisted her hand in the glove and punched the glass hard, several times, until it broke. She thrust her hand through the jagged hole and grasped the apple.
'With determination, some effort and a little danger, I have achieved my goal. The physical force I used was unleashed by my willpower.'
'I don't get it,' said Maxi. 'Why do you have to smash the glass? Couldn't you just imagine breaking it?'

196

'The glass symbolises a psychological barrier. Maxi, you have to punch through a pain barrier to get to your goal. Replacing the glass is not a problem.'

Sensei Minami went outside and moved the apple, placing it behind another window pane.

'Now it's your turn,' she said to Maxi. 'Here, put on this glove. Grab the apple. Go for it.'

Maxi hesitated.

'You have to break out of the box of your past behaviour,' said Minami. 'You can't edge up to the apple gradually. Smokers who try to quit gradually, never do. You can't half give up smoking. You need to make a complete break with your past. Maxi, you must act decisively, or you will never reach your goal. Go for it, now! Give it all you've got.'

Maxi punched, but her fist bounced back.

Lowering her shoulder to punch with full force, Maxi concentrated all her effort, smashed through and grasped the apple.

'How did that feel?'

'It felt reckless and exciting, even delicious, like an achievement. I unleashed my strength and it felt good. Does breaking a record have to be reckless and dangerous?'

'It's best to be deliberate, not casual,' said Riko Minami. 'You give your all. Weightlifters do it for a couple of seconds. Sprinters do it for 10 seconds. Elite marathon runners do it for about two hours. They use willpower and motivation to overcome pain barriers. You can do it too, Maxi!

'You willed yourself to get to your goal. A philosopher called Friedrich Nietzsche described a wilful and successful person as a superior type of being, an 'overman' who crosses an invisible line between non-achievement and achievement at will, daring to accept personal risk.'

'Maxi you're our superwoman,' said Corvid. 'You can get a job in demolition.'

They all laughed.

'Corvid adores Maxi,' thought Jack. *'So do I.'*

'Thanks, Sensei,' said Maxi. 'That was inspiring. I want to go to the beach and run up that dune again and get to my goal.'

'I'll come with you,' Jack said.

He ended the meeting and drove with Maxi to his parents' place, where they had a cup of tea before going to the beach.

It was mid-afternoon, sunny and warm, with hot, dry sand that squeaked underfoot.

They faced the dune.

'I'm going to do 50,' Maxi said.

She ran up the dune, with Jack counting the number of repeats.

As she ran, she remembered Stan's words: *'Facing your fear is the hardest thing you'll ever do. At this work rate, you could bonk. When your legs won't move and your lungs won't breathe, step up and open that door to freedom.'*

Her feet kept slipping on the loose sand and Maxi became angry and swearing.

When she turned at 40, she paused beside Jack, weeping.

'I think I'm getting close to bonking,' she said.

'They say it's like an orgasm in good sex,' he said. 'To make it last, you have to get as close as possible and then hold back.'

'You make it sound like withdrawal.'

'It is. Until you finish.'

'Love-making is spontaneous and fun. This is torture.'

'This is the first time. You'll like it more next time.'

She had almost reached 50 when her body became leaden, she stumbled repeatedly and passed out at Jack's feet, unconscious. He caught her as she fell. She lay on her back, breathing deeply, frightening him. He turned her on to her side, in the recovery position, and phoned for an ambulance.

'She passed out while she was running,' he said to the ambo. 'Maybe it was her heart. Not much sign of life. She's lying on Kings' Beach on the sand, near the path from Goulburn Park, about 200 metres north. Hurry!'

He had known this could happen but Maxi's blackout surprised and shocked him. He had watched bonking on videos and expected that a bonk would stop her, but not completely.

His first aid training had not dealt specifically with bonking and his position now seemed precarious.

Maxi could be dying and it would be his fault.

He waited anxiously, feeling for a pulse in her wrist, finding only a weak beat. He put his hand on her belly to detect breathing but movement was weak. He pinched her fingertips and toes. They reddened as if there was circulation.

Time dragged as he waited for the ambulance. After 20 minutes, she sat up and groaned.

'So that's what happens in a bonk,' she said. 'I thought I was dying.'

'So did I,' he said. 'You shut down.'

He used his phone to cancel the ambulance. 'Sorry. False alarm. She was unconscious but now she's sitting up and talking. There's no need for you to come. She must have blacked out from overexertion. She's a distance runner and it happens. She'll be okay. Sorry for the false alarm. Thank you for responding.'

She sat on the sand, recovering.

'What did it feel like?' he asked her.

'I had to fight pain,' she said. 'It made me angry. I went weak and couldn't move, the same as when I hit the wall at the pool. The difference was here I kept on going, with everything I had, until my body quit on me.'

'You found your bonk point by running to exhaustion,' said Jack. 'It took you 40 minutes until you couldn't maintain the pace. You slowed to a standstill. It came on too quickly as tiredness. Now you know the signs to look out for; you can delay bonking until you get to the finish line.'

Back at home with Jack, she called Stan.

'I bonked Dad!' she said. 'It was scary but amazing. I ran and ran until I dropped. I faced my fear. It was so liberating. It has put my head in a new and better place for enduring. You were right.'

'Congratulations. This is a new beginning. You could only get there by wanting it that much.'

'Thank you, Dad.'

Later, Stan had a word with Jack.

'Well done Jack,' he said. 'She has done for you what she wouldn't do for me. She must respect you. Now you need to bring this into her training plan. Derek and Riko will help you.'

'I need your input too.'

'I'd be pleased to.'

'She needs to put the anger she had running up that dune into her racing,' Jack said. 'Siri Lindley learned to commit to a goal, immersing herself, reaching new heights of constancy, effort, strength and endurance. Maxi has to change from running obsessed with winning, to running to improve her PB.'

'I agree,' said Stan. 'Instead of yearning to fulfil a destiny of top runner, she must learn to achieve her goal at every step of the way. She has to earn her way.'

'I'll call a team meeting to plan her training for her first marathon.'

In his biweekly phone call with his parents, he told them about coaching Maxi. They had met her several times. She had gone home with him for a weekend and they had liked her.

'When can we come and see her run?' they asked.

'The Brisbane Marathon is in about six months. Can you come?'

'Love to. Sebastian has a girlfriend, Wendy. Could they come with us?'

'I'd like that. I'll get tickets.'

'It'll really be something with you coaching her. She's bound to win!'

'Yeah, right,' he laughed.

CHAPTER 39

My home was two rooms in a converted former church. The living room had a wood-panelled ceiling and a stained-glass window. Maxi hadn't moved in with me completely yet, staying several days each week as a trial.

We had merged smoothly, except in the kitchen. She had been accustomed to Patti preparing her food at home. I did the shopping for us and cooked. Maxi was obsessive about her health and what she ate and I learned to prepare vegan food for her. When I shopped, I favoured vegetables and fruits in season, ease of preparation and quality for money.

But my approach was not entirely satisfactory to Maxi.

'Did you wash the fruits and vegetables?' she demanded.

It irritated me when she checked up on me.

I thought. *'I love her very much and will try to persuade her not to ask that question ever again.'*

'The suppliers washed them,' I said. 'If there was an infection and they didn't remove it, they could lose their supply contract with the retailer. If I rewashed them, I would not be able remove all flora and fauna. Sterility is neither achievable, nor is it desirable. Airborne pathogens can invade, or by contact with body wastes, from surfaces, from touching other people and from foods both washed and unwashed. When our immune systems are primed by regular exposure to pathogens, they produce lymphocytes able to counter threats and our bodies can deal with most hazards.'

'You must peel fruits and vegetables,' she said, disbelieving.

My nails dug into my palms. She was sceptical about science and gullible about pseudoscience. I had studied physiology and microbiology and read New Scientist magazine about the ubiquity of pathogens, the diversity of body flora and fauna and the paucity of technologies to prevent infections. She was unaware of, or did not understand, the orthodox scientific descriptions and theories. She preferred to rely on gossip and her stepmother's food prejudices.

'I don't like where this is going,' I thought. *'This is an issue that has festered since she moved in with me. I haven't lived with anyone before and it's turning out to be more difficult than I expected.'*

'Peeling fruits and vegetables can be harmful,' I said. 'I agree that peels from oranges and bananas are unpalatable and should be removed, but peels from apples, pumpkins, potatoes and zucchinis have fibre that benefits the digestive system.'

'When did you make this salad?' she asked me.

I gritted my teeth.

'Yesterday.'

She started eating it. She would eat salad up to two days old, but her question annoyed me.

'I'm offended that she's checking to see if I've sneaked in old food as if I'm irresponsible and would threaten her health,' I thought. *'She should trust that I would not serve food so old it could be dangerous.*

'Anyway, her body safeguards her against food that's bad. She'd be able to taste if it was bad and identify anything that was off. Anything harmful would be dealt with by her digestive processes.

'She's implied I care little for her well-being and could be so lazy, stupid or malicious that I would serve infected, unclean or unhygienic food. In fact, she seems to have aligned herself with a different concept of human evolution, in which humans distrust the hygiene of kin, confine themselves to packaged food and live in sterile environments. It's a future I reject as too discontinuous with my heritage.

'Sharing food prepared by a partner should create a loving bond from which trust builds. It is the first of the 'basic-four Fs', as neurologist Paul Maclean put it - feeding, fleeing, fighting and reproduction.'

When she had finished eating my salad, she did not comment on it.

'Did you find anything nasty in the salad, Joseph,' I asked her.

'Who?'

'Joseph Lister discovered asepsis. It's the method used in hospitals to prevent the spread of germs, by washing hands and surfaces.'

'That's what I want here.'

'Most people are aware there are germs everywhere, that can only be prevented by comprehensive sterilisation. Another theory is that we are bathed in potential pathogens that are held at bay by a strong immune system.'

'I know that.'

'Then why don't you accept that our bodies can deal with germs? Checking on the age of a salad won't protect you.'

'There are risks with old foods.'

'Achieving sterile conditions is difficult in hospitals. Everywhere else it is impossible.'

'It's not that hard. In my view, hygiene is worth doing well.'

'If I hand the job over to her, we'll be in strife,' I thought. *'She's never done anything in a kitchen since I've known her.'*

'I have better things to do with my time than washing vegetables without good reason,' I said. 'Babies with severe combined immune deficiency, or SCID, have been reared in plastic bubbles to avoid contact with pathogens. They become helpless dependents. You're trying to live in a bubble too. In a sterile environment, fed on crisp new salads, your immune system will atrophy. Outside, we have pathogens with us always. By cutting yourself off, you're setting yourself up to suffer badly from an infectious disease, one you would otherwise have been able to counter.'

'You're making all this up.'

She turned her back and picked up a magazine.

'I know more about this than you,' I said. 'I'm fed up with pandering to your special foods and trendy health nonsense. For example, the way you blindly accept food within its use-by-date is plain stupidity.'

203

'Why not?' she shrieked. 'If it's within the use-by-date it's okay.'

'It may not be okay. The UBD is merely a guide. You need to check the appearance and taste.'

She squinted at me as if to say 'How dare you correct me!'

'You take more risks than I want. I won't eat old food like you do.'

'Why not if it's okay?' I said patiently. 'We've evolved with our taste, smell, touch and vision sensitive to bad foods. There's no sudden toxic decomposition after the UBD expires. A UBD is conservative and has wide latitude. Some products are inorganic and hardly degrade at all, such as toothpaste. You throw enough good stuff away to keep whole families going.'

'I don't like your tone,' she said angrily. 'You're lecturing me.'

She had lost her temper before but only once had I seen her this worked up: when we had quarrelled about her ear stud, before I had realised it was a symbol of her self-determination.

'You may learn something,' I said scornfully. 'You seem to have fallen for every food fad going. When you go shopping it's like missionary work, trying to help people, animals and the environment. It's admirable, but our need is for good quality economical nutrition.'

'I try to help others.'

'So do I, by purchasing value for money,' I said, peeved. 'I demand it and they supply it. You reject foreign products as if Australians are the only people worthy to survive. You deny work to poor people overseas who may be starving. The good you do is at the expense of other people who you do harm to.'

'That's not true,' she said loudly. 'My interest is in where a product comes from and how it's produced. I buy sensibly and it helps me feel good about myself. I've noticed you go for the cheap stuff, without regard for real quality. It's short-sighted.'

'I buy value for money, whereas you splash out on trendy fetishes with deceptive ads.' It came out harshly, overstating my case.

'I support trends when they do good, like cage-free eggs.'

'If you really wanted happy chooks, you would stop eating eggs,' I said mocking. 'Being in a cage is a minor issue for a chook compared with the pain of squeezing out eggs day after day, until the final squawk.'

'You're in a mood! Go on, tell me what else is wrong with me?' she said taunting 'It's a good job I don't start on your strange ideas.'

'Like what?'

'You must be the only person who washes their hands *before* going to the toilet.'

'That's reasonable. I also wash my hands before preparing vegetables.'

I wouldn't rise to her bait. Nor would I become emotional, nor aggressive.

'I don't like being interrogated in the kitchen as if I am a poisoner,' I said assertively. 'I want you to have a more realistic approach to my food preparation efforts.'

'You're too lazy to prepare food properly,' she said nastily.

'Rudeness won't solve this,' I said. 'The 'properly' you want is weird. When I don't engage in a pointless, harmful ritual, like washing carrots, it isn't laziness. You're trying to impose your irrational prejudices on my liberty.'

'You should respect my wishes with food,' she said shrilly. 'When I'm rundown after a race, I can catch things.'

'I do not take risks with your health. There's nothing wrong with your immune system. You don't need to be in cotton wool all the time.'

'More of the time would be an improvement.'

'Let's compromise? How about you prepare the fruit and vegetables?'

'I have other things to do.'

'You could accept me the way I am,' I said. 'Have you heard of unconditional love?'

'You don't know what love is.'

I didn't like where this was going. I regretted having confronted her. I couldn't see a way forward.

'I suppose you do?' I said.

'I thought I did, but then you killed it.'

'What did I do?'

205

'You don't have feelings and you don't respect mine,' she said. 'You don't seem to like me anymore. You won't even wash vegetables for me.'

I didn't like it when she tried to make me seem weird and repulsive.

'Your constant demands are too much.'

'You're a self-centred bastard.' she said sadly. 'Do you want to be single?'

'No,' I said automatically, although right now it seemed attractive. My aspiration was to isolate myself from her unreasonable demands.

'We need a break from each other,' she said.

'For how long?'

'See how we go,' she said. 'A month to start with.'

'A month is a long time.'

'It will take that long to get over the yelling today and understand what has gone wrong between us.'

Our relationship, the centre of my life, had unravelled quickly. I was devastated.

Although it was late, Maxi packed her things and I drove her to the university, where she still had a room. After dropping her off, I remembered her good qualities and regretted not being more flexible. Because I loved her so much, I had wanted her to understand me and accept my values. It seemed like a paradox that my love for her had to be unconditional when hers was so demanding.

CHAPTER 40

Our team met again to plan for Maxi's run in her first Marathon in Brisbane.

'Maxi, what is your goal?' said Riko.

'I want to do 2h30. My PB for half the distance is 1h02. It seems much further.'

'It would take you 2.4 times longer,' Jack said, using his calculator. 'Will it take 2.4 times more effort?'.

Maybe even more,' Maxi said.

'More will,' said Riko. 'The same self-discipline, holding yourself on the right track. Self-discipline is like crawling out of bed on a cold morning. It overcomes base desires, such as withdrawal and laziness, a grudging and measured response. A marathon will require the same self-discipline but much more will, a bigger ambition.'

'How is will different from self-discipline?'

'Will enables you to unleash yourself, to overcome a barrier in your mind and spring out of bed.'

'How do you get more will?' asked Maxi.

'A determinist would believe you don't have any will, except by instinct or impressed on you by others,' said Stan. 'A determinist never chooses: they simply follow instincts, obey habits and carry out orders.'

'Perhaps there is some of that,' said Maxi. 'I have few choices when I run.'

'You happily accept responsibility, but not everyone does. The philosopher Schopenhauer regarded a person's will as a curse, causing him to strive all his days,' Jack said. 'Could will be a hunger for something, anything, to satisfy us, with causes beyond our control?'

'Is that what you think?' said Maxi. 'That I'm driven to run, like a moth to a light?'

'No,' said Coach Derek. 'You are free, with will, or personal volition.'

'Is will something I have in different amounts, from time to time?' said Maxi.

'Will is like the voltage put out by a car's battery,' said Jack. 'If you keep the car in the garage, the battery will run down and you won't have enough charge left to get started. Will has to be nurtured. Training and exercise keep a runner's will charged up, ready to apply it to the heavy demands of the race.'

'Could a long practice run under race conditions act like periodic deep discharge of a rechargeable battery, stopping the chemicals crystallising and becoming inert?' asked Blake.

'A good analogy,' said Corvid. 'In other words, a person's will can atrophy with neglect. The exercise of will develops muscle and ability. Weightlifters use their will to cross pain boundaries and you should too. Exercise breaks down the muscle with micro-tears that rebuild it stronger than before. A runner rebuilds her muscles every 15 to 30 days, needing smooth fibres for endurance and twitch muscle fibres for quickness. 'No pain, no gain' is the mantra. It explains how her body builds to protect itself from future stress. Similarly, will has to be exercised and rebuilt.'

The group's ideas ran fast and deep. Jack provoked discourse with controversy, iconoclasm, drama or emotion. He was at pains not to dominate and when there was too much dependence on his leadership, he would desert that post and begin a conversation with someone on the periphery of the group, bringing them in.

'Maxi, it took will to unleash yourself and smash through that pane,' said Riko. 'It has strengthened you. In our next Zen running lesson, you will run through a pain barrier to your goal.'

'Doesn't she need to stop when she comes up against a pain barrier?' said Patti.

'No,' said Stan. 'A pain signal begins as a warning with a large safety margin. Maxi knows each signal from experience and understands when she can keep going or choke.'

'Marathon running is as safe as houses,' Coach Derek said. 'If she's fit, she won't damage herself by over-exertion. Her body would shut down long before that could happen.'

'There are heaps of theories about limits on a runner's endurance,' said Jack. 'Every coach has favourite tweaks to improve physical and mental endurance.'

'What limits do we want Maxi to overcome?' asked Blake.

'Bonk point acts to keep her safe, issuing warnings. If she keeps going, it cuts the power and if necessary, shuts her down,' said Jack. 'Central governor theory is that her brain receives feedback like a car's computer system. It gets information about muscle glycogen, blood glucose, muscle damage and fatigue and can perceive that the car is out of stable control. We want Maxi to consciously override her brain's perception of instability.'

'It's partly psychology,' said Alice. 'Research has used a concept of toleration of perceived effort.'

'Derek and Stan's concepts of endurance have the brain overriding body processes,' said Riko. 'In Zen there is no dichotomy between mind and body. In archery, it is your whole being that strives to hit the bullseye. There's no concept of over or under exertion. There's only deviation. Archery requires physical strength as well as mental self-control. Enduring a marathon requires more than a cautionary mind. Mind is the basis of performance.'

'Which is more important, my mind or body?' Maxi asked them.

'Mind,' said Alice.

'Body can cause pain but mind can desensitize perception of pain,' said Corvid.

'Mind and body work in tandem and depend on each other.' Derek said. 'To rehearse mental toughness, physiology also has to be trained, like when Maxi ran up the sand dunes.'

209

'I'm not likely to forget,' said Maxi.

'When you do something new, your mind has imagined you doing it,' said Riko. 'In 1958 a four-minute mile had never been achieved and was considered impossible. After Roger Bannister ran it in 3:59:4, within a couple of years 30 runners including schoolboys had beaten the old record. They have called it The Bannister Effect. How do you explain it?'

'People need a nudge to do something new,' said Coach Derek. 'An old habit like choking at 4 minutes can bounce around like a pinball on a table, until something flips it onto a new path.'

'A larger prize,' said Blake.

Derek laughed. 'No. Bannister wasn't paid. He imbued the Oxford tradition of nonchalant superiority and eschewed training and coaching. Initially, there was volume in long distances, sometimes at walking pace. Training has had fads of volume and then intensity, in cycles (14).

'In the US, college runners going for the 4-minute mile record were getting full-time professional coaching. Bannister worked as a hospital intern and could train for only 30-40 minutes a day,' said Coach Derek. 'Bannister started interval running, an intense new training technique, doing countless 400-metre repeats.

'For his attempt on the record, he ran behind pacers and benefited from the slipstreaming effect of lower wind resistance, which could possibly be 1 second per 400 metres on a still day and into the wind even more. Running in a pack with others lifts performance. Pacing was banned in some marathons.'

'So it could have been pacing that caused his breakthrough?' said Blake. 'Besides the change to intense training, pacing can reduce wind friction and decrease self-control exertion.'

'They probably contributed to endurance performance, but there are other possibilities. A change in Bannister's psychology could have caused him to break the record,' said Coach Derek. 'Maxi, how do you know whether to slow down, stay at the same pace, or speed up?'

'I try to keep up with the leaders.'

'And when you are in front?' he asked.

210

'I run as fast as I think I'll be able to sustain the rest of the way to the finish line.'

'Does seeing your time on the race clock or on your wrist affect your performance?' Coach Derek asked.

'Sometimes.'

'Does spectator applause affect you?' asked Jack.

'Yes, always. It gives me a lift.'

'What about your mood?'

'My moods can vary in their effects.'

'When does time matter most?' asked Derek.

'When I need to know if I'm on track with my plan,' said Maxi.

'If you're going faster than you planned, you might slow down?'

'Yes, it happens,' she said. 'If I remember feeling better, the same, or worse at this point in a previous race, I might change my pace. My sense of time affects how I'm feeling. I've learned to rate my speed not only from timepieces, but from my imagination. If I am hungry for a win, or hear a crowd cheering, I might not slow down.'

'What does slow you down?' asked Derek.

'I may feel I have to,' said Maxi. 'I used to feel defeated and slow down when I was overtaken, but I've learned success is being on track for my goal. I trust my goal.'

'Does a runner deliberately vary their speed during a race?' asked Jack.

'Not much,' said Derek. 'Constancy is preferred for efficiency. Running with a group is usual. It is more constant.'

'Maxi runs at a calculated speed, without giving in to her feelings, but she has to drive herself with her will to endure,' said Riko. 'A runner has to develop her will.'

'Should Maxi train with many short sprints or a single long run?' asked Jack.

'It's an old chestnut,' said Stan, joining in the discussion for the first time that day. 'In the 1980s and 1990s, there was convergence on a mix of interval and endurance work, different for each runner. Aerobic exercise, or 'cardio', came in with the heart beating fast to deliver oxygen to the muscles, strengthening the heart, lungs and

211

muscles. Then there was both. Runners ran 160 kilometres per week or more and the interval training was severe enough to induce vomiting. By the 2000s, endurance training and total development were using a wide range of intensities from pure sprinting to slow jogging. I believe Maxi needs both, for both physical and mental development.'

'Maxi can develop her will by using it,' said Coach Derek.

'You can build your will on your strengths too,' said Alice.

'Will is a force that can achieve goals, or ambitions, like a yacht tacking to and fro towards a destination upwind,' Jack said. 'The crew have to strive to hold the rudder and sails into the best positions and aerofoil shapes. They force the yacht to perform well, like the way Maxi wills her body to run fast.'

'Forcefulness is what I need,' said Maxi. 'How can I get it?'

'By rehearsing your movements,' said Stan. 'Plan how you will run. Before a Wimbledon final, tennis player Chrissie Evert would spend several hours watching videos of her opponents' recent matches and rehearsing in her mind the shots she could need to make. Consequently, when she was on court, she responded automatically and quickly to opponents' shots, winning by being faster and making fewer errors. To concentrate like that takes will. Could you use a method like that, Maxi?'

'I've been doing it a bit,' she said. 'I run pictures of race situations forward in my mind to prepare. I aim for 'no surprises' because if I don't respond quickly enough, I could be set back badly. I have to prepare for things like competitor moves, course conditions, weather, disruption by a spectator and even professional fouls. I have to decide what I would do in the race.'

'Maxi your mental control has steadily improved,' said Riko. 'I believe you will soon achieve 'It': a higher awareness of goal achievement.'

'Well done, Maxi and Riko!' I said. 'I am going to call a halt there. Today we have explored some aspects of willpower. Let's meet next week to go into Maxi's goal setting.

'Would Derek, Riko and Stan stay please, to discuss Maxi's training? Everyone, thank you for your inputs. I want us to continue into goal setting. Can we meet again to talk about that? How about Friday?'

'Sorry, no,' said Derek. 'Riko and I have a dinner party. How about Thursday evening next week?'

'Is there anyone who can't come next week on Thursday? Okay, we'll meet then, at 6 pm.'

I coordinated the coaches in preparing a plan for Maxi's training activities. I would discuss it with them individually later.

'I really appreciate everyone's inputs,' said Maxi. 'These meetings and plans are great for my training. So far I have made great progress in countering choking and bonking. Thank you, everybody.'

I left the meeting feeling pleased that Team Maxi was working well. Training of Maxi's mental control had emerged as the priority and Riko expected a breakthrough soon. My PhD research was well underway. I was tracking Maxi's growing control over her performance time with three techniques: near-bonking, Zen meditation and exertion of will power. These methods all depended on Maxi pursuing a definite and intractable goal. I wanted to explore next the best way to set such a vital goal.

CHAPTER 41

Team Maxi met a week later to consider her goals. She had moved out from Jack's, back to the university, after their conflict about how to prepare vegetables. They were unreconciled and she went home at weekends, where Stan resumed coaching her.

'I'll keep you going until you and Jack come to your senses,' Stan said grimly. 'You were happy with him, weren't you? What happened?'

She was defensive. 'We had a difference of opinion and I left.'

'Couldn't you work out a compromise?'

'He refused to wash vegetables and I won't eat them like that.'

She felt a little foolish because everything else had been okay and their dispute was unexpected.

'Maybe your relationship was too fragile to last.'

'I don't agree. This dispute was one of a kind.'

'Have you talked it through together?'

'I tried,' said Maxi. 'He used science bullshit to claim the moral high ground. I thought you were bad like that, but he's worse.'

'Being rude won't help you,' Stan said. 'You can talk to him on Thursday at the meeting.'

'I doubt he'll talk to me.'

Before the meeting, Riko took Maxi aside.

'Maxi, I hope you and Jack will make it up,' she said earnestly. 'You're good for each other.'

'Thank you, Riko. I used to think that too, but he's unreasonable.'

Jack started the meeting. He avoided looking at Maxi.

'Would each of the coaches tell us what Maxi has been doing?'

'More of the same,' said Derek. 'She's done some strenuous interval work and distance runs of up to 10 kms, habituating to higher levels of effort.'

'She ran a full marathon on Saturday. She could be better than at halfs.'

'It was okay. My time was slow though.'

'You did well with half marathons,' Jack said. 'You were second in the National last year.'

'She could have won,' said Stan.

'He doesn't miss an opportunity to put her down,' thought Jack.

'She has potential,' said Coach Derek. 'Changing to full marathons is her decision and I approve.'

'Will you have much competition in Brisbane?' asked Blake.

'Yes, heaps,' said Maxi. 'There are large cash prizes; Annette Cummings won last year. Aisha Sayat came second by only a metre. Hoogly will be running: I beat her in Sydney. There are some top internationals: Theodore Kirwan beat me by a few seconds in the half in Sydney last year. Carol Kotan the Kenyan is coming. The favourite will be Wilhelma Luck from Ethiopia, who broke the record two years ago; and the New Zealander, Heidi Gartner.'

Jack imagined the challenges Maxi faced. His own distance experience was only a 86 kms walk from Lancaster to Manchester. He had been unfit, without training and wearing wrong gear. It was 23 hours of torture. He could imagine the ordeal to compete in an endurance event successfully.

Because of their separation, he didn't address Maxi directly.

'It seems to me that Maxi must have a goal to pull her along,' he said. 'Or does it take more than a goal?'

'Fear of losing?' asked Blake.

'No,' said Alice. 'Your factory workers doing piecework know they lose money if they are slow. In a marathon, push isn't enough. Fear of losing could keep a runner going but would not keep her at the front of the field. Maxi needs a goal that inspires her to produce an elite performance.'

'If her mind is concentrated on a goal, she might not notice the pain,' said Coach Derek. 'Can she focus on both her goal and her body at the same time?'

''Her body can be trained to automaticity, leaving her mind free to concentrate on finishing.'

'Her mind has to drive her body to the edge of bonking,' said Sensei Minami.

'If she is going to race on a knife edge, between going too slow or bonking, it will have to be carefully planned,' Blake said. 'Maxi needs a goal she can follow to the end.'

'Are you sure she needs goals at all?' asked Stan. 'Why can't she simply do her best? Aren't motivation, drive and reward enough?'

'They're not readily variable and measurable,' said Blake. 'She can relate her goal performance to accomplishment and get feedback.'

'I agree. She needs a performance goal she can monitor and recalculate while she's running,' said Sensei Minami. 'Goals are important for bringing order, security and hope, at the edge of the realm of chaos. A surfer's ride on a wave has a masterful balance between order and chaos.'

'I'm not sure she should dice with chaos,' said Jack. 'She needs a performance goal that inspires her to new levels of mastery.'

'This is her first marathon,' Riko Minami said. 'We okayed her goal of 2h30 at our last meeting.'

'2h30 could be too fast for her first marathon,' said Stan. 'The winner's time last year was 2h22 and the national record is 2h18.'

'I can run slower,' said Maxi. 'I'll be happy just to finish.'

'2h30 is reasonable,' said Coach Derek. 'Many of the skills are the same as for the 3000 and you've mastered those.'

Maxi said with patience: 'So 2h30 it is?'

'Yes, BUT,' said Coach Derek, his tone warning, 'it's NOT a try-it-and-see situation. You MUST achieve it. It'll be your toughest race yet. Hopefully, your fear of the unknown has gone. Our training will aim to teach you how to run closer to bonking than other runners, never quitting, always surviving and winning.

'We're training you to be savvy, to assess risk and run fast without bonking. You know the symptoms of a bonk from your water running and the sand dunes. A bonk may sneak up on you, coming as a shock. You have to be ready for it and turn down your effort level immediately to get to the finish. Somewhere between ignoring the symptoms and coming to a halt, there'll be an optimum way for you to continue. Your training has to teach you to find that optimum.'

'What type of training can find an optimum?' Maxi asked.

'Trial and error,' said Coach Derek. 'The optimum is a balance between too much and too little. You learn to delay your bonk point, your time before cutting out,' said Coach Derek. 'I want you to challenge yourself with a run every week at marathon pace, for 90% of your bonk point. What is your bonk point, Maxi?'

'2h30, my goal.'

He keyed his calculator.

'I want you to practice running at marathon pace for 2h15,' said Coach Derek. 'You won't fully bonk — you'll get tired and signal your body and mind to adapt. This training will improve your bonk point, which we can test every week. There are club runs you can do. By the time you run in Brisbane it will be old hat.'

'You'll unleash yourself the way Siri Lindley did,' said Jack.

'Maxi should be on a plant-based diet,' said Patti. 'When she runs, she has to carry in her body as much readily accessible energy as possible. Is that okay, Maxi?'

'I would give anything for a pork dinner with crackling.'

'That would slow you down in a big way. I have some photos of food you can look at while you're eating your soy curd,' Patti said.

'Maxi is shaping her ability like a work of art,' said Riko Minami. 'She must cultivate peace of mind in what she is doing and with her surroundings. Everything else follows naturally. The spiritual way of Zen is conveyed by the following chain of ideas:

'Peace of mind produces right values; right values produce right thoughts; right thoughts produce right actions; and right actions do work which will be a material reflection of her serenity at the centre of it all, a material reflection of a spiritual reality.

217

'Briefly, peace of mind causes right thinking, then action and then work.'

'What is right thinking?'

'Zen develops certain forms. Instead of forcing each stride by willpower, you'll let your legs look after themselves and your mind will be focussed on your art of achieving your goal,' said Riko. 'You have to let go.'

'Corvid, have you ever let go?' Alice asked mischievously.

'I always retain my civility,' Corvid said, rebuking her.

'No, I mean: gone all out for a goal?'

'I put everything into my PhD research,' she said. 'I found out today that my thesis has been accepted.'

'Woohoo,' said Alice.

They all clapped.

'Why did you ask me that, Alice?' asked Corvid.

'I want Maxi to give her everything, like you've done.'

'Legend,' said Blake. 'I don't think our Maxi will hold anything back.'

Because of his rift with Maxi, Jack took a backseat while they discussed the training plan.

'Should I change my pace to stay on plan?' asked Maxi.

'Yes, when possible,' said Sensei Minami. 'You may need to adjust for how much running you have left in you and what competitors are doing. You will need to gather information continually, frequently reviewing what you are doing. You have to be in total control.'

'Can you imagine that, Maxi?' said Derek. 'Being totally poised.'

'You mean I have to think about the race, not about myself?'

'That's right, float above your body's protests, never thinking about quitting.'

'What can I focus on?'

'Consider if you're in the right cadence or 'gear' for the terrain,' Coach Derek said. 'Are there other cadences you could consider? Could you go up a notch? Are your posture, your breathing, your pace, your stride right? Is your position with the other runners the best for now? Should you stay with them, or break away?'

218

'That seems okay. What else?'

'You will achieve your goal in small pieces along the way. Be thrilled when you achieve a piece, like when at halfway you're on target.'

'That makes it sound robotic.'

'That's the big picture. You need to stay alert in case someone tries to overtake.'

'How do I know when to let them go past and when to fight back?'

'Half the battle is to be ready for it,' Coach Derek said. 'You'll already have rehearsed most situations in your mind and will be able to respond immediately.'

After the meeting, as he was leaving, Derek said to Jack: 'I'm sorry that you and Maxi are at odds. She's special, like you. You deserve each other.'

'Thank you,' Jack said mumbling. He couldn't think of a reply less awkward.

Sadly, Jack went home alone.

He went to the track several times and sat in the empty grandstand, watching Maxi training. Corvid was down at the trackside, cheering her on, fussing over her as she recovered after runs, mopping her brow.

'Corvid wants Maxi badly,' Jack thought as he watched. *'So do I. I hope Maxi fends her off.'*

Without Maxi, Jack's life took on a despondent hue. After a week he called her.

'How are you getting on without me?' he asked.

'Okay,' she said. 'No, not okay. I've been lost without you.'

'Me too. Can we get back together?' he asked. 'The philosopher Immanuel Kant wanted people to treat each other *as inherently valuable, an end in themselves.* I have been treating you as a means to my ends, which was wrong of me. I have tried to use you. I'm sorry, Maxi. I've realised you're unique and you need a customised approach. I'll want to provide that.'

'What's going to change?' she asked.

'Is mutual unconditional love too much to hope for?' he thought.

'I'll wash the fruit and veg always,' he said.

219

'I'll keep out of the kitchen. I do appreciate your food.'

'Thank you.'

'What are you going to do for me?' asked Jack.

'Hmm,' said Maxi. 'I'll conserve energy and water in the ways you recommend, when I remember,' she said.

'You might be going to do those things anyway,' he said. 'How about making a real sacrifice?'

'I could run harder and make your coaching more successful,' said Maxi.

'Aren't you running as hard as possible already?'

'I am, but there's always room for improvement.'

'I'll accept that,' he said.

'Okay then. I'll come back tomorrow evening, for a trial.'

'How good is that,' he said. 'We compromised!'

She stayed the night and for the rest of the week. They argued a little, compromised a lot and valued each other highly.

She went home each Saturday to run 90% marathon distances at race pace around the Glasshouse Mountains, or along the coast, with Stan on his bike or with his drone overhead. She loved the panoramic views, from rocky peaks, across the blue haze of eucalyptus forest, to the distant ocean shore.

For a change, she sometimes ran 25 kilometres at a tempo pace along local beaches with a group from the Caloundra Athletics Club. When wet, the white sand was firm. She found that beach running was only fun for her first 10 kilometres or so. After that, the cute little waves became annoying, glare from the sand blinded her, sand got into her shoes, or flipped up on to the back of her legs.

'A 25-kilometre run on a long flat beach seems like fun until you do it,' Maxi said to Jack.

'Beach running does you good,' he said. 'Before John Landy lowered Bannister's mile record, he ran 100 miles per week, much of it along a beach.'

She enjoyed running through the surf to cool her legs. A month before the race, she began tapering off and relaxing.

CHAPTER 42

One rainy afternoon, Maxi was with Jack at his apartment when Blake came by with Alice. The four had coffee together.

'I'm glad to see you two are together again, ' said Blake. 'I guess you have plenty to do outside running?'

'Yes, heaps,' said Jack. 'We have been living 'in the moment' and going out to uni and events when we feel like it. I have been studying Zen, like Maxi. It has given me a different sense of time. I avoid worries by doing things right away, rather than later.'

'Is it escapism?'

'It is, in a way,' said Jack. 'I used to have milestones, the certainty of future days, weeks, months, years and birthdays that gave life texture. That's gone now.'

''Don't you need that?' asked Alice.

'Being without news of the world is no loss,' he said. 'I can do without the procession of natural disasters, divorces, terrorist attacks, wars, deaths, accidents and crimes. But I miss having plans for the future and relating to change in others, such as ageing.'

'Living in the moment stops me stressing,' said Maxi. 'Uncertainty is a part of competing and Riko is teaching me to tolerate and even enjoy it. She's been telling me about Ikigai, the Japanese way of reason for being, which strives to balance the spiritual with the practical.

'Ikigai gets me out of bed in the morning. I have stopped getting stressed seeking to do what I enjoy and now I enjoy more what I do.'

'Some physical stress may not be harmful,' said Alice. 'Few top sports people have died young from the physical stress of the activity, but mental stress can kill you, with diseases or suicide. The

221

uncertainty of competition can be stressful. Fear of uncertainty is like having a dog phobia when you even imagine a dog barking when it's not happening. The treatment is to objectify the uncertainty. Riko is exposing you to uncertainty, to learn to ignore all dogs. The worst you can do with uncertainty is to confront it.'

'The early existentialists wanted personal control,' said Jack. 'Kierkegaard, Schopenhauer and Nietzsche had their attention on the here and now. Existentialism and living in the moment are breakthroughs in my life.'

'The existentialists changed the focus to person-centred thinking,' said Alice. 'Until then, individual values were less important than lofty imperial, religious and ethical horizons. They realised that it took willpower to make choices, pursue power and ignore external effects.

'Hitler took up personal control in a big way, but he didn't respect other people.'

'Hitler's totalitarian existentialism had bad consequences,' Blake said. 'The hippies' opposition to the Vietnam war was existential too, but they were less domineering and more considerate of others. They rejected the central authority of 'the man' and founded the peace movement.'

'The difficulty is to get a balance between one's own and others' interests,' Maxi said, putting her hand on Jack's arm. He covered her hand with his.

'Is it possible to be individual-centred in a couple?' asked Alice.

'We have accepted making sacrifices and compromises,' said Jack.

'Really?' said Blake. 'Ayn Rand wanted man to live neither sacrificing himself nor sacrificing others to himself, following rational self-interest as the most profound assertion of his own needs and values. Are you sure what you call sacrifices aren't capitulations, subordinating yourself?'

'You're right,' said Jack. 'We don't keep an account of our compromises. Each of us is always in the black. Our relationship is more like a mutualism,' he said.

'I agree,' said Maxi. 'You scratch my back and I'll scratch yours.'

'You're a wonderful runner,' said Jack, ingratiating. 'I'm seriously a fan of yours.'

'You're an awesome physicist,' she said obsequiously, 'and a good running coach.'

'Okay. I get the picture,' said Alice.

'Kierkegaard wanted people to live passionately,' said Blake. 'I'm in favour of that.'

'Nietzsche dared us to let out our inner selves,' Jack said.

'Don't mind us being here,' said Alice. 'You go for it.'

For the last three years, Jack's passion for Maxi's running had fizzed and whooped. Her successes, instead of bringing certainty, raised the stakes. Causes of success could not be attributed with any confidence to any one of a multiplicity of variables. Passion was sometimes the only rationale Jack had for deciding what Team Maxi should do. He would hide it behind pretended contemplation, critical thought and creativity.

'Don't give me that bullshit,' Maxi told him. 'Your reasons aren't good enough. You're are just trying to have your own way, as usual.'

Maxi understood him instinctively, despising him and loving him simultaneously. He couldn't give her the certainty she wanted and nor could she give it to him. Their needs for each other were underscored by denial and derision. Alone with Maxi, confrontations blew up when no hold was barred. Their arguments were full-blooded, confronting, revelling in each other's differences. Their relationship was finely balanced by their genuine affection for each other.

'You would have won in Sydney if you hadn't choked,' Jack said, reopening the wound made by Stan.

'I didn't choose to choke. I was doing everything right. I won't accept I was at fault.'

'You're not perfect. Next time you won't be afraid of bonking.'

'Hah. What do you know about bonking? I know enough and all it means is I must hold back when I begin to fade. I won't win like that and it will be your fault!'

Like ping pong, they rallied vigorously until a winning hit was scored more by good luck than by calculation. That cleared the air when they would become attentive, kind and loving to each other.

At meetings, the team recognised the ambiguity of Jack's position in harbouring success and leading change. His passion inspired a certain admiration and even horror. They admired his robust ego, the pride of his subjectivity and curtailed his freedom when they thought his passion could lead to tyranny, fanaticism or could even grow violent.

'Turn it down, Jack!' Blake would say.

They gently opposed his authority, reining in his passionate outbursts. Afterwards, he would be embarrassed.

'Sorry everyone. I got carried away again.'

They forgave him. His belief in Maxi transcended individuality and time. His passion brought the group together around Maxi, in a way that mitigated the emotional austerity of a bureaucratic meeting.

'Did I build you up too much?' he asked her.

'Expectations are a fine line and when you create them, I try to meet them,' she said. 'When I succeed, your passion is vindicated. When I fail, the pathos of your position is palpable. If it happens often, you'll lose credibility.'

Coaching Maxi took nerve.

At home together, they talked only when necessary. Neither of them was a talker, nor wanted to entertain the other. Although they shared the same spaces at the same time, they acknowledged each other's presence non-verbally, for example preparing food for each other. Then they would hurry away to work, after full-body hugging and kissing that lingered.

Riko Minami had watched and waited patiently for Maxi's running to achieve the new level she wanted. One day, watching her run laps, the Sensei stopped the lesson.

'You got 'It' Maxi!' she was smiling. 'You ran into 'the zone'.

Maxi stared at her, bewildered. She had been so absorbed, she had not noticed the elevation in her awareness. She had worked for this a long time and air-punched her delight.

'Yay.'

'You noticed?' Riko asked.

Maxi was nonplussed. 'It was good but not much different,' she said sheepishly.

'It is a beginning,' said Sensei Minami. 'You didn't do anything new just now, but I observed your running has greatly improved. You ran into 'the zone', your sweet spot.'

In the following weeks, practicing as if nothing had happened, Maxi ran 'in the zone' regularly. She was attentive and recognised when pain and effort would fall away and enjoyment take over. Riko Minami had started her self-control.

'I run so much better 'in the zone,' she said to Jack. 'Do you know why?'

'I'm trying to find out. Does it matter?'

'I want to do it more, as much as possible.'

'My hunch is that you need a certain state of mind to stay 'in the zone'. Perhaps by becoming more aware of your thinking keeps you in the zone.'

'I'll try it.'

Maxi ran with growing self-confidence.

CHAPTER 43

The Brisbane Marathon began at a stadium, followed the Brisbane river into the countryside, crossed over a bridge and returned through bush country to the stadium.

On the day of the race, Maxi walked out on to the track from the player tunnel. Blake, Alice, Corvid, Derek, Sensei Minami, Brian and Sarah Cram, Sebastian and his girlfriend, Wendy waved from their seats in the stand, where a large crowd waited to watch the start and finish. It was Maxi's first marathon and she tried to ignore her nervous butterflies.

Her name was announced, bringing whoops, yells, whistles and applause. She went over to Jack and Stan at the fence.

'All right?' asked Jack.

'Yeah, good,' she said, her mind locked on to her target.

'Aisha Sayat has pulled out.'

'One less to worry about.'

'There's nothing to worry about,' said Stan. 'Enjoy yourself.'

She loosened up her legs and arms, jogging around on the grass beside the track. With her were 25 elite women. Another 1500 women waited in pens further back and would cross the same electronic timing mat a few minutes after they went. The runners milled around, not speaking, concentrating, their adrenaline poised for the starter's summons to the line.

The gun went off. Maxi sprinted until she was in front. Her heart rate red-lined and she eased off to 180 bpm. Several runners passed her. After 5 kilometres, at the drinks station, she was 4th in a group of 8, with 3 ahead of her by 100 metres. Jack sent her time as 15m20 for the 5 kilometres split, a little faster than the 15m30 in their plan.

She was in touch with the leaders and unconcerned. She felt good, her body working smoothly and comfortably. She resisted the temptation to overtake and lead. She would have plenty of time for that later. She wouldn't think about what was ahead and would concentrate on conserving her energy supply. Her plan was to be a follower at this stage, keeping the leaders within sight.

Her running was strenuous but not hurtful. She was in the second group and enjoying the race. Now every metre felt like she was achieving her goal, even when other runners overtook her. She was loving it, on a high, taking in her surroundings and the other runners. She paced herself, aware that this run would be twice as far as she had run before.

Jack was at the 10 kilometre drinks station.

'Perfect,' he called. 'You're motoring well.'

After 15 kilometres, she noticed it was taking more and more effort and she would have to slow down to ease the pain. She felt a flash of panic. She recalled her meltdown at the Gold Coast but she had run this distance at this pace in training. She would take her mind off the hurt by catching up with the runners in front.

The station at 20 kilometres was halfway and the furthest she had ever raced. The prospect of another 20 kilometres was daunting. She wondered why she had entered this race and whether there was any real evidence she would be able to run this distance. She wanted to sit down.

'Stay with it,' Jack called as she gulped water. 'Your time is terrific. Keep it up!'

The hurt in her legs demanded attention and she fought down momentary panic before reverting to thinking that she was halfway and on target.

After another 10 kilometres, she was having trouble hanging on to reality. The race was a hell that went on and on. The day had warmed up and she was uncomfortably hot. When she reached the 30 kilometres drinks station, her family and friends were there hollering and clapping. Patti's presence was a first.

Hearing them, she forgot her misery briefly. But it came back worse than ever and she berated herself for volunteering to do something so cruel, where she would look foolish when she quit. At the next water station, she grabbed two cups, poured them over her head then took two more and drank them. She squeezed an energy gel into her mouth. Her racing was in unfamiliar territory and she focussed desperately on putting her feet down one in front of the other. Her spirits were bumping along the bottom and the only thing that kept her going was her body had been in this space before during training.

With only a few kilometres to go, a silver lining appeared. Her time at 40 kilometres would put her at the finish in 2h23, an outstanding achievement for her debut race. Suddenly she had a bright new future. One of the leaders, possibly Wilhelma Luck, dropped back behind her. Maxi was in 5th place, 50 metres behind the leaders, in a field spread out over several kilometres.

When she saw from her GPS that it was one kilometre to the finish line, she eased forward gently past two other runners before turning on full power. Digging deep for energy she had saved for this move, she broke away from the second group. For a moment she imagined she was storming a sand dune, giving it everything she had, without fear. She had been here before and wasn't nearing collapse. She would know a bonk before it came and then she could ease off without being in any danger.

She passed Gartner and Kotan and was first across the line, in 2h25.12

She congratulated the others, hardly believing she had won The Brisbane Marathon.

'You were great,' Jack said, bringing her a drink as she sat exhausted.

After five minutes she stood up, stretched to clear the lactic acid and high-fived some kids watching. She wrote her autograph on programmes and arms, as she waited for the medal ceremony.

She stiffly mounted the podium, her body exhausted and suffering. They hung it around her neck and she used a mike to thank her coaches and supporters.

'This is the happiest moment of my running career,' she told the compere.

'How did you do it?' she said.

'I wanted it very much and I was helped by my team.'

CHAPTER 44

I watched Maxi as she slept, facing me. She stirred, opened her eyes and looked at me.

'Good morning,' I said.

'Morning Mark,' she said.

I was gutted.

'Mark? Who the fuck is that?'

'Oh, I mean Jack. Shit. I get names mixed up.'

'Who is Mark?'

'He was my first boyfriend. I haven't thought of him for years.'

'Did you sleep with him?'

'Not sex.'

'How could you forget my name?'

'I don't know. I forget the names of people I know well sometimes, even my family. A face may be familiar, but when I reach for the name, it isn't there, or someone else's is.'

'Why him now?'

'I don't know. It came to me from nowhere. Don't names ever come into your head?'

'Not often. Sometimes I think of a name. It may even be the wrong name. But calling me by the wrong name is weird.'

'You know I have difficulty with names.'

It was true. When we watched movies or were at the theatre together, she would ask me characters' names or roles.

'Is she married to him, or to that other one?' she would ask.

Fairly often she forgot a face, or could not put a name to one. It was difficult for her to follow the plot of a drama. At the theatre together, she would ask me who someone was, during a

230

performance, in the intermission or afterwards. I liked being useful to her. I mentioned it to Coach Derek.

'It's prosopagnosia, a condition that affects about one person in 50,' he said.

I Googled the symptoms. A person with prosopagnosia may not recognise faces, fear social situations, have difficulties with relationships and avoid social interaction. They may be unable to judge a person's age or gender, unable to read some facial expressions, nor able to recognise and interpret body language, nor recognise objects such as cars or places. They may appear rude or disinterested.

I quizzed Maxi about it.

'It must be difficult for you when you can't remember who someone is.'

'It is annoying,' she said. 'It can spoil movies and plays, unless I have help. I have been fortunate to have you.'

She seemed unaware it was a distinct condition.

I wondered if there was anything I could do to help her and asked Stan.

'She has difficulty keeping tabs on other runners during a race,' he said. 'I didn't realise it had a label.'

'Could it be a problem for her when she has to recognise other runners and officials?'

'I haven't noticed it,' he said.

'There's also the social side.'

'Parties are a challenge for her,' Stan said. 'She's popular but she prefers her own company. She's a bit of a loner.'

'Perhaps she finds it hard to connect?'

'She is coping, Jack. It is not a problem.'

'Should we talk to her about it?'

'I can't see it would do any good. She might use it as an excuse for giving up trying, making it worse.'

'If she was more aware,' I said, 'she could deal with challenges better.'

'It depends on how much you think she's missing out on. She already has strategies, such as getting me to tell her the names of other runners. I don't think she's missing out on much.'

'She may have gotten by so far, but it might not be so easy in future,' I said. 'Could she see a specialist?'

'It could put her off her stride. Talk to her and find out if she wants to see an expert.'

'OMG,' she said, when I told her it was a recognised condition. 'It explains everything, how I walk past friends and get people's names wrong. What can I do about it?'

'You could see a specialist.'

'What would they do?'

'I'm not sure. Maybe suggest strategies for coping.'

'I can cope. I don't need a specialist.'

'That's okay,' I said. 'There's plenty of time. Don't think you're on your own with this. I'll keep an eye on you.'

'Thank you. I'll decide what to do after my next run.'

A few weeks later at home, I noticed she was putting on lipstick without a mirror.

'You seem to remember your own face well enough,' I said, joking.

She didn't smile.

'Would you be able to shave in the dark?' she asked me.

'No.'

'You would remember the ins and outs of your own face, wouldn't you?'

'No.'

'That's how others' faces are for me. I don't remember them. I can look at a face I have known for years but in a new context, be unable to remember their name or who they are.'

'Does that make you feel bad?'

'It used to, but when I start talking with them, then I remember their names. Only a few people feel snubbed.'

'Is it a problem?'

'Not really, except when I don't remember them, I avoid people.'

'That's not friendly. Did you take up marathon running because it's solo?'

'No. I like to socialise with other runners.'

'Do you have any other strategies?'

'I like to have someone I can ask who people are, the way I do with you.'

'During a race, don't you need to know what's going on?'

'Ideally, yes, because competitors have different strengths and weaknesses and it helps to know who I am up against.'

'It's a challenge for you to get savvy with who's who in a race.'

'I can get by, like I do at the movies, with your help'

I was her coach and I could help her put names to faces if needed. So far she had performed unsupported without incident. Maxi liked me watching over her and I felt wanted.

CHAPTER 45

Jack called the next meeting of Team Maxi on an evening two weeks after the Brisbane Marathon. The coaches and researchers were there as Jack passed around some light snacks and candy bars.

'Maxi, how did you think you went in The Brisbane?' said Alice, munching. 'I saw you at the 30 kilometres station. You were lying 6th. You must have made a huge effort to win from there.'

'I finished 10 metres ahead in 2h25,' said Maxi. 'Second was Heidi Gartner and third Carol Kotan.'

They applauded her.

'Not bad for a first marathon,' said Blake. 'How many were you up against?'

'About 1500.'

'That's awesome.'

They all clapped again.

'Patti has created a wonderful website for fans to use,' said Maxi.

'Fans are cool,' said Blake, fanning himself with his hand. It was a warm evening and the church nave was without air-conditioning.

Patti told them that the website had information, images and events for reporters and activities for Maxi's fans to find out about her and what she was doing. Jack had collated her performance history. Maxi's advertising manager had posted details of sponsors. Donations could be made online, with a portion going to runners in developing countries. Patti posted photos of Maxi's foods and her recipes and apparel, with her comments on nutrition quality.

'Fans will love it,' said Corvid.

'I didn't do it all myself,' said Patti. 'I hired a digital marketing agency.'

'You've established my brand,' Maxi said. 'Now, all I have to do is keep on winning.'

'I want fans to feel they're sharing in Maxi's life and success,' Patti said. 'Can I post details of her training?'

'Not yet,' said Jack. 'Our methods are secret.'

'They're so secret, even we don't know them,' said Blake.

'That's because some of our methods are experimental,' Jack said. 'They haven't been tried out so we won't be telling the world about them until we know they work.

'Maxi's next race is the National marathon in Melbourne. She could be favourite but there's stiff competition. Aisha Sayat has run faster.'

'How did Sayat go in Brisbane?'

'She was sick on the day and didn't start,' said Maxi.

'How fast is she?'

'She's National champion, with 2h23 in Sydney last year. If I can run more in flow, I might be able get in front.'

'Maxi, would you tell us about your 'flow'?' said Derek.

'Two weeks ago, in the Brisbane, I was 'in flow' from about 5 kilometres out to 15 kilometres.'

'Did it feel good?' asked Jack.

'Yes, a sort of stoned ultra-realism. I've been practicing with Dr Minami. She calls it 'It,''' she said.

'Is 'It' like 'in flow' and the same as 'in the zone'?' asked Blake.

'The psychologist Mihaly calls it 'flow' and runners call it 'in the zone' or 'runners' high', said Alice. 'No-one so far has explained exactly what it is and how it improves performance.'

'Would you explain how it helped you,' said Derek.

'I had a fast start. I concentrated on achieving my target rate and got into flow. I didn't acknowledge the pain and cruised 'in flow' until about 15 kilometres. Then I was uncomfortable and got thrown out of 'flow'. After that, I was doing it tough. Near the end, I gave it everything I had, took the lead and stayed there.'

'Yes.'

'Are we sure it's a real effect?' said Stan sceptically. 'Could locking on to her goal really cause her to run faster?'

'It's a psychological condition of her mind that could cause her to run faster,' Alice said.

'Have any benefits been demonstrated?' asked Stan.

'It is contentious, but I'm convinced it has helped Maxi,' Alice said.

'I've experienced flow at my desk,' said Jack, 'but it may not be the same as Maxi's flow. It seemed to help me get work done. Did 'flow' help you, Maxi?'

'It's hard to say. It was comfortable and enjoyable.'

'Flow' might not do any harm,' said Stan. 'Whether it does any good is a different matter.'

'Do psychologists have any ideas how 'flow' works, Alice?' asked Jack.

'Have you ever been absorbed in something you like doing, using your skills, with all your attention taken and before you know it, several hours have whizzed past?' said Alice. 'You were 'in 'flow'. Most of us experience it from time to time in our work, recreation or hobby.'

'Like meditation?'

'It is a type of meditation,' said Alice. 'It's effortless and absorbing, enabling enjoyable timeless concentration, freeing up attention and energy to obtain more achievement. Mihaly called it 'optimal experience'. It's a sort of deep immersion characterised by automaticity. Self-consciousness disappears and sense of time becomes distorted.

'A runner's striding can seem predictable and boring, but 'in flow' it's not. Waiting for the kettle to boil can seem interminable but a year can flash past 'in flow' at an Antarctic station. Flow superimposes meaning that can transcend time.'

'Is it a type of play?'

'Yes. You're playing when you lose yourself in what you're doing, forgetting yourself and forgetting time. You're in it for goal achievement, not to get a reward.'

'Is 'flow' a mind trip, like a rush or intoxication?' asked Blake.

'An athlete in 'flow' can perform arduous feats, overcoming stress and pain by releasing adrenalin, like a buzz. But it isn't a trip.

236

The higher plane is goal-focussed and anything else is a distraction. A runner in flow would be diverted by background music.'

'I'm sceptical that 'flow' is real,' said Stan. 'When a runner performs well, they often tell us they were in 'flow', when it could be the exuberance of running fast and easily. A runner may convince herself that her buzz was 'flow' and that it caused her performance to be good, when in fact the buzz was caused by exhilaration from performance.'

'It is a 'post hoc ergo propter hoc' fallacy to confuse an effect with its cause,' said Jack. 'The notion that 'flow' induces high performance could be a tautology. They might even occur simultaneously.'

When the others' understanding was different, Jack had to hold back his disagreement. Their reflex was to deny his differing opinions because his credentials had yet to be established and their support was slow. But their acceptance improved as they realised Maxi respected his skills as an investigator and convenor of their meetings.

'It's not a tautology,' Alice said. 'Being 'in flow' and performing well are not the same thing. Being 'in flow' is a definite psychological condition.'

'You mean there's an organic change in the person when 'in flow'?' Jack asked.

'Yes, in the brain, affecting enjoyment, sense of time and performance. Neuroscience has observed certain changes in brains 'in flow'.'

'How does 'flow' work?' he asked.

'There are many theories but no incontrovertible explanation,' said Alice. 'It's often that way in psychology. The Bannister Effect could have been his overcoming choking.'

'Does it matter?'

'Yes,' said Alice. 'When we understand it, we may be able to exploit it. We could train her to control it and use it to enhance her performance.'

'Could 'flow' be a placebo?' asked Stan. 'If she is enjoying her performance and assumes it is because she is 'in flow', could she go on to a better performance?'

'It can't be ruled out,' Alice said. 'But I doubt 'flow' is as imaginary as you suggest.'

''Flow' benefits many facets of performance,' said Jack.

'Jack is right,' said Coach Derek. 'I'm sure the 'flow' effect is real. A runner 'in flow' can be so engaged in a race that they forget the pain of running, lose track of time and are surprised how far they've come.'

'I want that,' said Maxi. 'I want to get into 'flow' early and stay there as long as possible.'

'The literature has several types of 'flow', said Alice. 'Maxi, you've already experienced the Siri Lindley type, running at the edge, unleashing yourself and smashing through barriers. In The Brisbane you ran for 15 kilometres with total goal commitment. With training, could you extend it to the whole 42 kilometres?'

'Maybe,' Maxi said. 'It's not something I can turn on when I want to.'

'Siri Lindley used to choke until Frank Sutton set her difficult challenges,' said Jack.

'There's a theory that marathon runners are running away from something unpleasant in their home life,' said Coach Derek. 'Siri Lindley's parents divorced when she was four and she blamed herself, with feelings of inadequacy that made her throw herself into running and choke.'

'Maxi grieved when she was 5, after her mother died,' said Stan, kindly. 'You are over it now, aren't you Maxi?'

'I do think about Mum sometimes and get sad. It doesn't affect my running.'

'Maybe subconsciously?' asked Derek.

'The memories pain her,' said Stan.

'Sorry,' said Derek. 'Yes, of course. Maybe Maxi could unleash herself from the past the way Siri did.'

'Sutton angered her with difficult tasks.'

'Maxi got pretty mad running up that dune before she bonked,' said Jack. 'Maybe she's already unleashed,'

'Ask me,' said Maxi.

'Are you unleashed Maxi?'

'Yes,' she snarled.

Everyone laughed.

'She has been running well in 'flow' but we would like her to do it for longer,' said Jack.

'Could we train her to avoid whatever it was that threw her out of 'flow' in The Brisbane?' Derek said.

'I lost flow at 15 kms when the pain got to me. I couldn't get back for the rest of the race. My attention switched from my goal to my legs.'

'She has to stay concentrated on her goal,' said Alice.

'Could she top up her concentration, or stop herself being distracted?' asked Jack.

'Same difference,' said Derek. 'Her training should rehearse race conditions.' He turned to Maxi. 'What training would you prefer for the National?'

The four coaches looked at Maxi.

'Let's see,' she said coyly. 'Stan can challenge me like Sutton did Siri. Derek can train me to perceive less pain. Jack is going to train my mind to 'flow' over the pain. Riko will train a whole body spiritual response. Is that everything?'

'Not quite,' said Patti.

'Oh. Sorry, Patti, I didn't mean to leave you out. Would you feed me up for the best health and performance possible, in training as well as in the race? Thank you.

'I don't know which of you is more important to me but I'm grateful that you all came this evening. Thank you everybody.'

'What is your goal for the National, Maxi?' said Riko.

'I want to get my PB down by 5 minutes to 2h20,' Maxi said.

'Great,' said Coach Derek 'That goal has to be etched into your training. We will elaborate it in exercises and rehearsals.'

'You should get enjoyment from running 'in flow',' said Jack. 'Flow' has existential nowness, the way a musician plays in an orchestra. There's joy in being connected, keeping in time with others, the way musicians are inspired by audiences.

'In endurance running, 'flow' is a long phase of concentrated performance unmarred by disruption. A tennis player can stay 'in flow' for several hours. A pole-vaulter can jump half-hourly, staying 'in flow' throughout a half-day of competition, without disruption. Maxi can aim to stay 'in flow' throughout a race.'

'Zen is very powerful,' said Sensei Minami. 'Her actions will be stylised and automatic. She can learn to focus her mind totally on accomplishing her goal, using tunnel vision to shut out thoughts that distract her with dreams. She shouldn't imagine herself on a dais receiving a medal. Wishing won't help her run faster. Nor will thinking about breaking the record. She should concentrate on how she is delivering her performance.'

'Let's finish there for today,' Jack said. 'We've talked about some broad concepts of 'flow'. I am fascinated by the performance improvement and timeless aspects of 'flow'. We won't expect Maxi to join all the dots for her second marathon. We can do fine-tuning with her when we see how she goes.'

'The passionate mission of this group is to support Maxi in learning to run 'in flow', concentrated on her goal. We haven't experience of this technique used in this way and we have to be cautious, considerate and creative.'

'Thanks, everyone' said Maxi. 'I'm going for a run. Does anyone want to come with me?'

Jack, Blake and Alice went to change into jogging clothes.

CHAPTER 46

Jack observed his own behaviour to understand how he got more done 'in flow'. Without a deadline, time seemed to drag and his performance wilted. In the vacuous sterility of a waiting room, or in a queue, or at the traffic lights, when he was hyped up in flow, he clock-watched with his brain processing capacity exceeding the stimulation load, waiting with every minute seeming to last forever.

Out of 'flow', his time passed unevenly and less pleasantly. For example, if he had been busy and his mind was revved up when he went to bed, he might lie awake with his mind working, recalling events, planning responses and anticipating outcomes. In a period of 15 minutes by the clock, he might think in detail about many different situations. He generated thoughts, worrying uselessly. He did not feel tired. Although he wanted to sleep, the time might crawl around to 1.30 am with his brain jerking through a maze of worries.

It was better, though, to ignore the clock and get out of bed. Seated at his desk, Jack would lose himself in his work, 'in flow', enjoying the timelessness of the 'block universe', in which everything existed in the present. Time passed without him noticing.

Sometimes he stayed 'in flow' for many hours. His enjoyment of his work had an obsessive quality. It was different from the dependant workaholism he had experienced when he was younger. Now he had a definite goal, was using his skills and enjoying himself. Nor was it like his time addiction earlier, when he checked his watch continually to see if he was on schedule. Now he was free from the control of others. He concentrated and willed himself into 'flow' because he wanted to achieve something.

Time would pass more fluidly than Slessor's 'little fidget wheels' could tally.

'When Michelangelo sculpted David, he was probably not on a time schedule nor following a plan,' Jack thought.

Michelangelo probably achieved his artistic goals 'in flow'. Rather than time proceeding linearly with a pendulum beat, as in most scientific subject-object dualisms, an artist in 'flow' could merge their being into the subject, using the material and applying the technology, the way Jackson Pollock sloshed paint and spread it spontaneously across his canvass. The art had its own time, without the artist's conscious intention.

When he was 'in flow', Jack disconnected from his surroundings. A friend phoned him when he was at his desk working.

'How is the flood?' she asked.

'What flood?'

He looked out the window and saw his mailbox disappearing under a brown torrent. There had been hours of heavy rain, but he had been oblivious. He could have been in danger.

'It's easy when you're 'in flow' to be so blinkered that you shut out changes you should respond to,' said Coach Derek. 'Maxi has to be ready throughout her run to observe anything going wrong and apply alternative tactics. She has to rehearse responses in her mind. When she is racing, she has to be able to respond automatically to every possible eventuality.'

He had watched Maxi closely and observed that when she went into 'flow' her striding rate quickened, maintaining the same stride length and speeding up, as if with more power. She got more done before deadlines, doing more in the same time, in the moment, in a succession of moments, each of which lifted her performance to achievement of her goal.

'Goal differentiation as a succession of targets could explain the value of 'flow',' he thought. *'It is not a mechanism for faster running but demonstrates the autotelic nature of 'flow' described by Mihaly.'*

Jack decided to present his ideas when the team met again after a month.

'Maxi has trained steadily since our last meeting,' Jack said, starting the meeting. 'She goes to the national in Melbourne in two months. It will be her second marathon. She has several learning strands to bring together in her training.

'Public performers do amazing feats on stage within tight deadlines. Michael Jackson's control of time in his Moon Walk dancing presented highly rehearsed time-defying motion. Perhaps Maxi can run as timelessly, by intense rehearsal 'in flow'. She can control her performance time.'

'Are you sure I can control my time?' Maxi asked. 'It seems to me that when I run with more effort, my time reduces. Time is passing anyway, I just take less of it.'

'That's correct.,' said Jack. 'Your performance time is an outcome and your effort controls it.'

'My goal is 2h20,' she said to Jack. 'It is 5 minutes faster than my PB.'

'If you concentrate and run hard, you can lower your time and achieve your goal.'

It was an intense programme to prepare Maxi to run the National only five months after the Brisbane Marathon. The coaching team scheduled training runs to expose her to conditions she might encounter. She would practice running in 'flow', goal-focussed, with her effort controlling her time.

CHAPTER 47

Maxi was flying with Jack and Stan to Melbourne for the National. Jack's family had wanted to go with them, but Jack had talked them out of it.

'There wouldn't be much to see,' he said. 'Will you come instead to London next year if we get through?'

'Okay, but we'll be watching you on the box.'

Now they were in the airport coffee shop waiting to be called.

'You have a couple of days to acclimatise,' Jack said to Maxi. 'I can hardly wait to find out if your training has worked.'

'Don't expect a miracle,' she said. 'I doubt I can pull 'in flow' performance out of a hat, in the first race I try.'

'It has been getting easier, hasn't it?'

'Yes, but I may not be able to adopt the same mindset for the race as I've been using in training.'

'It should be easier to concentrate,' said Jack.

'Ignoring the pain will be hard.'

'Thinking about pain accomplishes nothing. You have to stop thinking about it, forget your worries, get comfortable, then 'flow' will happen.'

''Flow' is like a tightrope. It's easy to lose your balance.'

'There's no need for pessimism,' said Jack. 'It's early days. Our work with 'flow' is in its infancy. It could take years before you can get into flow on demand and stay there.'

'Jack is convinced that 'flow' is the solution to improving my performance,' thought Maxi. *'Distancing myself from my body is counter-intuitive for me, but I trust him and I'll try it.'*

244

''Flow' might have an effect after all,' said Stan when they discussed her progress. 'These numbers from her training show she speeded up since The Brisbane. She shouldn't have any difficulty in this race.'

Three days later, in the National, Maxi unleashed herself into flow from the start, keeping to her goal speed, allowing others to pass.

'How is it?' Jack asked at the drinks station after 10 kilometres.

'Good,' she smiled. Her time had flown by enjoyably and she was in a second group, 100 metres behind the leaders.

At the halfway drinks station, Jack was waiting.

'Who's in front?' she asked.

'There's Sayat, Omigachi and several others,' he said.

'Aisha Sayat?' said Maxi. 'Shit. I didn't see her go past. Her PB is two minutes faster than mine. I'll try to catch her.'

'I'm chasing Sayat,' she said to Jack.

'You're on target,' he said. 'Don't speed up unless you're sure you can keep it up.'

'I'll wait until the last few kilometres.'

The pace of the leaders was fast and Maxi's body and legs hurt beyond her previous experience. She lost concentration, slipped out of 'flow' and dropped back a little, but the two in front eased off too.

By the 30 kilometres station, Omigachi had faded, but Maxi toiled, having caught up but unable to gain on the runner she assumed was Aisha Sayat, 20 metres in front.

'My legs are a bit wobbly,' she thought. *'I could be close to bonking but I've slowed down and will put everything into reaching the line.'*

Sayat increased her lead to 200m and finished strongly in 2h20. Maxi ran in with 2h22.

'I am so proud of her,' Jack thought. *'If this is a dream, then Maxi doesn't have to win. She is perfect in spirit.'*

'You were a tad faster than in the Brisbane Marathon,' Stan said. 'It is good enough to nominate for the London Marathon.'

'Do you think I choked?' she asked him defensively.

'Did you?' he asked.

'No. If I hadn't slowed down, I would have bonked. It was that close.'

'You ran well today,' he said. 'I'm looking forward to London. You're going to win.'

Maxi glowed. Stan believed in her and she trusted him.

'I was able to get into 'flow' when I wanted to,' she said. 'When my legs acted up near the end, it threw me out.'

''Flow' may have helped you more than you think,' said Jack. 'If you had run the second half 'in flow', you would have won today.'

The result appeared in The Australian newspaper the next morning, with a photo of Sayat, Maxi and Omigachi on the winners' dais.

SAYAT AND FLEET SET FOR LONDON MARATHON
Defending champion Ethiopian Aisha Sayat sprinted the last 2 kilometres at the National Athletics Championships in Melbourne today, after running the first 40 in a time close to the Australian record. Her time of 2h20 qualifies her to run in the prestigious London Marathon in two months' time, where she will compete with Indihra Patel(2h17) Kenyan Vero Lamu (2h16) and Russia's Orva Kopotlek (2h18). Second at the finish was Maxi Fleet (2h22) from Caloundra, who also qualifies for London. It was Maxi's second marathon, after winning The Brisbane Marathon in March and the National Half Marathon Championship last season. Her times have shown a steady improvement. The competition in London will be fierce, but these two Australian women are no slouches.

Alvin Weller, Newscom.

'The stage is set for a battle,' Jack said.

'I'm not sure I'm up to The London,' said Maxi.

'You will be after you've practised.'

'I'm going to take a break and stay at home.'

'How long for?'

'I don't know.'

She seemed tired.

'I'll call you every day.'

'Thank you, Jack, but no. I want to be alone for a while. I'll call you.'

CHAPTER 48

After two weeks without hearing from Maxi, I was missing her and becoming anxious. When I called, her phone was switched off. I left a message. Then Patti called.

'It's about Maxi,' she said.

'Is something wrong?'

'I'm not sure. She spends all day in her bedroom. She's stopped running.'

'Is she ill?'

'She might be depressed.'

My heart sank.

'She won't talk to me or Stan. She won't go to a doctor. Would you talk to her? Don't let her know I called you.'

'I'll try. Can I come over now? You can say I called to find out how she was and you asked me over.'

'I'll tell her you're coming. Can you stay for dinner?'

'Maxi, Jack's here,' Patti called as she let me in.

The girl who came tentatively down the stairs was not the Maxi I knew; she was hesitant and hurting, a shadow of the way she had been at the National two weeks ago.

'Hello, Maxi.'

'Hello, Jack,' she said dully.

'How are you?' I asked.

'Not good.'

'How do you feel?'

'I'm not sure.'

"Is it anything to do with the National? You ran well.'

'No, I'm just having some time to myself.'

'Why?'

'I want to centre myself. The London will take everything I have.'

She seemed reluctant to talk. If there were just the two of us, she might tell me her problem.

'Would you come for a walk? We'll be back soon, Patti.'

We walked to her local park. It was a sunny afternoon. The new Maxi had none of her former talkativeness and ebullience. It was like being with a stranger.

'I've been missing you heaps,' I said.

She didn't say anything.

'How do you feel about us now?' I asked.

'I don't know.'

'Tell me what's going on with you?'

No answer.

'Has something happened?'

'It's gone,' she said so quietly I could hardly hear.

'What's gone?'

'My running. I've stopped training. I can't go on.'

'You'll come back to it.'

'No. I've stopped forever.'

I paused, thinking how to best respond to this awful idea.

'Why, when you could be the fastest woman marathon runner ever?'

'I'm not that good.'

'But you are. Everyone says so. You've been winning.'

'After the National, I realised I was ordinary. I'm not sure I can get to the Olympics.'

'Do you have to have certainty? Being a top athlete isn't a shoo in. It's precarious. Can't you be like Schrodinger's cat, with your outcome either winning or losing? One will occur: losing is a risk you can afford to take. You're so near the top. You were going to stop fearing uncertainty. Well now is the time to face up to it! '

'Stepping onto the international stage requires more courage than I have. I can't go on with it.'

'Did you imagine it would get easier nearer the top?'

'You seem conflicted by having a goal to be the best and coming second in a race. It's called cognitive dissonance. You don't always have to be best!'

She didn't answer.

'You're choking in your career. You have to either start winning or stop thinking you're best. Could you win? Would losing be so bad? Can you look at it like you did bonking, with nothing to fear but fear itself? You've managed your running career well so far.'

'No, Jack. My mind is made up. I'm quitting.'

Her voice was quiet and husky, shaping the words as if exhausted. I put an arm around her shoulders. She didn't pull away.

'What happened to you Maxi? I agreed to wash your vegetables. What other problems do you have?'

'I'm sorry I was so demanding. I use people. You would never be happy with me.'

'Nonsense,' I said. 'The time I've been with you has been the happiest of my life.'

She looked down at the ground. 'I'm not good enough,' she said. 'People are making sacrifices for me and they'll come to nothing. It's not just you. There's Mum and Patti, and the Team Maxi crew. You're all giving up too much for me.'

'You sound like Woody Allen, full of doubts about yourself, apologising for being alive. Don't you realize that we *like* helping you. We do it for ourselves, not for you. You brighten our drab lives. You make us happy. You're an amazing runner and a wonderful person. Tell the Woody Allen on your shoulder to shut up. He's pulling you down.'

I walked with her back to her parents' house. I stayed for dinner and then went home.

I came back the next day and we talked more about her concerns. She wanted to be the best and earn adulation. If she had liked herself more, it would have been narcissism. Her bubble of self-confidence seemed to have collapsed into Cold Feet.

She raised her eyes to mine.

'I'm not worthy of you. I'm not as good as you think I am.'

She wasn't fishing for a compliment.

'Self-doubt is quite natural but your performance times show you should be confident.'

She looked at the ground.

'I can't do it anymore,' she said.

'You can't quit! You can take the girl out of running but you can't take running out of the girl. You would be miserable. What are you going to do if you quit?'

'I'll find something.'

'What about us?'

She looked at me blankly, as if she hadn't thought about it.

'Without running, our romance will be over, won't it?' Maxi asked. 'Isn't it better to face that now before we get more involved?'

'No. Your journey as a runner is part way through. When you reach the end of the course, whether you are a winner or a loser, I will still love you. You'll always be the runner I love, even if you give up running. I believe you are a wonderful person with an exciting future and I want to spend my life with you.'

'Do you mean it?' she said.

She was weeping and her resolve seemed to melt. We had a long hug.

'When Aisha Sayat blasted past me, I lost confidence in myself,' she said. 'She's so good.'

'Maxi choked,' I thought. *'She could have won.'*

'You're better than Sayat,' I said. 'You were only a few metres behind her. She won't beat you next time. You've been improving and you'll continue to get better and better.'

'Maybe,' she said quietly to herself. 'I could try. I think part of the problem was I didn't recognise who had come up behind me and I let her get past. When you told me it was her in front, it rattled me. If I had known it was her earlier, I would have stayed with her. By the time I realised it was too late. I couldn't catch her.'

'Do you think a specialist could help you with it?'

'Thanks for your concern, but I can handle proso-whatsit, if that's what it is. I have learned not to be rattled by being overtaken. From now on, my running will be to reach my goal, not to finish in a certain position.'

Her eyes were still red from crying, but she had brightened up.

We went back to the house and I stayed for dinner with the family. She ate heartily. When she had finished eating, she stood up.

'I'm going for a run,' she said.

'On yer, Maxi.'

Everyone clapped.

I hugged her and kissed her.

I left then. On the way out I asked her. 'Will you stay at my place tomorrow?'

'Okay,' she said. 'I'll come after QIS.'

'There's a team meeting on Monday.'

'I'll get ready,' said Maxi. 'The team is my secret weapon.'

'I want you to take 'flow' up to a higher level,' I said. 'Too high for you to run down again.'

'Thank you for supporting me,' she said. 'You carried me through. My hopes and ambitions had folded, but you lifted me up. You gave me back my self-respect. Thank you.'

'It's okay. It's great to have you back.'

I went with her to see her other coaches. She explained to them what she had been going through.

'Maxi has taken a couple of weeks off from training,' I said. 'She is now back into it and has started preparing for the London Marathon.'

CHAPTER 49

Maxi bounced back into training for the London Marathon.

She stayed at my place through the week, a blissful time together. The barrier of our time apart after the National quickly dissolved and she recovered her poise. Her nose and upper face were sprinkled with fine freckles. She seldom looked in mirrors or wore cosmetics. Her ponytail was trimmed, infrequently, by a friend. Her eyes were deep-set with small furrows arching across between the twin barrels of her piercing gaze. She addressed events and people head on, giving them uninterrupted attention. She looked great and was perfect.

The psychologist Maslow defined outer beauty as having three elements: form, symmetry and balance. Maxi had all three in spades. Her outer form manifested inner spiritual beauty, that of a performer. She had style like Madonna and Taylor Swift, an all-round symmetry that caught your eye and kept it on her. She wasn't at all narcissistic, too active to be self-absorbed. Between performances, she was preparing for the next one. She would practice until her routine was perfectly balanced and incognisant of time. She lived to perform, a rare and exotic beauty able to hold millions enthralled.

'If I had to be with someone else, they would have to be exactly like you,' I said. 'You're perfect for me.'

She was not without flaws. Her ego grew and she preferred to be in control of proceedings. She was prickly, even tyrannical, at times holding her entourage in an iron grip, but she always treated me with respect and courtesy.

She was a star who shone for others. Her fans adored her and travelled around the globe to watch her run.

Her running performances expressed in her carefully rehearsed art. In these sessions, her persona seemed to adapt to a form she customised. Maxi was transcending from externally motivated performer to public icon.

CHAPTER 50

Jack was uncertain how much Maxi had been helped by flow in Melbourne.

'The first half was a breeze,' Maxi said. 'I made heavy going of the second half. Having Aisha Sayat in front threw me.'

He had not found research explaining how flow could cause an increase in physical performance.

'I want to find out how 'flow' works,' Jack told Maxi. 'It could be physiology, neuroscience or psychology, or something else.'

'How would that help?' she said,

'When something is understood, it can be controlled. When Newton had identified and explained gravity, ballistics and rocket science were developed.'

'Could flow really be as profound as gravity?'

'Absolutely. It could liberate human performance with consequences as far-reaching as the evolution theory was for ecology.'

'Hmm,' she said. 'You want flow to be part of a bigger picture, like my running is survival of the fittest.'

'Exactly. Flow could be one of many adaptations for survival.'

Jack talked with her then about how the flow phenomenon was manifest in many different situations of human individual performance in time, or extreme achievement. Jack looked for the effects of 'flow' when time for an activity was limited, such as in a race, or when escape from danger was wanted. The proponent would minimize their time to race a distance, or alternatively, to survive danger for as long as possible, as in gliding or extreme free diving. The condition that was essential was goal focus.

'Perhaps you can use flow to control your personal best,' he said.

'How could controlling 'flow' reduce my marathon time?' she asked.

'You have controlled choking and bonking by experience and understanding,' he said. "Why not control the whole performance with flow?'

'Can I use 'flow' like that, to control everything?'

'Why not?' Jack said. 'You can habituate to engaging fully in tasks, always concentrating, stopping clock watching, regulating your activities by when you start, not by duration.'

'What difference would that make?'

'You could be 'in flow' more often, when you wanted.'

'Are you sure it can be controlled like that?'

'I'm not sure, but I am trying it out on myself. Besides totally engaging at work, I am starting to go to bed and get up when I feel like it.'

'Bloody hell, you're going to be a pain to share a bed with,' Maxi said.

'Please try it. We can get into a phase that suits us both better.'

'Okay. But if it doesn't work for me, you may have to sleep in another bed.'

Their synchronisation had begun.

'I thought you'd be here an hour ago,' Maxi said when he met her at QIS the next day.

'Sorry. Time got away from me.'

He had stopped wearing a watch because he was habituating to being in 'flow'.

'We should have arranged a time to meet.'

'I don't want to be limited like that. Could I call you when I'm ready to leave, to see if it's convenient for you?'

'Do you imagine your time is more important than mine?'

'Of course not. It might be better if you call me when you're available.'

'Do you want us to meet only when neither of us has anything better to do? Our time together shouldn't be our least common denominator.'

'Maybe not.'

'Certainly not,' she said sharply. 'Have our activities together become a last resort?'

'No.'

'Being together should come first. We should fix a time in advance.'

'I don't want to have to fit my life around anything.'

'If you're going to be with me, that is going to happen,' she said fiercely.

He couldn't see a way around it, so he surrendered.

'I suppose in a relationship there have to be limitations on 'flow',' he said, musing.

'Duh. At last you've worked it out. Flow is solo; a relationship is not solo.'

Jack's interest in personal time led him to home in on the brain. Marathon runners broke records regularly as if the human race was somehow improving. Did superior athletic prowess reside in athletes' minds? Mihaly had described 'flow' as a psychological effect. Could 'flow' affect Maxi's mind? Could her time pass more slowly in flow, enabling her to get more done, run harder and finish earlier?

His investigation had now entered a new phase: testing. His hypothesis was that 'flow' was causing Maxi to run marathons faster. If he could demonstrate that 'flow' reduced her performance time, it could benefit performers in other fields besides athletics, such as sport, education, entertainment, personal health and general employment.

There wasn't enough data to separate a 'flow' effect from the background noise of runner improvement and changes in running techniques. Marathon running was changing. The men's record of 2h58 in 1896 had reduced to 2h01 in 2018, an average improvement of about 0.5 minutes each year. For the women's marathon record, the time had reduced more sharply, from 2h46 in 1970, to 2h17 set by Mary Keitany in 2017. Although it wasn't certain that the improvements had resulted from 'flow', it couldn't be dismissed as a possible cause.

Jack's task in measuring when a performer was in flow was difficult. No line was crossed in going into or coming out of flow, athletes had probably been getting into flow forever, but it had only been discussed and recorded recently. Developing flow as a controllable technique would be resisted by others trying to use the same or similar techniques. There could be a different technique for every runner.

'If you are the only one your flow technique works for, so much the better,' he said.

'Then it won't be a technique, it will be my ability,' she said.

He had leapt at the opportunity to coach Maxi in physics, partly because he loved physics. His interest in metaphysics of time had led him to study running and then to investigate 'flow'. He had realised that Maxi would be an ideal subject to test for effects of 'flow'. Her 1500 metre runs were done in just over 4 minutes, with insufficient time to determine effects of flow. Maxi's change to running marathons meant he could test her for runs lasting over two hours and his conclusions would be more confident. Of the many types of human performance that could benefit from 'flow', a marathon was most controlled.

CHAPTER 51

In the weeks since the National Championship, Maxi had filled out between her muscles and tendons. Jack was concerned: a marathon runner couldn't carry luggage.

'She's a bit buxom,' he said to Stan

'She'll soon run that off.'

'She could be eating too much. Have you mentioned it to her?'

'No. You do it.'

'Yes, Jack,' Maxi said, testily. 'I'm 3 kilos overweight. Patti is cutting back on my carbs. There's no need for you to be concerned.'

He did not mention it again.

She was often hungry but knew that carrying dead weight could jeopardize her performance. She was like an Apollo spacecraft, carrying a minimum of energy to burn at each stage, jettisoning wastes, retaining only enough fuel for brief de-orbit at the destination and for a re-entry burn. She took with her only enough to get to the finish line: fat and muscles that would not be used were not taken.

She ate only the foods Patti provided and soon was her lithe self again.

Jack and Maxi waited for the next Team Maxi meeting as the others arrived.

'Maxi is looking particularly svelte,' said Blake. 'Don't you agree, Jack?'

Jack was irritated by Blake's interest in his girlfriend.

'I hadn't noticed,' he said to Blake acidly. 'I don't objectify her the way you do.'

'Ouch,' Blake said.

It was their 6th team meeting.

'We are here to commence Maxi's campaign for the London Marathon,' said Jack. 'Maxi would you please tell everyone about Melbourne. Stan and I went, but the others need to know too.'

'I was stretched to be ready in time,' she said. 'I was recovering from The Brisbane.'

In top level marathon running, only one race per year was usual. Recovery, training and travel took many months.

'I prepared for a tough race and it was,' she said. 'It was only my second race at this distance and I was worried about burning out early. I planned to stay with Aisha Sayat because she had a PB like mine and was sure to be a front runner. But I didn't see her. I stayed with a group following the leaders. Pretty soon I slipped into flow and kept to my plan, staying behind, letting the front group get 100 metres ahead. I relaxed, felt great. I didn't notice time slipping by until just before halfway my legs began to hurt like hell. My mind hung up on the pain and it threw me out of flow and I stumbled to the halfway drinks station.

'Jack told me that Aisha Sayat was ahead. I hadn't seen her go past. She won last year in 2h23. I had intended to stay with her, but by this time she was well ahead of me in the front group. I had a few moments of panic. I wanted to quit but I wasn't going to let this race beat me and set off to close up to the runners in front.

'I kept putting my feet down one in front of the other. I tried to get my mind back to where it had been earlier, but I worried that I was doing something terrible to my body. This was the worst time.

'Seeing Stan and Jack at 30 kilometres was great. Thank you so much for being there, guys. It was downhill after that. When I realised I would finish, I went into 'flow' again and stayed in it until near the end of the race.

'With one kilometre to go I was 5th. I was only 200 metres behind the leaders but I had left it too late. I passed 3 of them, but Aisha Sayat was still 200 metres ahead, I couldn't catch her and I came in second. I was delighted because racing at this distance and level was new.'

She sat back and looked at Jack, who clapped with the others.

Only Stan and Jack knew Maxi had wanted to stay with Aisha Sayat but hadn't recognised her. When Jack had asked her if she wanted to see a specialist for her condition, she had declined. 'It won't happen again,' she said. 'I'm aware of the problem now.'

'Apart from that, I had a good run,' she said. The focus on will and on goals in my training had prepared me very well. I was 'in flow' for most of the first half and the last 10 km. In those sections, I sped along on a cloud of determination. Thank you, all of you, for your help with my training.'

Team Maxi discussed her preparation for The London Marathon.

'Thank you, Maxi. This evening we need to plan how to fine tune you, to run all the way in 'flow',' said Jack. 'Would you tell us what you were thinking about when you were 'in flow'?'

'I was thinking about achieving my goal. I was never bored, like when I run laps. I knew if I let my attention wander, I'd slow down. My body was sending pain signals, but I was used to them from training and paid no heed. Sure, if something new had started hurting, I would have considered slowing down, but it didn't happen. I kept my mind on performance.'

'Did you run to win?' asked Alice.

'I didn't think about that. I was trying to achieve my goal.'

'You succeeded very well,' said Riko Minami. 'In your first marathon, in Brisbane, you smashed through the mental barriers with a creditable time of 2h25. In Melbourne you ran a controlled race, staying in 'flow' for half the distance and bettering your time, to 2h22. In London, I want you to enjoy the whole race without driving yourself. Your goal requires willpower, not suffering. Your goal is to achieve happiness, not escape. You have to let go.'

'Isn't 'letting go' the antithesis of 'flow'?' Alice said. 'Doesn't letting go mean giving away concentration and self-control, letting it all hang out?'

'In an untrained person, letting go could be disastrous,' said Riko. 'For you Maxi, it would be unleashing your efficient biomechanical machinery into automaticity.'

'What's your goal for London?' Jack asked her.

'Last time I ran 2 hours and 22 minutes. I'll take off 5 minutes and try for 2h17.'

'Can you improve that much?'

'I'm not grabbing at too much. If I concentrate and stay 'in flow', I can do it. I'm feeling strong and fast.'

'Does anyone have any ideas for improving Maxi's performance even further?' said Jack.

'Could Maxi aim to stay 'in flow' for the entire race?' asked Alice.

'We can work on that,' said Coach Derek. 'There's a swag of tweaks we can try. We can raise her tolerance for perceived effort. Or she could practice kicking into sprints faster.'

'We can put those into her programme,' said Jack. 'Would the coaches stay to plan her training. Researchers, thank you for coming.'

Maxi wanted to train on six days per week, three at uni and three from home. She would average 100 kilometres per week, with a full marathon on Saturdays in a simulated London Marathon competition, to lengthen her bonk point. On the other days she would run 10 kilometre combinations, with various distances, climbs, paces and effort levels. The programme had variety to keep her interested. When she felt bored or stale, she would take time off and go to the beach or into the city with Jack.

They planned her training for the next 3 months. People's ideas didn't always agree, but Jack kept the discussion going until consensus was obtained and Maxi approved.

'If you don't state your objections and listen to the arguments, it's too late,' Jack told them. 'Here we put up or shut up.'

The meeting finished with Maxi's training agreed.

CHAPTER 52

'Riko's training is helping me a lot,' Maxi said to Jack the following week. 'Zen is perfect for getting into 'flow'.'

Riko had been having success with her other QIS athletes and her coaching was held in awe at the Institute. Maxi trained with her for an hour every day, either at the track or in the Japanese garden where she practiced archery.

When Maxi had loosed an arrow, Riko turned to her beaming.

'You did 'It', Maxi,' she said. 'Your mind had control. Congratulations.'

Maxi's shot seemed to her like the others, but Riko had sensed a spiritual change.

A news article in a running magazine reported on Maxi's training.

AUSTRALIAN WOMAN IN THE ZONE FOR LONDON MARATHON

Aisha Sayat (2h20) and Maxi Fleet (2h22) were 1st and 2nd in the marathon at the National Athletics Championships in Melbourne last year and have qualified to run in the London Marathon.

Sayat (Ethiopia) has been training near Addis Ababa.

'London will be tough,' Aisha said. 'The fastest women in the world will be running. I've been doing long runs in Bekoji, 3,200 metres above sea level, to build up my endurance. I have simulated the effort the race will demand. My training has habituated me to pain I could perceive in the race.'

For Fleet, who trains at Queensland Institute of Sport, it will be her third marathon ever.

'Whereas most runners train to cope with pain, I hope to improve my time in London by running enjoyably 'in flow',' Maxi said. 'A psychologist in the USA, called Mihaly, described the condition in his book 'Flow – The Psychology of Optimal Experience' published in 1990. My training is to run in 'flow' by mental control.'

Maxi Fleet is keeping details of her training methods confidential. Which will work better, her carrot, or Ali's stick?

The two will arrive in London this week to acclimatise for the event which will be held on April 26th. Live TV coverage is planned to be streamed on SBS, with the race starting at 8.00 am London time and 6.00 pm in Australia.

Alvin Weller, Newscom.

Maxi took her team with her to London, all except Alice, who had to attend a viva for her PhD in Brisbane. Maxi paid for them from a fund that received her appearance money, also donations from sponsors and well-wishers. An international marathon was audience-winning and brought a bonanza of international media attention, with fees for exclusive interviews.

Her team included a marketing coordinator, who reported to Jack. She franchised Maxi's brand logos and advertising images to marketers of food, footwear and clothing. Managers of products from cars to cornflakes sought to sponsor her. The amounts offered were increasing and difficult to resist. Advertising space on Maxi's running attire and merchandise attracted high prices. A prestige car manufacturer loaned her a limousine with chauffeur for her use in London, her name emblazoned on its bonnet and side panels. At the venues, fans queued up to buy expensive memorabilia and bling.

Patti went on a spending spree to Harrods and returned laden with designer clothes.

'How did you pay for that lot?' Maxi asked her.

'I borrowed your cards.'

'Patti!'

'You want me to look good, don't you?' said Patti. 'I've reached my credit limit. How about making me an advance?'

Patti was addicted to glamour and fashion and wore miniskirts, sheaths, high-low dresses and cutaway gowns.

'You dress like a whore,' Maxi said to her step-mother. 'Why don't you wear clothes for women your age?'

'You'd like to pigeon-hole me, wouldn't you? I dress to please me, not you.'

Maxi was pleased with the fan site Patti had created. Advertisers were contributing strongly to Maxi's finances. She gave in.

'I've paid off your card,' Maxi said. 'Thank you for your support.'

She retrieved her credit cards.

'Would you and Maxi like to come to a soccer match with Riko and me?' Derek asked Jack. 'It's Chelsea against Manchester United!'

'I'd love to go,' said Maxi. 'I've never been to a soccer match.'

'Nor me,' said Jack. 'It's a top game and Wembley Stadium will be electric.'

The crowd's excitement, mischief and noise amazed them.

'Why do people get so revved up?' asked Maxi.

'One theory of soccer crowd behaviour is that individuals lose personal consciousness and are controlled by a common mind,' said Jack. 'I suppose that's why they like to sing together. A different explanation is that people get the same stimuli and behave in similar ways, such as applauding. Another is that the crowd situation induces emotion, intensifying individual responses, which can lead to misbehaviour, such as angry fighting. Alternatively, it could be the Matthew Effect, with people imitating others and accreting into like-minded groups, such as fan groups. Jung's theory of unconscious induction proposes people have an innate ability for mob behaviour when inhibitions are removed, allowing irrationality and violence to rule. Their previous socialization becomes ineffective.'

'Not everyone is affected in the same way,' said Riko. 'Crowd responses can vary a lot during the game. If they perceive: 'Our team sucks!', their response may be subdued different from the violence when they perceive: 'We was robbed.''

265

'A group can enjoy various pleasures: sharing common experiences; being 'in flow' together, in music, sport, and work; or the sense of exhilaration they experience when their life together takes on full meaning,' said Derek. 'Communitas, or collective joy, is inspired fellowship. Watching sport and athletics can be mesmerising and joyful, when the group regard the athletes as part of their group or tribe, for example when watching a national team or the bonhomie of the Commonwealth games or the goodwill at the Paralympics.'

They enjoyed the soccer match, especially the singing and antics of crowd members. Jack explained to Maxi how primal atavism could cause powerful tribalism.

'What did you think of the crowd behaviour?' Jack asked her.

'It resonated with me once or twice,' she said. 'I wanted Chelsea to trash them.'

'Why, Chelsea? What's wrong with United?'

'I liked Chelsea's uniforms better.'

On the road, Maxi kept everyone at her beck and call. She was the performer who reigned supreme and she expected obedience. On the way to London, after Jack had spent most of the flight talking with Corvid, Maxi said to her: 'We won't be needing you any more on this trip. You can go home.'

The sharp dismissal shocked and hurt Corvid. She had dated Jack briefly six years earlier and had not realized how attached to Jack Maxi had become in the past two years. Corvid had become infatuated with Maxi herself. She was hurt when Maxi dismissed her. Jack intervened as Corvid was leaving to go to the airport.

'It was my fault,' he told Maxi. 'I tried to get your attention by chatting up Corvid. I was the disloyal one, not Corvid.'

'Why did you want my attention?'

'You were ignoring me and it hurt.'

'Don't ever try to get my attention by chasing another woman,' she said to Jack. 'If you do it again, I'll dump you. The way to get my attention is to show you appreciate me.'

Maxi's haughty manner was confronting, but Jack accepted it. She relented and Corvid stayed. Jack had to persuade Corvid to attend the next team meeting at the hotel.

'Maxi is a megalomaniac trying to control everyone,' Corvid said to Jack.

'Her greatest fear is worthlessness,' he said. 'She always has to look good and we took that away from her. She is vain and she's different. Can't you forgive her?'

'Hmmph.'

Corvid came to the meeting and she ceased to pursue Maxi.

During a timeout at QIS, Maxi came across Derek and Riko having sex in physiotherapy room.

'You can do that privately, not when you're coaching me,' she said. 'I need your attention on my training.'

It was unusual for her to give her coaches orders, but she was the performer and they respected her right to call anything that detracted from achievement of her goal. They could not have relationships that intruded into Maxi's space and would displease her. She was the super-being they had created.

CHAPTER 53

At Heathrow, a crowd with Australian flags waved and yelled welcome.

'I didn't know there were so many expats,' said Maxi.

'Some have come over with us,' said Jack.

'Why have they come all this way to watch me run?' she asked Jack. 'What is it to them?'

'They come from where you do and share in your greatness,' Jack said. 'The young ones love you because you're following your dreams and doing what makes you happy. They hope to do the same one day. Your striving inspires them.'

'What about the older fans?' she asked.

'They idolize you for following your dreams. They haven't and they know they never will. They admire your greatness and want to share in your success.'

'Is that sufficient reason to spend so much time and money in following what I'm doing?'

'You give them hope that anything is possible, by striving and self-abnegation like you do,' Jack said. 'Their sacrifice has been to save up fares, miss out on social activities, holiday at home and decline family life, all in order to be here. This self-denial hopes to enrich their lives.'

'I still don't see why they latch onto me, a complete stranger.'

'It's a connection to a part of the wider world they like and it makes them feel they belong. They're a member of your 'tribe' and on your side. When you win, they win too.'

'Fans' interest is enormously flattering,' Maxi said. 'It's what I like best about running.'

'Your fans are like a soccer crowd,' said Jack. 'Patti says they're really hitting on your website — Tweets supporting you have gone viral.'

'That's thrilling. I want to read their messages,' she said.

'Me too,' said Jack. 'I'm your most devoted fan.'

The team stayed in Prince's Gardens, at an Imperial College hall of residence, during vacation. Jack's room was in a separate wing but he slept with Maxi. He found a hotel for his family on Gloucester Road nearby. The hall accommodation was basic, but the location was excellent for training. Maxi trained daily in nearby Hyde Park, also at the College's indoor track and gym.

She practiced receiving messages on her wrist monitor from her coaches during runs. She would feel a message arrive as a vibration. Her monitor displayed elapsed time, projected finish time and kilometre splits from a GPS. She could regulate her speed precisely. Stan or Jack would message from their bicycles, or via a race drone, how far she was behind the lead and her position in the field.

Riko Minami had brought archery bows. Every afternoon, she and Maxi knelt in Prince's Garden and loosed arrows at a target. Afterwards, she would run in Hyde Park, with Riko correcting her style.

In the evenings, the Team met to discuss Maxi's training. They pooled their information about competitors' preparations. When the starting line-up was published, it included many of the World's fastest. Several had competed in the Paris marathon three months previously. Stan had an app with race results and statistics and another with videos of races. He screened them for everyone to watch together, identifying rivals' strengths and weaknesses, such as front-running and fast-finishing abilities. They also told Maxi any signs a runner gave when she was about to move up or drop back.

Stan received a media release from the race promoter.

MARATHON SHOWDOWN IN LONDON
Many of the World's fastest women distance runners will contest the London Marathon in two weeks time. In the Paris Marathon in

269

June, a group broke away and set a cracking pace: Vero Lamu (Kenya, pb 2h18) led Indihra Patel (Namibia, 2h15), Cindy Hirako (Japan 2h16), Desai (Kenya, 2h15), Pamuk (Canada, 2h17), Kopotlek (Russia, 2h18) and Rubinski (Finland, 2h17). At one kilometre from the finish, Pamuk dropped back and Hirako and the Finn passed Lamu, with Hirako having the edge at the line with a new pb of 2h15.

These runners will compete again in London, with Hirako starting as favourite. Two runners, Aisha Sayat (Ethiopia, 2h20) and Maxi Fleet (Australia, 2h22), did not compete in Paris but could also perform well. This will be Fleet's 3ʳᵈ marathon ever. She has been improving and could challenge her more experienced rivals. The race will be closely contested and if the weather is favourable, the World record of 2h17 set by Mary Ketany in 2017 could tumble.

Arden Lockwood for Australian Runners' World

There were media interviews almost every day. Maxi liked being feted.

'Publicity is paying our accommodation and airfares,' she said to Jack. 'They are throwing money at me for inspirational talks at conferences and dinners. I love turning people on to themselves and would do talks for nothing.'

'We need the money,' he said. 'Anyway, they appreciate it more when they have to pay.'

Maxi received all the media attention and the rest of the team none.

'When I make it to the top,' she said, 'the important role of you and the team will be recognised. At present people are more interested in whether I have the goods, than where I got them from.'

Maxi expected a lot from her staff, treated them well and they contributed strongly. The challenges for her coaches were to keep Maxi in peak physical and mental condition, through gentle exercise, rest and relaxation. The others provided nutrition and health support, marketed her appearances and products, gathered information on her competitors and their strategies and found entertainments for her. In the evening before the race, she mentally rehearsed what could happen, such as inclement weather or injury and how to deal with it.

After a Team meeting at the hotel, Maxi was alone with Jack.

'How would you like to relax this evening?' Jack asked her.

'We shouldn't have sex the night before,' she said, 'should we?'

'Some boxers' coaches believe it saps energy and don't allow it, but there is no evidence against it and some are for it. It will be okay if we take it easy.'

'A couple of rounds should be fun,' Maxi said. 'No uppercuts, though.'

This time it was different, gradual and slow.

CHAPTER 54

'For the last three days, I've carb-loaded you with spaghetti and foods easy to digest,' said Patti. 'Your muscles and liver should be full of glycogen. Protein takes too long to break down. Fat is worse. Your race is in about two hours from now and this breakfast will prepare you.'

Patti served avocado on crispbread, with a handful of spinach, a side of oatmeal and banana slices.

'You can top off your energy stores when you get close to the stadium, with an instant hit of glycogen from energy chews and Gatorade. Then during the race, I've put some candy and gels in your pack.'

'Thank you, Patti.'

To avoid the road traffic, they took the underground to Stratford Tube Station and walked to the stadium. The course wound from Greenwich along the Thames, crossing several bridges and finishing in St James Park.

Maxi parted to go to the dressing rooms.

'Good luck,' Jack said.

'I'm not counting on luck,' she said. 'I'll stick to the pace I have trained for.'

'You can do it. You're the greatest!'

As she toed the line at the start, she recalled Riko Minami's admonition to be unselfconscious, observant and respectful. Next to her were the fastest female marathoners in the world, but she would not be deterred. She sprinted away being careful to avoid colliding, stumbling or tripping. She unleashed herself, fine-tuning the cadence of her body's many instruments, seeking a symphony of concerted performance suppressing interest in the time on her wrist.

As she ran through the tunnel of spectators, she was immersed in London and its people. Her senses detected she was approaching the automaticity of 'flow'. Exhilarated, she flowed into the zone and took the lead.

At 15 kilometres, times for the split beamed to her showed her pace was a little above target. She slowed down to maintain her energy for later, dropping back into a group of 6 runners, with Rubinski in the lead.

The morning sun warmed the air and perspiration prickled her brow. It had rained and there were puddles. There were birds sitting on wires. She was reasonably comfortable and settled into the artful Zen forms and movements she had practiced in training. They didn't seem purposeless now. Focussing on her breathing, she established herself in the leading bunch and was aware of her competitors scrutinising her, as if they suspected her of being an impostor. Stan had warned her she would feel the chill of their greater experience, but she wasn't intimidated. She laid down her strides end to end, with the singular mindfulness and precision of a dot artist filling in a large canvas. She was serenely in 'flow'. After 25 kilometres, she noticed discomfort but put it out of her mind.

It didn't last. After 30 kilometres, the euphoria faded and her spirits descended steadily with disillusion lurking. Nietzsche's invocation of will-to-power saved her. She would dare to be great and nothing would stop her. She disdained the cacophony of protest from her body. The hurts were imagined ailments she would ignore.

Jack messaged her: 'Hang in there, doll!'

Her posture was hunched at the turnaround and Jack could tell she was suffering. He tried to divert her attention away from her body, to the race, so she could 'flow' again.

'You're going great, love, right on target.'

She smiled. His support put a glow inside her. She would win for Jack, because she could.

At 35 kilometres, with one-sixth of the distance remaining, she glimpsed a silver-lining. Ahead of her by 10 seconds were Hirako and Pamuk, pulling away from the field. She stayed with them as they sped up, with Vero and Rubinski close behind her. She would avoid over-exerting because her fuel was getting low. She could sustain this pace, because she had done it before.

Three kilometres from the finish, the race changed to a sprint. Maxi closed the gap using the finishing speed she had from 3000 metres racing. She caught up to Pamuk and passed her. Hirako's legs and arms were flailing, her mouth wide, desperately grabbing air, legs overreaching to finish. Maxi joyfully came alongside and passed her, taking more and longer paces, crossing the line a few metres ahead. She had won in 2h14.04, an improvement of 8 minutes on her PB and smashing the race record.

She recovered and as runners continued to stream in, she shook hands with Hirako and Pamuk.

'How did you make such a large improvement,' asked a reporter with a camera who followed her to the fence, where she acknowledged her support team and celebrated with them.

'The weather was perfect,' Maxi said, smiling for the camera. 'I enjoyed the kiss of wind on my face, the firmness of the ground under my feet, a million small natural things, they all made it my place, my time. I was in 'flow' most of the way, intent on my goal during almost every moment of the race.'

'What did you do to get into 'flow'?'

'I had trained under race conditions. I was calm, got comfortable, concentrated on my most efficient style and ran at my target speed with enough energy to finish. Getting into 'flow' was like putting on a favourite jacket. It felt good.'

Maxi hoped she sounded humble. She had been the fortunate instrument of a team effort. The journalist was disappointed that her success lacked privilege and illicit dealing, wanting her win to be both sensational and suspected of corrupting fair competition.

'It was a fast race,' said Maxi. 'In the front group, everyone improved their personal best.'

'Are you sure it was 'flow' that gave you the edge today?' said the reporter.

'No, we don't know that yet for sure. When there are more race results from others using the same technique, confidence can grow that it is effective. We won't know for some time yet.'

'Maxi, as European Marathon Champion, what advice do you have for other runners?'

'Set yourself an achievable goal, focus on it obsessively, practice over and over again under race conditions and when the gun goes off unleash your body. Don't drive yourself. Enjoy achieving.'

'What is your next race?'

'The Boston.'

'Do you expect to reduce your time?'

'By a few minutes.'

'Will you be increasing your training?'

'Our team will discuss that at a meeting.'

'How many people are in your team?'

'Besides me, there are seven. One couldn't come.'

'How much say do you have?'

'As much as I want,' Maxi said. 'Usually we try for consensus and decisions are unanimous. For an idea to be accepted, it has to get past everyone. I can veto but I haven't done it yet.'

'What expertises are there?'

'I do the running. Would you like to talk with the others?'

'Yes, that would be good.'

'Jack will take you to meet them,' she said. 'He coordinates the team.'

The reporter talked with them and took a group photo, with Maxi at centre.

'Smile for the camera please,' the reporter said. 'This photo will tell your success story. You're sensational. One, two, three. Thank you.'

CHAPTER 55

After she received her medal, a race official asked her to accompany him to the medical tent.

'Just some more routine tests, Ms Fleet.'

Before the awards ceremony Maxi had submitted blood and urine samples.

'What tests now?' she asked.

'Chromosomes and hormones.'

Jack was with her. 'What hormones?' he said.

'Testosterone.'

The male hormone measured in a female runner could indicate gender transgression. The IAAF had ruled that an intergender athlete with XY chromosomes had to have a testosterone level of less than 5 nanomoles per litre to run as a woman.

'Who asked I be tested?'

'There has been a complaint by a competitor,' said the supervising doctor.

Jack's was perplexed and Maxi dismayed. Questioning of her gender seemed offensive. Her ability to run as a woman would be determined by her testosterone level, regardless of her appearance and characteristics of her genitalia.

'There's no reason to think I'm XY,' she said.

'We'll do a chromosome test.'

'Will you measure her testosterone?' Jack asked.

'Yes. If she is XY, there is a possibility of hyperandrogenism, which would mean her body produces more testosterone than other women. Testosterone makes muscles bigger and bones stronger, and increases levels of oxygen-carrying haemoglobin in the blood.'

He pierced a vein in her forearm and began collecting blood, talking all the while, warming to his subject.

'More protein would be laid down within each muscle fibre and the fibres would increase in size and diameter. A larger amount of muscle bulk would improve performance – the size of the muscle tends to be linked to the power it can produce.'

Jack held Maxi's hand, knowing that with her career in the balance, she must feel threatened, out of control.

Jack was indignant. 'They must be grasping at straws, wanting to insult you, trying to subtract from your success today.'

The medic covered the puncture with a pad.

'There. Finished. Thank you.'

'How are you feeling,' Jack asked her.

She gave him a grim smile.

He turned to the doctor.

'How does this make running fairer?'

'It can disqualify XY women whose testosterone level is too high,' the doctor said. 'Performance differences between the sexes emerge at puberty. Males get ten times as much testosterone as females and a lean inverted V torso, small breasts and large biceps. These are advantages. The IAAF has provided for competition between females on a level playing field. Some women take oestrogen, which reduces their male characteristics and performances.'

Jack was annoyed. 'Testosterone level is arbitrary. Limiting it does not bring equality of opportunity. Why should it? A seven-foot basketball player is not required to play on his knees.'

Maxi spoke to him quietly: 'Patti once said to me: 'You look like a boy.''

'Whatever you once looked like and whatever this test shows, you are all female,' said Jack.

She had been a wiry teenage ectomorph, but in her twenties her slender shoulders and thighs had thickened into curvaceous mesomorphic shapes that Jack adored. He did not find her unfeminine or unattractive. Her femininity was sound. But, even if she was exonerated, some mud from the allegation would stick, as if

277

she might possibly have been cheating but hadn't been caught. It was unfair.

'Don't worry,' he said. 'It's just a formality.'

The tests found Maxi was an XX and her testosterone level was within the limit. Jack was annoyed.

'Dividing athletes into men and women creates a problem of how to distinguish them,' said Jack. 'Men's and women's events should be separate when their performances are significantly different. In the marathon, women's and men's performances are converging. In future the division may become unnecessary.'

'The solution could be for men and women to compete together equally, separated only by age and disability,' Maxi said. 'Like in primary school, when girls often used to beat boys.'

'I suppose gender differentiation allows for separate development of the dimorphs,' Jack said, musing. 'Males and females do have a few differences.'

'It fosters prejudices,' Maxi said.

'Exposing borderline individuals is unkind,' he said.

'That price is too high,' she said.

'I agree,' Jack said. 'Women and men should run together.'

CHAPTER 56

Maxi and I seldom talked about concerns or misgivings in our relationship. We depended on each other and were positive, discussing our hopes and dreams. We usually agreed. I was focussed on my research and Maxi's attention was on her running. When we talked about our feelings, we were honest with each other, like best friends. We talked about her running in 'flow' as a joint project.

'I want to develop 'flow' as a skill anyone can learn to perform many types of endurance activity,' he said.

'You don't know for sure it has benefits,' she said sceptically.

'I'm testing your performances to see if 'flow' has benefits.'

'If I run faster, there could be any number of causes.'

'I'll compare runs that differ only by presence or absence of 'flow'. If we discover 'Fleet flow' is faster, you'll be immortalised.'

'Jack, you're dreaming.'

'I'm dot painting, one dot at a time.'

'Why dots?'

'Each one is a race and adds its evidence to the picture.'

'What are you painting?'

'A picture of successful running.'

'What will be the attraction?'

'The dots are green when you win with 'flow' and red when you lose. A predominance of green will be irresistible evidence.'

'Sometimes I think your only interest in me is as a test dummy,' Maxi said. 'You haven't told me you like me lately.'

'I'm not into hype. If there was a problem, I would tell you.'

'It's not enough for me to be satisfactory,' she said. 'I try to please.'

'It's what I do, not what I say, that counts,' I said. 'What I do for you shows you please me.'

'You lack emotional expression,' she said.

'At school they told me I avoided emotional situations and hid my feelings,' I said. 'But I'm completely committed to you.'

'As your research subject?'

'Can't you tell that it is much more than that?' I said. 'You're the best thing that ever happened to me.'

'Me too,' she said.

'I suppose I probably love you.'

'Maybe I love you too, though we have different ideas about what love is.'

'That's okay, isn't it?'

'Do you think we could reveal ourselves more?'

'Maybe not,' I said. 'Talking can convey our emotions superficially, but our relationship is like an iceberg having two protruding peaks of consciousness. We have feelings and behaviour at the surface that pique each other's interest, whereas the feelings supporting our affection are submerged and don't get conscious attention. We know they're down there somewhere, supporting us.'

'Do we need to talk about deep feelings?' she asked.

'It could be difficult to get down to them.'

'You sound as though you don't think it's worth trying,' she said.

'What would you like me to do?'

'You could say nice things to me.'

'When?'

'When we're with Alice and Blake,' Maxi said.

'What would I say?'

'Show you're infatuated with me.'

'I could stare at you and lick my lips.'

'No,' she said. 'Say things that show you love me deeply.'

'You want me to say loving things they can hear?'

'Yes.'

'Are you sure?'

'Don't look at me as if I'm weird. For women, love is social.'

280

'It is peculiar,' I thought. *'Females need public displays of affection whereas most men are reserved or even covert. Perhaps women need to feel secure socially, whereas a man needs his psyche boosted.'*

The taxi reached my place and we crunched leaves as we walked up to the entry door.

'We have trialled living together several times,' I said. 'I want you to move in with me permanently.'

'Were the trials successful then?'

'Yes: we're still together.'

She thought for a moment. 'Okay. But you need to show me more affection in public.'

'Alright,' I said. 'Would you remind me, until I get the hang of it?'

'Are you humouring me?'

'No way. I wouldn't do that. I know you're serious. You want adulation, whereas I want non-attachment.'

She thrived on adulation. I had wanted Maxi to video her running experiences to present to audiences, but then I realised what she wanted was worship by a live audience.

'Can your non-attachment work in a relationship?' she asked.

'If you allow me to be detached, I'll worship you.'

'Sounds okay. I want the tenancy to the apartment to be made joint.'

'I'll have your name put on the lease.'

'I'll bring the rest of my things.'

She would be over-controlled with me as her coach and her landlord. When she moved in and gained equal rights, it evened up. Living together was more than a convenience: it kept our minds connected. We talked together in the evenings.

'What are you thinking about?' I would ask her.

'Whether you really like me.'

'If our relationship is like a living plant, should you keep digging it up to look at the roots, to see if it is growing? Or is there another way?'

'I suppose I could observe us and what we're doing.'

'Yes. Are you worried about us?'

'No. I suppose it's a habit.'

'You don't worry about your running.'

'I focus on my goal.'

'Could you have a goal about us?'

'Yes. To stay together always.'

'That's my goal too. You don't need to worry any more. Think about what you need to do to stay with me.'

'That is a worry,' she said laughing.

'Not as bad as wondering how much I like you.'

'It's not much of a choice. Maybe I should give you the flick.'

'That's not possible.'

'Why not?'

'Our goal is to stay together always.'

'I forgot. Okay then.'

'I'd like to watch the news now.'

I put my arms around her and drew her towards me. 'Would you?'

'Okay.'

CHAPTER 57

Everyone arrived for the 7th team meeting. Some of them hadn't seen each other since the previous meeting in London. They chatted, catching up.

At 6.00 pm, Jack said: 'Let's begin. I want to welcome Wayne, who is our new advertising manager and Ingrid who is taking on media coordination.'

He read a brief resume' for each newcomer and there was polite applause.

'They won't be staying because today's meeting is about coaching. We will need their expertise later, in preparing Maxi's campaign for Boston. Thank you, Wayne and Ingrid.'

They left.

'Brenda is starting as business manager, but she couldn't be here this evening and I'll introduce her another time.

'Now to what's been happening. Some of us watched Maxi win The London Marathon with a new PB of 2h14.'

Everyone clapped and Alice whooped.

'Her improvement was an amazing 8 minutes. After the race, they tested her for every drug known, but they found nothing, of course.'

'Thank you, Jack, for not mentioning testosterone,' Maxi thought. *'I hope never to hear that mentioned again. It is so embarrassing.'*

'Maxi mainlines on physical training,' said Stan.

'Mental performance enhancement is allowed,' said Blake, 'unless it uses illegal substances.'

'Neuroscience and brain physics training can boost her performance legally,' said Jack. 'They leave no traces detectable by chemistry.'

'That's because they don't have any effect,' said Stan dismissively.

'Stan, just because something isn't visible doesn't mean it doesn't exist. Maxi's running has improved and it could be by flow. I am going to explain my theory of time dilation. Its effects can include faster running, but the causes exist in the brain and are undetectable. There are three basic ideas and they require concentration to understand. Don't worry, they are easier to understand than, say, how a mouse can take cheese from a mousetrap without getting caught.'

They looked at Jack, puzzled.

'What the fuck has that got to do with it?' asked Stan.

'It's so you don't get bogged down by relativity, which is harder to understand. You can ease our long journey with travel along a scenic by-road.'

'Could the mouse be too small to get caught in the trap?' asked Blake.

'Good. That's one way: the hammer wire could miss it. Can you think of any other way? Tell us presently. Now, back to dilation of time.

'Einstein did a thought experiment about a spaceship. An astronaut inside it flashes a pulse of light across the spacecraft, setting off a timer and reflecting back perpendicularly from a mirror to the timer again. The travel time across the width is T seconds and can be calculated from light speed, or alternatively, read from the timer.'

'Is the spacecraft stationary?' asked Stan.

'Yes.'

'Does the pulse travel across and back in T seconds?'

'Yes. T is a tiny fraction of a second, about 30 nanoseconds.'

'It takes one nanosecond for my nan to hide her purse away when I go round there,' said Blake.

They laughed.

Jack continued: 'If the spaceship moves forward at the speed of light, would the travel time T across the spaceship and back be the same as when it was stationary?'

284

'Why not?' said Blake.

'We could think its travel would take more time, because the path of the light pulse would be further,' Jack said. 'When the spaceship moves forward, if we look inside through a porthole using a telescope from Earth, we would see the light pulse, revealed by illuminating dust particles in the air, going along a diagonal path. It would go to the mirror in its new position, being reflected off the mirror and coming back along another diagonal, completing a dogleg (23).

'If that seems too hard, imagine a mouse coming out of its hole and smelling the cheese. It would think: *'How can I get the cheese without being caught?'* What would be your advice? Tell us presently. Now, back to the spaceship.

'Can the light follow the dogleg? It can if it obeys these three conditions: 1. The path is further than perpendicularly across and back; 2. It must arrive by time equal to T; and 3. It cannot go faster than the speed of light. Could all 3 happen?'

'No,' said Derek. 'To go further along the dogleg in the same time, it would have to go faster. But if it was already at the speed of light, it couldn't go faster, nor could it arrive by time T.'

'What if time stretched?' said Minami. 'If each second lasted longer, it would be logical. We don't think of seconds varying in duration, because we imagine a pendulum beating out regular portions of time. But a pendulum can be slowed and the light pulse can pass along the diagonal in T longer seconds also. Thus, a longer distance can be travelled in T longer seconds.'

'You can't make seconds longer, can you?' asked Maxi.

'Why not?' said Riko. 'The duration of a second is fixed by a clock, so why not by logic?'

'It wouldn't be scientific,' said Blake. 'A second has to last for a certain number of caesium crystal vibrations.'

'That's Newtonian science,' said Jack. 'Einstein allowed time to dilate, so it could pass across the moving spaceship.'

'What is 'time dilation'?' asked Alice.

'Time stretches due to relativity,' Jack said. 'Einstein has an equation calculating exactly how much for different speeds. There is most dilation near the speed of light.'

'When you watch pylons passing at regular intervals from a train travelling at constant speed, if the gaps widen, you will assume you have slowed. Would your time have dilated?'

'No. It's an illusion called the Kappa effect. Time dilation is different. It is real. Seconds last longer.'

'A second can't be longer than a heap of vibrations of a caesium crystal, can it?'

'That defines clock time and is as regular as the rotation of the Earth. I live in my own time which is different from timepieces and different for every individual,' said Dr Riko Minami. 'I run my life with my spirit, not by any 'little fidget wheels' as Slessor called them. My seconds are as long as I want them to be.'

'Don't we all have identical little fidget wheels?' asked Blake.

'Different individuals do have identical sub-particles in their atoms that orbit at identical speeds,' said Riko. 'But the processes they are engaged in, such as molecular diffusion of nutrients in cells, proceed at rates determined at higher levels within bodies. They depend on the extent of their energy at that time and molecular processes would be faster at some times than at others and at temperatures that differ between individuals. There is no universal time regulating living things.'

'I agree,' said Jack. 'We're made of different atoms in different compounds in different cells,' said Jack. 'Our hearts don't beat in unison, nor do our billions of atoms, march in lockstep to the same pendulum beat, each with its swarm of sub-particles. At the Sydney Olympics, the winning marathon runner had a resting heart rate of 35 beats per minute, whereas 70 is normal. Each person's body is different and has its own metabolic time. Maxi's experience of time is hers alone.'

'Does each person, each system and each organ keep its own time, or can they coordinate with others?' Patti asked.

'Each has its own time. Complex animals function independently but we notice when their times do coincide, such as the simultaneous hatching of birds' eggs. Another example is when women who live together start menstruating on the same day of the month. These are the exceptions. Ordinarily, individuals' times differ because their bodies operate independently.'

'All humans stand upright, so couldn't their individual times be the same too?'

'Standing may not be a time process. Why should their time be the same?'

'Gravity is acceleration in time and approximately the same wherever people live,' said Blake. 'Perhaps that's why they stand upright.'

'If individuals align variables that cause their speed, their activity times could converge. Their times can coincide, but usually they don't. A person's time to run a marathon is like them cutting a piece from an infinitely large pie. Everyone can cut their piece differently. Their hearts and breathing wouldn't be in sync. Personal time varies between individuals.'

'Personal time is a new approach: it isn't the universal time measured by timepieces.'

'No. A person's time is what they make of it.'

'I suppose differences between species are greater. Would an elephant's time be in sync with a hummingbird's time?'

'No, definitely not. Hummingbird hearts seem to be in a faster timeframe with their time more dilated. But we'll ponder this later. Consider how the mouse can get the cheese without getting caught?'

'Could it move fast enough to dilate time?' Maxi asked.

'Good idea,' said Jack. 'If it moved near the speed of light, it would hardly take any time at all to grab the cheese and scarper.'

'No way,' Blake said. 'A mouse would keep stopping and sniffing.'

'It could take steroids.'

'Moving that fast is just too far-fetched for me,' said Blake impatiently. 'Why did Einstein have the spaceship going at the speed of light?'

'So no-one could see he was wrong,' said Stan.

'I agree with Stan,' said Blake. 'The problem with these theories is they can't be tested.'

'Hmm. It's good to be sceptical, but Einstein's theories have been tested. His thought experiment deduced when two time frames are moving at different speeds, the one near the speed of light would have its time dilated.'

'If the premises are wrong, deductions would be wrong. Einstein began by assuming the speed of light is the fastest movement possible. How smart is that?' said Blake. 'Not.'

'Nothing has been measured to go faster,' said Jack.

'The fastest human travel has gone is only a fraction of light speed,' said Alice. 'Has the amount of time dilation observed been significant?'

'With the fastest technologies now existing, time dilation is almost imperceptible,' he said. 'As speeds approach light speed, time dilation would increase until time stops. Ultimately the light pulse would be too delayed to transmit.'

'Yes,' said Jack. 'Clocks in aircraft run slow. Long-haul airliners have their clocks set forward a little to match stationary caesium clocks.'

'GPS navigation in a car has timers for signals to 4 satellites that correct for time dilation. Using four satellites allows solving for length, width, height and time. Unless they allow for time dilation, your car would be calculated a long way from its true position.'

'Perhaps the mouse could evade the hammer by dilating time to get in and out quicker.'

'Mice have evolved to be quick,' said Alice. 'A mouse pup could inherit its parents' speed. The slow ones would get hammered and never become parents.'

'What if the mouse trained to be faster, for a quick snatch?'

'How?'

'It could practice by biting a cat and getting away.'

'Could Maxi practice by running up mountains?'

'I wouldn't be fast enough for my time to dilate.'

'Your body speed doesn't have to be fast. But your nerve impulses could approach the limit for electromagnetic transmission speed.'

'Is that bad?'

'No, good. Einstein's Special Relativity theory is that near that speed an observer in a slower time frame would see the impulses slow down, by time dilation.'

'What would they actually see?'

'A stationary observer would see motor responses to the stimulus in dilated time. But I'm getting ahead. We'll break there and afterwards consider how to get Maxi's time to dilate. Mountain running could develop the strength she would need in dilated time to speed up. But other training is needed too. Let's take a break.'

They stopped for coffee, biscuits and cheese.

CHAPTER 58

'How are you getting on with the theory?' Jack asked Maxi during the interval. 'Are you ready to take on another wodge?'

'I don't get all of it,' she said. 'You'll have to be patient with me, but I'll give it a go.'

'You'll manage, I'm sure,' he said. 'Einstein's theory concerned travel in space and we need to understand it to apply it to time dilation in your brain.'

'Is this your theory?'

'It is Einstein's theory applied to the microscopic level of nerve impulses.'

'Then it's your theory, sort of,' Maxi said. 'I hope it's right!'

'So do I,' he said with a wry smile.

'Let's go everybody,' Jack said and they came back to the table and sat down. 'We'll continue with the mouse problem presently. Are you ready to do some thinking? Einstein published his Special Relativity theory in 1905. It was explicated in the Twins Paradox, a celebrated thought experiment. No-one has ever refuted it. I have adapted it for Maxi's running.

'Identical twins aged 20 are both marathon runners. One becomes an astronaut and travels in space until she returns to Earth 60 years later, after travelling to a star 24 light years away and back at a speed at 0.8 of the speed of light. That's 24 X 2/0.8 = 60. Only 36 years have passed as recorded by the spaceship's clock, as predicted from the Lorentz factor at this speed and distance (22). 60 years have passed on Earth. When she climbs down from the hatch, she is 20 plus 36 equals 56 years old, comparing with her sister's 20 plus 60 equals 80 years. The traveller's physical and mental appearance is consistent with being 80 - 56 = 24 years younger. Supposing the traveller has no muscle wastage, the sisters, 80 and 56, could live on Earth and run marathons, adding years to their lives by the calendar. The returned traveller could expect to live longer than her sister by 24 years.'

'How could one sister be physically younger than the other?' asked Stan.

'Good question' said Jack. 'Who has the answer? If you want to try something easier, think if there is any other way the mouse could get the cheese, without having to be quick?'

'She stayed physically younger because the clock on the ship was running slower and her calendar had shown only 36 birthdays,' said Jack. 'Back on Earth again, her physical decline would resume at the same rate as other 60-year-olds.'

'On the spaceship, was her life slowed, delayed, truncated, decompressed, expanded, or what?' asked Blake.

'None of those,' said Jack. 'Her time dilated or stretched. Her body processes worked the same as usual with the clock running slower.'

'Would she be in slow motion by the on-board clock?'

'No,' Blake said. 'She would be moving around the same as on Earth without being aware that the on-board clock was running slower.'

'What about if they watched her from Earth through a porthole?'

'She would be seen in slow motion, 36/60 = 0.6 of normal. Astronauts on the International Space Station are ageing just a bit slower than people on Earth. Now, is there another way the mouse can get the cheese?'

'I know,' said Blake. 'Softly, softly, catchee monkey!'

'Good idea, Blake. The mouse could take the cheese gently from the trap without depressing the catch. Now can you answer: Which one of the twins would finish a marathon first if the traveller runs around a track inside a rotating spaceship, held down by a centripetal force of rotation? The traveller would complete the marathon distance in 36/60 = 0.6 of Earth time.'

'But Maxi does not have a spaceship!' said Corvid.

'Psychologists often speculate by analogy and modern physics does too. Her nerve impulses travel through neural space. We'll see later that there is evidence that time dilation can occur in the brain. It's a real effect and Maxi can use it to get an edge on rivals.'

'Each of Maxi's nerve impulses is like a spaceship, travelling very fast at electromagnetic speeds through pathways from her brain to her legs and back again. It is the same medium we considered in space to experience time dilation.

'All our sensory apparatus also rely on electromagnetic interactions. Even our nerves transmit information via electromagnetism; hence our brain functions via electromagnetism. This is the crucial point. It all means that our sensory experience of the universe is mediated by electromagnetism.' (20).

'How are electromagnets involved?' asked Blake.

'There aren't any. The nerve impulse is a wave with wavelength and frequency on the electromagnetic spectrum, which has a range from long slow radio waves to short fast ultra-violet. Nerve impulses transmitted through neurones penetrate the emptiness resonating sparse particles. A nerve impulse is something like a subsonic tremble in air, an electrical wave passing through nerve cells.'

'How can there be a wave of electricity?'

'A nerve impulse, like a lightning strike, is an electrical phenomenon but without the large potentials that cause high temperatures. Electricity has caused Volta's frogs' legs to twitch, hearts to defibrillate and electric shock therapy to overcome mental illness. Nerve impulses can invisibly cause Maxi to speed up.'

'How would that happen?'

'Signals from her brain as nerve impulses that would be transmitted through nerve cells and across intervening. They have evolved causing sensors to detect, brain functions to analyse and motor neurones to react, enabling an organism to escape from a predator by muscles that freeze, flight or fight.'

292

'How would a nerve impulse have to travel further like the pulse of light in the spaceship?'

'Electromagnetic impulses would have maximum speeds much slower than 300,000 kms per second for light through the vacuum of space. As density of the medium increases, light is slowed and refracted in glass. In air, sound slows with increasing density as temperature rises. Rutherford discovered that the mass of an atom is in a tiny nucleus and electromagnetic transmission through air, glass and human tissue would encounter mostly empty space.'

'A nerve impulse is nothing like a spaceship in space.'

'There are many differences, I agree, but regarding electromagnetic wave transmission, there are similarities. Nerve impulses and light are both electromagnetic waves. Differences between the media of transmission, space and neurones, are superficial. We do not have to think less of the relevance for dilation of opaque materials in the human body nor of the very small scale compared with space travel. The tiny diameter of a brain dendrite filament does not diminish its significance as a site where time dilation can occur. Nor does the tortuous course of neural pathways, with impulses bouncing between parts of the brain like a Pachinko ball, reduce potential for time dilation. Although transmission distances within the nervous system would not be in light-years, there would be enough time for a runner's time to dilate.'

'How would Maxi's time dilate?'

'When she is stoked in flow, Maxi's neural pathways would be congested with impulses travelling through neurones and synapses near their maximum speed, about 430 kilometres per hour. With her brain nearing overload, response times could dilate, as they would inside a spaceship near light speed, or in a longer brain pathway like the dogleg, we considered earlier.

'Why would an impulse take a longer pathway?'

'To increase her cognition, for example. She would need time to dilate.''

'How would that affect her running?'

293

'Observed from a slow timeframe, like a telescope through a porthole, she would be running in slow motion with fewer longer seconds, completing the distance earlier. Because neural transmission speed is approaching maximum speed, time has to dilate for the neural impulses to coincide with a direct reflex response from the spinal cord.'

'Would her running be observed from outside with normal reflex responses expected before she engaged in flow and her time dilated. The observer timeframe would be like that of the twin who stayed on Earth with time on a calendar and timepieces, when her sister took off.'

'How certain are you Maxi would take less time?'

'Einstein's thought experiment can't be tested, except for logical consistency. We can't see inside brains or neurones and measure signal speeds, so experimenting is not possible. Like the astronaut, her reaction would be earlier. If the two sisters would continue with the second part of their runs, the traveller will have saved 60 - 36 = 24 years in the first part, having conserved more energy and having stayed younger.'

'Whoa. My brain is overloaded,' said Blake.

'Einstein predicted that if an event needs more time to complete than is available, time can dilate,' said Jack. 'Let's think about something easier. Is there any other way that the mouse can get the cheese, without risking depression of the catch?'

'Stan has depression of the catch when he comes home from fishing,' said Patti.

There was laughter.

'The mouse could hunker down in the centre and duck under the hammer wire, so it snaps past without impacting.'

'Now, what about the mouse getting the cheese? Any more ideas?'

'Could it set off the trap without being caught, then eat the cheese,' said Riko.

'Far out, Doctor. It could use its tail to set off the trap.'

'Yeow,' said Corvid.

'It could wait for another mouse to set off the trap, then eat the cheese,' said Blake.

They all looked at him.

'A light bulb moment,' said Stan. 'Well done Blake.'

'You are mean, Blake, but I like it,' said Corvid laughing.

'Would a mouse really wait for another mouse to set it off?' asked Maxi.

'It's what the oil company I worked for used to do with new technology,' said Jack. 'Everyone raced to be second.'

'Me too,' said Blake. 'It's the best way to win.'

'The mouse could loiter and pretend to be uninterested in the cheese,' said Maxi, 'waiting for another mouse to come and set off the trap.'

'Some of my physics colleagues are responding to my thesis as if it is a baited trap,' said Jack. 'They're waiting for me to have my risky ideas sprung, so they can move in fast and grab the credit.'

'Could Maxi suck competitors into taking the lead and bonking, then pounce?'

'I'm like that fucking mouse,' said Maxi impatiently. 'But I'm not going to be caught.'

'You have to speed up.'

'Are we talking about seconds or minutes?' Maxi asked.

'It doesn't have to be much. Bannister improved a few minutes over several years, then in his record run, shaved off a few seconds to get under 4 minutes.'

There was silence as they thought about it.

'What do your physics people think of this time dilation idea, Jack?'

'They don't like that it is untestable. If Maxi keeps on winning, they could eventually come around.'

'It's only a thought experiment, but it's a good one,' said Coach Derek. 'I want Maxi to train to dilate her time in flow. I'll get some of our other runners at the Institute to try it too.'

'The evidence is a bit skimpy,' said Blake. 'But it's an awesome fucking theory! I want Maxi to try it.'

'That's nice for you, Blake,' said Maxi.

'It would be for your benefit,' he said, 'if you can appreciate that, with your brain so overloaded.'

'Ouch.'

'The lack of evidence may only be temporary,' said Jack. 'I believe the dilation phenomenon exists. There is a wealth of circumstantial evidence in various fields and it is only a matter of time before its significance is widely accepted.'

'This theory is peripheral to Maxi's success,' said Stan. 'If you believe in it, you'll believe in anything. We shouldn't put all our eggs in one basket.'

Jack was silent as he reflected that Stan's contribution to the team varied between heavyweight lifting and being a dead weight who had to be carried.

'Thank you, Stan,' said Jack. 'This evening we have found the mouse can deceive another to take the rap, or it can move fast enough for its time to dilate, to grab the cheese and get away before the hammer descends. Now all we need is for Maxi to dilate time and finish in front. Let's meet again in a week's time to work out a detailed programme.'

Jack finished the meeting.

CHAPTER 59

Maxi was a performer and I was her greatest fan. I was in awe of her, marvelling at her endurance in training and in races. My own endurance at desk research was physically less challenging but not without mental difficulties. Her training had a gruelling schedule with frequent repetition and fine-tuning, whereas I could vary my activities but lacked concrete results to guide the way. We were like chalk and cheese, an unlikely pair to share our lives, but we had lived together almost a year now.

When not at work, we wanted different lifestyles. For example, she used her phone a lot, watched movies, went to running socials and made celebrity appearances. She gave interviews at home, had visitors and was noisy, talkative and laughed a lot. I preferred to read and write quietly by myself. We got under each other's feet but learned to be flexible and compromise.

She was meticulous about her diet because of its importance to elite performance. The food she wanted was healthy but too bland for my taste. I preferred steak, but it was expensive.

'Let's eat out,' she said.

'Let's eat in,' I said. 'We ate out last week.'

'I'll pay,' she said. 'I'll put you on a salary.'

She phoned Brenda, her new Business Manager, who was already earning 10 times my research grant by selling Maxi dolls and smartphone apps. The Maxi fan business was thriving.

'Brenda, I want to pay Jack a salary. How much can we afford?'

She turned to me. 'Is $5000 a month okay?'

It was generous. I nodded, stunned that the love and dedication I had been giving out freely would now be bought. I wasn't comfortable becoming dependent on Maxi and I resisted, until I realised we were a unit and the money belonged to both of us. She was the running part and I was the coaching part. I deserved a share in earnings, but how much less than her we didn't discuss. I got all I wanted. It was wonderfully kind and supportive of her and enabled me to concentrate on my studies.

We were both struggling to deal with the welter of opportunities that her prominence in the media created and the stresses her meteoric rise to fame had brought. With her success, we lived our lives publicly, more seriously, with less time for relaxation and recreation.

We were good for each other. I was proud of her competence at running and she was proud of my expertise in science. The passion and strong affection we shared flowed from our mutual admiration and support.

Maxi made demands on herself and others close to her, but behind her hard edge, she was soft and vulnerable. Her tendency was to keep busy with running matters, giving little time to getting in touch with her feelings. I had a bigger picture of her running career and was able to advise her, helping her realise alternatives and consequences.

CHAPTER 60

It was a week later and Team Maxi was meeting to continue working out a training programme for The Boston.

'Do you have a goal, Maxi?' Jack asked.

'2h10.'

'I like it,' said Riko. 'It's 4 minutes faster than you ran in London. It's a challenge, but do-able.'

'In London, you were 'in flow' for most of the way and in Boston you can aim to 'flow' all the way,' said Derek.

'I agree. Not only should she aim to be in flow, but her mind should be near overload for her time to dilate,' said Jack.

'How could her brain be caused to overload?' asked Blake. 'Would heaps of action cause her to max out.'

'Nerve impulses travel very fast and have a maximum speed, like light,' Corvid said. 'The neural system has a limit. I have heard that stimulus overload can cause a person's brain to shut down.'

'Before shut down can be reached, her nervous system would become congested and reach peak capacity,' said Alice. 'Mihaly, a psychologist, has described 'flow' as a condition of full cognitive engagement. Could flow be a near-overload condition?'

'The behaviour is similar,' said Corvid. 'But it may not be the same thing.'

'Mihaly's full engagement sounds like a fade-out, whereas Corvid's overload is like blowing a fuse,' said Jack. 'Which would Maxi experience?'

'Mihaly explains flow as transient hypo-frontality,' said Corvid. 'It reduces stress reactions by limiting prefrontal responses of fear, fright, flight and fight.'

'Maxi's brain overload could go either way, into a frazzle or into 'flow',' said Jack. 'One way is dysfunctional and the other is bliss.'

'Why bliss?' asked Maxi.

'Flow eliminates stress and is enjoyable.'

'How would I get that?'

'Instead of becoming frazzled by overload, you would go into 'flow',' said Alice. 'Your time could dilate, allowing you to complete actions blissfully without fading out or jamming.

'There you have it,' said Jack. 'That's the last part of my theory.'

'It makes sense,' said Derek. 'Dilating time to work out a smart move is a better alternative to pumping adrenalin for a fight or flight response.'

'It explains that 'flow' evolved under stress with more time to escape.'

'It predicts the timelessness people notice when they return from 'flow' to normal time,' said Maxi. 'When the time traveller returns, she finds her time has slowed down. Is there a simpler explanation?'

'Yes,' said Stan. 'When running is enjoyable, time flies and runners who have run fast attribute it to being 'in flow'.'

'That doesn't explain how they perform better in 'flow',' said Jack.

'Are you sure they do?' Stan asked.

'There is some evidence,' Jack said. 'Do you perform better in 'flow' Maxi?'

'In London, I was in 'flow' during most of the race and ran my PB. So yes.'

'Other explanations are possible, such as training hard.'

'If she continues to win running in 'flow', would you be convinced then?'

'More convinced, yes.'

'Do I really need to overload my brain to reduce my time?' Maxi asked.

'Yes,' said Jack. 'Time dilation occurs when nervous impulses in your central nervous system are much faster than reflex responses in your local nervous system.

300

'So the evidence for this theory of yours is circumstantial, meaning that it indicates higher performance but not conclusively?' said Derek.

'Yes, but there is no other explanation of Maxi's steady improvement that is as convincing as flow and time dilation.'

'Could my time bend enough for me to overtake someone?' asked Maxi.

'Why not?' said Corvid. 'When a person responds to a stimulus travelling through the nervous system at a maximum speed of about 430 kilometres per hour, at the speed of a high-powered rifle bullet, the delay in the brain is 10-40 microseconds. Stimuli are processed in the vision, auditory, memory and intuitive parts of the neo-cortex. Your stimuli could travel longer neural routes in your engaged brain than for your reflex responses. These are relatively slow in shorter pathways, typically not going to the brain, with responses coming from the spinal cord in a stimulus-response time of 300 milliseconds. The responses by the brain would travel further and could dilate time. The resulting muscle contractions in your legs in the dilated time could allow more strides. Your running could be faster than an adversary whose time for striding is not dilated.'

'When time dilation kicks in, would she spurt forward?' asked Blake.

'No,' said Jack. 'There is no boost effect. She gets the opportunity to run harder. She only gets the benefit of more time by claiming it, with striving.'

'After 40 kilometres, I don't have more ability and strength, but I can have more striving. With Jack's theory, I get extra time. I used to wonder why being 'in flow' felt like magic and now Jack's theory explains it.'

'Your winning would be the best evidence,' said Jack.

'Does your PhD depend on me winning?' said Maxi.

'It doesn't depend totally on you, sweetheart. But if you win, it will be a big help.'

Maxi turned to Alice. 'He called me sweetheart! Get that!'

'He's using you. Don't trust him!'

'I don't,' said Maxi. 'He wants more than my body.'

'Don't let him fuck up your head,' said Blake. 'You think too much, Jack. Your brain seems to be stuck. It's overloaded and fused.'

'It's a theory,' said Stan. 'All theories are head fucks.'

'It's a harmless theory,' said Jack. 'If there's nothing in it, we'll have wasted our time talking about it, that's all. Maxi's training runs would be the same. There's no downside. Do you see that, Maxi?'

'How will getting into 'flow' make me run faster without trying harder?'

'You do have to try harder. I'm making an educated guess that it will cause you to run faster.'

'Flow can improve your performance in four different ways,' Jack said. 'First, you'll be focussed on it and able to concentrate. Second, you'll enjoy the running as an end in itself.'

'Third, you'll have automaticity from our training and be able to achieve optimally.'

'Fourth, we will have set thinking tasks to overload your brain during the race so your time will dilate and you can run faster.'

'If overloading their brains reduced running times, wouldn't runners already have discovered it and be doing it?'

'Some might have. We don't know which runners dilate time,' said Riko Minami. 'The Bannister Effect could be everywhere.'

Blake looked around the room, pretending alarm.

They all laughed.

'Bannister's breakthrough could have been from changing his coach, or runners who set the pace for him, but he made gradual improvement. In the year before, he sped up by about 8 seconds. Only his last runs were with pacers.'

'It took only a small time reduction to break the record,' said Coach Derek. 'Was the Bannister Effect time dilation or something else?'

'It is time dilation by Bannister's imitators that is most intriguing,' said Jack. 'What caused all those relatively unknown runners to speed up.'

'Bannister's success smashed a glass ceiling,' said Coach Derek. 'His improvement could have inspired imitators to gain: motivation,

302

adrenaline, willpower, practice, attention, concentration, focus or time. Take your pick.'

'I think time dilation was important,' said Jack. 'Those milers' brains were pumped up and congesting. High performers' brains often are. Prodigious feats in many fields could be due to both 'flow' and time dilation: in nature, athletics, sport, entertainment, dance, music and chess. When a flock of starlings swerves in concert, time dilation could facilitate their coordination. A concert pianist may need his brain time to dilate as he races to keep up with the conductor's time.'

'They might have had girlfriends watching. There was reason a-plenty for their minds to by maxing-out. After Bannister broke the record, those athletes ran faster than any milers had ever run. I deduce it may be possible for Maxi to dilate time by a brain-congesting performance.'

'It is strange to encourage an athlete to be mentally active during a performance,' said Coach Derek. 'It is more usual to seek alleviation of the runner's anxiety and stress.'

'Maxi has to overload her brain,' Jack said. 'She has trained to run in flow, with concentration on her goal, full mind engagement and control of her actions. To induce congestion near overload, her attention might have to be induced to consider other matters.'

'What other evidence is there?' asked Coach Derek.

'Runners' self-reports and their performance statistics. They indicate flow has a positive effect. I would like to have your view of a piece I found in this book by Adrian MacGregor, about Cathy Freeman. He describes her run in the 200m final at the Commonwealth Games in Canada in 1994.'

He read:

'Freeman ran the most storming last 80m of a 200m sprint seen in women's athletics for many years. The key to Cathy's speed is her lightness of tread, her ability to lift her feet off the track quickly to take the next stride. She doesn't possess great power in her legs because she doesn't need it. She has spring instead. And like animals on the veldt, to increase speed she doesn't take more steps, she increases the length of her stride. Thus Cathy, Gainsford and Onyali

303

ran almost the entire last 80m in identical stride cadence, with almost military precision. In video slow-mo, the three ran the last 35 strides in perfect step. But Cathy was taking longer strides.

'It is not enough just to be a long strider, it has to be long AND quick. Like Cathy, who overtook Onyali with just three strides to go.

'It was in this race that Cathy experienced the sense of lifting off the ground . . . . She was 'in flow' where effort is effortless, where energy is endless, where feet take flight. It looked all of that as she steamrolled Onyali with sheer will and self-belief. She won the gold medal in 22.25 s, a new Commonwealth Games and Australian record.

''It happens quickly,' she says. 'You start to feel good, and you feel yourself lift and come out of yourself. Like you feel you're high above the ground and something happens to you, and you lift to another level. You lift and you just feel like magic. You feel, wow! It's a great feeling, just amazing.' Her voice soars, her face is luminous. 'It's more than just running, it's . . . Flying! You want to win so much and whoever's got the biggest heart, whoever's the most honest with themselves on the day, wins.' That day it was Cathy, by a mere 0.1 s.'

Jack put down the book. 'Macgregor's idea is that Cathy won from a last-minute display of physical strength. My interpretation is different. This report has evidence of time dilation from 'flow'. Cathy's longer strides were dilated in time due to cognitive overload. More than the other runners, she was wilful, wanted very badly to win and she was pumped up in front of a crowd, high on the excitement of her landmark statement about Aboriginality the previous day, when she ran a lap of honour draped in the Aboriginal flag, attracting world media attention. Her brain was racing and her time had to slow, with more time for each stride than her competitors. The identical stride cadence reported by Macgregor was possible because Cathy had more time and did more work than the others.'

304

'It's not obvious but it's possible,' said Coach Derek. 'You're saying it was driven by more mental engagement. You seem to be disagreeing that Cathy's win came from superior physical ability.'

'The evidence supports it. Cathy lengthened her stride by her time dilating more than the other runners', without the usual slowing down. Her longer strides needed more time but they were in her dilated time and it allowed her to maintain her cadence without changing down a gear or suddenly having to produce power from nowhere. McGregor claimed she did this by being lighter on her feet, springing like a veldt animal or by lifting her feet off the track quicker. I don't think so. Cathy was well known for her long stride. She had strength in her quads, thighs and hamstrings from her training with weights. She could swing her femurs further forward in the same time, using fast twitch fibres she had developed. She had a priori time to accelerate, rather than from starting to use strength and ability she had not accessed previously, as MacGregor claimed.

'My interpretation is that time dilation in her busy brain enabled her to do more running in the time available. She was in 'extreme-flow', or superlative flow and able to speed up. She did it again in the Sydney Olympics in 2000, winning gold in the 400 metres. Again, she was hyper-focused by the expectations and excitement of representing her people and her nation in a competition that for the first time was fair to her as an Aboriginal. Cathy Freeman's performance was super-human, which denied that when Europeans arrived in Australia the culture of Aborigines resembled the earlier 'stone-age' in Europe due to primitive intellect.'

'You make it seem that going faster is there for me to take when I feel like it,' said Maxi. 'It isn't that easy. Going faster is the outcome from imagining what I want, visualizing it and busting through the barriers.'

'A barrier that Freeman had to overcome was the low expectations of Aboriginal accomplishment held by a racially prejudiced general population. Another barrier was competition from experienced elite runners. She overcame both with her courage.

'Your conquest will be psychological, not ethnic,' said Jack. 'Don't let your competitors' experience discourage you. You are unique and the only one who can beat them. Let's finish there today and we'll meet again in a week's time to complete your training programme.'

CHAPTER 61

At their next meeting, Jack passed around a bowl of peaches.

As he held a peach ready to bite it, Blake said to Maxi: 'I imagine your bottom looks like this.'

'You'd do better to imagine my fist in your face,' she said, annoyed.

'Children, please!' said Jack. 'I want us to consider how we can use the overload theory we talked about last week to prepare Maxi for the Boston in 3 months' time. She needs a training programme.'

'Would it be self-defeating to rehearse brain overload?' said Corvid. 'Her brain could become habituated to congestion, less responsive to stimuli and less active.'

'Not if she is in extreme-flow,' said Jack.

'Would this extreme-flow improve her performance?' asked Stan.

'Yes,' said Jack. 'Dilation is greatest when an object is moving very much faster than the observer, close to the maximum speed. The closer her brain activity gets to the limiting neural speed, the more her time will dilate. Extreme-flow would speed up neural impulses close to system capacity, much faster than local reflex responses, enabling her to respond in dilated time and complete her run earlier.'

'Are you saying anyone can perform better simply by getting into flow that is extremely engaged?'

'Yes,' said Jack. 'Marathon runners and others whose performances embrace endurance with cognitive vigour, can bolster their time, bit by bit, crossing finishing lines earlier, inserting additional accomplishment and staying younger.

'A busy mind has been prescribed for running before. Author Alan Sillitoe wrote in The Loneliness of the Long Distance Runner, about a runner who was thinking as he ran '. . . *I wonder if I'm the only one in the running business with this system of forgetting that I'm running because I'm too busy thinking . . .'*

'He was probably busy thinking about running away from his juvenile detention centre,' said Stan.

'Is prodigious mental activity associated with high performance elsewhere?' asked Blake.

'In academia, organisation leadership and entertainment,' said Patti.

'Boxing requires fast thinking,' said Jack. 'A boxer's training routines build speed, timing and endurance. Fights are psychological encounters, between adversaries whose responses are conditioned by hours of training to overcome their opponent with speed.

'Muhammed Ali's fast thinking, fast footwork and fast right-hand leads got the better of George Foreman,' said Coach Derek. 'The action happened so fast, George didn't have time to do it back to Ali.'

'Rehearsal could enable a boxer's time to dilate.' Jack said. 'A boxer reacts with automaticity practised in months of training. He studies his opponent's style. The trainer and boxer together come up with a basic plan for the fight. He fights 'in flow' with high engagement. The action is often a blur. He must adjust in the moment when things aren't going his way. He won't have anticipated everything and he may have to adapt and get the advice of his trainer between rounds. There is cerebral overload and it is the fighter's rehearsed responses in dilated time that enable him to inflict more damage than he receives.

'It's the same in a marathon: it's how a runner grabs time that can take her past rivals.'

'Wouldn't automaticity acquired by training smooth the action, preventing congestion and overload?' asked Coach Derek.

'No, the effect is opposite,' said Jack. 'A fighter who is content to trade blows reactively will lose the fight. Automaticity is a springboard to launch surprise tactics. Maxi won't win by staying on automatic, like percentage tennis. She needs the edge provided by extreme-flow.'

308

'If her neural traffic loads the brain lightly, such as when she reads a good book or watches an exciting movie, she might be 'in flow', but without enough brain congestion for her time to dilate.'

'Can a person really get 'in flow' reading a book?' asked Blake.

'Absolutely,' Jack said. 'A reader can escape into her imagination.'

'Timelessly?'

'Yes. It could be by time dilation.'

'Is there evidence that extreme-flow has resulted in time dilation?' asked Stan.

'Yes. People have come to terms with dire circumstances and suffered near-death traumas in slow motion,' said Jack. 'Outstanding performers have testified that their exceptional performances seemed timeless to them. Alice's base-jumping may dilate her time.'

'The buzz of bending time is part of the attraction,' Alice said.

'When a runner dices with bonking, it could be timeless like a near-death experience. We're wanting Maxi to run at the edge of bonking, which could be optimal for extreme-flow and time dilation.'

'Don't go overboard with all this mental stuff,' said Stan gruffly. 'If Maxi dilates her mind, she will still need her body to get her to the finish line quickly. A smart bike rider needs a fast bike. Her body has to be fast.'

'Stan has a point, but his rejection of Zen is because he doesn't understand it,' Jack thought.

'What do you say to that?' Jack asked Riko.

'A bicycle is a machine you can prepare, but you can't prepare Maxi's body without preparing her mind at the same time,' she said. 'In Zen, her mind and body are one.'

'That answers Stan nicely,' Jack thought. *'We can do without his negativity.'*

'Stan, would you please train her to run at the edge of bonking?' said Jack. 'Patti, will you provide her with food to delay bonking? Riko, will you teach her a Zen mental posture that she can use to defend against bonking? I'll work on getting her to run in extreme-flow? Maxi, all you have to do is give it everything you have, without ever quitting. We're counting on you.'

'I feel honoured and will try to be worthy,' Maxi said. 'Thanks, guys.'

'How much training should she do?' Jack asked.

'It's up to her,' said Coach Derek. 'Enough to challenge her in every area but not so much she becomes stale. I think we can suggest a schedule and leave it to her to tell us when she wants a timeout.'

'Could the coaches stay behind, please, to nut out a training programme?'

'Do I need to stay?' said Maxi.

'It's essential,' said Coach Derek. 'You're the one who will do it.'

The others left them to it.

'Maxi needs to develop mental endurance, strategic automaticity and relentless goal achievement,' said Jack. 'Let's start with mental endurance. What exercises can she do?'

'QIS has digital software for brain endurance training,' said Coach Derek. 'An annoying stimulus keeps coming at you on the screen. There are drills that train you to restrain an impulse; withholding a reaction is less fatiguing than reacting. The training makes you stay more focused and sharp when you get tired. Your perception of effort will not be as high compared to if you only train the physical. The mind will not limit what your body can do and slow you down.

'Maxi, you can look forward to spending a few hours online doing mental workouts.'

Stan interrupted. 'I'm not convinced she can become a better runner by sitting in front of a computer.'

'I agree it's not obvious. She can try it out and see if she likes it and if there are any gains.'

'What about strategic automaticity?' asked Jack.

'There are brain development exercises requiring physical participation,' said Jack. 'She can train with armed services

310

personnel who rely on mental prowess to survive, endure and succeed in combat and counter-terrorism.'

Jack's ideas had been tentative earlier but now to avoid being seen as an exploiter of Maxi, he had to compromise his ideas and accept others' proposals. Conversely, he would not become so beholden to them that he fell into their servitude. Achieving his freedom depended on him respecting theirs.

'Holy shit!' Maxi said. 'How is counter-terrorism training going to help me run marathons?'

'You need to develop instant access to full mental power, making rapid and correct responses.'

'I would rather run away,' she said.

'If you run fast, that could be good!'

'Finally, how can she develop relentless goal achievement?' asked Jack.

'Marathon runners are good at it,' said Stan.

'She needs absolute commitment to her goal,' Riko said.

'She has improved,' said Jack. 'Earlier, she varied from her plan sometimes, just for the hell of it.'

'That's not fair,' said Maxi. 'I had reasons . . . good ones.'

'Sorry Maxi,' he said. 'You almost always stay on plan now. Congratulations. Further improvement is up to you.'

'I'm helping her,' said Riko Minami. 'The Zen way is total mental control.'

'We all have exercises to do that will prepare Maxi mentally. That's our plan, folks. I'll write it up and send it. Let's finish there for today.'

CHAPTER 62

It was not unusual for a coach to be in a relationship with his or her athlete. It was working well for Maxi and me. We seldom were opposed and we often had synergy. Our trust built into total commitment.

Maxi was preparing for the Boston Marathon, where she would compete with the World's best at her event. Her training exercises were designed to enhance her extreme-flow capability with ability to dilate her time. Her practice runs carefully simulated the race conditions we expected. On an army obstacle course, she prepared responses to intermittent threats.

She respected me as a scientist who could hold up a mirror to her performance, for her to realise what she was doing and make corrections herself. I was a taskmaster who helped her fulfil her goal commitments supportively rather than critically. Her show was mine too.

It would have been easy to slip into a 'tough love' mode where I cajoled, chivvied and goaded her like Stan had. She responded to me better by consideration, kindness and good humour.

Top marathon competition had sensational media coverage and publicity was precarious. A newspaper article about her had the headline: 'Australia's Running Champion'. High expectations for top performance in The Boston had a negative effect on her, magnifying her natural fear of failure. Her antidote was to relax with activities she enjoyed and forget the ordeal that loomed. I gave psychological support sustaining her self-confidence and preventing distraction by media.

'This race matters more to me than to you,' she said to me. 'If I fail, you have other career possibilities. I don't. I have nothing else.'

In my dream of Maxi, I heroically provided her with a winning training formula, but extreme-flow was out on a limb. It had never been tested but she had agreed to try it. A day of reckoning was fast approaching when my theory could fail miserably, Maxi could suffer and I would be humiliated.

'My PhD could crash,' I said. 'I would have to go back and do the type of work I detest.'

'You poor thing! You could have to get a regular job!' she scoffed. 'I don't know what job I could do. All I can do is run.'

I watched Maxi run at the QIS track on alternative weekdays. When she became despondent, I worried about her.

'Has your ante ratcheted up to a dark place?' I asked.

Her reply was a sullen mumble and revealed I was closer to the mark than she was prepared to admit.

'You're the favourite because you're the best,' I said. 'There has never been anyone before as good as you. People are excited because you could do very well, even win. You should be feeling confident, not inadequate.'

'How would you know how I'm feeling,' she said. 'You don't even know I have feelings.'

'Ouch,' I said. 'I do want to know your feelings. I'm aware you're doing it tough and I want to help you. You're being too hard on yourself.'

'How can I escape from their expectations? Everyone has a piece of me, stroking me with hype. People are getting up my arse.'

'You sound angry. How do you feel?'

'Tired.'

'You know what to do about that.'

I had asked her to go away with me for a couple of weeks on a rainforest trek.

'I can't quit the programme,' she said. 'A lot of people have invested their time in me and depend on me. I have employees who expect to get paid. I have to compete and I have to win.'

313

'People want you to enjoy running and have fun.'

She glared at me and her words were vehement.

'Those long training runs are hardly fun,' she said indignantly.

'They used to be. You told me once that when you were 'in flow', it was not just ordinary enjoyment, but your favourite thing ever. I want to help you get back to that, to be happy.'

'How can I be happy walking along the edge of a cliff?'

'You have me as your safety net. You can live in the moment. I want you to do well, for you, but I will love you just the same if you lose.'

'Then stop pulling the other way,' said Maxi. 'Pull with me. It's so hard to keep going sometimes.'

She wanted help but wouldn't ask for it because it would admit to weakness she wanted to hide. She was fiercely independent. She leapt over tall buildings while I made my way through at ground level.

'Your research is taking forever,' she said. 'Why are you dotting all the i's and crossing all the t's?'

'That's how we do academic research,' I said.

'We're running out of time!'

'Good,' I said. 'With a close deadline, time can dilate for us.'

'I wish you weren't so gung-ho about this damn time dilation thing. I don't know what to believe.'

'You have nothing to lose by believing and much to gain,' I said. 'Can't you just accept it could be true?'

'That's easy for you to say, but I'm the one who has to flog her ass along 42 kilometres of track on a whim. If I'm to put my heart into something, it has to be a sure thing.'

'Committing to extreme-flow won't lose you anything.'

'Will I ever know if your theory works? How can I be sure that extreme-flow is faster?'

'Bannister, Freeman, Prefontaine, Muhammed Ali and Michael Jackson all rose to new high levels of accomplishment under duress. You will be too.'

'Because they tried harder?'

314

'Of course. They didn't pull it out of a hat. They were already at the tops of their games and they did it by engaging extremely so that their time dilated.'

'They could have had potential not realised previously.'

'It doesn't explain what they did that was different.'

'What do you think they did?'

'They thought hard, with their brains racing in extreme-flow. In the movie 'Bannister' he recounts his self-talk while he was breaking the record. He was worried he was too slow, then he relaxed and detached 'in flow', marvelling at his effortless speed with exultation, his mind racing and in control, driving him forward interminably, until he crossed the line and collapsed.'

'How can you be sure his time dilated?'

'It isn't something you can see. The conditions were present for it to occur. A lot of so-called scientific theories are like that, evolution, for example. You can't actually observe it happening. Nor can you see gravity causing Newton's apple to fall. Many theories are inferred to be true. When you win, you'll be convinced. It could be false, but there's no harm in thinking it's true. Cathy Freeman's brain went nineteen to the dozen when she was racing and what she did for 49 seconds you can do for most of two and a half hours. There is heaps for you to think about, as we have practiced.'

'What if I lose?'

'Don't think about that. I'll love you just the same.'

She hesitated.

'Okay, I'll give it a go.'

I had not been aware until now how difficult it had been for Maxi to believe in my theory. My credibility as a coach rested on our unique rapport. She trusted in me. Gradually, she had suspended disbelief and accepted my theory. We had a shared belief in something beyond the physical world, our fortunes in spin. We were optimistic. If she won, I would win too. If she lost, I would lose too. Our overriding belief was in each other. Our faiths in each other were scaffolded by our faiths in humanity. We believed what we were doing would be highly valued and widely.

'Will you still want me around after you break the record?' I asked.

'Will you still want me around if I don't?' she said.

I denied my interest in her would diminish, but I didn't voice my main fear, which was that we might not last together if she lost. The glue in our relationship was her running goal and without it we could come unstuck. Our dare had danger.

CHAPTER 63

Jack showed a video at the start of their next meeting.

'This interview was broadcast yesterday in Performance Space on Fox News.'

A TV host faced Maxi before a studio audience.

'Good evening, viewers. I'm Robert Renfrew. In three weeks, my guest: Maxi Fleet, will line up in Boston with 20 elite runners and 30,000 of the World's best women marathoners. Maxi, will you tell us why you run marathons?'

'Good evening, everyone. Thank you for having me on your show, Robert. I like running and I hope this race will be particularly enjoyable. Also, I want to win.'

She gave a confident air punch and the audience clapped.

'Would you tell us something about how you became a marathon runner?'

'I started running 1500 metre races at school in Brisbane. I liked to be in front of a crowd and distance running enabled me to put on a performance. I went on to 3000 metres, then half marathons and for the last two years I have run marathons. I enjoy the preparation that goes into running 42 kilometres. I have been fortunate to train at the Queensland Institute of Sport and have the support of coaches, family and friends.'

'Why not play a team sport?'

'I prefer to be in a team of one.'

'You like to be in control?'

'I like to be free to run my own race.'

'Do you always win?'

'No. In the national half-marathon at the Gold Coast three years ago, I over-exerted and collapsed, finishing 23rd.'

They watched a video of Maxi wobbling into the barrier, collapsing, then getting up and staggering across the line.

'I don't like watching that,' Maxi said.

'Sorry,' said Renfrew and turned it off.

'I did get up and finish,' she said.

'Did it change what you do?'

'I have learned to run with less striving, in flow.'

'Flow is when you run 'in the zone' isn't it?'

'Yes.'

'When do you do that?'

'As much as possible. Ideally throughout the race.'

They watched a video of the London Marathon with her finishing first.

'Were you 'in flow' when you won?'

'I was 'in flow' during most of the race.'

'What was that like?'

'I was on automatic, goal-focussed and timeless.'

'Can you tell us about your training?'

'Our methods are experimental. We're not telling people about them just yet, until we are sure they work.'

'Have they helped you much?'

Maxi smiled. 'It's difficult to know. I won the London Marathon in a PB of 2h14. It was 8 minutes faster than my previous race in Melbourne, so we think the training had a good effect.'

'How do you expect to go in Boston?'

'My goal is 2h10, 4 minutes faster than I ran in London, but even if I improve that much, it may not be fast enough to win. Several others have run similar times.'

'Thank you, Maxi and good luck in Boston.'

Applause.

Jack switched the video off.

Everyone applauded.

'You spoke well, Maxi,' said Jack.

318

'Why didn't you mention that you dilate your time?' said Alice.

'I don't want competitors benefiting. People are okay with 'flow', as if it is a gimmick, but if time dilation gets out, it could stir up opponents and create a controversy.'

''Flow' is not a gimmick,' said Alice. 'It is more like a philosophy.'

'Time dilation is our secret weapon,' said Jack.

'Why does it have to be secret?'

'When the media realise Maxi's techniques could have contributed to her running 8 minutes faster than in London, they could want her excluded from The Boston.'

'What could they say?'

'That it endangers the runner, gives an unfair advantage, could result in injury and would bring running into disrepute.'

'Are they likely to say that?'

'Yes.'

'It would be false.'

'That wouldn't stop them. We must keep quiet about time dilation until after the race. Agreed?'

Jack had abandoned the notion that an objective reality ruled. There was none, only individual subjectivity, arbitrated by the media. Performers were pawns in corporate games that lacked rules and ethics. Anything could happen and they had to be careful.

The secret of Jack's theory brought hope and excitement to their preparations. They united in gathering intelligence of course conditions and competitor abilities for Maxi to have in her head, besides the confidence she knew they had in her.

CHAPTER 64

Maxi and her 10-strong team, with Jack's family, flew to Boston a week before the race. On the plane, Maxi met with team members, considered business issues with Jack used her devices. She liked to analyse statistics of past performances, looking for patterns such as trends. She asked questions of fact or opinion on everything, even the best colours for the running gear she would wear.

Obtaining the standards she wanted took persistence. When he booked accommodation for everyone, he emailed the hotel a list of her requirements. Her bedroom must have a window area totalling at least 8 meters wide by 3 metres high and a balcony 3 meters wide and 6 metres long. There had to be a sitting room of at least 6 metres square with a ceiling of at least 3 metres over it. There were other stipulations for staff quarters and for a conference room.

Maxi was uncompromising.

'My bedroom has less window area than I require,' said Maxi to a hotel manager when they arrived. 'Change me to another bedroom.'

'There is no other bedroom with windows large enough, ma'am.'

'Jack, would you find another hotel for us? There must be one that has decent-sized windows.'

He found another hotel and they transferred there in a fleet of taxis, with all their baggage. It became a part of her myth that Maxi got what she wanted.

As her closest confidante, companion and lover, Jack advised her on much more than science. He was chief of staff and supervised the Team, including his own personal assistant. Her hair, her clothes, her public appearances, her business, her finances and her medical specialists all fell within his ambit. Not least was his role supporting her celebrity lifestyle. Her father, stepmother and several close friends had come with them to Boston to be with her too. Jack reminded her of their special occasions, such as birthdays, with a choice of gifts and messages she could send to them.

Maxi was the boss. Jack, her manager, had to be stoical. Seneca had described his stoical position like a dog tied with a long rope to its master's chariot.

'If I want to follow I am pulled, my action coinciding with necessity,' he said to Blake. 'I am compelled to follow what is destined.'

Nevertheless, he was content, for the moment.

Maxi's wilfulness was admirable in races but could be a hazard for those who worked with her at close quarters. When she wanted something, she had to have it right now or she might scream. A quite trivial matter could explode unpredictably. As the race got closer, they had to make allowances for her.

She could be prickly and temperamental like Evita Peron, the Argentinian nightclub singer who soared to stardom and won the hearts of the nation. Authenticity radiated from Maxi like a beacon and adoring fans travelled around the globe to watch her run.

Maxi had employed her friend Zadie as Events Manager. Her engagements and training were planned meticulously from her arrival until the race.

The team met at 7:00 am each day, at their hotel, the Lenox on Boylston Street, where the race would finish. They discussed her training. Afterwards she ran for several hours in the park and inside on a track. The city vibrated with marathon fever and there were so many runners it was difficult to find space to train. Maxi spent afternoons doing interviews, meeting with sponsors and promoting her brand. The team met again every evening at 5.00 pm. Afterwards she went through her race plan with Jack and mentally rehearsed alone for the coming race.

Everyone on the team helped with preparing Maxi in an atmosphere that was tense. The star's life was public without enough privacy for relaxation. When the rigour became too demanding, she would break out.

'Come on Jack, let's get out of here.'

Leaving her security guard behind and taking the hired limousine with driver kept on standby for her, they went downtown to a nightclub. They would dance for hours, she drinking only water. She was a vigorous dancer and exhausted Jack. People recognised her from photos in the news by her charisma, physical beauty and imperious demeanour. They would queue up for her autograph and she would linger over the signing, charming them.

'I love having fans,' she said. 'They make it all worthwhile for me.'

Jack read aloud in their morning meeting an article in the Boston Examiner.

AUSTRALIAN COULD WIN IN BOSTON

Marathons have been run in Boston since 1897. There is a festival atmosphere here for the race on Saturday. With 30,000 runners, 20,000 officials, and one million spectators along the course from Hopkinton to Boylston Street and 2 billion looking at TVs globally, the Boston Marathon is one of the most-watched sporting events in the World.

Maxi Fleet from Australia is a favourite to win after coming first in The London Marathon. I talked with Maxi at a track where her training is tapering off in preparation for the race.

'Boston is more aware of and involved in its marathon than anywhere I have run,' she said.

Her training over the past year has been far from traditional.

'Maxi has learned to run in 'the zone' or 'flow' as we call it,' said Jack Cram, her manager, who is researching physics for a PhD. Athletes performances seem to benefit when they run 'in flow'. I believe this is why Maxi's results have improved.'

Maxi said: 'My goal is 2h10, compared with my time of 2h14 in London last year.'

After the London Marathon, she was tested for illegal substance use by the UK Athletics Association, without any being found.

Her coaching team includes Queensland Institute of Sport's Derek Tracker, Zen specialist Dr Riko Minami, her father Stan Fleet, Alice Lamont, a psychologist, Blake Holocene, an engineer, Corvid Feir, a neuroscientist and her mother Patti who is the Team's nutritionist.

I asked coach Jack Cram: 'Is the optimal experience claimed for 'flow' a physical outcome as well as a psychological effect?'

''Flow' is too subjective to measure,' said Cram. 'Runner self-reporting is unreliable and our relating 'flow' to outcomes has not come very far.'

I telephoned Dr Rohan Baxter, of Queensland University's Physics Department.

'Is Maxi Fleet's running part of a physics experiment?' I asked him.

'We are investigating effects of high brain activity levels on athletes' performances,' he said. 'Experiments are difficult to control and our study is expected to take several years. We will be watching The Boston and hoping that Jack Cram's theory will help Maxine Fleet to a winning performance.'

Eyes will be on Maxi in the race on Saturday. Competitors are not required to disclose their training methods. In the past, new mental regimens have been allowed.

The first placed woman will receive $250,000 prize money. Sponsorships and media contracts would be worth much more.

Cindy Hirako from Japan will be a strong contender. Bostonians are expecting Susan Walters, the reigning champion from the USA, to run well. It is a strong line up and if the weather is fine, record-breaking can be expected.

Victor Eckman, Associated Press.

'Maxi won't be the only runner trying to run 'in flow' in this race,' said Alice. 'Other runners have taken up flow. But we have time dilation up our sleeve.'

323

'There could be crazy people in the crowd and we have to protect her from accusations of drug-taking,' said Jack.

CHAPTER 65

On the day of the race, the weather was atrocious, cold, wet and windy. 2 million people usually packed the sides of the streets along the route, but under these conditions fewer were expected. Security personnel lined the route wearing yellow and orange visibility vests.

Maxi ambled around in the marshalling area, shaking loose her muscles, watching drone views of the crowd on a huge screen. There were 4 drones overhead at the start, two scrutinizing for threats to security and two monitoring runner performances. Coaches used the official drones, via satellites, to communicate with their runners' monitors. Media would show videos of the race around the globe.

Drones would be 100 metres above, navigating with radar to avoid colliding. In an earlier race, a pacesetter drone she was following had crashed, breaking her concentration. She would take direction from the drones, obtaining her pace from independent feeds to her wrist monitor. They had cameras able to zoom in from 2 kilometres to track a runner's facial expressions. Maxi welcomed the distraction from pain and weariness of scrutiny by a global audience.

The wind-chill temperature today was below zero as Maxi toed the start line, wearing a sleeved shirt, leggings and toque. She lined up with the 20 elite women who had qualified with times below 2h35. The race record was 2h12. They would start at 8.40 am. Different ability levels would run off in waves, the faster ones getting away first to minimise overtaking.

The men's course record was 1h55. The first wave of men would follow 20 minutes after the women and catch up to finish together.

Maxi subvocalized the checklist Riko had taught her to start correctly.

'Speak these words 30 minutes before every run, in a quiet space.

'Double-check the knots in my shoelaces and that I have everything I need. Relax my breathing while visualising the course and imagining finishing exhausted.

'Start the run and focus on rhythm and cadence. Listen to my feet and turn the small sound into music in my mind, like a drum beating. Listen to my breathing and how each inhalation and exhalation relates to the rhythm my feet are making. Stop hearing the sound of my feet, focus on my breathing and relax. When I'm aware that I'm moving, I'm no longer 'in flow'.

Maxi memorized the ritual and obeyed it automatically, to settle her nerves and get into 'flow'.

The starter called them to Get Set. Beside her Cindy Hirako from Japan toed the line and held a crucifix dangling from her neck.

The gun fired and the peloton galloped along the wet road, their breaths condensing to steam. Maxi listened to her breathing. She eased into the lead, with Desai from Kenya at one shoulder and Cindy Hirako at the other. After 1500m Desai kicked to the front. Maxi accepted second place. Desai drew steadily away. Maxi used her monitor to check the pace. She was going fast enough. Desai might not keep it up. When she was 50m ahead, Maxi sped up, running along the double yellow line at the centre of the turnpike, the rest of the pack at her heels.

She was wet but felt good, turning 200 steps per minute, well above the efficient average of 180. She wore a pink long sleeved running top with a collar, her hair swinging in a golden pony tail and gold running shoes. Her rhythm was steady and smooth, her body comfortably straight and slightly forward, legs and arms reciprocating smoothly. Her mouth was open for easy breathing and her gaze intent ahead, with occasional glances around her. She scrutinised her path carefully for holes and bumps that could cause her to trip. They were difficult to see in the glare from the shiny road and under puddle surfaces rippled by the wind.

Maxi let her mind rove. She recalled that Desai had run 2h16 in London, but the conditions today were more punishing and their times would be slower. Desai dropped back and was absorbed in the group behind. Buffeted by wind, with cold rainwater running in her eyes, down her face and soaking her shirt., Maxi was in the lead, 'in flow' despite discomfort.

At Mile 5, Framingham, someone 'got off the bus' and the convoy reduced to 18. The route was mostly flat and the runners were conserving energy for the uphill work late in the race. After Mile 8 they entered Natick and Maxi stepped up the pace a little. Behind her, the pack unravelled into small groups, strung out over hundreds of metres.

There was a big crowd at Mile 10, Natick Center, whooping and cheering as Maxi came through leading the front group. Although the first 10 kilometres had been downhill, the pace was slow because of the wind and cold. Someone was tucked in 50 metres behind her but she couldn't recognise who it was. She hoped it was Hirako because she had beaten her in London. She couldn't see who was catching up behind her. Damn this prosopagnosia. It could be the American, Susan Walters. She was reputed to be a strong finisher. Assuming it was Walters, Maxi sped up. She would fight her now before she caught up and used her as a shield from the driving wind and rain.

She was soaked and her toque let water through, flowing down her forehead and into her eyes and mouth. Gusts blew leaves across the road. She had not raced in conditions as bad as this before. The cold would reduce her energy supply. Some of the women wore leggings thicker than hers. She wore gloves and her arms were covered but her torso and legs were in cold wet cotton and felt uncomfortable. She concentrated on conserving as much energy as possible while keeping to her performance goal.

At Mile 13, halfway, she ran through the Scream Tunnel at Wellesely College, with the girl students' yells amplified in a wall of sound. There were colourful signs, high fives, hugs, and kisses to cheer on the runners as they streamed past. Because of the weather, the crowds were thin.

Maxi was still ahead but the gap with Walters or whoever had closed to 50 metres and Maxi was concerned she would be caught. She sped up again.

Now there was just two of them. At Mile 15, after the sharp descent at Newton Lower Falls, Maxi lifted her pace to the fastest rate she figured she would be able to sustain up the four hills ahead. Only Walters stayed with her. They quickly opened a lead of over a minute and the rest of the field dropped out of view.

Maxi was determined not to be caught and swung into Newton at Mile 16, across the overpass with the cold wind buffeting her and rain at 4°C driving in and soaking her. Despite the inclement conditions, she was focussed. Her lead was 20 metres with 16 kilometres left to run. The conditions would reduce her time, but her aim was now to equal her previous PB. A glance at her wrist monitor confirmed she could achieve it. At this point in the race she was free of fatigue.

She was passing spectators huddled beside the road under umbrellas, when a gust tore one away and it sailed across the road straight towards her. She was unable to avoid it, ran into it and tripped over, falling forwards onto the road, going down on to her knees and hands. She rolled sideways, leapt up, kicked her feet free and continued running. She had lost only seconds and still had a lead of 40 metres. Her ankle was hurting — it had twisted when she went down. She was running awkwardly, feeling pain.

She approached the first three of Newton's hills, Firehouse Hill at Mile 17. The fall had reduced the fuel in her tank down to the dregs. It took tremendous effort to slowly climb the hill.

'I am going to finish,' she thought. *'I've had bad luck and I may not get all the apple, but I'll punch through the glass and get as much as I can.'*

She was so exhausted she could barely climb up the terrain. Her resolve was reeling. Whereas she had planned to float above hurt throughout this race, she was now mired in pain and limped up hills through the cold, wet and gusting wind. Her fuel was nearly gone and she expected to bonk at any moment. Her legs felt like concrete, her quads were cramping and she was panting in shallow breaths because it hurt too much to breathe more deeply. Her solar plexus was stabbed by pains like cramps. She feared permanent organ damage. Her toes hurt as if the nails had come off.

Her muddled thoughts questioned why she was here running a marathon in bad weather. Beside the road undeterred by the rain were pretty Columbine flowers. She considered how they grew; 'they toiled not; neither did they spin'. They survived in all their beauty. Perhaps they had an inner purpose, as she did.

She stumbled on up City Hall hill at Mile 20. After three hills, she had reached the most difficult part of the course. Although the total rise was only 540 feet, she now faced a winding half-mile climb up Heartbreak Hill from Center Street to Hammond Street, 91 feet above, a punishing 3.3% gradient. At Mile 21, Boston College, the course plummeted down, difficult for her on shaky legs. Much of the course so far had been downhill, wearing her quads down to searing aches.

Now Maxi tried to speed up, but pain everywhere in her body prevented her overcoming the exhaustion and cold. The crowd thickened with university students. Maxi glanced behind her and was surprised to see not Susan Walters, as she expected, but Cindy Hirako. She had caught up while Maxi was slowed down by her fall. Maxi had put all her energy into staying ahead of someone who was not a threat, because Maxi was a faster finisher. Walters' disappearance was a mystery.

Jack was there at the final drinking station. Pausing only to grab a paper cup of water, she hid her pain from him as she hid it from herself.

'Almost there and you're in front!' he said. 'You can do it!'

For 8 more kilometres, she kept her lead with Hirako slowly getting closer, but she had nothing left with which to fight back.

Finally, it was the last kilometre and the leading elite men overtook her up the slight rise. When Maxi took the left turn into Boylston Street, Cindy Hirako hurtled past her. Maxi picked up and stayed with her but was unable to sustain the kick and by the time she reached Copley Square and crossed the finish line, she was 30 metres behind. She dropped into Jack's arms. Her time was 2h22, well short of her goal of 2h10 and her PB of 2h14. The weather and the unexpected umbrella had taken their tolls.

She sat with Jack and Stan in the stand beside the finish, sheltering from the rain, dispirited but not abject. They considered what to do differently next time.

'That umbrella was bad luck,' said Jack, who had watched the incident on a screen. 'You would have won easily.'

'You let it rattle you,' said Stan. 'It delayed you seconds and you accepted second place.'

'Stan! Stop it,' Jack glared at him.

'I blew it,' said Maxi. 'I thought it was Susan Walters behind me and I used up my energy trying to get away, because of her strong finish. It turned out to be Cindy Hirako behind me, but I was spent by then and she took the lead from me.'

'You ran brilliantly,' said Jack. 'In future, when there's bad weather, you'll be ready for unlikely events.'

No-one voiced what they all knew, that Maxi had run too hard too early, due to mistaking who was behind her. Her recognition error could have cost her the race. It was a concern that could be left until later. In post-race discussions, it was customary not to blame the athlete. Setbacks could not be shortcomings of the runner. Causal factors could be specific, like the lone umbrella, or external like umbrellas in general, or all hills, because they could be encountered in any race. For now, it must be assumed she had done as well as she possibly could, this being reason for authentic happiness, preventing depression, hastening the athlete's recovery and improving training for the next performance — if she could somehow get a place on Australia's Olympics marathon team.

If Stan had more criticism, he kept it to himself. They would analyse her performance later.

CHAPTER 66

Maxi qualified for the Australian Team to go to Cape Town for the Olympics. Team Maxi met to plan her campaign. Everyone was sitting in pews around the altar table in the community room. This was their first meeting since returning from Boston three months earlier. Maxi had been away travelling in Europe with Jack and today was a reunion.

'Have you had a good holiday, Maxi?' asked Blake.

'Yes, thank you.'

'Did you take a break from running?'

'Mostly. I went jogging a few times.'

Jack started the meeting.

'Our congratulations to Maxi for making the Australian team.'

'Way to go, Maxi,' said Alice.

Everyone clapped.

'Hayley Thomas from QIS has also been selected,' Maxi said. 'She ran 2h25 in the National last year, only 3 minutes behind me. I invited her to our meeting to see what we do.'

Hayley acknowledged their applause.

'Could you run with Hayley in Cape Town?' asked Alice.

'Pacing is banned,' Maxi said, 'because it would advantage nations with several runners. In any case, it's easier to concentrate alone.'

'It is strange how cycling allows teamwork and running doesn't,' said Jack. 'Perhaps it's because collective success is part of cycling tradition.'

'Today Hayley and I ran 20 kilometres together,' said Maxi.

'How was it?'

'I'm out of shape but it won't take long to get back.'

'I have been on a break too,' said Hayley. 'Today's run was hard work for me.'

'Hayley, we're going on to talk about Maxi's training,' said Jack. 'I hope you won't think us rude to leave you out for the moment. You are welcome to stay. You could want to meet with your coaches soon and you can get an idea of what we are doing with Maxi.'

'Thank you, Jack,' said Hayley. 'I would like to find out about Maxi's training.'

'Maxi and Hayley could train with me every morning and I hope the other coaches will work with them together too,' said Coach Derek.

'Is Hayley going to join in with Maxi's Zen work?' asked Corvid.

'Maxi is more advanced and the two will do exercises separately,' said Riko.

'Could Hayley catch up before we depart for Cape Town?' asked Stan.

'She will have the basics,' said Derek.

'I've booked everyone on a flight on May 6$^{th.}$, a month before the race,' said Jack. 'Maxi and Hayley will be in the village and the rest of us at the Mandela Hotel.

'Today, we need to learn what we can from Boston and review the various techniques we are planning to include in Maxi's training for the next four months, until we go to Cape Town. Maxi, will you tell us about Boston. How well do you think you ran?'

'It was difficult to stay focussed with all that weather. It took longer than I expected to get into 'flow',' she said. 'I was going into the wind and rain at point position and using a lot of energy. When I did get into 'flow', I was uncomfortable and by the time I reached the hills I was having to push myself to keep up my pace.'

'Did being 'in flow' help you at all?'

'It helped me to hold the lead from about Mile 3 to Mile 16, until the accident. After I fell, I couldn't get back into it.'

'What was your time when you fell?'

'About 1h25.'

Jack used his calculator.

'That's 18.5 kilometres per hour, a tad below your target of 20.'

'The weather slowed everyone down.'

'The last 16 kilometres was even slower,' he said, 'only 17 kilometres an hour. Why was that?'

'I struggled up those hills. My legs almost quit and I slowed down, but I couldn't pull back from the edge. It was like being in a long partial bonk. My lead had been a minute, but by the time Cindy Hirako caught up, I had no fight left in me. I was hurting and limped to the finish.'

'I won't mention that I wrongly perceived the runner behind me as a threat and burned up too much energy trying to stay ahead,' she thought. *'It makes me seem foolish. I don't need everyone to know about my prosopagnosia.'*

'Could you have avoided the umbrella?'

'It caught me by surprise.'

'Afterwards, did you lose confidence and choke?'

'It wasn't just the umbrella, or the fall. It was the weather, the terrain and the stage of the race. It all went bad at once.'

'Could your sense of time have been dislocated by the umbrella, so that you slowed down without intending to?'

'I was emotional for sure and maybe not thinking straight.'

'What is your goal for the Cape, Maxi?' Jack asked

'2h10'

'There could be another incident like the umbrella,' said Derek. 'It is difficult to prepare for how to deal with a disruption, or with a group breaking away.'

'Perhaps Jack could rush out in front of her during her training at random intervals with an umbrella,' said Blake.

'Or Derek could overtake her,' said Riko. 'If he still can.'

'I'd be too fast,' said Derek, laughing. 'I'll get the QIS squad to race against Maxi, maybe in a relay.'

'It would bring out her best performance,' said Stan.

'What if my squad beats her?'

'It won't matter to me,' said Maxi. 'My performance time drives me, not my ego.'

'How are you going to learn to vary your pace?'

'I need to stay alert for any change in conditions. I ran into the umbrella because I wasn't flexible enough.'

'You need to project your goal into every stride,' said Riko. 'You can keep alert by constantly reviewing your options, asking yourself if your energy is enough to finish, or whether to slow down.'

'Achieving a piece of your goal can keep you going, like achieving your half-way target, or staying with the leading group, or taking the lead, or letting someone pass you when you know you can take the lead back later,' Coach Derek said. 'As you come to milestones and potential disruptions, you have to be ready with all the options.'

'Do my decisions have to be ready-made?'

'Yes,' said Jack. 'When you're at the back of a group, there are few choices, but further forward there are many. Nietzsche wanted people to proactively choose their own future.'

'Jack's right,' said Coach Derek. 'Will yourself to move forward through the field to achieve a new PB. If you have a challenging goal, your performance will be new territory and exciting.'

'I need to judge accurately my fastest sustainable pace,' said Maxi.

'That's what training is for,' he said. 'When your energy has faded and you predict you are about to bonk, you learn to slow down.'

'How would I know when to make a move?'

'When you have had some success, you can go for more,' he said. '"Flow" can inhibit your brain's amygdala and you might take a risk you don't need. Positive feedback and applause can lower your perceived effort and cause you to grab too much.'

'So Maxi has to be prepared to be decisive. What else can she do to improve?' asked Jack.

'Could she try for flow that's more extreme?' asked Alice. 'Perhaps she wasn't getting the full benefit in The Boston.'

'I'm not sold on extreme-flow,' said Maxi. 'Why do I need that?'

Jack rolled his eyes. He had gone over this with her several times.

'It will create more time to run in, a faster result and more enjoyment,' Corvid said. 'Impulses to your brain will stretch your body time compared with external time. You'll be able to get more done, hit time targets and achieve your goal. If you exert your will and maintain extreme-flow, your running should look after itself.'

'It's just a theory,' Maxi said. 'Why should I believe it?'

'Does she want to be convinced or is she just testing?' Jack thought. *'I hope she is more believing than she sounds.'*

'Having faith will cause you to run faster,' said Coach Derek.

'Faster than what?' she said.

'Faster than otherwise. Your minutes will stretch and you will have extra time to put in more or longer paces. Your endorphins will enable you to tolerate more pain and adrenaline will cause you to run faster, allowing you to overtake. You'll feel good, push past your previous best and you could even break the event record.'

Jack smiled happily. Until now, he had been ploughing a lonely furrow all alone. Now Derek's support made it all worthwhile. A top coach was using his theory.

'Can all of that be achieved by faith alone?' asked Maxi.

'You have to be physically able to sustain a pace to achieve your goal,' said Coach Derek. ''Stan will prepare you physically and Riko will prepare you mentally.'

'Thanks, Derek,' said Jack.

'Okay,' Maxi said, capitulating. 'I do believe extreme-flow will make me faster and I'll strive to get into it and stay in it.'

'Believe it with fervour and your brain will stretch time for you to get done,' said Riko.

'How can I fire up my cognition enough?' asked Maxi. 'Flow is too preoccupied.'

'You have to be totally mentally engaged with the race,' Riko said. 'Brain engagement is the new paradigm in distance running: gone are the days when marathoners meditated placidly or day-dreamed. Your brain should be a hive of furious activity.'

'Should I be adjusting my pace to stay on target?'

'Yes, whenever possible,' said Coach Derek. 'You need to identify abnormal conditions requiring intervention and remediation. Your plan may need you to adjust for how much running you still have in you, for the weather, or for other competitors. You'll be in extreme-flow, in total control, thinking of everything except being limited. You'll be unleashed. Can you picture that?'

'Me in control?' she said. 'I can imagine that! I'll give it a go.'

'You're a natural,' said Blake.

'You're already doing 'flow' well,' Jack said. 'Now we need you to reinforce it with extreme-flow.'

'After this meeting, we coaches need to create a training programme for Maxi right through to the Olympics,' said Coach Derek. 'Okay Riko, Stan, Jack?'

'Maxi is going to be a race favourite,' said Patti. 'Australia has never won an Olympic medal in the marathon, except for Lisa Martin's silver in 1988.'

'The hopes of millions are on my shoulders and I'm weighed down,' said Maxi.

'It will get worse!' said Alice.

'Only if you think about it,' said Minami.

'We'll finish there, unless anyone has any questions,' said Jack. 'Hayley, have you been able to see what we do?'

'Yes, thank you.'

'I will send you Maxi's programme if you like and then you can choose sessions where you want to join her?' Jack asked.

'I would like that.'

CHAPTER 67

When Maxi had first started running, Stan coached her. With Derek and Riko training her at QIS on weekdays, I started Team Maxi to coordinate her coaches. My influence had steadily increased, with the coaches adopting training ideas from my research. During the last few months of Maxi's preparation for the Olympics, I kept her programme together, with the others putting her through her paces. I supervised her time dilation work, coached her overall performance and managed her business.

'I'm uncertain how I should respond to being overtaken when I'm racing,' she said. 'I don't know when to move over and when to resist.'

'Do you need to be certain?'

'It's worrying me. I wake up at night with someone overtaking me.'

'Thinking about it won't help you,' I said. 'Anxiety and loss of sleep can pull you down. Forget about your competitors. You can't predict all the possibilities, so don't even start. Concentrate on what you can control: your own running.

'You're a strong runner like Prefontaine. His desire to control put him in the lead from the start of each race. Mo Farah worked his way up through fields of runners, by mental strength, going into the lead by the end of each race. Siri Lindley's strength, after she overcame choking, was to 'unleash herself' by running in the 'flow' of the moment.

'Your training has featured extreme-flow, causing you to run further in less time than other runners. You can race on automatic, the way you have rehearsed.'

Maxi listened to me, or seemed to. I wasn't a certified coach, but I had tried to understand her needs, how she learned and how she communicated. We were as one, her hand in my glove. I protected her from risks she would encounter during her performances.

All Maxi's retinue and our families flew with us to Cape Town two weeks before the race. When she encountered security procedures at airport departure, I kept her calm.

'Why should I remove my ear-stud?' she said. 'They're trying to depersonalise me. I'm not a fucking sheep. It's part of conditioning me to become a passive passenger. It's the opposite of running a marathon. They're stopping me from being an individual. They should let me be and try to catch villains and nutcases. If I thought it would do any good, I would refuse to comply.'

Maxi was wound up and unwilling to be herded. Somehow I got her on to the plane, through the flight and off again.

When we arrived, Maxi went on a training run with some others around the Olympic marathon route. She trained daily, a light programme.

When the Games opened, she marched with our countrymen and watched some of the 400 events in 40 sports. The marathons would be held on the final day of competition.

That morning before her race, a journalist interviewed her at the Australian house in the athlete's village.

'Cindy Hirako will be running,' she said to Maxi. 'How will you deal with her?'

'She ran 2h14 in London, a few metres behind me.'

'Can you beat her again?'

'My goal is 2h10.'

'What will you do?'

'I'll hang with her, keep tabs on her for the first half.'

'Will you be in 'flow'?'

'Most definitely. I'll make her take the initiative, make her run my race.'

I leaned against a locker listening, anxious about what Maxi would say next. Maxi disdained journalists whose interest was to sensationalize. She might become angry.

'But Maxi,' said the journalist, 'will Cindy let you? I mean, she could — '

Maxi interrupted. 'Going into the last lap in the stadium, I'll be right on her tail, see, all the way into the last turn.'

'But her kick — '

'I can stretch my time with a shortcut across the infield, sprint down the pole vault runway and lean at the tape. Works every time.'

Maxi winked at me.

CHAPTER 68

As Maxi struts purposefully out of the tunnel from the changing rooms, every seat in the Olympic stadium is occupied and abuzz. Built for the 2010 World Cup, the grandstand has been modified for 80,000 people to watch the start and finish. They will watch the rest of the race on massive screens. Maxi saunters around in the marshalling area, waving to her team seated in a row near the start and talking over the barrier with Jack and Stan, who hand her a water bottle.

The men have already gone and the best 80 women runners from international competition are waiting on the track, not more than two from each nation, all qualifiers below 2h30. The sky is overcast and the temperature fresh at 17°C, with 20°C forecast at noon. The conditions are good and the race should be fast. Maxi stands near the starting line with the others, moving a little to relax. When the TV camera reaches her she smiles pleasantly.

Most of the women are wearing bikini bottom briefs, with bare midriffs and skimpy tops with shoulder straps. Maxi is in a gold top with green shorts, pink knee socks, yellow running shoes, her ponytail held by a fluorescent yellow scrunchy. Hayley Thomas is further across, also in green and gold.

Maxi gives Hayley an air punch, which Hayley returns. It doesn't get Maxi's blood up like yelling the QIS war cry would. She runs through her pre-flow checklist.

She adjusts the position of her bib, checks her wrist monitor and waits restlessly, shaking thigh and leg muscle bundles to prime them. She listens to her breathing and concentrates.

The umpire raises a flag and the crowd instantly falls silent.

The runners move up to the line, 15 across in ragged rows about 5 deep, standing where they can find a space. Champions take front positions, where fewer people will be in their way as they sprint for a position in the lead.

'No cheating, bitch!'

Cindy Hirako, the gold medal holder from the US, shoulders Maxi aside and pushes in front of Maxi. Three months previously, in the Boston Marathon, Cindy had taken the lead from Maxi after she fell. They are legendary rivals with no love lost between them. She had been second in London and it could have been her who asked for Maxi to have a gender test.

'She competes by putting others down with lies,' Maxi thinks. *'She may even believe them.'*

Some mud had stuck and Maxi is still under a microscope. The accusation had angered her but she is over it now and Cindy's bad behaviour is a problem for Cindy.

Harassing an opponent can disrupt their concentration so they will drop out of 'flow', forget their race plan and make mistakes. Maxi claims her space in the front row, getting comfortable next to Cindy, defying her hostility. Hayley is outside her. Further outside are the Kenyans, including World record holder Rona Iftake. Maxi pushes away an idea that tries to sneak in, that she, Maxi, is the outsider in this austere company.

'I know exactly how to deal with them,' she thinks. *'I'm a Ferrari; I can leave their pissy Fiats in my dust.'*

A steady cam is carried across the line, but there isn't time to announce everyone and media commentators are left to read some of the names from the runners' bibs. After an age of waiting the starter calls: 'Get set.'

Drones overhead have pictures of the line up on the stadium screens. The pistol fires. All 80 runners lunge forward, many going hard to get into a front position. In the crush, it takes Maxi 10 seconds to reach the electronic timing mat, her bib-tag registering when she crosses it, as it will again at the end of the 42.195 kilometres course.

Maxi sprints and side-steps around slower runners, jostling, forcing through to the front. As they wheel out of the stadium, she is leading the charge, with the media truck 40 metres ahead. The mob settles into a stampede along the road that leads towards the hills.

Maxi lopes along, eating up the distance. She glances at the monitor on her wrist. She is pacing at 100 strides per minute, her GPS measuring 20 kilometres per hour, her heart is beating at 180 per minute, her breaths at 60. It is all good.

They run along Beach Road for 4 kilometres, then double back 7 kilometres and go off along Helen Suzman Road, around the foot of Signal Hill on Long Street.

At 5 kilometres, the herd is in two groups, 50 metres apart. Maxi is leading 10 frontrunners, including Hayley and several Kenyans. Her split time is 15 minutes and her monitor calculates 20 kilometres per hour, a little above the 19.5 she needs to achieve her goal of 2h10.

Cindy Hirako is running off her right shoulder and Hayley is behind on her left. As positions freeze, Maxi slides into automatic.

Following her race plan, she gives a burst and pulls away, taking the others with her on an elastic band. Then an Ethiopian and a Namibian drop back and there are 7 remaining in the group: two Australians, three Kenyans, Cindy Hirako and a Finn. The Russians and Chinese must be in the second and later groups, with the remainder of the 80 runners still close enough to threaten.

Maxi is slender and sleek, running smoothly and fluidly, with economy of effort, pink knee socks her conspicuous trademark, her thigh muscles rippling. Speeding towards her target, she feels fulfilled. It doesn't matter how it will turn out because she is following her plan precisely and that is all that matters now. If other things should have been considered and her instruction was incomplete or wrong, responsibility for that is shared with her team. She thinks fondly of Jack, scrambling on a bike to the next drinks station. She is looking forward to seeing him there.

She glances around at the other runners. Cindy is a pace behind her.

'We may not be as equal as it seems,' she thinks. *'My running is in 'flow' and optimal. I could be using less energy. I will achieve my*

342

goal by sticking to the speed I need. Time dilation should enable me to sustain.'

After 8 kilometres the two groups are 100 metres apart and with runners strung out in ones and twos. Maxi is at point position, with Cindy off her shoulder. She keeps an eye on her.

'I am managing my running subconsciously,' she thinks. *'I'm alert for trouble, actively scanning the environment, checking opponents and race conditions. I'm continually reading and analysing my performance indicators on my wrist monitor. My mind is as busy as it can be, in extreme-flow. I am stretching out time. What a blast!'*

Maxi feels enervated. Her nerve traffic must be near capacity. She watches Cindy Hirako labouring beside her. Maxi notices that although her effort is steady, her speed is surging a little on her monitor. Her brain is in 'flow' and flat out, thinking furiously, going over her checklist of controls with signals veering off through longer pathways, with speeds of the impulses at maximum. The responses would fall behind, but they have to react in time and dilation is making it happen. She speeds toward the 10-kilometre drinks station with Cindy in her wake.

CHAPTER 69

Maxi has an achievable goal and is on automatic. She is in the lead and her time is on target as she gulps a mug of water. Jack is there, but she is locked onto her goal and can manage only a small smile for him.

'That last 5 kilometres ran themselves,' she thinks. *'Pure magic! I have 32 kilometres to go. I must watch Cindy like a hawk. I'll slow a little and let her take the lead for a while, then take it back. That could do her head in. I'm enjoying this. For the magic to continue, I have to stay precise, monitoring and reviewing my tactics are optimised.'*

'My legs are hurting, but I won't pay attention because I'd drop out of 'flow,' she thinks. *'My mind is flowing nicely and ruling my body.'*

Her team had discussed how 'flow' numbed pain.

'When football players are fully engaged, they don't notice injuries,' Stan had said. 'Flow releases endorphins and oxytocin, which relieve pain. After the game, when they come down off their high, they may need medical treatment.'

'I'm up there,' Maxi thinks. *'My neural traffic speeds must be near maximum.'*

Behind Maxi, Cindy gulps water and follows her out of the station. She tries to kick level, but Maxi has her response ready and fights her off. They run shoulder to shoulder until Cindy drops back.

The course turns back around Company Gardens after 12 kilometres, past the Houses of Parliament and Cape Town City Hall. Then they go through District Six, Woodstock, Observatory and Rondebosch Common to halfway.

At 20 kilometres, Maxi is still in front, when a spectator leaps onto the road in front of her with outstretched arms, blocking her path. She has anticipated this in her training and responds immediately, fluidly side-stepping around the intruder. Cindy follows her. Glancing back Maxi sees security officers grab the intruder.

'No harm done,' she thinks.

They pass the halfway point, grabbing up two cups of water each from the drinks tables and slosh them over themselves. They wend their way back through Cape Town suburbs with luxurious houses and manicured gardens.

At the 25 kilometres mark, she and Cindy are neck and neck, with a commanding lead of 200 metres over the second group with 8 runners.

Cindy kicks to pass her and Maxi lets her go.

'She can have the lead for now,' Maxi thinks. *'When she slackens off, as she must at this pace, I'll take it back. I'm going to wear her down. I'll revert to my target speed. If she comes back at me, I'll do it again and again, until the last two kilometres, when I'll stay in front.*

'I don't care who is in front of me now. I don't have to be in front. I don't do ego. Like me, Cindy Hirako has never run at this pace before. She's having to work harder than she is used to and could burn out.

'We've done the easy part of the race. Now it's getting serious. All my training has led to this, a contest of mind over matter.'

Her feet are lumps of suffering. Her toes stab pain as if blood vessels are bursting under the nails.

'Shit. There go my toenails. They could come off, even during the race. It won't slow me down.'

At 35 kilometres, Maxi takes back the lead from Cindy, surging ahead with her back straight, a picture of efficiency. Cindy follows Maxi closely but is toiling. She is hunched up and struggling to keep a rhythm, as if her legs want to do something different.

They are 300 metres ahead and Maxi's wrist monitor shows she is a little slower than planned. She decides to press Cindy with a killer pace and speeds up. Cindy tracks her, labouring desperately.

Cindy begins to wander, drifting away to the side of the road, where spectators crowd. Without warning, she moans, staggers and pitches onto the grass verge. Maxi looks back without slowing and sees Cindy has collapsed. There is no other runner in sight and she is in position to win. She pounds on at the same record-breaking pace.

When Jack arrives at the stadium on a bicycle, he cycles in as close as he can get to the finish line, then drops the bike and elbows his way through the crush of onlookers and watches a screen. It shows a drone's view over the heads of the stadium audience, to the Somerset Road approach where the crowd is 10 deep on both sides. In the distance, matchstick figures come around a corner on the horizon, crawl into view and approach in a bunch. An expectant buzz starts in the crowd.

On a large digital screen, he sees drone photos with an aerial view looking directly down on 5 women running in a line behind each other, with Maxi 300 metres in front and drawing away. A distance indicator on the screen shows they have come 40 kilometres. The camera goes back to where a group of race officials stand near Cindy Hirako, collapsed by the road. She lies face down on the grass, her legs writhing, trying to get traction to regain her feet. By a Herculean effort, she levers herself vertical and wobbles another 100 metres on jelly legs, before colliding with the barrier and falling heavily. The crowd look over the railings at her and take photos. Officials arrive but do not dare touch her, in case it would disqualify her. When her prone form becomes still, medics stretcher her away to an ambulance.

The runners have meanwhile reached the stadium. Maxi is striding evenly, urgently, filling the screen, the musculature of her legs rippling, with every sinew and tendon taut and highly tuned.

'*She looks great!*' he thinks. Her long loping strides and arms work like piston rods, each pace consuming distance, using the last of her energy efficiently.

'Can she keep this up?' he wonders. The runner behind begins to catch up. Maxi glances over her shoulder, lengthens her stride and the challenger fades.

When the group enters the stadium, Maxi has a lead of 200 metres with two laps to go, well inside the World record. Her body is straight, inclined slightly forwards, placing her feet with precise repetition. People in the stands are yelling and chanting: 'Max — i! Max — i!'.

As she comes around the bend towards him and goes past, Jack scans her face anxiously and sees the euphoria of her 'flow'. She is oblivious to her depleting energy and revelling in the fulfilment of a goal that she has tortured her for the past 10 years. She is achieving it with dignity, driving all the way to the line, where she throws herself across and sinks to her knees.

Her face is hidden by the race officials around her and Jack fears she is damaged, but she stands up and raises her arms in triumph. She looks for Jack, sees him at the barrier and gives him one of her hundred percent smiles. He relaxes. She isn't damaged.

She high-fives some watchers trackside. The other runners are streaming in around her. Rona Iftake will get silver and Hayley Thomas bronze. The screens have Maxi's time as 2.09.34, a minute under the World record. Her historic achievement causes an uproar in the stands, where everyone is standing and yelling.

She comes over to Jack at the barrier, her eyes radiant. She is smiling, pleasure crinkling the corners of her eyes, her mouth upturned and teeth wide.

His concern turns to joy deep inside him. They are going to be okay.

'*This isn't a dream,*' he thought. '*It's real, wonderfully real. For 6 years since I met Maxi I have lived my life under her spell. She has been my reality. I knew it would end one day but I didn't imagine it would be as dramatic and pleasant as this. She was my dream and she is come true.*'

347

Wearing an Australian flag like a cape, Maxi and Hayley jog side by side around the stadium, wobbling a little. As they pass a medical trailer, they wave to Cindy who is reclining on a trolley bed. Cindy waves back.

Stan, Riko and the rest of the team arrive and bend over the fence to hug her. She thanks each of them. It has taken their combined strength to smash the World record.

'How good was my luck to meet you and join in this giddy adventure,' Jack says to Maxi.

'Your time dilation made the difference,' she says.

'No, it was you. My theory only explains what you did.'

'You told me how.'

'Perhaps it was a team effort.'

Jack and Stan go with Maxi to the sampling room where they test her for performance-enhancing substances.

'This is so unnecessary,' says Maxi.

'Chill,' said Jack. 'Runners could be using new enzyme blockers. There is research showing an enzyme blocker in mice is beneficial for endurance exercise capacity, reducing running time and increasing running distance. If the enzyme can be altered in humans, they could get super-endurance capabilities.'

'I imagine they could outlaw enzyme blocking,' Maxi says. 'Mental engagement would be harder to prevent.'

'They could require a low IQ to qualify,' he says with sarcasm.

'That would contradict our tradition that distance champions and record breakers are smart.'

'Maxi's 'flow' technique will soon spread to every other event,' says Stan. 'They won't be able to stop it. There has never been a generic new technique before. There have been new techniques that lifted records in swimming and high jumping. When freestyle came in, it was separated from breaststroke. In the high jump, the scissors was discarded when the Fosbury Flop raised the bar. But 'flow' could be taken up in many events and break many records.'

The drug testing results are negative.

Maxi goes to the changing rooms to dress for the medal ceremony. When she sees blood in her urine and vomits black mucous her elation is replaced by fear, until she recalls these are common in endurance running, believed to be due to the bladder walls slapping together causing traumatic blood loss.

She is totally spent and it will take six months for her to recover. She won't decide what to do next until then. Her remaining obligation is the medal ceremony.

Maxi follows in solemn procession the bearers of the Olympic and Australian flags as South African voices sing the mellow harmonies of Nkosi Sikelei. She steps up to the winner's podium, flanked by Rona Iftake and Hayley Thomas. Advance Australia Fair plays as she bows her head and the South African Prime Minister hangs the medal around her neck.

Afterwards, Jack organises photographs. All eyes are on Maxi. She is confident and chic, with glamour and poise. She has star-quality as she poses for the television cameras and for her fans, who crowd in all around. She waves, blows kisses and throws her arms wide to embrace her audience.

'Here is Maxi Fleet. No woman has ever before run a marathon in 2 hours, 9 minutes and 34 seconds.'

There is explosive applause.

The compere hands her the microphone and she holds it delicately.

'Thank you everyone for coming today and encouraging me,' she said. 'It took our team six years to do this. Your support made all the difference. As you could see, it was a close-run race. Cindy had me worried back there. She ran brilliantly and she's going to be okay. Give her a big hand, please. Now I want to thank you, my fans and my loyal team.'

After the medal ceremony, the crowd are chanting Max - i, Max - i. When she steps forward to a mike again, there are excited screams, a cascade of sound spilling down from the tiered audience.

'I've climbed up here from the bottom,' she says. 'Today I'm living my dream, the culmination of hours and hours of training. I started running at school. For years I have lived in hope that I'd make it here. This moment is every bit as good as I hoped for.

349

'I want to read some words written by Robert Persig: *'Mountains should be climbed with as little effort as possible and without desire. The reality of your own nature should determine the speed. If you become restless, speed up. If you become winded, slow down. You climb the mountain in an equilibrium between restlessness and exhaustion. Then, when you're no longer thinking ahead, each footstep isn't just a means to an end but a unique event in itself. This leaf has jagged edges. This rock looks loose. From this place the snow is less visible, even though closer. These are things you should notice anyway. To live only for some future goal is shallow. It's the sides of the mountain which sustain life, not the top. Here's where things grow.'*

'That's from a book called Zen and the Art of Motor Cycle Maintenance. During my climb to here, I was kept going by beauty that gave me joy. I met people who inspired my long journey and I am forever thankful to them. As I ran today I saw many wonderful things that nurtured my spirit. Your support today was the greatest inspiration of all. Thank you.

'Now I've reached the top, I'm so grateful to all of you. This is the best day of my life. It makes a huge difference to have your goodwill. I want you to be aware your part was important in the achievement you helped me to accomplish, step by step, day after day.

'Thank you especially to all my team.'

She calls them forward one by one, each receiving applause.

'First, my parents: Stan and Patti.

'Now my partner and physics coach: Jack Cram, the man who coordinated my team and discovered my training method.'

'Thank you to Queensland Institute of Sport Coaches Derek Tracker and Riko Minami.'

They walk up hand in hand, their relationship accepted now that Derek is separated from his wife.

'My friends and research scientists: Blake, Alice and Corvid.

The three come forward together, hand in hand. Blake bows to the audience and the women curtsy.

'There are others in our team who helped me too: there they are, waving.

'Thank you all for your contributions.'

She steps down and walks over to the barrier fence, to touch hands with the people straining forward. She has a camera and takes selfies with her fans. She autographs programmes and shirts.

Maxi goes to a studio for interviews and Jack goes with her.

A talk show host asks her on camera: 'After winning at the Olympics today, does the rest of your life seem easy?'

'No. Why should it?' she answers. 'Winning the marathon was a narrow achievement. Living a good life needs a wide range of abilities. I'm ordinary at almost everything else. Doors could open for me, but my path to happiness needs a worthwhile challenge to fully engage me, with a definite goal. I need to 'flow' and I need a goal.'

'When you 'flow' do you go into timeless activity?'

'That's right. Anyone can do it; you don't need to be a runner.'

'Did you train to run in 'flow'?'

'Yes. We simulated race conditions as closely as we could, rehearsing the volume of running and the intensity.'

'What will you do next? More running?'

'Maybe. I'll wait to see what offers I get.'

As her fame spreads, awestruck scientists are eager to investigate her. Maxi is a phenomenon they want to understand.

CHAPTER 70

On the plane returning from Cape Town, Jack was sitting with Maxi.

'When will you finish your PhD?' she asked. 'It's been 5 years since you started.'

'I hope to submit in a couple of months.'

'Will it be plain sailing after that?'

'It could be heavy going.'

'Why?'

'My thesis is a paradigm-shift in the metaphysics of time. They may not accept it.'

'Why not?'

'After 120 years, Einstein's theories are still being interpreted. My theory of brain time applies them in a different context and it could be a long time before that is accepted.'

'Could it be refuted?'

'Einstein's preoccupation with light in his Special Relativity theory was to relate kinetic objects to the ultimate energy of light. He could have been concerned with visual appearances because these are dramatic and influential. He defined light precisely and it defined time visually by visible solar revolutions, diurnal dawn and dusks. We have it now the same in every corner of the planet, taken from the vibration of caesium crystals in 'block universe' theory of time that is the same everywhere. My theory applies it within an individual's nerve cells, where times can vary widely under personal control enabling living in the moment. there isn't much unequivocal evidence for it, nor is it likely to be rejected outright by scientific methods. It is most likely to be held in abeyance awaiting evidence.'

'Wouldn't absence of rejection be enough support?'

'No. There is time to obtain more supporting evidence. Einstein said: 'You never fail until you stop trying.''

'My reduced running time is evidence, isn't it?' asked Maxi.

'Yes and no. Yes, because since you have been running in flow, your times have improved. No, because the improvement could be attributed to: your will, your self-control, your concentration and your motivation. Or from physical changes due to your training.'

'Shit. Just about anything could be doing it. Could flow ever become flavour of the month?'

'Recognition of time dilation could be slow. It could take many runners, repeating identical runs in and out of flow, many times, before the benefit of flow is accepted.'

'Do you have enough evidence?'

'I think so. A PhD thesis doesn't have to report an open and shut case,' Jack said. 'I've made a start. When you win more races and other runners copy our technique and win, it could persuade them that the theory is correct.'

Jack's research supervisor, Baxter, questioned Jack's epistemology. Jack had explained his logical inference that transmission time for impulses in a person's nervous system would dilate, but Baxter expected claims in physics to be backed by experimental data.

'Flow is psychology, time dilation is physics and the brain is neuroscience,' Baxter said. 'It's not usual to mix up disciplines. Could you submit it as metaphysics? Or could it be philosophy?'

'Universities find it difficult to approve interdisciplinary research like mine,' thought Jack. *'I would have to start again. Baxter's lack of support now is like a betrayal. Until now he's gone along with my ideas. Perhaps he has been hiding his scepticism. He's supposed to be for me, but behind his charisma, he could be against me.'*

'Are you certain that this time dilation effect is real?' Baxter asked.

'Her performance changed spectacularly — she broke the world record.'

353

'Your training methods will be accepted even if you don't box-tick a PhD. Running people will beat a path to your door. The examiners will need evidence that her improvement was not from another cause, like motivation.'

'We did nothing to change her motivation.'

'Could she have gained self-confidence from your theory?'

'He's deconstructing my achievement,' Jack thought. *'I can't argue against the possibility of other improvement alternatives.'*

'Could the enjoyment of running in 'flow' have motivated her?' said Baxter, toying with Jack's precious idea.

'The bastard is negging me. He's supposed to support me.'

'Yes, there could have been a little of that,' Jack said. 'But the main improvement was by time dilation.'

'That's an inference based on circumstantial evidence. It won't convince them.'

'Shit,' he thought. *'Circumstantial evidence is all there is in psychology. He's a physicist and physics people like evidence to be direct or indirect — with the exception of compelling logic using mathematics.'*

'QIS's Hayley Thomas also ran the Olympic marathon in extreme-flow and her time improved too,' Jack said.

'Self-reports are unreliable: there isn't control over extraneous variables, such as her training,' said Baxter.

'QIS have other runners training with extreme-flow and improving too.'

'The examiners will be interested, of course, but improvement needs a definite link to a time dilation phenomenon.'

'Dilation of time can be inferred from evolutionary biology,' Jack said. 'When an animal has insufficient time for a considered response, it does not freeze in homeostasis, nor go into slow motion, nor become incoherent. It responds in its own time. We can infer that animals have evolved by natural selection to respond in time that is different for each species. If an animal did not respond fast enough, a predator could grab it. Response times have adapted by time dilation. The brain times of surviving individuals have had to dilate to allow escape. If their response times slowed for intellection, predators would pick them off.'

'Are you saying that the fittest survivors under stress could have dilated their time?'

'Yes. It is proximity of neural traffic to the maximum speed that would dilate their time.''

'Would their responses be limited by brain capacity?'

'Yes. Natural selection could favour both bigger brains and release of endorphins under stress. They would maintain response times by time dilation.'

'Interesting,' said Baxter. 'Another explanation is that predators or deadlines simply cause people to hurry and get more done.'

'I am not denying that. Hurrying can observe an external clock and cease when the deadline is reached. But a person's time can dilate within a sequential series of deadlines, continuing on and on until a finish. A runner in extreme-flow nurtures that.

'A marathon requires a runner to keep up to their goal pace, like meeting a series of deadlines. In extreme-flow they are totally engaged, hurrying throughout, furiously thinking about alternatives and dilating time.'

Baxter rubbed his chin.

'I see. What is the greatest application of your theory?'

'Every individual can have their own time, if they assert it,' said Jack. 'Chairman Mao Tse Tung is reported to have run his household in Beijing on a 48-hour cycle. He may have spent many hours in 'extreme-flow' – exploring mental algorithms to decide his actions, like a chess grand master. His time could have dilated requiring less sleep, less often. Another prodigious thinker, Karl Marx, seldom slept at all.'

'Those commies were inconsiderate bastards.'

'I agree. They kept to their own sense of time, which would have made it difficult to coordinate with others. When Einstein's astronaut returns from her thought experiment of travel in space, decades younger than her twin sister, she could go on to run a set distance faster than her sister. Maxi dilated time like the twin space traveller, doing in her brain what the space traveller did in body: more travel, fewer birthdays, faster performance.'

'Is there evidence that dilation of personal time actually happens?'

'It is customary to attribute extraordinary performances in time to born ability, when in fact they could be achieved by rehearsal. Dancers like Michael Jackson and Madonna could have practised their moves with such extraordinary existential energy and persistence that their brain time dilated, as if they were in a space-ship at light speed, relative to their audience stranded here on earth, ageing faster than they are. When a performer's movements are rehearsed to ultra-precision, they could compete in dilated time, as revealed in the intense facial expression of determination and complex rapid movements of gymnast Nadia Comanechi.'

'Her determined look may not indicate time dilation. How would it affect her performance?'

'She could do more and faster moves,' Jack said. 'The time from stimulus to response is in a faster timeframe with time slowed enabling extraordinary performance.

'Endurance sportswriter Matt Fitzgerald observed that runners limit themselves when they observe external time, commenting as follows.

'Most serious runners don't realize their potential. They simply stop getting faster and don't understand why. The reason is simple: most runners are unable to run by feel. The best elite runners have learned that the key to faster running is to hear what their bodies are telling them.' (8)

'Interesting,' said Baxter, musing. 'Your thesis explains how improvement can occur and how training can achieve it.'

'At least he's not refuting me now,' Jack thought.

'In physics, Einstein assumed that the speed of light is constant and that is the basis for calculating time dilation. But the 'river of time' is probably flowing at variable speed.'

'What is this 'river of time'?' asked Baxter.

'Physicist Kenneth Chan has said: *'Time is only relatively constant: it may vary and we are unable to detect that. Timepieces*

356

relate time to electromagnetic transmission. We are simply unable to experience the speed of light varying because both our perceptual apparatus and our brain function via electromagnetic transmission. (20)'

'Physical time may not be constant but it is measured with caesium clocks, according to Einstein's assumption, electromagnetic radiation is at constant speed in space,' said Jack. 'Measurements used to calculate light speed have circular logic that deceives us to believe its speed is absolute, when it is relative. It's circular that light is at constant speed. It is like trying to measure the speed of a train from inside another travelling beside it at a different speed. An observer can be deceived with false impressions of time and speed. Constancy of light speed cannot be tested. It is an assumption and it is consistent with there being time dilation.

'Interesting,' said Baxter. 'But it simply highlights that the constancy of light is a convenient assumption and we could perceive time dilation in the brain as well as in space. There is an ocean of inconstancy engulfing physical quantities, which drowns objectivity in extreme contexts. You have exposed the interpersonal subjectivity of a metaphysical quantity: time. I agree there is a possibility, if not a certainty, a runner could experience dilation of time, enabling faster performance. I will endorse submission of your thesis.'

'Yay,' Jack thought, with enormous relief, 'at last I have an ally who will help me.'

'Thank you.'

'You must write it up to be acceptable to the external examiners. I will talk with them to align their conception of a runner's dilated time with ours.'

'Wow. Baxter has come good,' Jack thought, *'How wrong I was to doubt him.'*

He could now submit his thesis, his goal for the past 5 years.

CHAPTER 71

Under my coordination, Maxi had attained extreme prowess. The venture had been precarious and now she had triumphed, the danger was past, but I wasn't sure she was still there for me. I had reached for the sweetest apple on the highest branch, but I did not yet have it.

Was she less committed to me than I was to her? Our post-Olympic relationship seemed to be on an even keel, balanced as it had been earlier. We were invested in each other, but the continuance of our relationship into further adventures was not assured. This far, we had shouldered the risks together like comrades in arms. Our lives had interwoven. Now we had entered a new space with our roles undefined and I felt vulnerable.

I trusted that Maxi loved me. Nietzsche's injunction was that wrong love is better than being in doubt and without love. It had been right for me to love her, but would it turn out right or wrong? We needed to maintain our momentum. I would not allow delusion to get a foothold.

I had started my perilous journey, daring to love high-flying Maxi for the fun of it, knowing I might live to regret it. I had soared with her, me on an intellectual up current, knowing I had to come down one day.

'My PhD is risky,' I said when Maxi and I were at dinner with Blake and Alice.

'How dare you!' Alice quipped.

'I've dared to design a way to dilate time.'

'You have allowed a person to have as much achievement as they want,' said Blake, 'by locking on and overloading their brain. Can anyone do it?'

'If they are capable of goal performance and push to their mental limit, they get enough time,' I said. 'Maxi ran in ahead of the others. She wanted it enough to break the record.'

'You're lucky she has faith in your theory,' said Blake. 'The daring is mostly hers.'

Blake was suspicious and wanted to protect Maxi, warning her against relying on a theory that could not be tested.

'Einstein's theory is full of holes,' said Blake. 'What you need is some real data, from experiments.'

'There are too many variables,' I said. 'Runs can't be repeated keeping everything the same, so we can't deduce causes by elimination. Without knowing causes, improvement is a lottery.'

'Trial and error.'

'Exactly,' I said. 'A pattern may appear if she continues to win.'

'I don't need that pressure just now,' said Maxi.

'Is the nasty man pressuring you?' said Alice to Maxi, consoling.

Maxi nodded, smiling. 'A little. He doesn't get it all his own way, though.'

'Maxi's running is a pattern, like a dot art painting,' I said. 'Her art is artless, like her archery, all form and aimless.'

'Jack is like an organ grinder with a temperamental monkey — me. He wants me to keep winning and amassing data supporting extreme-flow and gets shirty when I suggest anything else.'

'I started doing a PhD because I wanted to be independent,' I said. 'We had a mutual interest, but now Maxi has collected hers and she wants to pull out.'

'You ungrateful shit,' said Maxi. 'I'll have you know I do my best for both of us. I can't promise to always win, much as you'd like me to.'

'Now, now children,' said Alice. 'Jack, it wasn't very nice of you to suggest that Maxi is unreliable. She's the most reliable person I know. Maxi, I'm sure Jack wasn't being critical.'

'I don't like being cast as a monkey!'

'Sorry, Maxi. You are reliable, the talented part of our partnership,' I said. 'What I was trying to say was that I've had to trade off independence, becoming dependent, with more uncertainty.'

'That's better,' said Maxi. 'That could be my mantra too.'

'Karl Popper, the science philosopher, says that uncertainty is all there is,' said Blake. 'Loosen up, Jack. Nietzsche wanted us to dare to be great.'

'When I look back on where I've come from, I have gone along the edge of a cliff,' I said. 'Now is the first time I can look down and enjoy the view.'

'Me too,' said Maxi.

'Is your enjoyment of success proportional to the risks you've taken?' Blake said.

'Absolutely,' I said. 'Relief is part of it. Alice, after a base jump, are you on a high?'

'Definitely. Very high.'

I turned to Maxi. 'We must have jumped and are stuck on a ledge?'

'Maybe. But I wouldn't have got this far without you,' said Maxi.

'I wouldn't have discovered how to use flow without you,' I said. 'Our perilous enterprises have coincided and we have shared uncertainty. We have dared to live dangerously.'

'And now we are sharing success — on a ledge,' said Maxi.

'Let's drink to that!' said Blake.

'What's next for you two?' Alice asked.

'This week we're going into a studio to make a reality TV show. Patti wants to publicise Maxi's Olympic success. An audience will find out aspects of Maxi's life previously unknown to them.'

'I don't want my life to be made public,' Maxi said.

'Don't worry, there won't be any negatives,' I said.

'Reality TV is sensational and mindless,' Maxi said.

'You need to think of all of us,' I said. 'We can make a lot of money and promote our global lecture tour.'

'It doesn't get much better than that,' said Blake. 'You have a deadline, the possibility of an extended honeymoon and all the time you want.'

'I'm not going to think about anything,' said Maxi, 'until it happens.'

CHAPTER 72

A studio audience is applauding as Patti sashays onto the set with strobes flashing, music pumping. She is wearing a gold lame' jumpsuit, cut away to display cleavage, wearing gold flying boots, her hair swept over and bobbed. She poses on her dais under the spotlight between two panels, with four men seated in a row on one side and four women in a row on the other.

'Good evening, viewers. I'm Patti Fleet. I will be your host and here is my fast step-daughter: Maxi.'

Maxi is spotlighted on a dais on the audience's right. She is in running gear, a singlet with the Olympic rings, her hair frizzed and big, loose-limbed and confident. She graciously acknowledges the adoration of the audience and the applause.

'Hello, everyone. Thank you for being here.'

'Maxi, tell us, are you recovered from Cape Town?' asked Patti.

'You bet. No problems. I'm back in training.'

As the applause subsides, Maxi's spotlight turns off.

Patti is spotlighted and introduces a group sitting further back.

'Here are the rest of Maxi's team: my slow husband Stan, and Maxi's partner, scientist Ripper Jack. Maxi's other running coaches are from the Queensland Institute of Sport: Derek and Riko; also her researcher friends: Alice, Blake and Corvid. Together they guided Maxi to success.'

More applause.

'Maxi has kindly consented to tell us what her feelings were while she was breaking the World record. We invite you at home to join in, as our two panels, men and women, compete to guess Maxi's feelings.

362

'The women are: (she names each in turn); and the men are (she names them). These panel members are without running experience. Can they correctly imagine Maxi's feelings? The panels will select her feelings at 10 different times during her World record run, shown on the screen behind me. I will then ask Maxi the same questions. When a panel is right, they will get one point.

'We will find out who is right more often: men or women? Give them a big hand.'

The camera turns to the beaming faces of the audience as they cheer and applaud.

'Two months ago Maxi set a new World record for the marathon. We will begin, as Maxi did, with her training.'

Patti and the others on stage face a large screen at back centre. The lights dim and the screen has a country road, at sunrise, through a tunnel of trees, with a distant runner approaching. They hear the dawn chorus, then the sound of a drone helicopter approaching and passing out of view overhead. Maxi runs up to the camera.

Patti reads: 'Question 1: You're seeing a recording of Maxi in training for the Olympics last year.'

Her face is tense, grimacing, as she reaches the camera.

'Now it's your turn. Which alternative describes how Maxi is feeling at this moment?'

Four words are displayed on the screen.

Patti reads.

'Alone

Accompanied

Bored

Excited.

Would the members of each panel get together and lock in their selection. Maxi, would you make your choice. If the a panel has the same word as Maxi, they will get one point.'

Panel members whisper in their teams and their choices are screened. Then Maxi reveals hers. Patti reads:

'The women have chosen 'Alone', the men 'Accompanied', Maxi 'Accompanied.'

Maxi's spotlight turns on. 'The men are right,' she says. 'I felt accompanied because a drone was with me and my coach was watching. I was running at race speed and it was too demanding for boredom but too predictable to get excited. I had my team with me by phone when I wanted and the drone keeping an eye on me nearby. My fans could follow my training from streaming of pictures from the drone. I liked being watched.'

'Is training by yourself ever lonely, Maxi?'' asked Patti.

'Lonely is when you want friends to be with you. I prefer to train alone. I get together with friends outside training.'

'So the men get one point. Well tried women.'

There is applause.

The screen changes to the interior of a large room and the camera pans around 9 seated people, members of Maxi's Team. The camera looks over Patti's shoulder, seated, as team members discuss, controlled by chairman Jack.

Patti reads: 'Question 2: Months before the race, Maxi was in a meeting with her coaches and advisers discussing her training programme. Which one of the following describes how Maxi is feeling at this moment?'

Patti reads:

'Important.

Unimportant

Bored

Excited.'

'And the answers are: Women 'Important', Men 'Bored', Maxi 'Important.'

Maxi says: 'I felt important because people were there to support my campaign and I felt responsible to them to do my best. Our meetings are seldom boring for me because we workshop ideas about training that I'll put into practice. They need me to agree, so my point of view is important.'

'We tell you off if you come on too strong,' Stan said, laughing.

'That's a win for the women,' says Patti. 'One all.'

The screen is filled with Maxi, her raised arms outstretched, pulling back an archery bow with an arrow nocked.

'And now for the third question: 'Maxi trains by Zen archery her mind, as well as her body. How does she feel at this moment?'

'Concentrating

Loose

Controlled

Spiritually aware.'

'I'll give the panel a few moments to collect their thoughts on this one. Here we have their responses. Women 'Spiritually aware', Men 'Concentrating', Maxi 'Concentrating'.'

Maxi says: 'I was concentrating, with my mind in control, my muscles striving to obey. I held the bow precisely as I had practised many times, comfortable, not loose, not caring where the arrow went, spiritually aware, in touch with all the parts of my body. It was like meditating with my feet firmly on the ground.'

'Why didn't you care where the arrow went?' asks someone in the audience.

'I'll answer that,' says Dr Riko Minami. 'Maxi had learned to form certain movements that would cause a required result. I gave her feedback to correct her form. Form is everything. Missing the target is nothing, merely bad form.'

'With practice, my mind shoots the arrow into the bullseye,' says Maxi. 'My body is controlled by my mind. That is how Zen running works.'

'Thank you, Doctor Minami. That's one to the women,' says Patti.

The scene is now inside the hubbub of the Cape Town stadium, with Maxi on the start line of the Women's Marathon. She smiles for the camera and then switches back to serious.

The commentator announces the runners: 'From Australia, Maxi Fleet winner of the London Marathon. Next to her is Cindy Hirako from Japan, winner of the Boston Marathon.'

Patti says, "This is question 4. How does Maxi feel?

'Fearful

Confident

Happy

Angry'

365

'What do you think at home? Here's our panel responses. Women 'Fearful', Men 'Confident', Maxi 'Angry.''

'I was angry because one of the runners had stuck an elbow in my face,' said Maxi. 'I wasn't quite calmed down as I took my position. It seemed deliberate. She could have been trying to throw me out of my race plan.'

'Was it Cindy Hirako?' a voice calls from the audience.

Maxi looks at Patti. 'I'd better not say.'

'Did it put you off?' asks Patti.

'It made me a little angry. I had to hold back from starting too fast.'

'You would be used to that sort of thing, wouldn't you?' says Patti.

'We had clashed previously, but you don't get used to bad behaviour.'

Patti says: 'No-one scored and the women are still in front with 2 points.'

She turns to the screen and describes the action. 'The camera is mobile and moving abreast of the front group of 15 runners, 40 metres ahead of a second group.

Your 5th question, contestants, is: 'The start has been fast and the girls are settling into a slower pace. They have run 5 kilometres and are out in the suburbs. Maxi is in the middle of the leading group. How does Maxi feel?

'Terrified

Confident

Disembodied

Focussed'

They answered: Women 'Confident', Men 'Focussed', Maxi 'Focussed'.

The men have it.'

'I was focussed on my goal of 2h10', says Maxi. 'I was running in 'flow', timelessly. I wasn't confident at this point, in fact, rather apprehensive.'

'Remind us what 'flow' is, please?' Patti asked her.

'Some people call 'flow' being 'in the zone'. It's a psychological condition of optimal achievement. It's when I'm totally absorbed in achieving my goal and oblivious to time passing.'

'Is it like meditation?"

Maxi shakes her head. 'Some meditation is tranquil. In 'flow' my mind is racing, the opposite of repose. I'm not spiritually transcended.'

Patti says: 'With the game half over, both of our teams have 2 points.'

The camera shows a crowd lining the course at the halfway drinks tables as Maxi runs up, grabs two cups of water and sloshes them over her head and face.

'This question might be the decider,' says Patti. 'How does Maxi feel?

'Hurting
Revelling
Striving
Relaxing

'I'll give the audience a few moments to consider what their answer might be. I think the panels are taking their time too. Yes, we have our responses: Women ''Striving', Men 'Striving', Maxi 'Striving'.'

'Both teams guessed right. Marathoners are often hurting but constant striving can push the hurt aside. I was in 'flow', enjoying the run with my mind stretched out, hyper-focussed, dilating time, thinking how to get to my goal. After the race, when we have recovered, then we party, revel and relax.'

Patti says: 'Tell us, Maxi, what does 'dilating time' feel like?'

'I was totally energised and in the moment. I'm giving it everything I can afford and still finish.'

'Both teams get a point and have 3 each. Who will win?'

The next scene is of Maxi coming through yelling crowds lining a road with the stadium in view. Cindy is beside her, wobbling, staggering and falling beside the road.

'And now the pressure is on for our panel. Question 7,' Patti says: 'Maxi is 2 kilometres from the finish and has run 40 kilometres when Cindy Hirako goes down. How does Maxi feel?'

'Happy

Sad

Concerned

Pleased.'

'I want honesty here. What does an athlete feel when a competitor goes down? Let's find out: Women 'Sad', Men 'Happy', Maxi 'Pleased'.'

Laughter.

Maxi hesitates: 'Cindy was in agony and I've experienced that myself. A marathon runner faces the possibility of meltdown in every race. Cindy's exit took the pressure off me. Her exiting was a relief and I was pleased.'

Patti asks: 'Could you have helped her?'

'No. It's against the rules to help another runner and she could be disqualified.'

Patti says: 'No-one guessed right and the teams stay at 3 points each.'

An aerial camera shows Maxi a half lap ahead on the track inside the stadium, sprinting, grimacing, the crowd on their feet gesticulating and yelling.

'The runners are getting close to the finish line,' Patti says: 'Your 8th question. Maxi is finishing in record time. How does she feel?

'Agonised

Confident

Disdainful

Humble

'Think about these, because there's quite a range of feelings there. Okay. Women 'Agonised', Men 'Disdainful', Maxi 'Disdainful'.'

Maxi says: 'I'm thinking I'm going to piss all over this record. I disdain it and will beat it into submission. I'm converting contempt into anger to push past the terrible hurt my body is suffering, beyond agony, kept under control by my willpower.'

Patti says: 'The men guessed correctly. Well done. I would have gone for agonised.'

Maxi says: 'Agonised is when the dentist hits a nerve and you shrink. I wasn't shrinking. I was more than confident, feeling arrogant. I had felt confident earlier as I ran into the stadium. This is what I was born to do. I'd felt like I couldn't put a foot wrong if I tried. But now I still had to nail it. I'd trained to have contempt, to disdain barriers, to hate them and bust through them.'

Patti says: 'Thank you Maxi. That makes it Men 4, Women 3.'

On the screen Maxi is at the Finish line, the crowd ecstatic and the camera cutting away to the race clock which had stopped at a time well inside the World record.

'Question 9,' Patti says. 'How does Maxi feel as she crosses the line?'

'Relief

Disappointment

Happy

Recriminating

'How does it feel to finally reach your goal? Let's see what the panels think. Women, 'Relief', Men 'Happy', Maxi 'Relief'.'

Maxi says 'If I'd been outside the record I would have been recriminating, blaming myself for not achieving my goal. But I wasn't and felt huge relief, euphoria, to have finished well. I could be happy soon, but not quite yet.'

'Didn't you feel at all happy?'

'Happy is like carefree and at this point, winning hasn't fully sunk in. I've been concentrating and it takes a few moments to adjust into happiness mode!'

Patti says: 'The two teams have 4 points each. We have the decider next.'

Runners are finishing and collapsing behind the line as Maxi mixes, shakes hands and gives hugs.

'Think carefully, panel. The final question is 'How does Maxi feel?'

'Competitive

Superior

369

Smug

Respectful

'How quickly can a feeling change? Let's see if our panels can pick it. Women 'Smug', Men 'Superior', Maxi 'Respectful'.'

'All the rivalry is sucked out of me,' Maxi says. 'I respect my opponents, too much to feel superior or smug, including Cindy Hirako, who is in the medical tent. It is a close result and I respect their ability.'

'Didn't you feel at all superior?'

'Not at all. That would imagine I existed on an elevated plane. I'd won using certain skills I'd learned. My advice to runners is to stop dreaming about being on the podium and concentrate on running faster.'

Patti says: 'That one went to the women and they've narrowly won the game. Congratulations, women, for your better understanding of Maxi's feelings. There wasn't much difference and it would be a brave person who tried to read gender ability into this result. Even when pooling their experience, the panels were right only about half the time, because they had to guess Maxi's feelings. How did our audience get on? Did anyone match Maxi's answers on all 10? One person! Wow. You can be an Olympic champion too, if you can run!'

The audience clap loudly.

'Thank you, Maxi and to the panels for playing this game so well.

'On behalf of The Real Fleets, we hope you have enjoyed the show, gained an insight into Maxi's world and are interested in supporting her future running. You can make donations at this phone number: 13 98 92. See you next week, at the same time and same place, when you'll find out about Maxi's training methods, mental and physical. I want to leave you with the thought that our champion athletes are not predictable like robots. They are flesh and blood with complex feelings, struggling to control their effort levels, overcoming extraordinary difficulty and pain.

'Good night, everyone!'

The Team gather around Patti and Maxi as the camera scans the audience's happy smiles and energised faces.

370

CHAPTER 73

During our 5 years together, Maxi and I had discovered different and delicious ways of relaxing. One was to indulge each other's fantasies. I would pretend to be a servant who would supply her with whatever she desired. If we reversed roles and I summonsed her, she might play masseuse, rubbing my body with fragrant oils. Our fantasies usually led to love-making.

We played with talk too.

'If I was the Queen of England,' I said to Maxi, 'I wouldn't stand for any nonsense.'

'If I was President of the United States,' she said, 'I wouldn't stand for The Queen of England.'

'If I was in the United States, I wouldn't stand for the President.'

'If I was in a state,' she said, 'I would be all het up.'

'Het up, you say?' I did my plantation drawl. 'Ain't nobody het you up yet, Brer Rabbit. Hain't no Presidenty gonna heat you up heither!'

'No way, dude,' she said. 'I too cool for him!'

And so on. We would continue such repartee until we ran out of interest. Sometimes Alice and Blake would join us in verbal horseplay over a game of scrabble.

'Is xylem a word?' Maxi asked.

'It's a place for insane people,' I said.

'It could be a funny place, like Har-Harlem.'

'You're too late: the bird has phloem.'

'What are you talking about?' asked Blake.

'Xylem is the woody part of a plant that transports water, while phloem is another part that transports nutrients.'

'Xylem pays 18 times 3 equals 54,' said Alice. 'You could win, Jack. If I didn't like you so much, I would hate you.'

We told each other stories we made up, beginning with a first sentence supplied by the other. I began: 'Once upon a time a pirate ship was wrecked on a deserted island and the survivors discovered an ice-cream mine.'

She continued: 'After they had dug up and eaten their fill, they built a rowboat from the wreckage and sent out a trading party.'

IIt was my turn and I continued: 'They discovered another island where guns were made. They traded ice-creams for Kalashnikovs.'

We would continue, trying to outdo each other in improbability, violence, sentimentality, nostalgia, or even banality, until we reached a natural end-point, for example when pirates conquered the Universe.

Our friendship with Blake and Alice went deep. When we were together, time flew by. It might even have dilated, because our minds churned as we wisecracked. These interludes helped Maxi and I to appreciate each other, beyond the serious business of her running. When we travelled to races, we took time to relax together. I realised what a wonderful person she was and how lucky I was that she was my partner.

Our postures when travelling were different from each other: Maxi liked to be noticed whereas I preferred to be inconspicuous.

'I wouldn't tour any community that would let me tour it,' I said.

'You have a streak of twisted passive resistance,' Maxi said. 'If you swallowed a nail, it would come out of your arse a corkscrew.'

'I'm benign,' I said, 'which is more than can be said for you and your naked narcissism.'

'That's rich, coming from you,' Maxi said. 'What is the difference between your egomania and my narcissism?'

'I do not inflate myself like you do.'

'My self-aggrandisement is because you don't value me,' she said.

'What's sauce for the goose is sauce for the gander,' I said. 'If you valued me more, my increased value would rebound on you as my partner and you would be aggrandised.'

'Haha.' Maxi said. 'We should stop this game before someone gets hurt.' Honesty and wit don't go together.'

'There are no honest games, only honest players,' I said.

'Games always have an element of chance,' she said, 'and cheats never prosper.'

'In a long game of poker, chance evens out,' I said. 'It's the ultimate game of skill.'

'Is the skill deception?'

'Certainly,' I said. 'You're good at it.'

'Do I deceive you?' she asked.

'Would I know to complain?'

'You can count on my honesty.'

'But you are a wit and you said that wit doesn't go with honesty.'

'I meant it as a joke.'

We laughed together. At last we had time to be with each other, relaxing as free partners, away from the worries of our running business.

Corvid cornered me one day on the staircase.

'Are you having a good time?' she asked.

'Yes, thank you. Are you?'

'Do you realise we have been here 5 years.'

'That long?'

'You'll stay with Maxi, right?'

'Why wouldn't I?'

'Is winning the Olympics a hard act to follow?'

I wondered if Maxi had said something to her. Perhaps Corvid still had a crush on her?

'We're not together just for the running,' I said. 'I'm in love.'

'What do you see in her?' she asked. 'I'm curious to know.'

'How long do you have?'

'I mean, what is it about her you really go for?'

She could be checking up my intentions with her friend were honourable.

'She's beautiful, intelligent, funny . . . extraordinarily determined . . . amazing.'

'Oh.'

Corvid seemed satisfied with this answer as if I might have been taking advantage of Maxi.

'I have to trust that Maxi loves me,' I thought. *'We don't talk about what we see in each other but we do things together and agree matters. There is a balance between us, a mutualism.'*

Perhaps Corvid couldn't see that we worked well together. Corvid had a dark side and I never knew what she would do next.

When I ran into Blake, I asked him the same question about Alice: 'What do you see in her?'

His reply adulated Alice's intelligence and kindness.

'What do you think of her base-jumping?'

'I'm not rapt. A friend of hers was killed the other day. They think he misjudged the height of a promontory and crashed into it.'

'Does she ever think of quitting?'

'No.'

'Do you think she disdains living?'

'She says base jumping is no more dangerous than crossing the road.'

'Do you worry about her?'

'Not when she crosses the road. She has a lot of base jumping experience. I hardly worry about her at all.'

'I'm happy for the two of you.'

'It's cool.'

It wasn't hard to see they were in love. The attention they gave each other seemed equally balanced, like ours. There were as many kinds of love as there were couples, but I was sure Maxi and I had the best.

It had taken years together to be able to show my emotions to Maxi with complete honesty. She had been the same with me. When we opened up our thoughts, we didn't always know what we were getting into. I had no fear for us, because although she might not like a blind spot I had or something I had done in the past, I knew she would be on my side. She knew my flaws and vulnerabilities I kept from everyone else. She brought difficulties to me alone, honouring her trust in me. Her weaknesses, in my eyes, were strengths that bound us together. We were two people living as one organism.

CHAPTER 74

After the Olympics, Maxi took a long break from running. She made a movie with the story of her career, did television shows and made public appearances. She licensed manufacturers to use the MAXI brand and distributed her products globally. A manager had taken over publicity, with Maxi presiding and Jack as CEO. She had toured America, Europe and Africa, with Asia planned.

Before everyone headed off for Christmas holidays, Team Maxi had a social gathering in a QIS conference room, with waiters serving drinks and finger foods.

'When will you finish your PhD?' Derek asked Jack.

'About a month.'

'What will you do until then?'

'Wait to hear from the external examiners. I'm keeping busy finding out how natural selection caused time dilation to evolve.'

'Wow,' said Alice. 'Would you tell us about that, Jack?'

'I've uncovered some surprising information,' he said. 'Geoffrey West (3) suggests animals die after their hearts have made two billion heartbeats.'

'But individuals vary?'

'The differences between species are greater than within species,' said Jack.

'Not all deaths are from heart failure.'

'No,' he said. 'Leaving out deaths from disease and accident, animals with slower hearts are likely to survive for proportionally more time, taking longer to accumulate their two billion beats. A hummingbird's heart beats 20 times faster than an elephant's and an average elephant lives for 20 times more time, 70 years, compared with the bird's 3.5 years.'

'That's amazing. Does each heartbeat take away the same fraction of a lifetime, whether it is a hummingbird or an elephant?'

'Yes.'

'Is it the same for all species?'

'Yes. The wear and tear on a heart from a heartbeat is about the same in both slow and fast hearts.'

'Each species has a different ecological niche and cadence, a different pace,' Jack said. 'A butterfly's brief frenetic flitting might not be more life-consuming than an elephant's ponderous browsing. Animals seem to enjoy an existential peace. Their tranquillity has been replaced in humans by hurrying to keep to clocked schedules.'

Maxi had joined him talking to Derek and Alice.

'Living by clock time is recent in human history,' Maxi said. 'Jack and I have retrofitted our lifestyles to pre-industrial conditions. We don't use timepieces. Our bodies know nothing of hours, minutes, seconds, or any quantity of time, except a day lasting between sunrise and sunset. We don't judge amounts of time. Our systems, organs, tissues and cells respond to each other and rather than to outside events.

'After six years' of study, Maxi has become a Zen master and taken total control of herself,' Jack said. 'Her training doesn't have fixed starting times, nor durations. It has sequences, distances and effort levels, of her own choice.'

'I keep time for myself without a clock,' said Maxi. 'I run at a rate I choose and get into 'flow', where I am unaware of time and stay engaged timelessly. The quality and quantity of my life are under my control.

'Every one of us can use Maxi's towering Olympic achievement as a lighthouse to guide us, through the darkness of unawareness of our abilities, into a safe harbour,' said Jack.

'That's a bit over the top,' said Maxi.

'No. I mean it. You have shone a narrow beam brightly for us to follow to success.'

'Can people live longer, more enjoyable, lives?'

377

'A study has shown that gold medal winners relax and live longer lives than silver, with silver better than bronze.'

'When a person focuses intensely on anything, they can 'flow' timelessly,' said Jack. 'When I do my research work, I use clock time hardly at all. I work when I feel like it. I go to bed when I feel like it. If I don't get to sleep, I get up and catch up on my sleep later.'

'That's what you think,' Maxi said, smiling. 'You share your time with me too.'

'We make time for each other.'

'It sounds like endurance,' she said. 'Perhaps our relationship is at an edge.'

'It wouldn't be bad if it was,' Jack said. 'It could be a paradox of the human condition that optimal enjoyment is experienced at the edge of endurance. Perhaps the cutting edge of evolution is where there is a balance between Nietzsche's daring to be great and the banal, stoical living that brings home the bacon in hard times.'

'My win has restored the balance,' said Maxi. 'I endured years of training without freedom and now I have carved out a niche which has individual freedom.'

'You have not walked over the backs of others to gain your freedom,' said Derek. 'Those you have beaten have had the same opportunities as you. You did not need their approval for your freedom and your success could even have pleased them. You have truly earned your freedom.'

While they had been talking, the others had gathered around, listening.

'Maxi, it won't be easy for you to escape from the rest of us on your rocket to freedom,' said Alice. 'Your actions could severely affect some of us. If you retired some in your team could lose employment, lifestyle and overseas holidays. I am not concerned myself, because whatever you choose to do, I do not have obligations to you I do not want.'

'I want you all to be able to cut loose from me without a backward glance,' Maxi said. 'I don't want to take away anyone's freedom!'

378

'Maxi has not created any dependants,' said Jack, addressing them sombrely and it seemed like an ending. 'You are free to go whenever you wish.'

'Maxi, your freedom is in spades,' he said. 'You hold all the tricks. So far, my own hand as your partner has complemented yours. My life's role derives from my primate ancestors, who foraged on the savannah in a group with others, in a full circle until today, when once again I compete with others by endurance. From being a hunter and then a herder, I eventually became an indentured labourer in the fields at my home on our family small-holding, then a compromised learner trying to assemble knowledge at Caloundra High School, then a project technical analyst, with an ulcer, on Oilco's treadmill. I broke free and investigated at university how endurance runners perform. I was fortunate to discover 'flow' and met Maxi who I could 'flow' with. We have flowed in a herd of running people, across a savannah of marathons, where we achieve in the timeless present and where high performers survive.

'It was my good fortune to find my personal freedom with you, Maxi, as have others here. When you showed us how to perform at the edge of endurance, it helped us to make better use of our time.

'I have been fortunate to lead a loyal and creative group, Team Maxi. We grappled with more variables than we understood and somehow have come through with flying colours. It was an experience with amazing positivity and the credit for that goes to all of us. Perhaps we have made a dent in the firmament, pushed back the darkness and chaos beyond. I feel launched into an unfolding reality, living on an exhilarating wave of existential change created by Team Maxi. Thank you for being with me. Whatever we do now, we have a great beginning. Thank you, Maxi for inspiring all of us.'

His face flushed and breathing quickly, Jack suddenly stopped. Team Maxi broke into spontaneous clapping.

'Thank you, Jack,' said Alice.

'Does anyone want to come for a pizza? Jack is buying,' said Maxi

'Oh? Why is that?' he asked.

'One good idea deserves another,' she said. 'This is mine.'

CHAPTER 75

'The hunter returns,' Maxi said brightly when I came home from the bottle shop carrying wine.

I liked it that she saw me as a 'hunter'. It recognised my desire to be a provider, even though her contribution to our joint finances eclipsed mine. Her affirmation of my role was good because now we had arrived, my role wasn't as clear as it had been when she was on the way up.

For the past six years since we met, Maxi had shaped me with her feedback. She had noticed my personal strengths and weaknesses, bringing them to my attention, to exploit or correct. She had moulded me into a different person, less controlling of others, more in control of myself, under her command.

I was still besotted, unable to define her or objectify her. She was vibrant and mysterious. Her determination was difficult to oppose, but I had not let her impose on me. Her tendency to dominate was caused by her vaunting ambition, but she was often kind and generous with her time. She had great understanding of people, including me.

To keep going with her demanding training schedule and improve performance, she had needed me and her other coaches to feedback frequently. During races, she wanted her family, friends and coaching team watching her. When she won, she had savoured the crowd's applause, the adulation of fans and stayed on the podium for as long as possible, getting the media attention her psyche needed.

Two years after the Olympics, Maxi still enjoyed being in the public eye. She received invitations to talk to audiences and selected those that would best help deserving people to succeed. She employed a social secretary. She liked doing interviews and making public appearances. Her driver was also her bodyguard and protected her from enemies, exploiters, over-enthusiastic well-wishers and stalkers. I wondered how long she would want to continue this lifestyle, because there were aspects I regarded as superficial, such as feeding the hungry maw of public attention that fickle media cultivated.

My exploitation of Maxi's marathon training techniques had reached a plateau with a choice for me of several career pathways. I could stay in academia writing and teaching, or I could coach other runners, or I could coach Maxi again for her next race. I would not want anyone else coaching her. I could want to do something else, depending on what she wanted to do.

'You've reached your goal,' I said to her. 'What's your next apple?'

'I'm not sure yet.'

'Could it be an orange?'

'Hmm. Something like that. I know what you can do,' she said.

'What.'

'Learn to glaze windows. I'll be breaking more glass barriers.'

'What is there to fix?'

'I run at the edge. I could get hurt.'

'So what can I do?'

'Discover any sharp edges for me to avoid.'

'You mean repair smashed barriers?'

'Nah. I want you to keep me from wrecking my body and my brain.'

'When you overload your brain, your time dilates and it fails safe,' I said. 'It won't wreck.'

'I want you to lookout for any rough edges,' she said. 'Breaking through could have dangers.'

I supposed she was thinking of other running competitions, wanting a change.

I would continue to coach her if she wanted it. Coaching an elite runner was exciting. We had developed our own formula for endurance training. I realised I wanted something more. Our Olympics conquest was a hard act for us to follow.

CHAPTER 76

Corrections and changes to Jack's thesis, required by the examiners, were taking forever. He worked at his desk with total concentration. If a gorilla had walked in front of him, he would have been oblivious. In neuroscience, an 'adequate stimulus' must exist in the eye of the beholder, or there can be inattentional blindness because we register only a very limited slice of the world. Jack was blinkered with his attention on what interested him most, imagining how he could best present his thesis.

'My thesis is the most I can do for my community,' he thought.

He was producing something like the economist Adam Smith's baker, who supplied bread to his community for a profit, thereby doing the best he possibly could for them. It was his type of happiness: eudaimonic, with virtue from pursuit of excellence.

Jack was in 'flow', revising the umpteenth draft, with ideas roaring like express trains through the subterranean passages of his mind. As he scrolled through his manuscript, images flashed by and thoughts bounced like pinballs around the table of his mind, sometimes dropping into unwanted emotional associations, like his rejection by Oilco and the pain of having his twin brother separated at school.

In Jack's theory, which elaborated Einstein's, every individual can have their own time. Had his twins paradox concerned two blind girls, the changes in their physical appearances with aging during their race would not have been evident to each other and perhaps of little consequence. The dilation effect would be evident to the traveller by the results of her longer time awarded by Einstein's logic. If she had the physical ability to maintain her effort level, she would finish the distance before her sister, who would hear the roar of the crowd ahead. When personal time dilates, it can enable better performance in many time-dependent variables: staying younger; running faster and much more. But the effect is difficult to see, even with vision, because brains are not easily observed.

Jack didn't dwell on his past. He was fully engaged, processing information at his maximum rate. He melded ideas and created new sequences in paragraphs he rewrote. His engagement in his research was precious. He wasn't expecting to be interrupted or distracted by anyone or anything, not by his phone, not by anyone visiting, nor by anything at all. He was in flow using his skills and would continue alone until he was ready to stop.

When he did stop, he saw that 3 hours had passed. He had edited 2 chapters, taken out a duplicated section, redefined a concept and fixed dozens of syntax errors. His information processing rate had been high and his time had dilated. He wished he could measure how much his time had slowed, like the twin who had aged 36 years in space while her sister had aged 60 years on Earth. His own journey in Maxi's space had encompassed more than seemed possible and in only 8 years he had gained understanding of time and endurance running.

Jack made himself a cup of coffee and took a few minutes out for reflection.

Perhaps there was a way of measuring time dilation. He could monitor his hair and nail growth over six months, comparing three high flow months with three non-flow months. If flow had slower growth, it would be evidence of time dilation. This evidence would be sufficient for his theory to be accepted widely, that increased mental engagement improved performance time.

He had come to dilating his own time gradually. He had been frustrated at Oilco that he lacked control over his activities. He had changed to a physics research project. His contemplation had been timeless, beyond the doleful beat of a pendulum or a caesium crystal's vibration. He learned of 'flow' from endurance running and equated it with serene enjoyment. He had achieved a personal lifestyle that allowed him to be 'in flow' often when focussed on a definite goal under his control and volition.

He believed he had discovered a useful mental training technique and he was frustrated that it could not be readily validated by experimental science.

In extreme-flow, Jack hurried to edit the concluding chapter. Meanwhile a clock on his wall was unobserved as it meted out several hours. Jack was having too much fun to care about the time. Later, he joined Maxi at daily archery practice, fine-tuning their minds and bodies to do what they wanted.

Team Maxi continued to meet a couple of times a year to support Maxi's career.

Riko's and Derek's personal best was yet to come. They had found each other, made a beginning and shared goals they could achieve.

Patti gave Roly a job caretaking their new mansion. She continued to expand the Maxi brand into a household name. Stan was busy with training camps for endurance runners. He had converted Maxi's success into vindication of his methods, adding 'flow' to his repertoire as if he had been its proponent.

Blake and Alice completed their doctorates and announced they would solemnize marriage to each other in a single ceremony with all The Team invited. They said: 'Despite our times being independent, we figure we have the best prospect of a lasting relationship if we both coincide at our wedding.'

Maxi's partnership with Jack was now 8 years old. He had been her tutor, coach, lover, team manager and CEO. Marathon running, with its unrelenting training, was gruelling and her journey had been harder than his. Her busy mind had been up against a speed limit in responding to stimuli and she rose to the challenge by putting more strides inside longer seconds than other runners.

A marathon race was a metaphor for survival by natural selection. To survive there had to be endurance, with concentration, patience, resilience and persistence. Perhaps homo sapiens had been inspired to be top dog by ancestral runners' endurances in pursuit of quarries.

Maxi spoke to audiences, fostering their daring and empowering people to grasp their own time. As a legendary public figure, her exploits were broadcast and shared, inspiring others to high achievement in all walks of life.

She employed people to take care of her and her businesses. She had changed from the leggy shy schoolgirl Jack had met 8 years ago, into an inspiring strong, confident, iconic woman, who had become a household name. She had pursued endurance to the apex of achievement and fame had been thrust upon her.

Maxi lived with Jack not far from a beach. They swam and body-surfed often. Maxi's physical accomplishments still held Jack spellbound. Her physical and mental repertoire was like a champion figure skater's. She displayed with ease combinations of elegant mental and physical metaphorical twirls, leaps, spins and graceful swoops. Never still, she was always creating and making public appearances, delivering speeches and giving interviews. When she wanted Jack's attention, he was there for her.

She had been considering her future with an Olympic encore in Delhi. Then she put forward a different idea.

'I could have a baby,' she said.

Jack was surprised. It was what he most wanted. Their legacy could be partly genetic.

'I'll be in on that,' he said. 'Will you retire?'

'I'm 25 now and can go back to running after, if I want,' she said.

'Good idea. Why not have two babies and then return with your best runs ahead of you?'

'What about you, Jack? Are you sure you want children? It will change everything.'

'Not everything. We won't let it take over. We can wait until after you have finished racing, if you like, with IVF as a backup.'

'I don't want my baby made by technology,' she said. 'Waiting is not the way to go.'

'Okay,' he said. 'Let's smash through and do it now.'

'You may lack subtlety, but you sure know how to help a girl set her goals. I made a great coach out of you.'

~END~

BIBLIOGRAPHY

1. Mihaly Csíkszentmihályi, 'Flow: The Psychology of Optimal Experience' (Harper & Row, 1990).
2. Daniel Kahneman, 'Thinking, Fast and Slow.' Penguin, 2011
3. Roy Baumeister, 'Willpower,' 2012.
4. Eugen Herrigel, 'Zen in the Art of Archery,' Vintage Spiritual Classics, 1953
5. Alain De Botton, 'Essays in Love,' Picador, 1993
6. Geoffrey West, 'Scale,' Penguin Press, 2017
7. Matt Fitzgerald, 'How Bad Do You Want It?' Aurum Press, 2016.
8. Alain De Botton, 'Essays in Love', Amazon, 2015.
9. Alain De Botton,'The Pleasures and Sorrows of Work,' Vintage International, 2009
10. Pirsig, Robert M, 'Zen and the Art of Motorcycle Maintenance,' Vintage 1974
11. McGregor, Adrian, 'Cathy Freeman,' Random House, 1998.
12. Seligman, Martin. Learned Optimism, Random House, 1991.
13. Seligman, Martin. Authentic Happiness, Free Press, 2002.
14. Steve Magness, https://www.scienceofrunning.com/2010/06/evolution-and-history-of-training.html?v=6cc98ba2045f
15. Movie: '4 Minute Mile,' Director Charles-Olivier Michaud, 2014
16. Movie: 'Chariots of Fire,' Director Hugh Hudson, 1981.
17. Schneck, Daniel J. Basic Anatomy and Physiology for the Music Therapist, JKP, 2015
18. Magness, Steve. The Science of Running, 2014

19. Sillitoe, Alan. The Loneliness of the Long Distance Runner
20. Chan, Kenneth. Why Relativity Exists, April 28, 2016 Kenneth Chan http://kenneth-chan.com/physics/why-relativity-exists/
21. Movie: 'First Four Minute Mile, HQ,' Roger Bannister 1954, 2012
22. Wikipedia. Twin Paradox. https://en.wikipedia.org/wiki/Twin_paradox
23. Giancoli, Douglas C. Physics, Chapter 26, The Special Theory of Relativity, Pearson, Esses, UK, 2016
24. Lawson, Lorraine. Lorraine's Squad Training Guide, Self-published, 2017.
25. Herrigel, Eugen. Zen in the Art of Archery, Vintage, 1953.
26. Movie: 'The Game Changers,' 2019, Netflix.

ACKNOWLEDGEMENTS

My interest in writing this story began when I presented Einstein's Special Relativity theory to school students in general science and found they could be interested in this abstract theory if I recounted Einstein's thought experiments. It gave a boost to non-science students unaccustomed to abstract reasoning to engage with the logical reasoning processes of that extraordinary patent examiner and thinker.

I became interested in Einstein's time dilation from the diagrams of Giancoli (23). I studied others' views of time in philosophy, art and history. I read widely on the topic of time in science: physics, neuroscience and psychology. I fell under the spell of Zen when I read Persig (10). Chan (20) convinced me that there is a tendency to expect time to be absolute and not apply relativity when it could affect observation. By good fortune, I stumbled on a condition of perceived timelessness called 'Flow' in Mihaly (1). I linked flow to time dilation and this led me to write a story about an endurance runner. I drew especially on Fitzgerald (7) a renowned endurance sports journalist. I was intrigued by Nietzsche's philosophy of will and Baumeister (3)'s psychology of free will. For my story, I am indebted to Alain De Botton for his dissection of a love relationship (8). My characters draw on a lifetime of experiences with people in industry, education, sport and in relationships where people are guided by goals and endure, for better or worse.

I wish to thank the following people for their help and forbearance during the writing of this book.

Donna Munro, author of The Zanzibar Moon, Kendwa's Secret and Elephant Creek, was my multi-talented publisher, graphic artist and website developer for this book, as she was for previous books.

I am indebted to Brad Ahern, Ross Allen, Denise Thomson, Dave Jones and Lorraine Lawson for reading, commenting and editing parts of the manuscript.

Roger Wooller was helpful with biological and physiological information.

Friend Dr Bill Richards, whose psychological and psychiatric experience was invaluable to my understanding of behaviour and encouraged my project.

Daughter Dr Zoe Knox provided insights into aspects of marathon running.

Daughter Dr Tessa Knox supplied experience of teamwork in groups and of science research protocols.

I am grateful to Dianne Bishop for her encouragement with his book. She accompanied me to endurance events, athletics meets and training conferences. Together we watched many movies about running.

Seville Writers Group heard me read aloud many of the chapters of this book and discussed them, with insight and good ideas. Prominent were Nancy Cox-Millner, Alan Holzl, Robyn Martin and Jack Russell.

Alain Guillemain corresponded with me on philosophical and physics aspects of my theory.

Dr Guy Barry of Queensland Institute of Medical Research provided helpful feedback about brain science, limits of empiricism and the theory.

Professor Darryl Eyles input helped with his neuroscience viewpoint on the theory.

Vince Katuske's neuroscience experience answered many questions I had about the neural basis of 'flow'.

Greg Lewis kindly supplied information about endurance in the boxing ring and his book 'Fifty Fighters Who Changed Boxing,' 2007.

I studied Einstein's theory and existentialism in Beginners' Philosophy at U3A and the discussion was a springboard into exploring the metaphysics of time 'in the moment'.

Our 'thinking about current issues' class at U3A considered issues with time, such as development of new time technologies and measuring the speed of light.

I attended discussions at the University of Queensland Students Philosophy Association, touching on issues in my story, such as willpower, determinism, liberty, virtue and trust.

Meetings of the University of Queensland PAIN physics association provided opportunities to discuss relativity and Einstein's theories with students.

AUTHOR BIOGRAPHY

Martin Knox graduated as a chemical engineer from Birmingham University in the UK and worked in the petroleum industry in Canada. He researched alternative systems of government at Imperial College, London. He emigrated to Australia and was employed in mining development. He became a high school science teacher, coached sport and wrote textbooks published by the Queensland Department of Education.

He has been writing fiction novels full-time since 2013: speculative, love, crime and satire. He is involved in public policy-making, proposing an underground railway for Brisbane and reasoning about climate and Covid-19. He meets with writing and reading groups and studies philosophy. He writes letters, plays the guitar, sings badly and does outdoor gym. He is divorced with children and grandchildren.

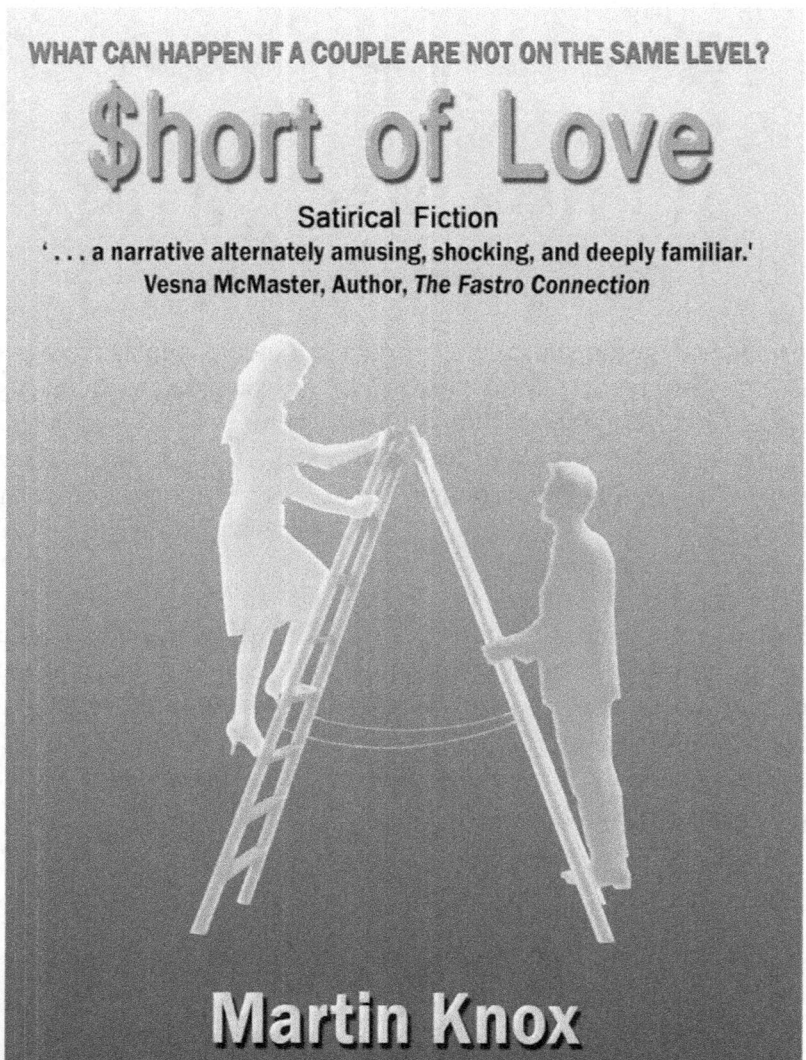

WHAT CAN HAPPEN IF A COUPLE ARE NOT ON THE SAME LEVEL?

$hort of Love

Satirical Fiction

'. . . a narrative alternately amusing, shocking, and deeply familiar.'
Vesna McMaster, Author, *The Fastro Connection*

Martin Knox

BUY THE BOOK AT:
https://www.amazon.com/Short-Love-Martin-Knox/dp/1920699570

THIS BOOK COULD CHANGE HOW YOU THINK
ABOUT PARTY POLITICS

PRESUMED
DEAD

A political crime fiction thriller

Martin Knox

BUY THE BOOK AT:

BUY THE BOOK AT:
https://www.amazon.com/Grass-Always-Browner-Martin-Knox/dp/1921731699